Dear Reader,

When anyone asks which Temptation book is my favorite, I always come back to *Mr. Valentine*. And Jack Killigan. How could you not fall in love with a guy sensitive enough to write great romance novels and gorgeous enough—once he cleaned up a bit—to pose for a cover shoot? Oh, and make no mistake, Jack's all man. His day job involves a hard hat and forklift. Does a fantasy get any better? I think not!

Mr. Valentine was also the first official project in which I joined forces with Brenda Chin, editor extraordinaire, and it was my twenty-fifth Temptation novel. All the stars were aligned for this book. I'm thrilled that it's part of Temptation's Twentieth Anniversary celebration, and even more thrilled that my friend and fellow Temptress Leslie Kelly joins in with a terrific novella. Happy birthday, Temptation!

Warmly,

Vicki Lewis Thompson

VICKI LEWIS THOMPSON
LESLIE KELLY

READING BETWEEN THE LINES

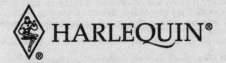

HARLEQUIN®

TORONTO • NEW YORK • LONDON
AMSTERDAM • PARIS • SYDNEY • HAMBURG
STOCKHOLM • ATHENS • TOKYO • MILAN • MADRID
PRAGUE • WARSAW • BUDAPEST • AUCKLAND

ISBN 0-373-83633-3

READING BETWEEN THE LINES

Copyright © 2004 by Harlequin Books S.A.

The publisher acknowledges the copyright holders of the individual works as follows:

MR. VALENTINE
Copyright © 1997 by Vicki Lewis Thompson

THRILL ME
Copyright © 2004 by Leslie Kelly

CONTENTS

With gratitude to Ed Hoornaert
and Donna Lepley for inspiring this story.

And to all the unsung heroes laboring behind
female pseudonyms in the romance industry.

Will you be my valentine?

MR. VALENTINE

Vicki Lewis Thompson

1

"WELL, CAT, I HOPE to hell this is sexy enough."

From her basket next to the computer, a butterscotch tabby watched with an unblinking stare as Jack Killigan packaged up the romance novel he'd just written.

"Had to go back into the old memory bank," Jack continued, "considering it's been a while since I've had any hands-on experience." He scratched behind the cat's ears and looked into her green eyes as she began to purr. "But if you'll pardon me for bragging, I make damn good love on paper. Damn good."

He smoothed the label onto the envelope, running his fingers across the pseudonym he'd chosen for the project. *Candace Johnson.* Although Manchester Publishing had invited any unpublished novelist to enter a manuscript in its Valentine's Day romance contest, Jack firmly believed a woman stood a better chance than a man.

A chilly dawn forced its way through the drizzle of another November day on Puget Sound. He had just enough time to climb into his coveralls and rain gear, make the wet motorcycle trip to Rainier Paper and clock in at the shipping dock at eight. He'd mail the manuscript on the way.

Krysta would chew his butt again all through lunch about not getting enough sleep. He took off his glasses to massage the bridge of his nose. Then he put them back on and smiled. He doubted that she knew how much he enjoyed the self-improvement lectures she delivered on a regular basis while they shared a lunch table in the company cafeteria. Or how much she'd inspired this latest book.

KRYSTA LUECKENHOFF WALKED into the contracts office of Rainier Paper at ten minutes before eight, the first one in the office, as always. She started coffee perking, turned on her computer and straightened the papers on her already neat desk in an effort to quiet the turmoil in her mind. The routine refused to comfort her today. She'd planned so carefully, yet nothing was working out the way she'd hoped. It looked as if she wouldn't be able to afford live-in help for her father in September, after all.

She picked up a framed picture on her desk and brushed a speck of lint from the glass. She'd taken the snapshot the previous June, when all four of her younger brothers had managed to get the day off from their summer jobs to celebrate Father's Day. They'd had a picnic on the beach, her dad's favorite place to eat, and for the picture his sons had lifted him out of the hated wheelchair and propped him against a large piece of driftwood. Then they'd clustered around him, their young, strong bodies obscuring his wasted legs, and for the first time in years, Krysta had caught a glimpse, through the camera lens, of the man her father used to be.

Krysta put the picture down with a guilty start as Rosie Collins came into the office shaking rain from her umbrella.

"Hi, there," Krysta said, flashing a smile.

"Don't put on that fake grin for me." The dark-skinned brunette had become Krysta's friend in the two years they'd worked together in the contracts department. "When I first came in, there was tragedy all over that pretty face. Something's wrong."

Krysta sighed. "After you left last night Juliet called me in and told me she won't accept the vice presidency even if they offer it to her."

Rosie gazed at her with compassion. "Sorry, girl."

"Yeah. That means there's no promotion for Krysta, either." Krysta ran her fingers through her hair. "I can't blame her. She's decided to adopt a child and doesn't want the added responsibility."

"No kidding?" Rosie took a mug from her desk drawer and

walked over to pour herself some coffee. "Bancroft's adopting a kid? That's a shocker."

"A little girl from China, no less. It's a very humanitarian thing to do, and you have to admire her for it, but I was so sure she'd accept the vice presidency and I'd get her job. And her paycheck."

"Listen." Rosie walked around behind Krysta's desk and gestured toward the picture of her family. "Ask those guys to help pay for your dad's live-in help. I never thought it was right that you're taking on the whole responsibility in the first place."

"They can't, Rosie. Not and keep going to school, and that's so much more important. Maybe if I request a transfer to marketing, I'll have a better shot at a promotion."

Rosie shook her head. "All this jockeying for position makes my head spin. It wouldn't kill your brothers to sit out a year and—"

"It would kill me. Once out, they might never go back. And education is the key. They have to finish."

"Okay, Mother Teresa." Rosie squeezed Krysta's shoulder and headed back to her desk. "I hope all these guys you're shepherding along appreciate you."

JACK CARRIED HIS TRAY over to the corner table where he and Krysta usually ate and waited while she hung her purse over her chair and took a seat before he settled down himself.

Krysta cast a quick glance over Jack's tray. "Coffee and carrot cake. My good friend, I hope that's not all you're having for lunch."

"Doesn't carrot cake count as a veggie?" He nudged his glasses back into position. He really had to get the broken earpiece fixed one of these days. Tape wasn't working worth a damn.

"No, carrot cake does *not* count as a veggie." She positioned her napkin in her lap before giving him a little smile. "Which you very well know."

He gestured toward his tray. "Actually, this isn't all I'm having."

"Thank goodness for that. A salad would be a very good idea, Jack." She took a dainty bite of hers, a concoction full of things like sprouts and fresh spinach.

"I was thinking in terms of three more cups of coffee. It's made from beans, isn't it?"

Krysta laughed and shook her head, causing her hair to ripple and glint like antique gold under the cafeteria's fluorescent lights. "You're a hopeless case. Clever but hopeless. You need the coffee because you spent another night in front of the tube, I'll bet."

"I did." It wasn't a lie, exactly. Computer monitors and television sets were similar, and he wasn't about to tell anyone about his writing until he'd sold something. He felt more hopeful about that today than he had in a long time. Even he had to admit that his mysteries had been clueless, his horror too tame and his science fiction was on a technical level with Tinkertoys.

"Jack, you have such potential." Krysta dabbed at the corner of her mouth with her napkin. "You may not appreciate my bringing this up, but in high school you pulled down a B average, despite all the partying."

"Maybe it was *because* of the partying. The grindstone doesn't rub everyone the right way, you know."

"I worked in the school office. I happened to see your SAT scores. Ninety-ninth percentile, Jack. You should be making better use of your brain than muscling paper bales by day and sitting in front of the television by night."

"That sounds like a line from my parents, if ever I heard one."

Her expression turned adorably serious. "If I repeat what your parents say, it's because I happen to agree with them." She put a hand on his arm. "Look, I know it will be hard to go back to college again after so many years, but education is extremely important. Don't you realize your innate intelligence will atrophy if you don't use it?"

He knew he shouldn't tease her, but he couldn't seem to help himself. "I subscribe to *Motorcycle Mania*. Some of the articles are pretty good." He grabbed a napkin as a sneeze took him by surprise.

"That's another thing. You get no sleep and then you ride around in the rain on that big old Harley of yours, catching colds." She reached down and dug around in her purse. "Take these," she said, shoving a bottle of vitamin C tablets in his hand.

"No. They're yours." He set them back in front of her tray.

"Please take them. I'll pick up some more, but I know you won't. Maybe that bottle will get you through the worst of the rainy season, although I wish you'd consider buying a car. I'm sure you could qualify for a loan."

"Why would I want a car? They use more gas than my bike."

She rolled her eyes. "Because," she said with elaborate care, as if talking to someone of marginal intelligence, "no one will think of you as executive material if you hang on to that motorcycle. And you could use a good haircut. The shaggy look is out, Jack. I honestly wonder what you're spending your money on. I hope it's not something obnoxious like calling those nine-hundred numbers." She wrinkled her nose in obvious distaste.

He couldn't help laughing at her suggestion that he might be interested in phone sex. "No, I don't call nine-hundred numbers." He didn't tell her that he'd sunk all his spare cash into the best computer and printer he could find, because then she'd want to know why.

"Then what's your secret passion?" Fortunately she didn't pause for an answer. "I suppose you have one of those sound systems that drives the neighbors crazy." She took a drink of her mineral water and set the glass down with a decisive click. "Night school, Jack. That's the way to get ahead. My management class was invaluable, and now the public speaking class is a perfect complement. Do you have a catalogue from Evergreen Community College?"

"No."

"I'll get you one. The fall semester is half over, of course, but you could certainly enroll for the spring. You really need to rev up the motors on that brain of yours."

"You seem more into this improvement business today than usual. Did you get another set of instructions from the folks back home telling you to work harder on reforming me?"

A hint of vulnerability flashed in her eyes, then was gone. "No, no, I didn't."

"Something's eating you." He paused. She always prided herself on being upbeat and in charge, a walking advertisement for the power of positive thinking. That brief glimpse of a chink in her armor was unsettling. "Is it something about your father?" Last Jack had heard, Hans Lueckenhoff had been forced by weakening leg muscles into using a wheelchair. Maybe his condition had deteriorated even more.

"Everything's fine, really," Krysta said, looking deliberately cheerful. I—" Her gaze slid over his shoulder and up. "Oh, hello, Derek."

Jack grimaced. Derek Hamilton, the youngest vice president in the history of Rainier Paper, was apparently standing right behind him. Jack could guess why Hamilton was lurking around the company cafeteria instead of spending his lunch hour in the executive dining room. Company gossip reported that Hamilton had a thing for Krysta, and Krysta seemed to welcome the attention. Jack would have loved to find something to criticize about Hamilton, but there wasn't much wrong with him except a slight tendency toward nerdiness. In today's world, that might be a plus, he thought.

"Excuse me for interrupting, but I have the symphony tickets for tomorrow night," Derek said. "Shall I pick you up about sixish? We'll have a drink, and then a light supper after the performance."

Krysta's answering smile made Jack clench his back teeth together.

"That would be great, Derek," she said. "You know Jack Killigan from shipping, don't you?"

Jack pushed back his chair and stood. Turning, he stuck out his hand. Hamilton took it and initiated a bone-crushing handshake, a technique Jack had encountered a few times from men shorter and slighter than he was. After months of working on the dock, Jack could have broken several bones in Hamilton's fingers if he chose to retaliate.

He didn't. Hamilton had the power to get him fired, and he still needed a regular paycheck to support his writing habit. The job was perfect, a purely physical one so he could keep his brain fresh for the nightly writing sessions. "Nice to see you, Mr. Hamilton," he said.

"For heaven's sake, call me Derek." Derek retrieved his hand. "Shipping's one of our most efficient departments. I'm glad to meet one of its members."

"Jack's family and mine know each other back in Mount Vernon," Krysta said.

Jack wished she hadn't felt obligated to explain that, as if that was the only reason she was sitting at the table with him. Maybe it was. What a depressing thought.

"Really?" Derek looked relieved by the news that Jack was an old family friend. "It's a small world, isn't it?" With that, he made a show of consulting something that looked like a Rolex.

Jack observed the gesture with malicious intent. A Rolex second hand made a clean sweep of the dial; an imitation jerked with each second that passed. Hamilton's watch jerked. Jack smiled to himself.

"Gotta run," Hamilton said with breezy efficiency. "Big meeting with marketing in five minutes."

"Are you planning to present my idea?" Krysta asked.

"I certainly am. I'll tell you all about it tomorrow night."

Krysta's smile was dazzling as she looked at Hamilton. "See you then, Derek."

"What idea?" Jack asked when Hamilton was out of earshot. He didn't even want to think about the impending date for the symphony.

"Rainier's been researching materials other than lumber to use for making paper. I suggested doing an infomercial that might boost the company's image."

Jack nodded, impressed. "So Hamilton's going to present your idea to marketing?"

"That's right. And that's how you can get ahead, Jack," she continued. "By demonstrating your abilities to the people who count."

"Hamilton can count, too? The man's a veritable genius."

Krysta frowned. "That's so typical of you, joking around when I'm trying to make an important point."

He wasn't joking around. He really disliked the idea of her dating Hamilton, which wasn't fair. Hamilton had several things to offer Krysta that Jack couldn't, and he should be happy for her. "I'm sorry. Please make your important point. I'll be good."

"Just like they said in my management course last semester, it's important to make a plan and then follow it. And it's obvious to me you have no plan, Jack. If you had one you would have had more to say when meeting Derek, some discerning comment that would make him notice you."

"I thought about saying 'Love your fake Rolex.' Guess I should have."

She put her hand over her mouth but her eyes gave away the smile. She cleared her throat and composed her features. "You promised to be serious. And besides, that is *not* a fake. Derek told me he bought it from a reputable jeweler in Seattle."

"Probably the reputable kind who conducts business on the sidewalk."

"Your attitude is terrible. You know that, don't you?"

Jack grinned at her as he stretched his tired muscles. "Blame it on lack of sleep." He pushed back his chair and picked up his tray. "Well, gotta run. I have a meeting with a two-hundred-pound bale of paper in five minutes."

"Jack, Jack, Jack. I'm concerned about your future."

"That's okay. You have enough future for both of us." He stood. Then he paused and gave her a long look. "Remember, if you ever need anything, I'm here. And I'm a good listener."

The vulnerable expression returned. "Thanks, Jack."

He set down his tray and returned to his seat. So he'd be late. "Talk to me, Krysta."

Immediately her expression cleared, and she gave him a big smile as she stood. "Don't be silly. Everything's fine. But it won't be if we don't get our fannies back to work. See you tomorrow. And take the vitamin C."

THE FIRST WEEK IN JANUARY, Krysta came into the office earlier than usual to get a head-start on a contract that had to be finished that morning. Lately she felt like a person running a foot race on a frozen lake. The transfer to marketing didn't look as if it would happen anytime soon, and her personal relationship with Derek was becoming sticky. He was pressuring her to go to bed with him, and she'd discovered that no matter how hard she tried to be attracted to him, he left her cold.

On paper Derek was everything she wanted in a man. He had position, reasonably good looks, ambition and cultured tastes. And he was polite and considerate. But he was also as boring as broccoli and his kisses made her gag. She'd never have guessed that would happen, and it was extremely inconvenient. Instead of making an ally of Derek she chanced making him an enemy if she kept holding him off.

Then last week her nineteen-year-old brother Henry had lost his part-time job, which meant he'd need a subsidy in order to continue in college until he could find another job. And her brother Joe had been offered a scholarship at the University of Puget Sound in Tacoma, which was where he wanted to go, but it clinched the need for live-in help for her father beginning in September.

And to top everything off, Jack Killigan hadn't improved one whit. He'd dawdled about enrolling in a night class and missed the cutoff date. He still hadn't gotten a decent haircut, and his dark hair was longer and more unruly than ever. Down in shipping they'd started making him tie it back in a ponytail while he worked. He still held the earpiece of his glasses together with tape, ate an atrocious diet and seemed to get no sleep whatsoever. She'd considered giving up on him and telling her father and the Killigans that it was no use trying to save Jack from himself. But every once in a while the fatigue would fall away from Jack's blue eyes and they'd shine with an intelligence that took her breath away. So she soldiered on, although she appeared to be wasting valuable time on him.

With a sigh Krysta turned on her computer and called up the file with the contract that needed to be finished.

A few minutes later, Rosie came in and hung up her trench coat. "No word on the marketing department job yet, huh?"

"No." Krysta looked up from the screen. "I'm surprised, considering they're using the infomercial idea I suggested through Derek. That should have made an impression on somebody." She reached for her coffee mug, but paused in midmotion. Jack Killigan had just walked through the door. To her knowledge he'd never set foot in her office in the eight months he'd worked for Rainier Paper.

Rosie turned toward the door, obviously motivated by the expression on Krysta's face. Rosie glanced at the name embroidered over the chest pocket of Jack's coveralls and smiled. "You're Jack." She held out her hand. "We've never met because I'm one of those people who blow their money going out for lunch, but Krysta's mentioned you."

Jack shook her hand and returned the smile, but he seemed very distracted. "She probably told you I'm a hopeless case."

"She did, as a matter of fact."

By this time, the agitation evident in Jack's manner had Krysta on her feet and moving toward him. "What is it? Has something happened?"

"I wondered if I could talk to you for a minute."

"Sure."

He glanced at Rosie. "Uh, in private?"

Krysta frowned. She'd never seen him like this, so full of nervous energy that he couldn't stand in one place. "There's a little conference room down the hall. We can go there."

"Great."

She led the way out the door, and he fell into step beside her as they moved down the carpeted hallway. They met Juliet Bancroft coming toward them, hurrying as she glanced at her watch. She gave Krysta a puzzled look.

Krysta paused. "I'll be back in a minute. I know you want to go over the Stevenson Corporation agreement first thing. I'm already working on it."

"That's good," Juliet said. "Derek said he wanted it ready by ten."

"It will be." Krysta had noticed Derek was setting tighter deadlines for the contracts department lately. She figured he was getting pressure from above to improve efficiency.

As she and Jack continued down the hall, she expected some crack about Derek, but Jack stayed uncharacteristically silent. She became more curious than ever as to why he was so preoccupied.

She opened the door to the windowless conference room and flipped on the overhead lights. A polished wooden table and eight chairs upholstered in blue tweed commandeered most of the space, and a large dry-erase message board covered with diagrams from a recent meeting dominated the wall at the end of the table.

Jack closed the door behind them and glanced around.

Krysta pulled out a chair that rolled easily on its casters and sat down. "Is this private enough?"

"I guess so." Jack moved around her to the next chair, but he leaned against the back instead of sitting in it. He pushed his glasses up on his nose and glanced at her. "I don't know quite how to explain this."

"You're in trouble with the law and they've tracked you down?" She'd always wondered what he'd been up to after he quit college and went adventuring around the countryside for several years.

The corner of his mouth lifted. "You don't think very highly of my character, do you?"

"Jack, people can usually put past mistakes behind them. Maybe I can vouch for you when—"

"Okay, I'll just say it." He gripped the back of the chair. "I've been spending all my nights writing books."

Whatever she'd been expecting, it wasn't this. She stared at him.

"So far I've only had rejections." He pushed away from the chair and took a deep breath. "Then yesterday Manchester Publishing called my apartment, and they want me to call back today, collect, and..." He paused. "God, I'm so afraid to jinx this by saying it out loud."

"You've sold a book?" She couldn't have been more shocked if he'd revealed that he was an international jewel thief.

"I think so." Suddenly his grin flashed full wattage. "Yeah, Krysta. Yeah, I think I finally did it."

"Jack, that's marvelous!" She sent the chair thumping against its neighbor as she leaped to her feet and threw her arms around his neck. "I knew you weren't a loser!" And then, surprising them both, she kissed him soundly on the mouth.

2

KRYSTA HAD A BRIEF few seconds to register a citrus-scented after-shave, a mouth that fit almost perfectly against hers, a solid chest, and a very pleasant zing of feeling before she came to her senses and pulled away. Kissing Jack! She must be out of her mind. In all the years the Killigans and the Lueckenhoffs had been friends, she'd never thought of Jack in that way. Never.

She put a hand to her heart and steadied her breathing. Somehow she had to pretend she hadn't just done such a ridiculous thing. Jack was like one of her brothers, for heaven's sake.

"So all this time," she began, her voice quivering only a little, "when I thought you were a couch potato, you've been writing a book?" she said.

He gazed at her without speaking for several seconds. Finally he cleared his throat and pushed back the glasses she'd dislodged. "Several books, actually. That's why I've been working on the dock. It's the perfect job for a writer, because I don't have to think much and I still feel creative when I get to my computer each night."

She shook her head, dazed by his revelation. No wonder she'd reacted so uncharacteristically and kissed him. "We need to tell your parents, Jack. They should know that you—"

"Absolutely not."

"But Jack, they think you're a lost cause!"

"First of all, we don't know yet if I've sold this book because I haven't called Manchester Publishing, and second of all, I'm not sure my parents will be all that impressed when they do find out."

She was slowly regaining her poise, although her lips still tingled. "Of course they will. And why haven't you called the publisher back? It's—" she glanced at her watch. "—already ten minutes after eleven in New York! Another half hour and they might be at lunch! What are you waiting for?"

"You."

She really shouldn't have kissed him. No telling what sort of ideas he might get from that. The kiss meant nothing, of course, but in her experience men tended to respond quickly to such stimulation. She schooled her expression into a professional mask. "I don't understand."

"I wrote a romance."

"A what?"

"You know. A love story. Manchester was having a Valentine's Day contest for unpublished writers and I—"

"I *know* what a romance is, Jack. I read them all the time. I just can't picture you writing one."

"Why?"

She opened her mouth to reply.

"Never mind." He sounded vaguely irritated. "I'm not sure I want to hear your answer. At any rate, I was afraid the publishers would react exactly the way you're reacting if I sent the book in under my own name, so I made up a woman's name, figuring that would help my cause. I don't know if it did or not, but I'm not taking any chances on messing things up now. I want you to call and pretend you wrote the book."

"Me?" She drew in a lungful of air. "I don't think so."

"Please, Krysta. You're the only one I can trust to do this."

"No, Jack! They could ask me something about the book, and I won't know what it's about or anything. Just tell them who you are."

"I promise there'll be nothing to it. If they want to buy, they'll probably offer me—you—a contract. All you have to do is accept it. If they start talking about the book, just say you'd rather have those comments in a letter because you're better at visual communication."

Krysta's eyes narrowed. "Did I just hear you say that all I have to do is accept the contract?"

"That's right. Just accept it and get off the phone."

"Oh, no, you don't!"

He looked puzzled. "Oh, no I don't what?"

"You *never* just accept a contract. You *always* negotiate."

"You don't understand. I would pay *them* to publish this if I had the money. I don't care what they offer, as long as the book will come out. It's a reputable publisher. I don't think they'll try to low-ball me. But even if they did, I wouldn't care."

Krysta was beginning to understand the situation and now realized she needed to make this phone call for Jack. As usual, he wasn't prepared to watch out for his own interests. "Okay, I'll do it."

His eyes sparkled. "You will? Fantastic!"

"When did you want me to make the call?"

"I thought we could call from your office during the lunch hour, when everybody's gone. I don't want anybody else to know about this yet."

"Why not? You'll be a published author, for heaven's sake. Not many people can say that." Her mental image of Jack was undergoing a rapid transformation. And she'd thought he had no enterprise in his soul. She'd been so wrong.

"Well, for one thing, the guys down on the shipping dock will never give me a moment's peace if they find out I wrote a book. Then, if they find out it's a romance, my life won't be worth living."

She nodded. "I see your point. Romance writing is rather an unusual field for men." She had a million questions about how a smart-mouthed guy like Jack had managed to write such a book, but she had to get back to the Stevenson contract before she put her own job in jeopardy. "Well, you can trust me to keep your secret."

"I know that."

She looked past the disreputable glasses into blue eyes that for a moment held hers captive. Her stomach gave a funny little lurch, and she glanced away. She couldn't imagine what was wrong with her. She'd looked into Jack's eyes a thousand times before, and her stomach had always behaved itself. "Why don't you come up to the office about fifteen minutes after twelve?" she said. "Everyone else will be gone, and you can listen in on the conversation when I make the call."

"Perfect." He reached for her wrist and looked at her watch. "We're both late. I'll probably catch hell. See you then." He was out the door and loping down the hall before she could say anything.

She stood in the open doorway and looked after him while she unconsciously massaged her wrist. When she realized what she was doing she stopped and glanced down at the spot where his fingers had gripped her gently. Her skin seemed to vibrate where he'd touched her. In all the years of playing tag, arm wrestling and exchanging high-fives, she never remembered a tingle like that. It was disconcerting, to say the least.

JACK BARELY AVOIDED maiming himself while working on the shipping dock that morning. A potential book sale and a kiss from Krysta in the same day would be distracting enough on a full night's sleep, let alone on the two hours' rest he'd allowed himself between four and six.

He wandered in front of moving forklifts without looking and came within a half inch of dropping a paper bale on his foot. Fortunately the guys in shipping were used to his muddled ways, and for some reason the foreman had taken a liking to him and routinely excused his blunders. If he had to hold down a regular job, he couldn't ask for a better one than this. And there was also the fringe benefit of seeing Krysta every day.

As kids growing up together they'd never dated, partly because they'd known each other too well and there was none of the mystery so critical for teenage romance, and partly because Krysta had been too much of a goody-two-shoes for Jack's tastes at the time. Then they hadn't seen each other for years, until he landed this job at Rainier. Her attitude toward him had remained exactly the same, but Jack had taken one look at Krysta and wondered how he could have been such an idiot for all those years.

Unfortunately, Hamilton had already gained the inside track when Jack arrived on the scene. Besides, Krysta had never given Jack the slightest indication she regarded him as anything other than an old friend. Until this morning. Not that he should put much importance on that kiss. She'd reacted on impulse and caught herself right away. But for a moment...

Finally noon arrived and he clocked out for lunch, washed up and headed for the service elevator. His stomach grumbled from nervousness and lack of food. He wondered if he could be building castles in the air. The night before he'd played the phone message over and over until he had it memorized.

This is Stephanie Briggs, senior editor at Manchester Publishing, calling for Candace Johnson about your manuscript Uptown Girl. *I'd like to discuss the book with you. Please call me collect at your earliest convenience.*

Then she'd given the number and her extension. He couldn't believe an editor would give that out unless she was serious about a manuscript. But then again, he still had a lot to learn about this business. He had to prepare himself for anything. By the time he walked into the contracts office, he was sweating.

"You look awful," Krysta observed helpfully.

"Thanks. I feel as if a whole bowling team is practicing in my gut." But he felt calmer from the moment he saw her sitting there, perfectly groomed in her kelly green suit and white silky blouse, her hair burnished as if she'd just given it a hundred strokes with a hairbrush. A chair was positioned beside her desk. He took it and drew a deep breath. "Got a pencil? I'll give you the number."

She lifted her eyebrows. "You didn't write it down?"

"Didn't have to." He was loathe to admit he'd played the

message about a hundred times and wouldn't be able to forget the phone number if someone gave him a lobotomy.

He recited the number, and although she shook her head in disapproval, she wrote it carefully on a notepad. She put a line across her sevens, European style, and he found that kind of sexy.

"You're calling Stephanie Briggs, senior editor at Manchester Publishing," he added, and Krysta wrote that down, too, her writing full of little angles and squiggles that intrigued him. He realized he could be quite happy sitting here for hours watching her do her job. "And your name is Candace Johnson."

Her gaze flicked up from the notepad and met his. "Candace, like your mother?"

"Yes. Candace and John's son," he finished for her. "I know it's corny, and they might not appreciate it when it appears on a book jacket, but I needed a woman's name, so I came up with that."

"I think you're wrong about your parents. I think they'll be very impressed."

He grinned at her. "That their only son is masquerading as a woman?"

"Oh, for heaven's sake. I think it's a wonderful choice, and so will they."

"Besides, *J* is close to the middle of the alphabet, so on a bookstore shelf the book will show up about eye level."

She gave him an approving glance. "It's good to know you can think in practical terms sometimes." She wrote the pseudonym on the notepad. "Candace Johnson. I think it's perfect." She looked up at him again. "What's the name of your book?"

Gazing into the warmth of her eyes, he couldn't remember. "Jack?"

"Uh, *Uptown Girl.*"

She glanced down at the notepad and started to write. Then she paused. "I can't remember if *uptown* has a hyphen."

"No hyphen." Released from the magic pull of her gaze, he

was able to regain his equilibrium and smile at her perfectionistic tendencies. "But I don't think that will matter on the phone."

"You're right. I'm just so used to typing faxes." She finished writing and tore the paper from the pad with a crisp movement. "I really wish I knew more about this book, Jack."

"All right. Here's a quick synopsis. Jake, a guy from the wrong side of the tracks, falls in love with a CEO's daughter, Christine, after they accidentally spend the night together. She doesn't want anything more than a fling and they part. Jake becomes a labor leader fighting her dad's company. A bunch of stuff happens, but in the climactic scene, she chooses Jake and his world over life in the fast lane." He watched her expression to see if a heroine named Christine would alert her to his use of her as inspiration but no awareness dawned.

"Sounds good." She regarded him with interest. "I guess I didn't know you as well as I thought when we were growing up. You never seemed to take anything very seriously. I had no idea you wanted to write."

"Neither did I. The only reason I went to college was because they offered me a football scholarship. Then I took a writing class because somebody said it was an easy credit. That class hit me like a lightning bolt, and I suddenly knew how I wanted to spend the rest of my life."

"Then why on earth did you drop out of college? I would think more classes—"

"Nope." Jack shook his head. "My writing teacher was very unusual. She said I had a gift for storytelling, and too much time in creative writing classes might screw that up. She suggested I spend a few years gathering experiences and reading all kinds of popular fiction instead of sitting in classrooms. I think she was right."

Krysta frowned. "I'm not sure I agree with that advice, but I can't argue with the results."

"We don't know what the results are yet," he reminded her, his anxiety returning.

"Oh, yes we do. They want this book, Jack." She pushed

back her chair. "You sit here at my desk and I'll use Rosie's so we can see each other and give hand signals." She pointed to a desk directly across the room that faced hers. Then she pushed a button on her telephone. "I'll use that line. When I give you the thumbs-up sign, you pick up the receiver, very, very carefully."

His hands had begun to shake. "Maybe I shouldn't try to listen in."

"Nonsense. I want you to hear all the wonderful things that—" she consulted the paper in her hand "—Stephanie Briggs has to say about your writing."

He sat at her desk while she crossed to Rosie's and settled herself there. Then she grinned at him and started to dial.

He gripped the arms of her chair as if he were in a rocket about to launch. Eager for distractions, he skimmed a glance across her desk and noted the monogrammed desk accessories, a bud vase with a single pink rose—probably from Hamilton—and a framed photograph taken at the beach of her brothers and her father. Jack remembered vividly the winter sixteen years ago when her mother had died. It had been his first funeral. At the ripe-old age of eleven, Krysta had taken charge of the family of four younger brothers and a handicapped father. No wonder she was such a dedicated little caretaker.

Then he heard Krysta give her information for the collect call to the long distance operator, and he looked across the office, his stomach churning. She raised her fist, thumb pointed at the ceiling.

Although he doubted he'd be able to hear anything over the roaring in his ears, he reached a shaky hand toward the receiver.

"Ms. Briggs?" Krysta said, sounding cool and professional. "I'm Candace Johnson."

Jack fumbled the receiver and cursed under his breath.

Krysta winced at the noise. "Sorry about that, Ms. Briggs. These darn shoulder gadgets for the phone are a nuisance, aren't they?"

Jack brought the receiver to his ear in time to hear Stephanie Briggs laugh.

"I take it you're calling from an office, then," said the senior editor.

"Yes. I work for Rainier Paper here in Evergreen."

Jack frowned. He wouldn't have volunteered that. Too much information might be dangerous.

"Really?" Stephanie said. "So you're one of those stalwarts who works a day job and writes by night."

"That's right," Krysta said, glancing across at Jack. "Existing mostly on sugar and caffeine."

Jack made a face at her and she winked back.

"I'm always impressed with the things writers sacrifice for their craft," Stephanie said. "But now comes the reward for all that lost sleep, Candace. *Uptown Girl* is wonderful. You're the hands-down winner of our Valentine's Day new author contest, and I'd like to make you an offer on your book."

Jack nearly dropped the receiver, and even Krysta lost her cool for a second as she yelped into the phone and punched her fist in the air.

Stephanie's tone was indulgent. "I rather thought you'd be pleased."

Krysta took a more professional tone. "Yes, I am. And I'm delighted that you like *Uptown Girl*. It's special to me, too."

Jack drew his finger quickly across his throat to signal Krysta to shut up. She was getting carried away with the moment and heading straight for trouble.

"I can tell that it is," Stephanie said. "That scene when they both fall in the drainage ditch and later wash each other clean is incredibly sensuous. I wondered what your inspiration was for that."

Krysta's eyes snapped open wide and she looked straight at Jack. "Uh, well, you know we have a lot of water here in western Washington, Ms. Briggs."

Stephanie laughed. "Call me Stephanie. And of course you're right. That explains all the water images. The rain scene, and the time they make love beside the waterfall in the park. You have a deft touch with love scenes, which is critical to our readership.''

"Th-thank you." Krysta focused on Jack, her gaze curious.

He kept his expression purposely blank.

"I also wondered if Candace Johnson is your real name or a pseudonym?"

Jack sat up straighter.

"It's a pseudonym," Krysta said smoothly. "But I plan to use it as my professional name, so you may certainly call me Candace."

Jack relaxed a little.

"Then if it's not your legal name at this point, would you consider changing it slightly?" Stephanie asked.

Krysta lifted her eyebrows as she gazed at Jack.

To what? he mouthed to her.

"To what?" Krysta repeated to Stephanie.

"Well, your first name actually started us down this road. Our vice president in charge of marketing suggested Candy instead of Candace."

Jack winced. He'd pretty much accepted the idea of using a feminine name, but Candy was a little further than he'd planned to go.

"I personally prefer Candace," Krysta said.

But then again, Jack decided, he'd be Minnie Mouse if it would help the sale of the book. He got Krysta's attention and was about to signal her to accept the nickname when Stephanie spoke again.

"Well, it would be up to you, of course, but marketing has a whole campaign mapped out, and it's going to be dynamite. By this time next year Candy Valentine's novel will be the talk of the publishing world."

Jack stared at Krysta, who stared right back, obviously in shock.

"Excuse me?" she said at last.

"Candy Valentine. We hadn't thought of it until we looked at Candace and started tossing ideas around. Sure, it's hokey, but that's okay. In fact, it's more than okay for this Valentine's

Day promotion we have lined up. And believe me, with Valentine as a pseudonym, you'll own the holiday, hands down."

"But—but won't the book be on the bottom of the racks, shelved under *V*?" Krysta asked.

Stephanie laughed. "No, dear. You'll have your own thirty-six-pocket display dump in the front of the store."

Krysta looked frantically across at Jack for some direction. Bless her, he thought. Despite the lure of a thirty-six-pocket display dump, she didn't want to sacrifice his precious pseudonym without his permission. He closed his eyes, silently apologized to his parents and nodded his assent. Candy Valentine. Good Lord.

"Well, in that case, I guess Candy Valentine it is." Krysta made a face at Jack.

"Good. That kind of team spirit will come in handy during the next year. And speaking of that, let's get to the nuts and bolts of this offer. We'll pay you half the advance upon signing the contract, and the second half when the book is accepted for publication."

"Isn't it already accepted?" Krysta asked.

"Essentially, but I have some revision suggestions, and I'm turning the book over to an assistant editor, so I'm sure she'll have some suggestions, too. Once you've completed the revisions and they've been accepted, the second half of the advance will be paid."

"But you're planning this big campaign, even though the deal isn't really final?"

"Oh, we have to, in the interests of time. If, in the end, the book isn't acceptable, we'll just have to change our plans. I doubt that would happen, but this is how the publishing world works, Candy."

"I see."

Jack watched Krysta's expression become intent. She'd obviously slipped into her business mode.

"And what is the advance?" she asked without a quiver of uncertainty in her voice.

Stephanie named an amount that Jack thought sounded quite fair considering it was his first book.

Krysta tapped her pen against the blotter and let a full three seconds elapse before she answered. "That's quite low, wouldn't you say, Stephanie?"

Once again Jack had to make a grab for the receiver, which he almost dropped. He pushed back his chair and stood, waving an arm frantically at Krysta.

"Low?" Stephanie seemed at a loss for words. "It's our standard advance for a first book."

"That may be true, but you said *Uptown Girl* is wonderful. And you're planning to put it in a thirty-six-pocket display dump. Surely you expect to make a lot of money."

Jack moved around to the front of the desk and as far as the telephone cord would reach in an effort to get to Krysta before she ruined his life. The cord was a good six feet too short.

"The book is wonderful, and we *hope* to make money," Stephanie said. "But—"

"Would you say it's better than your standard first book?" Krysta asked.

Jack danced, waved and cursed silently. Krysta gazed at him for a moment before swiveling her desk chair around to face the wall.

"Yes, I suppose it is better than the usual," Stephanie said.

"Twice as good?"

Jack closed his eyes. He was doomed.

"Perhaps," Stephanie said cautiously. "But I warn you that overpaying on a first book can backfire. If you don't earn out the advance, then—"

"It will earn out," Krysta cut in. "And I want twice your original offer."

Jack stifled a groan of despair. The chance of a lifetime, and it was slipping through his fingers because he'd allowed Donald Trump to negotiate the deal.

"I'll have to discuss this with a few people," Stephanie said.

"That's fine."

No, that's not fine, Jack raged to himself. *It's over.*

"I'll call you back in a couple of hours."

"Good. I'll still be at the office then. You can contact me here." Krysta gave the number of Rainier Paper and her extension. "It was nice talking to you, Stephanie."

"Same here, Candy. We'll be in touch." There was a solid click.

Jack practically threw the receiver into its cradle. "Are you insane? You killed my sale!"

Krysta swiveled around to face him, replaced her receiver with care and steepled her fingers. "You were ready to give that book away for nothing, weren't you?"

"Yes!" Jack shoved his glasses back on his nose with a vengeance. "Because it would have been a beginning! A huge beginning! My own display in the front of the store! The money doesn't matter."

"The money always matters. If you don't value what you do, others won't value it, either."

"This is *not* the time to take a stand on money." He pointed a finger at her. "I can guarantee you they won't call back. They'll choose another winner for the contest, and next week the manuscript will arrive in the mail, just like all the rest, and—"

"No, it won't. Weren't you listening to her? They like the book, Jack."

"Not twice as much, they don't." He paced in front of Rosie's desk. "I can't believe you did this. I wonder if you could call back and say that you'd had a little out-of-body experience just now, and you'd be willing to accept the original offer."

"I'd refuse to do that, even if you were dumb enough to ask me! You're lucky you had me call. If you'd done it, they'd immediately figure out they had a pushover on their hands and they'd probably take advantage of you."

He spun to face her. "And I wouldn't *care.* I want my name—or Candy's name—on a book jacket, Krysta. I've wanted to publish a novel for years. If Manchester will do that, they can push me over as many times as they'd like."

"Which is precisely why you need someone to take care of business for you." She folded her arms. "You're going to thank me for this, Jack. Now, shall we put all this aside for the time being and go down to the cafeteria and grab a quick bite?"

He stared at her. "How can you even think about eating at a time like this?"

"Relax." She stood and came around the desk. "They'll call back and you'll have more money. Trust me, this is the way to handle contract negotiations. Don't forget, I've spent two years in the contracts department here at Rainier, and I know this end of the business inside and out. You operate from strength, not weakness, independence, not neediness."

He had forgotten, in the excitement of having her agree to call for him. Belatedly he remembered that she'd made a point of saying a contract was never accepted without negotiation. He'd glossed right over that little statement of hers.

If he'd been paying better attention, he might not have asked her to make the call, although God knows who else he could have asked. Since taking this job and focusing on his writing, he'd given up all claim of having a social life. No, Krysta had been the only one he could turn to, and she'd shafted him. Unless by some miracle she was right. But he didn't think so.

"Come on." She took him by the arm and guided him toward the door. "You can even have cake and coffee today and I won't say a word."

3

HARD HATS WERE REQUIRED on the shipping dock, so when Jack saw Krysta approach him without one, his stomach churned. She was looking straight at him and not paying the slightest attention to what was going on around her. He hurried forward and guided her out through the double doors into the main part of the building. Once inside the tiled hall, he took off his hard hat and his safety goggles.

She turned to him. "Jack, I came to tell you—"

"I know what you came to tell me," he said in a voice tight with strain. He didn't want to hear this, but he especially didn't want to hear it in the hallway, where one of his fellow workers was heading toward them after a trip to the break room for a cigarette. "The foreman's office should be empty right now, since he's on the dock. We'll go in there." He indicated a gray metal door stenciled with Bud's name and position. "I don't think he locks it."

Fortunately Bud had left the office open, and they slipped inside the small enclosure that was barely big enough for the metal desk and the couple of chairs that occupied it.

Jack closed the door and put his goggles in his hard hat before tossing them on a chair. Then he faced her and steeled himself for the bad news. "Okay, what'd they say?"

She looked like a kid on Christmas morning. "They went for it."

"You're kidding." His brain refused to assimilate what she was saying. He'd decided during their brief lunch that he was incapable of staying angry with Krysta over this. It was his game, and he'd gambled and lost. The best thing to do was forget it and go on.

"No, I'm not kidding." She was so excited she was trembling. "Now, listen carefully, because maybe you'll learn a valuable lesson from this. Stephanie said she was impressed with my bargaining skills, and that she liked working with someone who valued her own talent."

Jack adjusted his glasses, as if that might make him hear better. "You're sure you understood her right?"

"They're buying it, Jack." Her voice hummed with delight. "For twice the amount."

The truth finally hit him, and without thinking, he grabbed her and swung her around, nearly colliding with the desk in the process. "They went for it! I sold a book! I really sold a book!"

"You sold a book!" she echoed, hugging him tight.

He glanced down at her. Her mouth was so close and he was so damned happy that he couldn't stop himself. A moment like this came once in a lifetime, and it deserved to be celebrated. As his lips touched hers, he knew this kiss would beat a bottle of Dom Pérignon any day.

He claimed her with all the triumph he felt, and she responded. Good Lord, did she respond. Within seconds he forgot about the book sale, the shipping dock and even Rainier Paper. There was only Krysta, coming alive in his arms, making him ache with a ferocity he hadn't allowed himself to feel in a long time.

Then, just as quickly, the moment ended as she eased away from him. Her face was pink and she lowered her gaze. "Congratulations."

He took a moment to get his bearings. Wow. "Thanks."

"Stephanie said she and the assistant editor would get their notes together on the revisions and send you a letter," she said, still not looking at him. "But you're not to touch the love scenes."

"Oh?" His heartbeat slowly returned to normal. "Why not?"

Krysta lifted her head and tried for an impersonal gaze. She almost succeeded. "The love scenes are luscious, I believe she said."

"Mm." His arms and chest still felt the imprint of her body, and her scent filled his nostrils. He'd better usher her out of here before he really overstepped his limits. He had to remember that she'd pushed him away. Nothing had really changed between them. "Well, I can't thank you enough. I guess we'd both better get back to work."

"I guess so. But there is one other thing, and I'm not sure what you want to do about it."

One other thing. He should have known. "They've decided not to publish the book for another three years?"

"No, no. Nothing like that. They want to stay on schedule with the Valentine's Day promotion next year, just like Stephanie said on the phone. But before I hung up, she asked for a bio."

His anxiety level dropped several notches. "No problem. I'll just leave out the football and emphasize the writing class. A bio doesn't have to reveal my gender."

"That's true, but I think a picture will."

"They want a picture of me?"

"No, they want a picture of Candy Valentine."

He cringed anew at the pseudonym. "I hope you told them you weren't photogenic. Ugly, even."

"I tried, but she said they didn't care. I said I had nothing recent, but that didn't matter to her, either. She was getting very suspicious, and I was afraid she might start asking the wrong questions, so finally I agreed to come up with something."

Jack rubbed the back of his neck. Then he glanced at her. "Would you consider it?"

"Sending a picture of me? I don't know what else we can do."

He caught her use of "we." She considered herself part of this project now. At least there was that. "I'd sure appreciate it if you could find a picture, then. This should be the last thing I have to ask of you."

"It's no problem, really. I believe in finishing what I start. And obviously this isn't quite finished."

"No," Jack said, gazing at her and remembering the explosive nature of their kiss. "I guess not."

AT LUNCH THE NEXT DAY Krysta sat down and placed a manila envelope next to her tray. "I went home last night and started going through pictures, but I didn't have very many of myself." She glanced at Jack. Much as she tried to retain the sisterly attitude she'd always had toward him, it was slipping fast. "I guess people don't keep a lot of pictures of themselves around. Just of other people." She didn't mention that while searching for the right picture she'd replayed their shared kisses many times over in her mind. That second kiss had really rocked her. She'd never been kissed with such abandon or responded with such gusto herself. Thank God she'd come to her senses and pulled away. Once again she'd put her reaction down to the unusual nature of the moment. Discovering Jack wasn't the person she'd imagined had flustered her more than a little.

"I hope you didn't spend much time on this picture business." He slathered his hot dog with mustard. "We're just throwing something at them to satisfy their public relations department."

"You sound as if appearances don't matter."

"They don't, in this case. All that really matters is the manuscript." He took a large bite.

As she watched him ingest the preservative-filled hot dog she reminded herself that although he might have given her the most exciting kiss of her life, he was still just plain Jack, a guy who needed direction, both in matters of diet and business. She'd concentrate on the most important first. "I agree the manuscript is important, but so is your image. Stephanie already has a mental picture of Candy Valentine as a competent, imaginative person with a lot of confidence in herself. The picture we send should support that mental image."

He finished chewing and swallowed. "How can we miss?

You're a competent, imaginative person with a lot of confidence in yourself. I'm sure that comes across on camera." He reached for the envelope. "Let's see what you've got."

"Wait." She snatched it back. "Let me present them and explain my reasoning for each one. Then we'll choose."

He chuckled and shook his head. "Good thing I didn't let you proofread my manuscript. It'd probably still be in rewrites while you searched for that last little typo."

She gasped. "You didn't send it in with *mistakes*, did you, Jack?"

He leaned toward her, his blue eyes serious behind the wire-rimmed glasses. "Yes, Krysta, I probably did, exhausted as I was. But I threw caution to the winds and sent it in, anyway. And look what happened."

"You were lucky!" She wondered how Jack had made it this far in life, disorganized and sloppy as he seemed to be. "Mistakes undermine your credibility. I'm certainly glad I didn't know about this before I bargained on your behalf yesterday. I might not have had the confidence to push so hard, knowing there were probably misplaced commas and heaven knows what else lurking in that manuscript."

"Lots of good sex."

She looked into his eyes and saw the teasing light there, but behind the teasing burned a more potent fire, one that brought back the memory of their explosive kiss from the day before. "So Stephanie said." She took a quick gulp of water and opened the envelope. "Okay. I narrowed it down to three."

"Sounds like plenty of choices to me."

"I'm not so sure." She pulled out the top one, a black and white shot she'd had taken to mail out with her resume three years ago. "This is actually the most correct thing to send. But it may be too polished for someone who's just a beginner. Not spontaneous enough, after the way I protested about sending a picture in the first place."

Jack took the picture by the edges. She was surprised he handled it with such care, given his general tendencies.

He studied it intently before looking up at her with a critical eye. "The photographer didn't capture your spirit. This is quite beautiful, but it's also a little flat."

She bristled. "He's an excellent photographer with a studio in Seattle. I told him I wanted this for professional purposes, and I think he made me look very professional. Derek complimented me on that picture when he saw it in the personnel files."

"I'm sure he did. It's Hamilton's sort of picture."

"Which points out his good business sense. This picture helped me get the job here at Rainier. You're awfully hard on Derek, Jack. He's never done anything to you, and you could probably learn some things from him that would help you now that you're moving into a new career."

He looked so much like a belligerent little boy who'd been chastised that she laughed. "Be honest, now. Derek is not a bad guy."

The belligerence cleared from his eyes and he smiled. "You're right. In fact, he's a real inspiration."

She didn't trust that kind of turnaround from a man like Jack. And she had a new respect for his use of words now that she knew about his writing. "That didn't sound particularly sincere."

"It should, because I mean it." He shifted in his chair. "What else do you have?"

She picked up the second photograph, one of her sitting in Juliet Bancroft's gazebo during a garden party Juliet had hosted for Rainier employees the previous summer. Krysta had borrowed a lace dress and picture hat from Rosie's sister for the event, which had been held a couple of weeks before Jack had begun work at the paper plant. Juliet had taken the picture, saying Krysta looked like something out of *Victoria* magazine against the latticework of the gazebo and a riot of climbing pink roses. That party was where Derek had first noticed her.

"Now, this is certainly romantic enough to be Candy Valentine." She handed it to him, waiting while he wiped mustard from his hands with a napkin. "Maybe too romantic," she added. "They might not take a woman like this seriously enough. But I thought you might go for this one, so I put it in."

Jack's gaze softened as he looked at the picture. Once again he glanced up at her, as if to compare the real woman with the photograph. "Better. Much better. But deceptive. You're not this sweet."

"I beg your pardon!"

He laughed, which dislodged his glasses. He pushed them back up on his nose and grinned at her. "Sorry. But remember that I listened in on the extension while you put the screws to Stephanie Briggs, esteemed senior editor of the prestigious Manchester Publishing House. You won't be able to pull the demure routine on me any more."

She couldn't help smiling. He was absolutely right, and after the first shock of indignation she discovered she preferred his assessment of her to Derek's, who had recently thought he was complimenting her by telling her she was a "lovely, uncomplicated girl." Derek underestimated her, and maybe that was one reason why she couldn't warm to him.

"Hey, nice pictures," Bud, the foreman from shipping, commented as he walked past their table carrying a loaded tray. He paused to look at the studio portrait and the gazebo shot. Then he glanced at Krysta. "You entering some beauty contest or something?"

Her brain went blank.

"She has a pen pal in Tasmania, and she was wondering what picture to send to her," Jack said smoothly.

"Oh." Bud consulted the pictures again. "The roses one. The other one doesn't look very friendly."

"Thanks," Krysta said.

"Anytime. And next time you pay us a visit in shipping, get a hard hat from my office first, okay?"

"I promise."

Bud looked at Jack. "See you at the dock in twenty minutes,

Killigan. You can't make us any money looking at pen pal
pictures."

"Right."

As Bud moved out of earshot, Krysta let out a sigh of relief.
"You came up with that pretty fast, Jack."

"Don't forget I write fiction. And we do have to hurry
along. What's the last one you brought?"

She withdrew the final picture, a snapshot her brother Ned
had taken of her during the Father's Day picnic on the beach.
Everyone had brought cameras and they'd produced a stack
of shots—the free-for-all volleyball game, everyone taking
turns cooking hamburgers, the furious activity surrounding
the sand castle they'd built, and her father hoisting a beer
with a happy smile on his face. Then, at sunset, Ned had
posed Krysta against the same gnarled piece of driftwood
she'd used for her shot of her father and his sons. The breeze
had ruffled her hair and the joy of the day shone from her
face.

Jack took one look at the picture and nodded. "That's it."

"I don't know. I mean, shorts and a halter top aren't very
professional. I'm even barefoot, and my hair's all askew."

"It's perfect." Jack focused on the picture. "Who took it?"

"Ned. Why?"

"He has a great eye. Maybe he should go into it profession-
ally."

"I don't know. Isn't that kind of a risky occupation?"

He glanced at her. "Every occupation is risky. Today's hot
career is tomorrow's unemployment line. You can't guarantee those four brothers of yours a steady living, Krysta."

She lifted her chin. "Maybe not, but I want them to have a
darned good head start, which means getting a degree. You
may do fine without one, but you're the exception."

He regarded her steadily. "I'd say your brothers' greatest
asset is having you there cheering them on."

"Oh, I doubt that." Her cheeks warmed.

"I don't. At least Ned knows your value. He's captured it in
this picture. Is it the only print?"

She became more embarrassed. "Well, no. All my brothers reacted like you have to the picture, and Ned had to make copies for everyone. My dad has an eight-by-ten on his dresser. I told Ned he certainly didn't have to make a print for me, but he said he might as well as long as he was getting copies. He told me to give it to a boyfriend or something."

"So how come Hamilton doesn't have it?"

It was a puzzling question she had no answer to. "I guess I forgot," she said.

"His loss, then." Jack opened the flap of the chest pocket on his coveralls and tucked the picture carefully inside.

She still had misgivings about such an informal shot. "Are you sure that's the right one? To be honest, all three of them have some drawback, in my opinion. I even considered getting somebody to take a roll of me so we'd have more choices."

Jack shook his head. "Somebody could take six rolls of film and not get anything better than this." He patted his pocket. "You look happy, confident, full of life. If they need a mental picture of Candy, this is the one I want them to have."

She realized she'd just lost control of the decision. She was used to Jack being more tentative, but in this matter he seemed to know exactly what he wanted, and he didn't plan to consult her further. Well, it was his career, after all, even if it was her picture he was using.

He glanced at the clock on the cafeteria wall and pushed himself away from the table. "I'd better get back to the dock. Thanks for the picture, Krysta. This really should be the last thing I have to bother you about."

"It's no bother. I've enjoyed it."

He smiled. "Especially the power negotiating part, right?"

"It worked, didn't it?"

"Yes, I have to admit it worked. Left to my own devices, I would have been a poorer man."

"When will you get the money?"

"Not for a while, I suppose. I've read some magazine articles that say it can be weeks or even months before the contract shows up. Then I have to sign it and return it before the first check will arrive."

"Don't you dare sign that contract without letting me go over it, Jack Killigan."

He winked at her. "Pretty soon I'll have to offer you a cut for all this business management advice."

"You most certainly will not! I'm helping you out of friendship, Jack."

He picked up his tray and gazed at her. "And you've been a good friend, Krysta," he said. Then he turned and walked toward the tray cart.

Krysta watched him leave the cafeteria, his physique disguised by the bulky coveralls that everyone in shipping had to wear. She'd never paid much attention to his body before. After all, he'd been just plain Jack, the happy-go-lucky Killigan kid, a boy going nowhere. Not the sort of person Krysta, who planned to do something significant with her life, could relate to.

But she'd related to him with embarrassing enthusiasm when he'd kissed her yesterday. She'd become aware of broad shoulders, strong arms, and a very talented mouth, attributes she'd never associated with Jack Killigan before.

She needed to forget that kiss, because she had no intention of becoming involved with Jack. Perhaps she hadn't guessed that he was a writer but otherwise she knew his personality very well. He wasn't at all her type.

4

AFTER KRYSTA PROVIDED the snapshot of her at the beach, Jack's view over his computer improved considerably. Before he sent the picture to Manchester Publishing, he took it to a print shop and had them copy it as a two-by-three-foot poster that he tacked on the wall. His second romance novel had been going pretty well, but with the extra advantage of Krysta smiling at him with such tenderness every night, he found his fingers flying over the keys.

His villain was taking shape nicely, too, thanks to Krysta's suggestion that Derek Hamilton could be useful to him in his new career. Jack agreed with Krysta that Derek wasn't such a terrible guy, and he probably didn't deserve being skewered as the villain in this book, but Jack took great pleasure in doing it, anyway.

And Jack's stray cat had a name. One night as he was petting the cat's thick fur he realized it had much the same shading and color as Krysta's hair, which might have been why he'd allowed the cat to adopt him in the first place. Even the cat's green eyes reminded him of Krysta's.

He should have figured out sooner why he'd developed such an affinity for the animal, but he'd probably tried not to acknowledge his growing feelings for a woman he couldn't have. She had her sights firmly set on the likes of Derek, and if that was what she wanted, that was what he wanted her to get.

He'd counseled himself to be satisfied with the friendship they shared, which had been strengthened by their collaboration on his career. Every lunch hour she'd begin the conversation by asking if he'd seen any sign of the contract yet, because without that he couldn't begin to expect his first check.

Krysta had spent that money several times over. A haircut was first on the list, but that wouldn't take much. Then she'd suggested contact lenses. He'd worn them all through high school and college, but then he'd lost one, and money had been tight, so he'd gone back to an old pair of glasses. After the contact lenses she wanted him to buy a car. He'd tried to sell her on the charisma of a Harley, but she'd insisted that a motorcycle was cold, wet and impossible if you wanted to arrive somewhere looking like a person instead of a drowned rat.

Jack had let her rave on about all the things he should do to improve his situation when the money arrived. He planned to put the whole advance in the bank. Maybe, if he kept saving, he'd be able to quit his day job and write full time. Now, that would be heaven.

That and having Krysta near him full time. But that was truly out of reach, so he'd concentrate on the other goal and hope that in the chasing of it he'd ease the persistent, painfully sweet ache in his heart.

TWO WEEKS HAD PASSED uneventfully when Krysta appeared once again on the shipping dock. This time she'd perched a yellow hard hat on her honey-blond hair, and she wore a winter white pantsuit that defined her trim figure beautifully. Jack threw the forklift into neutral and sat there staring at her for the pure joy of it. He must have been blind back in high school.

She walked over to the idling machine and tipped her face up to look at him. Her gaze was anxious. "Can I see you for a minute? We've got trouble."

Heart hammering, Jack glanced over at Bud and held up his hand, fingers spread, to indicate he needed a five-minute break.

Bud waved his approval.

Jack shut down the forklift and swung to the ground. Trouble. Dammit, he'd known something would go wrong with the book deal. Somebody had read the manuscript and objected to any advance. He still had no contract, and he wasn't sure what a verbal agreement was worth, especially if it came out that he hadn't been the one agreeing.

Once again they headed for Bud's office. Jack held the door for her, followed her inside and closed it securely. "What kind of trouble?"

She faced him and took off the hard hat. She was trembling. "I knew it was a mistake for me to pretend to be you. I knew it from the beginning. I can't imagine what we'll do now, Jack."

Her agitation required him to be the calming influence for a change. It was a nice change. He pushed aside his own fears and placed both hands on her shoulders. "Take it easy. We'll work it out, whatever it is. Just tell me what happened."

She took an unsteady breath. "It was the picture. They loved that picture. Before they got it they were just going to announce the winner around Valentine's Day in some magazine I've never heard of."

"*Publisher's Weekly*. I know. It was in the contest rules."

"Well, now they want to do more. They want to make the announcement a big deal in New York on Valentine's Day, and, Jack, they want Candy to be there!"

"To be there?" Stunned, he released his grip on her shoulders. "You must have misunderstood. They don't treat first-time authors like that."

"That's exactly what Stephanie said! But they've revamped their plans, considering the picture, and the...bigger advance—"

"Aha!" He stabbed a finger in her direction. "*You* helped us get into this mess!"

"Jack, I had no idea this would happen." Her green gaze pleaded with him. "You'll have to tell them. You'll just have to tell them the truth."

He went cold at the prospect. They'd bought Candy Valentine as a package, a package that now included a beautiful, promotable author. Now they were planning a big reception in New York for their latest find, who'd had the guts to demand more money for her book.

He turned the matter over in his mind and could only come up with one solution. "I don't think it would be wise to tell them now," he said carefully.

"You have no choice!"

"Yes, I do." He gazed down at her. "If you'll help me."

She backed away as far as the little room would allow. "Oh, no, you don't. I can't do this, Jack. Negotiating on the phone is one thing. Sending in my picture was okay, too, but I'm not—"

"Krysta, my career hangs in the balance." He was playing shamelessly on her caretaking nature, and he knew it. Later he might feel guilty. Right now he was desperate. "I'll coach you. You'll be great. I know you'll be great."

"If you think I can go to New York by myself and pretend that I'm the person who wrote that book, you're crazier than I thought you were!"

Necessity became the mother of invention. "You won't be alone. I'll go with you."

"They're offering one first-class plane ticket, one suite at the Marriott Marquis. It would be inappropriate to ask to bring a guest on a business trip like this."

"They'll never know I'm there."

"You'll hide?" Her shocked expression gradually gave way to a giggle of laughter. "Jack, what *are* you suggesting? This is real life, not one of your books."

Her laughter brought a smile to his lips. This disaster was beginning to show its more appealing side. "You said it was a suite, right? Plenty of room for me, and nobody at Manchester has to know. I'll be around to coach you before each meeting and debrief you when you come back." *And we'll be together in that room all night.* "It will work, Krysta."

"You're crazy." She shook her head, but a smile still played around her mouth.

He could tell she was intrigued by the novelty of the plan, so he added another inducement. "Ever been to New York?"

"Of course not. It's a very expensive place to visit."

"Well, I spent time there during those years I knocked around the country. It's an exciting city. And it sounds as if Manchester is ready to lay Manhattan at your feet."

"No, *your* feet," she corrected him.

"*Our* feet, then. What do you say?"

"I don't know, Jack." She lowered her gaze to her clasped hands. "You'll have to give me some time to think about this."

"How long?"

She glanced up at him. "I told Stephanie I'd call her back tomorrow with an answer."

"And of course you know you can trust me to be a complete gentleman at all times." *Unless you beg me not to.*

"Oh, of course. That's no problem."

He wished she hadn't replied to that with such complete conviction. She obviously still thought of him as good old Jack. She had no idea what being a gentleman in this situation would cost him.

KRYSTA SETTLED INTO the leather luxury of a first-class airline seat and sipped a mimosa the flight attendant had given her soon after takeoff. The champagne and orange juice combination heightened her sense of unreality. It was difficult to believe she was on her way to New York, traveling in a style she'd only seen portrayed in the movies.

She'd told her father and brothers the same story as everyone else, that she'd won a free weekend at a health spa. They'd all been so happy for her she'd felt incredibly guilty about the lie, but she and Jack had agreed they couldn't chance letting anyone, not even her beloved family, know the truth.

Gazing out the window at the blanket of clouds below, she tried to appear nonchalant about the trip. Her every action would reflect on Jack's reputation, and she was determined to represent him to the best of her ability. Thank heaven no one occupied the seat next to her. She wasn't up to answering the kind of questions chance traveling companions often asked.

"Ms. Valentine?"

Krysta didn't respond.

"Excuse me, Ms. Valentine." The flight attendant touched her arm.

Krysta jumped before realizing that she hadn't answered to the name on her airline ticket. She'd have to work on that. "Sorry—" she looked at the attendant's name badge "—Holly. I guess I was daydreaming."

The flight attendant leaned forward, her expression solicitous. "I promise not to interrupt you again, but I need to get your order for lunch. We have beef tenderloin or a very nice tuna filet."

"The tenderloin would be fine." She tried to sound patient and slightly bored, as if she were asked to make that sort of decision on a regular basis while cruising thirty thousand feet above the ground.

"Good choice." The flight attendant straightened and turned toward someone who was standing in the aisle beyond Krysta's line of vision. "May I help you?" she asked in an imperious tone.

Krysta leaned forward and saw that it was Jack standing there, a large envelope in his hand. The flight attendant looked ready to march him straight back to his seat in coach.

"It's okay, Holly." Krysta said. "I need to speak to this gentleman a moment."

Holly looked Jack up and down. He wore a corduroy blazer that had seen better days and was a little tight across the shoulders, a red flannel shirt, jeans and weathered running shoes. His dark hair was caught back with a rubber band and his glasses were still held together with tape.

Jack met her appraisal with a calm gaze. "I promise not to contaminate the area for long, Holly."

Holly flushed. "Oh, I didn't—"

"Hey, it's okay. I realize it's part of your job to keep those of us in steerage from penetrating the velvet curtain." Jack's devilish grin transformed him into quite a rakish character, in Krysta's opinion.

Holly's attitude shifted. She smiled back. "Take as long as you like," she murmured, and gave him a sidelong glance before returning to the galley.

Jack plopped into the empty seat next to Krysta. "What're you drinking?"

"A mimosa. Orange juice and—"

"I know what's in a mimosa." He stretched his long legs and worked his shoulders into the padded leather seat. "Not bad up here. Thanks for putting in the good word for me, or I'd have been tossed out on my ear."

Holly reappeared and gave Jack a brilliant smile. "Can I get you anything?"

Krysta stared at the flight attendant. Jack had made a conquest. Somehow Krysta hadn't pictured Jack as the conquering type, yet with one disarming smile he had Holly eating out of his hand. Or maybe it was the tight jacket that emphasized the breadth of his shoulders that had caught her attention, or the light in his blue eyes. But she was definitely interested. Krysta glanced over at Jack, who seemed oblivious to the effect he was having on the flight attendant.

"Nothing for me, thanks," he said. "I'll just deliver my package and be on my way."

Holly leaned closer to Jack. "No one's sitting there," she murmured. "As long as Ms. Valentine doesn't mind, I don't think it would hurt anything if you—"

"Highly inadvisable, Holly," Jack interrupted, his grin flashing again. "Disturbing the social order is a dangerous business. If people like me start infiltrating first class, next you'll find us storming executive dining rooms, then invading private clubs." He nudged his glasses back onto the bridge of his nose. "And before you know it—anarchy."

Holly laughed. "I hardly think so."

"Besides, I'm sure my seatmates miss me already." Jack

handed Krysta the fat envelope he'd been holding. "In all the rush I forgot to give you some reading material for the trip."

"Oh!" Krysta took the package, which probably contained his manuscript. She'd asked to read it on the plane and then had forgotten her request. As he eased his large frame out of the seat and into the aisle, she glanced up at him. "What seatmates?"

"I think they said they were traveling to a beauty pageant or something."

"And I suppose you're in the middle seat?" His sudden transformation into Don Juan was quite irritating.

Amusement sparkled in his eyes. "It seemed like the gentlemanly thing to do. See you later...Ms. Valentine."

Krysta watched him stroll down the aisle and push aside the curtain dividing the first class cabin from coach. Then she became aware that Holly was also watching his departure.

"You know who he reminds me of?" Holly said.

"I really can't imagine."

"Clark Kent. I can just picture him whipping off those glasses and turning into Superman."

Krysta resented the dreamy expression on Holly's face, and the thought of Jack sandwiched between two beauty pageant entrants didn't improve her mood. "I'd like another mimosa, please, Holly," she said.

"MS. VALENTINE?"

Krysta left the page she was reading with great reluctance to look up at Holly. "What?"

"We'll be landing soon. I'll need to have you stow your tray table and return your seat to the upright position, please."

"Landing? In New York?"

"That's correct. We should be on the ground in fourteen minutes."

Krysta glanced at her watch, unable to believe that hours had passed while she'd been totally engrossed in Jack's book. She vaguely remembered cutting the tenderloin all up so she could feed herself with just her fork while she continued to read.

In those hours she'd become the characters in Jack's book, and through them she'd experienced anger, joy and sorrow. She still had two chapters to go, but already she'd been drawn into a love so deep it brought tears to her eyes. And in its wake she'd felt the characters' sexual desire, felt it with a visceral response that had left her restless and aroused. Stephanie's comments about Jack's love scenes hadn't prepared Krysta adequately for Jack's expertise in that area. Expertise on paper, Krysta reminded herself. Just because Jack could write about making love in such sensuous detail didn't mean that he'd be that kind of lover in real life.

Not that it mattered what kind of lover he was. Jack might have managed to finish a book and sell it, but deep down he still lacked the sort of drive and ambition that she sought in a man. His willingness to take a low advance was proof of that. She suspected he'd never be particularly concerned about how much money he made on his writing so long as someone continued to publish him.

Yet his ability with words intimidated her a little, truth be told. Talent like that didn't come along every day, although Jack was the sort of man who might squander his impressive talent. She'd do her level best to make sure that didn't happen in the next four days, at least, although it was a frightening responsibility now that she knew what Jack had to offer the world.

Derek's intellect had never frightened her, and he had never squandered a single opportunity in his upward journey, according to the tales he told. She admired that sort of drive, but she wondered if reading Jack's book might help Derek learn to kiss better. Jack's description of a long, lingering kiss had made her tingle as she read it. Her two personal experiences with kissing Jack hadn't been like that at all. The first had been her idea, and it had been over before either of them had quite realized what had happened. The second kiss had been more like a bomb detonating than the slow, sweet seduction Jack had written about so well.

Jack probably just had a good imagination, Krysta thought as she handed her glass and crumpled napkin to Holly and stowed her tray table in the arm of the seat. He'd only created a fantasy, after all, she mused while gathering the pages together and returning them to the envelope. Real life could never live up to the sort of pleasure Jack had depicted between a man and a woman. Only a fool would think differently, and she was no fool.

She fastened the envelope's clasp and held the package on her lap as the plane descended. When the plane hit an air pocket she gripped the envelope with both hands in a sudden possessive gesture. It was, she thought as the plane's wheels skidded on the tarmac and the New York skyline appeared in miniature outside her window, a very good book.

JACK'S HEIGHT ALLOWED him to hand down parcels stored in the overhead bins to the two women who had sat on either side of him during the flight. While in Seattle for a genealogy convention, they'd loaded up on souvenirs for their respective grandchildren. After several hours of anecdotes and accordion-folded snapshot holders, Jack could recite the exact ages, names, hobbies and cute little habits of Sadie's six grandchildren and Bernice's five. He'd heard about Sadie's battle with gallstones and Bernice's recent knee operation. And he knew more than he'd ever cared to about the problems of menopause.

He'd been delighted with the nonstop conversation because it had kept his mind off the nerve-racking idea of Krysta sitting in first class reading his book. Sending it to New York hadn't taken as much courage as walking it up the aisle to the front of the plane. If she hated the book she probably wouldn't tell him, but he'd know, anyway. Her opinion meant more to him than he'd ever imagined it could when he'd proposed this crazy scheme, and he was really sweating her response.

At least he wouldn't have to face her immediately. First class would deplane ahead of coach, and all she'd brought was a rolling carry-on bag, so she'd be down the jetway and whisked off by a waiting limo driver before he made it into the terminal. He'd take a bus. Fortunately he knew his way around New York and could get to the Marriott Marquis using public transportation. To say he was on a budget this trip was a gross understatement.

Knowing he was in no rush, he offered to help carry Bernice's and Sadie's packages, an offer they accepted after some protest. He blocked the aisle so they could climb out and then followed them, his duffel bag slung over one shoulder and a bulging shopping bag in each hand.

"You should come to my hairdresser in Brooklyn while you're here, Jack," Bernice said over her shoulder as the two women preceded him down the jetway. "I'll bet if you had a nice haircut, you'd be surprised how the girls would flock around."

"Thanks, Bernice. I'll consider it." Jack smiled to himself. Bernice seemed to have taken lessons from Krysta, except that Bernice's goal was to marry him off, not send him up the corporate ladder.

"I could get you a discount on a better pair of glasses," Sadie added. "That has to be uncomfortable, with the tape and all."

"I'm used to it, but thanks."

Outside the jetway two middle-aged men stood waiting and Bernice and Sadie rushed toward them, arms outstretched. Jack followed with the bags and was introduced to the husbands, each of whom clapped him on the back and invited him home for a good meal.

In the flurry of goodwill Jack almost missed seeing Krysta wander right past the limo driver holding a sign with "Candy Valentine" written on it. He glimpsed her mistake in time to excuse himself from the two couples and sprint after her.

"Candy!" he called.

Paying no attention to the name, she continued down the

terminal pulling her rolling carry-on. He muttered a curse as
he dodged through the crowd after her. They'd agreed not to
use her real name here in New York so the publisher
wouldn't be able to trace her in any way and discover dis-
crepancies in her story.

Finally he got near enough to grab her arm. With a cry of
alarm she swung her purse at his head.

He ducked. "Hey! It's me!"

"Jack!" Color drained from her face as she stood there
trembling. "I thought you were a mugger."

"Sorry. Let's move out of the center of traffic." He propped
his duffel bag on top of her suitcase and took command of the
handle while he used his free hand to guide her away from
the flow of people.

She leaned against the wall and put a hand to her chest
"Whew. Adrenaline rush."

"I didn't mean to scare you, but you missed the limo
driver. He's back at the gate."

"I didn't see anyone."

"He was holding a sign that read Candy Valentine."

"Oh." She took a deep breath and gave him a sheepish
smile. "I really should have practiced more with that name.
That's twice I've spaced out about it."

"If you hurry, I'm sure you can catch him. It was a big
plane, and I imagine people in the back rows are still getting
off."

"But he probably saw me walk right past him. What will I
say?"

"Tell him the truth. It's your new name and you still aren't
quite used to it."

"I'll do that." She straightened and peered down the length
of the terminal. "Can you see him from here?"

"Yeah. He's wearing a navy uniform and a billed cap, just
like you'd imagine a proper chauffeur would."

"Where?" She stood on tiptoe.

"Over this way." Taking her by the shoulders, he pointed
her in the right direction to see the chauffeur. Beneath the fab-

ric of her suit jacket, her body felt warm and supple, and he
caught a whiff of her delicate cologne.

"I see him now."

He released her with reluctance. "I'd better not walk down
with you."

"That's okay. I'll be fine." She smiled at him. "Sorry to have
tried to clobber you like that. It's just that I've heard all those
horror stories about New York, and when somebody grabbed
me, I reacted."

"Good. I'm glad you have that kind of reaction. You probably won't have any problems because you'll be with people
all the time you're here, but it's a good idea to stay alert. The
crime here doesn't match the reputation, but you still have to
be reasonably careful."

"I will be." She gazed at him with a warmth that he found
disconcerting. "I liked your book, by the way."

The book. Ah, yes, the book. He swallowed. "You did?"

"Yes. You're quite a lover on paper, Jack. See you at the
Marriott." She turned and walked toward the uniformed
chauffeur.

Jack stared after her, his heart pounding. One thing was for
sure. Krysta Lueckenhoff could deliver a hell of an exit line.

5

WHEN KRYSTA WALKED through the door of the suite it took real effort to stifle a gasp of pleasure.

"I trust this will be satisfactory," the bellhop said as he wheeled her suitcase through the door.

"It will be fine," she said.

"Would you like me to unpack your things?"

"No, thank you." She extended her hand with the folded bill she'd decided on for the tip. She hoped it was enough.

The bellhop took the money and smiled. "Thank you. Enjoy your stay."

After he left, she gave him some time to walk down the hall before she let out a whoop of delight and spun around in the center of the room. Then she approached the floor-to-ceiling windows carefully, her stomach churning, both from the thought of being so high above the city and the excitement of a wide-angle view of Times Square. Just as Jack had predicted, Manhattan lay, literally, at her feet. She'd give anything if her father and brothers could see this. Joe, especially, would go crazy. But she didn't dare even take pictures, because she was supposed to be at a health resort.

She'd been reading travel guides for days in preparation, but to actually see the band of illuminated news parading around the top of the triangular Allied Tower gave her goosebumps. Chips of light dotted skyscrapers as office switches were thrown to greet the approaching night. Krysta's gaze swept outward, and the chips became sparkling pinpoints that finally blended into a dazzling necklace of gems stretching to the horizon.

The faint bleat of taxicabs drifted up from the streaming activity on the rush-hour-filled streets, but Krysta felt wrapped in the serene isolation of privilege. On the forty-fifth floor she smelled no carbon monoxide, only the fragrance of a huge bouquet of flowers sitting in the center of a banquet table placed near the suite's wet bar.

She wandered over to the bouquet, so big she couldn't get both arms around it. The card read, "Welcome to the Big Apple, Candy. Manchester Publishing."

So Jack's publisher had arranged for the bouquet. The gesture reminded Krysta that she wasn't here on vacation. Tomorrow morning Stephanie Briggs would be waiting in her office for the arrival of Candy Valentine. The reality of what she was attempting slashed Krysta's fantasy balloon to ribbons.

For the next three days she was supposed to be romance novelist Candy Valentine, an author with impressive skills, and she'd never written anything more creative than a personal letter. The people at Manchester Publishing would see through her facade immediately. She'd end up embarrassing herself and ruining Jack's career before it even got started. This was the dumbest stunt she'd ever tried. If she was smart she'd—

The sound of the telephone made her jump. The ring seemed to be coming from everywhere, but she located a phone next to a flowered sofa. She crossed over to it, then hesitated with her hand over the receiver. It could be Stephanie from Manchester. Answering the phone would commit her to this charade, once and for all.

She walked away from the phone and into the bedroom, which had no windows but was lit softly by bedside lamps flanking the broad expanse of a king-sized bed. The phone next to the bed was also ringing, and a third ring seemed to be coming from the bathroom.

She investigated, and sure enough, there was a phone in there, too. As she gazed at it, all the phones stopped ringing. She let out a sigh of relief and walked into the bedroom to sit on the edge of the bed and think.

Within thirty seconds the ringing started again.

"Oh, all right!" She grabbed the receiver, figuring she could always pretend to be very sick. In fact, that was an excellent plan. She made her voice sound low and throaty. "Hello?"

"Krysta? Where the hell have you been? And why do you sound like one of the Budweiser frogs?"

"Oh, *Jack.* I thought you were Stephanie. I was pretending to be sick."

"What on earth for?"

"I—I'm getting cold feet, Jack."

"Is that why you let the phone ring about twenty times without answering before?"

"Was that you, too?"

"Yes, that was me, and as the phone kept ringing I pictured you passed out, tied up, murdered by the bellhop, you name it. I can't decide whether I'm mad as hell that you're okay or faint with relief. Anyway, I'm glad nothing's wrong."

"Something *is* wrong. I can't do this. I don't know anything about writing, and I can't possibly—"

"Give me the room number so I can come up."

"Okay, but I'm warning you that we might as well call Manchester right now and confess everything."

"What's the room number, Krysta?"

She told him.

"Be right there."

While she waited for him, she paced and rehearsed a speech about honesty being the best policy. Finally, a firm knock sounded on the hall door, and she checked through the peephole before opening it. Her speech was on the tip of her tongue, but when he walked in, his expression a mixture of hope and determination, she couldn't say a word. He was counting on her to come through for him, and she couldn't let him down, no matter how scared she was.

"You okay now?" he asked, looking into her eyes.

"I'm okay."

"Good. I know you can do this."

She felt ashamed of her momentary loss of confidence. Jack didn't need her to fall apart on him, and she vowed not to do it again. "Can you believe this place?" she asked.

He surveyed the luxurious suite. "Wow. This isn't bad." He dropped his duffel bag in the middle of the room and crossed to the windows. "Not bad at all. I would say Manchester thinks a lot of Candy Valentine."

"Definitely." She gestured toward the flowers. "Those are from them, too."

"No kidding?" He went over to inspect the bouquet and read the card. "Very classy," he remarked, tucking the card back inside the arrangement. Then he glanced at Krysta. "You look right at home here, you know. I guess suites at the Marriott are your style."

"I've never stayed in a place like this in my life."

"Stick with Derek Hamilton and it'll probably be one fancy hotel after another."

Before she could stop herself, Krysta grimaced at the thought.

Jack's eyebrows lifted. "Do I detect trouble in paradise?"

She turned away from his perceptive gaze and walked toward the windows.

"Come on, Krysta." Jack walked over to join her by the windows. "You can tell old Jack."

She sighed. It would be nice to confide in someone. She hadn't dared tell even Rosie about her aversion to becoming intimate with Derek. But after reading Jack's manuscript, Krysta had an idea that he'd understand. She concentrated on the news flashing around the Allied Tower's perimeter. "Derek is the perfect sort of man for me," she began. "He's going places and he can help me go places, too."

"I absolutely agree. So what's with the sour face when I mention the very same thing?"

"I...don't like kissing him. And if I don't like that part, I can't imagine I'll like...the rest," she admitted softly. When Jack didn't respond to her statement, she glanced sideways at him. "Did you hear what I said?"

He stared straight ahead, his hands jammed in his jeans pockets. "Uh-huh."

"Do you think that's a legitimate problem?"

His stance didn't change. "Sure."

"What do you think I should do about it?"

He turned to her slowly, his hands still in his pockets, his eyes hooded. "I haven't the slightest idea."

She felt disappointed. Jack was no help at all. "Maybe I'm being too picky. I mean, it's not as if real life can be as romantic as your kiss-in-the-rain scene, for example."

A subtle change came over his expression and a soft light grew in his eyes. "You could try dragging Hamilton out in the rain and find out."

"Oh, Jack, be serious."

"This is as serious as I get."

"In the first place, I can't picture Derek standing in the rain without an umbrella."

The corners of his mouth twitched. "Well, now, that's a damned shame."

"You *are* making fun of this, aren't you. I should never have—"

"Of course you should have. That's what friends are for. I'll give this some thought, I promise, and get back to you on it. Now, shall we unpack?"

"Okay." She started toward her suitcase and paused to look back at him. "I don't want you to think there's anything *wrong* with Derek. I'm sure, with some help, that he could improve his technique."

When Jack just gazed at her, she put both hands on her hips. "What?"

"Maybe it's not Derek at all. Maybe it's you."

Chagrin heated her cheeks. "Well! That was certainly blunt."

"I didn't mean that you weren't good at kissing or making love," he said more gently. "I meant that you're just not attracted to him. No matter what he did, it wouldn't be exciting to you."

"Oh." Her wounded ego began to recover. "I've thought of that, but why wouldn't I be attracted to him? He's good-looking, ambitious, clever and polite."

"You sound as if you're placing an order in a catalogue. I'm sure you know love doesn't work that way."

"There's nothing wrong with having a list of qualities you want in a man."

"Not if you understand yourself well enough to know which qualities you need."

She really didn't care for his tone. "Well, I do, and if you put it that way, then kissing isn't really that important."

"Not if you don't think so."

"Honestly, I don't. Not really. It's a small problem. I shouldn't have brought it up in the first place." She grabbed the handle of her suitcase and without thinking started toward the bedroom. Then she realized that she couldn't just appropriate the bed, especially considering the suite was more for Jack than for her.

She turned back and gestured toward the bedroom doorway. "You can have the bed, if you want, and I'll take the couch."

"No. I asked you to come along. The bedroom's yours."

"But I'll get all those meals meant for you, and the night out at the theater, and heaven knows what else. Besides, it's a king-size and you're too tall to be comfortable on the couch. You take the bed."

"Want to flip for it?"

She gazed at him and smiled. She did enjoy this playfulness of Jack's. "Okay."

He fished a coin from his pocket. "Winner gets the bedroom, loser bunks on the couch." He spun the coin upward. "Call it."

"Heads."

Jack caught the coin and slapped it on the back of his hand. Then he looked up at her. "You win."

"Really? Let me see."

He pocketed the coin. "You doubt my word?"

She did, as a matter of fact. When the coin was in the air, she'd had a premonition Jack would make sure she won the toss. "Thanks, Jack."

"You're welcome. For my next trick I'll buy you dinner."

"That's not necessary. I have money to—"

"Manchester suggested that Candy order room service tonight, remember? And get rested up for the big day tomorrow."

Krysta laughed. "I had forgotten Manchester would be paying. I accept your offer. Go ahead and order whatever sounds filling that we can share while I change into something more comfortable."

JACK WISHED KRYSTA hadn't phrased it quite that way, which presented images of her reappearing in a revealing negligee, leaning seductively in the open bedroom doorway and crooking one manicured finger in his direction. Sometimes his active imagination was a curse. He didn't even want to see the king-size bed she'd mentioned.

He tossed his duffel bag into a spare closet next to the wet bar and hung his sport coat in there, too. Then he located the room service menu.

So she hadn't slept with Hamilton yet, he thought as he perused the menu. He probably shouldn't take any solace from that, because she still seemed determined to fashion Hamilton into the ideal mate for her. With her determination, she might succeed, especially if she was willing to settle for adequate lovemaking, as opposed to the kind capable of toppling a kingdom or beggaring a prince. Jack had never experienced that kind of passion, either, but he'd flirted with the possibility a couple of times, and he definitely believed it existed.

He had the receiver in his hand and was about to dial room service when he remembered that Candy would have to do it. Maybe it was an unnecessary precaution, but he'd rather not take a chance on any members of the staff discovering there was a man staying in Candy Valentine's room.

He crossed to the closed bedroom door and rapped on it.

"You'll have to call in the order, Candy, my sweet." He figured she'd think the endearment was a joke, so he could get away with it.

She opened the door, her hair mussed from pulling on a powder blue sweatshirt that matched the sweat pants she wore. Her feet were bare. She looked up at him, her face pink and glowing after being scrubbed free of makeup. "Candy, my sweet," she repeated, rolling her eyes. "Really, Jack."

He shrugged.

"But you're right," she said, moving past him into the living room. "And when the meal arrives you'll have to hide, just like in those situation comedies."

He'd imagined her coming out in a negligee, but somehow her casual attitude at sharing this suite, along with her mussed hair and her bare feet, had nearly the same effect on him. She seemed so damned relaxed and approachable that he wondered what would happen if he just walked over to her and took her in his arms. He already knew how she wanted to be kissed. Hell, he'd written the book on it.

She reached for the telephone and pulled her hair behind her ear as she placed the receiver over it. "What are we having?"

He noticed she'd taken off her earrings, her watch, and the rings she wore. *At home with Krysta.* God, it was an appealing thought. "Seafood pasta, a large spinach salad and a bottle of Pouilly-Fuissé," he said.

She turned, the phone still to her ear, and stared at him. "That's very *good*, Jack. I didn't think you had it in you to eat food like that."

"The pasta and spinach salad are for you and the wine's for me."

"Oh, no, you don't. We have to review our strategy tonight. I want you fed and sober."

He'd settle for just having her want him, period. "I think we deserve the wine. We don't have to drink much of it." Come to think of it, he might be forced to finish off the bottle after she went to sleep. His writing schedule had turned him

into a night person, and he might need the sedative effects of
the wine to counteract his normal schedule, not to mention
the added stimulation of having Krysta in the next room all
night.

She punched in the number for room service. "All right. I'll
order the wine, but I'm monitoring how much you drink. I
need to be fully briefed before I head out tomorrow. I haven't
even finished—" She paused and returned her attention to
the telephone. "Hello? This is Kr—, uh, Candy Valentine. I'd
like to order dinner, please."

After ordering, Krysta went back to the bedroom to finish
unpacking and Jack pulled the proposal for his second book
out of his duffel bag to look it over. After the reception for his
first book, he figured he should feel confident about this second idea, but he didn't. Krysta would be his first reader, and
he was more than a little nervous about her reaction.

Krysta came back out of the bedroom just as the knock
sounded on the door. "Quick, into the bedroom," she whispered.

"I wonder if this is what a married woman's lover feels
like," he murmured as he walked past her.

"It speaks well of your character that you have to ask. Now
get in there and close the door. Don't come out until I come to
get you."

"Yes, ma'am." He followed her instructions and shut himself inside the bedroom. The scent of her cologne assaulted
him immediately, and he closed his eyes and breathed
deeply. When he opened his eyes, the first thing he saw was a
huge bed that teased him with all sorts of possibilities. Worse
yet, she'd tossed a flowered nightie across the pillow. It didn't
surprise him that super organized Krysta laid out her night
things when she unpacked, but it certainly unnerved him.

Knowing it was a terrible mistake, he walked over to the
bed and ran a hand over the nightie. The yellow-and-white
daisies suited her personality, and the softness of the material
hinted at a sensuality that he'd suspected for some time.
Hamilton wouldn't make her happy. Not in bed, anyway.

Jack wasn't sure enough of himself to think he could, either, but he'd give anything to be allowed to try.

He glanced into the bathroom at the array of lotions and potions she'd arranged in a neat row. He'd always been fascinated by women's beauty routines and aroused by the myriad cosmetics they employed to make their soft bodies even more enticing. Leaning against the doorjamb, he allowed himself to fantasize what it would be like if he and Krysta were here as vacationing lovers instead of being involved in this crazy plot to pass him off as a woman writer. The thought made him ache with longing.

"Jack?" Krysta opened the bedroom door. "I'm sorry. I swear that was the slowest waiter in the world, but he's finally gone. You must have been bored stiff waiting around in there."

He pushed himself away from the doorjamb. Little did she know. And that's probably the way he'd be wise to keep it if he didn't want to face big-time rejection. "Actually, I've been trying on your underwear."

She rolled her eyes. "Someday that wise-cracking tongue of yours is going to get you into big trouble, mister. Let's eat. I'm starving."

So was he, and the seafood pasta tasted far better than he'd expected. Maybe there was more to life than Cheetos and Milk Duds, after all. Even the spinach salad wasn't half bad.

He speared a few more leaves onto his fork. "I'm getting into this green Popeye stuff," he said.

"It's the dressing. I take it you don't cook."

"Sure I do." He stabbed a piece of shrimp from the plate they were sharing. "You should see me nuke a bag of popcorn. Nobody can touch me in that department."

"Popcorn's not as bad as some of the things I've seen you eat. It's a wonder you keep going, a guy as big as you are, with the type of things you put into your body."

"I have a highly efficient metabolism." He poured himself another glass of the Pouilly-Fuissé and gazed at the panorama of lights outside the window. He'd forgotten how stim-

ulating New York could be. Or maybe, just maybe, it was the
company that made the difference. He lifted the glass to his
lips.

"You'd better take it easy on the sauce, Killigan. Don't forget you're using a water glass, not a wine goblet. The glass
holds more."

"So do I."

She sighed and shook her head. "I can see you're going to
be difficult. We'd better go over your new proposal now before your thinking gets too muddled."

"Does your thinking ever get muddled, Krysta?"

She gave him a long look. "In what way?"

"You always seem so in charge of everything, so sure of
your direction." He swirled the wine in his water glass and
took another swig. "I just wondered if you ever get confused."

Her gaze became wistful. "I guess I never thought I had
that luxury."

"Everyone has that luxury. It's called being human."

Her answering sigh revealed more than she might have intended. "Oh, I'm human, all right. Sometimes I just feel like
saying to hell with everything and running away to raise
flowers or something."

He decided to pursue it. Maybe the wine had loosened her
up a little bit, too. "And why don't you?"

She stared into her wineglass. "Because I'm afraid they'd
all fall apart without me," she said softly.

"Your brothers?"

She nodded. "And Dad. He'll need a full-time nurse in the
fall, when Joe goes away to college. That's why I've been trying so hard to get this promotion, so there would be enough
money to pay for that."

"Krysta, your brothers are all good guys. I can't believe
they expect you to take on that burden alone when you can't
really afford it."

"You're right. So I've led them to believe I can afford it.

That way, they won't be tempted to drop out of school to help pay."

He started to object to such self-sacrifice.

"Don't say it. I've heard it all from Rosie a dozen times. But you see..." She paused and gazed out the window. "How my mother would have loved this view."

"You still miss her."

"I think of her almost every day. She had such high hopes for all of us. One night when she was very sick, I got up for a drink of water and I overheard her tell my dad that they should have taken out life insurance on her so there would be money for everyone's college tuition. That's when I knew she would die."

His throat constricted. He dared not reach out for her and risk breaking the mood. She probably didn't let many people see this side of her.

"When I'd cried myself out that night, I made a silent promise to her that I'd see to it, that I'd get the boys educated. I knew with my dad's problems he wouldn't have the means."

"But you would."

She faced him, her gaze calm. "I have, and I will."

His inability to help filled him with frustration. It was such a heavy responsibility for one young woman. Not that she couldn't do it. But the price might be very high. "Hamilton can greatly affect whether you get that promotion, I guess."

"You'd better believe it. If I hadn't agreed to go out with him in the first place, it wouldn't be so awkward. But we've been dating for several months now, and naturally he expects..."

"You deserve better." He knew it was the wine talking, but the wine spoke with more truth than he dared.

"I don't know how you can say that, Jack. He's an educated man with a bright future. He'd do anything for me."

"As long as you do one little favor for him."

"Watch it, Jack. I certainly don't think in those terms, and I'm quite sure Derek doesn't, either. But the reality is that I've indicated an interest and accepted his invitations, and now the reasonable thing would be—"

"To pay up?"

Her green eyes flashed. "That's enough. I will not have to go to bed with him to pay for the attention he's given me or to get that promotion."

He hated the thought that Hamilton had so much power to grant or crush her dream. "I hope you're right, but we're living in an imperfect world, with imperfect people, and you'd be naive not to consider that it might be his price."

She glared at him, obviously ticked off. "You are a very maddening person, Jack."

He leaned forward, nose-to-nose with her. He longed to take her in his arms and vow to protect her from the world, but he wasn't sure what that vow would be worth at the moment. "That goes double for you, Krysta."

6

KRYSTA MET JACK'S challenging stare as long as she could. He had a real knack for getting past her defenses, and there was no question that she was becoming attracted to him. Maybe it was because they'd just been discussing her potential sexual relationship with Derek, but she couldn't help thinking about the love scenes she'd read on the plane and wondering if Jack would be that kind of lover. Probably not. No man could live up to the idealized picture he'd painted. And yet, he'd written it, so he might come very close....

No. Jack might be attracting her on a physical level, but she had to stay focused on her goals, and his lack of drive would eventually erode any transitory pleasure of two bodies meeting.

"More wine?" he said.

"No, thank you." She forced her gaze away from his. She had a job to do. "Let's go over our plan for tomorrow and then I'd like to take a look at your new book proposal."

"Maybe we should forget about the proposal on this trip. You can say it's not quite ready, and I can mail it to them later."

"But it is ready, isn't it?"

Suddenly he looked very vulnerable. "I don't know."

"Let me see it," she said gently.

"I think it would be better if I reworked it after we get back. Then I'll just send it—"

"Give me your proposal, Jack." She held out her hand.

He slipped from his chair, took her hand and dropped to one knee. "Marry me, Krysta. I know I haven't much to offer except a kiss in the rain, but—"

"Oh, for heaven's sake." She jerked her hand away before he could tell that it had started trembling. *A kiss in the rain.* She'd begun to daydream about the magic of such a kiss, about making love to Jack. A marriage proposal, even in jest, set her pulse racing. "You're impossible," she said, grabbing the dishes and stacking them on the room service tray. "I want those pages and I want them now."

He stood. "If you get the pages, I get the Pouilly-Fuissé."

"No, you don't." She picked up the bottle and carried it over to the couch. "After we've finished with business, we'll see about the rest of this wine."

He crossed to an end table beside the couch and picked up a stack of papers. "Now I understand why your brothers called you *Sarge.*"

She hid her agitation in the only way she knew, by taking on an air of brisk efficiency. "And they quickly learned that discipline was the key to success. I'm sure you know that, Jack. You stayed up all night to write."

"You don't understand." He held the book outline, reluctant to give it up. "I sacrificed sleep out of love, not discipline. I didn't force myself to write. It forced me."

She was taken aback by the statement. "Is that really true?"

He held up two fingers. "Scout's honor."

"I've never felt like that." She didn't minimize the significance of such an admission. He was obviously born to do this. "I envy you."

"Nevertheless, what I've produced while under that need to create can still be crap, you know."

"I seriously doubt it." She held out her hand again. "Give it here, Jack."

"Okay, and while you read, I'll just step out to the window ledge. If you don't like it, tap on the window and I'll jump."

"I am *sure* it's wonderful." She practically wrested the papers from his grasp, took them over to the couch and sat down to read.

Titled *Primary Needs*, the story was about a woman raised in foster homes and a politician who had much to learn about those less fortunate than he. In the beginning they squared off as enemies, but the groundwork was laid for them to become friends, lovers, and then enemies again when election time came and the issue of social welfare came between them.

Although she was engrossed in the story, Krysta finally became distracted by the steady rhythm of Jack's feet as he paced the floor in front of her. She glanced up. "Go do something."

"Like what?"

"I don't know. Do you have a deck of cards?"

"No."

"Well, you can't watch TV. That would bother me even more."

"I could take a walk," he suggested.

"That's silly. I don't have that much more to read. But you're driving me crazy pacing like that."

"I'll take a shower," he muttered, and retreated to the bedroom.

A moment later the water started, and with a sigh Krysta relaxed against the cushions of the couch and continued her reading. The story was, as she'd imagined it would be, wonderful. Even within this outline he'd captured the characters so well that she could see them in detail and hear the way they moved and talked.

More than that, she could see how they would come to love each other, both emotionally and physically. It was an explosive combination. Jack deserved even more money for this book, but she decided not to tell him that yet after the way he'd reacted to her last round of negotiating.

She picked up the outline and tapped it into shape again before heading for the bathroom.

Jack was just coming out, a towel wrapped around his waist and droplets of water still clinging to his mat of dark chest hair.

"The proposal's terrific," she said, thinking of nothing but the need to reassure him. After living with five men for most of her life, a towel-draped man was nothing out of the ordinary, anyway.

"You really think so?"

"Yes. The story has the potential to be even better than your last book, and I already told you how much I liked that one."

"God, Krysta, you don't know what that means to me." His smile flashed.

The brilliance of that smile shifted Krysta's attention dramatically. In the space of a few seconds, she forgot all about Jack's writing as she finally registered the sight of broad muscled shoulders, a flat stomach and lean hips that barely held up the towel Jack had knotted around his waist. He'd laid aside his glasses, and his long hair looked quite appropriate on a man dressed in something resembling a loincloth.

At the beginning of this escapade, she'd kidded herself that she'd be sharing a hotel room with good old Jack, a guy she knew so well he'd become nearly invisible. Well, he was invisible no longer. Not only was her roommate the most intelligent, gifted man she'd ever known, he was also a hunk.

Glancing away from the Adonis standing before her, she focused on the proposal in her hand. "I f-found a typo on page two." She fumbled with the paper and pulled out the offending page.

"You did? I went over it several times."

She realized her tactical error when he walked around to peer over her shoulder at the manuscript.

The fragrance of clean male filled her senses as he leaned closer. "Where?"

"You've spelled the word *passion* with only one *s*." Out of all the words he could have mistyped, it had to be that one.

"Guess I'll have to correct it in pen." His breath caressed her cheek.

She swallowed. This was ridiculous. Her heart was beating frantically, yet it was only Jack standing close to her. "Or I could find out if the hotel has a computer we can borrow." Doggone it, there was a definite quiver in her voice.

"Too much trouble. You'd better fix it, so it'll be consistent in case you end up having to write out anything else while we're here."

"I'll take care of it right now." She moved away from him and headed into the living room.

He followed her. "Use a black pen. I don't like the look of blue on a manuscript."

She glanced back at him. She had to get him to put some clothes on, and fast. "The curtains are open, Jack."

"So what? We're forty-five floors up."

She gazed at him, unable to come up with another excuse, yet unwilling to confess the truth—that his towel-clad body was giving her ideas she had no business having. Didn't *want* to have, under the circumstances.

Apparently she didn't have to say anything. Gradually, awareness dawned in his expression, along with a slow smile of male satisfaction. "I'll get dressed," he said, walking over to the closet and taking his duffel bag out. "And thanks, Krysta."

"For what?"

"For noticing me."

"Jack, I've always—"

"Not like that," he said quietly. Then he walked into the bedroom and shut the door.

JACK DECIDED NOT TO PUSH his luck. And luck seemed to be what he was having. He'd decided on a shower as a last-ditch distraction while Krysta finished reading his proposal. He'd thought about taking one earlier because he'd felt grubby after the bus ride to the hotel, so it seemed like killing two birds with one stone to take one while Krysta was reading his proposal. She had surprised the heck out of him by walking right into the bathroom, but he'd figured that was even more evidence that she didn't think of him in sexual terms.

And she probably hadn't before that moment. But one thing was sure. She did now. She probably wasn't too thrilled to realize she was physically attracted to him instead of to the guy she wanted to lust after, middle-management king Derek Hamilton. So Jack decided not to act on his newfound knowledge yet and see how Krysta would handle living with him for the next few days.

Consequently he was the perfect gentleman he'd promised to be while they had another glass of wine and talked about Candy Valentine's schedule for the next day.

"I'll give the proposal to Stephanie when I get to Manchester for the tour of the offices," Krysta said. Her bare feet were propped on the coffee table as she sat on the couch and sipped from her wine goblet. "That will give her maximum time to read it before Sunday morning, when we leave."

"I doubt if she will read it before we leave." Jack had chosen to sit in a club chair across from the couch. That didn't put him as close to Krysta as he would have liked, but he had the advantage of being able to study her when she wasn't looking. It was a luxury to record little details like the shade of pink she used on her toenails and the pattern of freckles across her nose, freckles that were usually covered by makeup and powder.

She crossed her ankles and scooted down lower on the couch. "I think she'll read it, and I think she'll make Candy an offer before we leave."

"Don't get your hopes up." Jack decided he liked her eyelashes better without mascara. There was a sweetness and vulnerability in her green eyes tonight. Then again, maybe that had nothing to do with the lack of makeup. He considered moving over to sit next to her on the couch but soon rejected the idea. No point in scaring her away just when she might be starting in his direction.

He picked up the typed schedule Stephanie had sent along with the airline tickets. "After the tour you're supposed to have a makeover. I'm not sure I like the sound of that."

She laughed. "It's a girl thing. We love makeovers."

"You wouldn't let them dye your hair or anything, would you?"

"I don't know. Would that be so terrible? Maybe I'd look great with ash-blond hair."

"What color is that?"

"Almost white, instead of this goldish brown I have."

He winced as he pictured her like that. The polished bronze of her hair was one of the things he treasured about her. "Don't let them change your hair color, okay?" He knew as soon as the words were out that they were far too revealing. "I mean, how would you explain that when we get back?"

"Everyone already thinks I'm at a health spa. They'll just consider the makeover as a part of it. Don't worry, I can cover my tracks."

Dammit, he liked her just the way she was. No telling what some New York salon would do to her. "But they were all crazy about that picture of you, so why would they want to change anything?"

"They probably liked the potential they saw in that picture, but I'll bet they want a more sophisticated look."

"I think you're sophisticated enough." To hell with it. He'd beg, even if it did tell her too much. "Please don't let them bleach your hair lighter."

Her gaze was assessing. "Okay, I won't."

With a sigh of relief he went back to the typed schedule. "Good. So then you have a photo session, then a Broadway show, the exact one to be announced."

"Whatever they can wrangle tickets to, I guess. I'll be excited to go to anything on Broadway."

"It should be great," he agreed. "Then you have dinner at Sardi's." He glanced up. "Doesn't sound like I'll see much of you."

"Which is precisely why I'm taking the tote with the tape recorder in it, so I can replay all the comments for you when I get home."

"I wish you'd reconsider that. If somebody at Manchester discovers you're taping the conversations, it could blow the whole deal."

"Come on, Jack." She waved a hand in dismissal. "I can

manage it. You agreed to it originally. You have to know the gist of the conversations to properly coach me on what else to say. I don't trust my memory to keep it all straight."

He knew she was right. "Okay, keep the tape recorder, but forget about smuggling food back to the room in that tote of yours. That's out."

"Don't be silly. I've heard about these five-course dinners at New York restaurants. I couldn't possibly eat it all. Don't you dare buy dinner. I'll bring you plenty, believe me."

"Don't do it, Krysta."

She got that smug little look on her face and he knew she had no intention of doing what he asked.

He resisted the urge to go over and kiss that smugness right away. "I can just imagine you coming back tomorrow night with pâté oozing out of the bottom of your tote bag."

She raised her eyebrows. "You know what pâté is? I'm impressed."

He rested his elbows on his knees and leaned toward her. "You seem to be under the impression that just because I don't eat exotic and health-filled items that I don't know what they are. I know all about them. I'd just rather have a hamburger and fries."

"You liked what we had tonight."

"Probably because I was starving to death." *Probably because you were there to share it with me.*

"Junk food is just a bad habit, Jack. If I were in charge of your diet for two weeks I'll bet you'd lose your taste for those things that are so harmful to your body."

He'd be willing to put her in charge of his diet for a lot longer than two weeks, but a few other stipulations would be included. He didn't think she was ready to hear about that. He reached for the nearly empty wine bottle. "Want to finish this off?"

"Actually, no. Considering the day I have ahead of me, I think I'd better get some sleep."

He pictured her going into the bedroom, taking off her sweat suit and slipping into the daisy-print nightie before climbing into the big bed and nestling under the covers. He could already tell it would be a very long night.

She stood and stretched. "Good night, Jack."

"Good night, Krysta."

She stopped in midstretch. "Oh! I need to loan you a pillow and blanket from the bed. I'll be right back."

He didn't have the heart to tell her it was wasted effort. He'd conditioned himself to function on very little sleep. Between his usual night-owl behavior and the stimulation of knowing Krysta would be in the next room, he'd be awake for hours.

"Here you go." She positioned the pillow at the end of the couch and arranged the bedspread over the cushions, tucking it in at the end with a practiced hand. She glanced over her shoulder at him. "Or would you rather I left this loose? Do you like to stick your feet out of the covers?"

Her endearing habit of caretaking really got to him. How he yearned to go over there, pull her down to the couch and show her how he'd really like to spend the night. "The way you have it is fine."

"I don't know." She stepped back, hands on her hips, to survey her handiwork. "This doesn't look very comfortable for a man your size. I think you should take the bed and let me sleep out here."

"It'll be fine. Besides, you're the one who has to represent me tomorrow. If anybody should get a good night's sleep, it's you. Can't have bags under Candy Valentine's eyes."

"I guess you have a point." She turned to him. "I brought some melatonin capsules for jet lag, if you want some to help you sleep."

"No, thanks. I'll be fine."

"I'll go get the bottle, in case you change your mind." She went into the bathroom and returned with a small plastic bottle. After shaking out a couple of tablets, she recapped the bottle and set it on the wet bar. "They're right here if you need them."

"Thanks, but I won't."

She sighed. "Sometimes it's so hard to help you out, Jack. By the way, what do you have planned for tomorrow? Obviously you can't stay in the room and let the maids see that you're staying here."

He laughed. It was so typical of her to worry about his day as well as her own. "Are you kidding? I wouldn't consider staying in a hotel room when I'm in the middle of one of the most exciting cities in the world. I'll be on the move all day, drinking it in."

"Gathering material for your work."

"You've got it."

A wistful look came into her eyes. "I wish I could go with you."

He met her gaze and allowed her to see a little of what he was feeling. Just a little. He'd hold off on the heavy-duty stuff for now. "I wish you could, too."

She didn't speak for several seconds. He could almost see the debate going on behind those green eyes. He was pretty sure she didn't want to walk into that bedroom alone any more than he wanted her to, but it would be a big leap for her to invite him to go with her. He didn't think she'd make that leap tonight.

She took a deep breath. "Good night, Jack."

"Good night, Krysta."

7

THANK GOODNESS she'd packed her melatonin to help her get a good night's rest, Krysta thought as her travel alarm beeped her awake. Jet lag might have messed up her sleep schedule, but not nearly as much as thinking about Jack would have. She'd never imagined that he could create such a hunger in her. Wanting to make love to Jack was definitely not part of the plan.

Fortunately such uncharacteristic behavior on her part could easily be explained by the unusual circumstances. First she'd read Jack's sensual manuscript on the way to New York. That had started her mind working in the wrong direction, and then she'd been stupid enough to walk in on him as he was coming out of the shower.

Probably most women would react the way she had, given that particular scenario. As long as she didn't read any more of Jack's work and gave him a wide berth when he was dressing or undressing, she'd be fine. She could go home to Derek with a clear conscience.

Well, almost clear. She'd had to tell him the same white lie she'd told everyone, about winning the health spa getaway contest. She and Jack had worked out every detail they could think of to protect the identity of Candy Valentine.

The only snag had been when they'd realized Manchester planned a photo shoot for a dust jacket picture. They both knew there was a chance someone might recognize Krysta when the book hit the stands. But after some thought they'd decided she could just laugh off any comments and put it down to a strange coincidence. The makeover would probably help, too. In Krysta's opinion, professional photographs seldom looked like the subject, anyway.

And that make-over and photograph session was today, Krysta reminded herself. She got out of bed and went over to the bedroom door to listen for some indication that Jack was awake. The total silence encouraged her to ease the door open and peek out.

Jack lay sprawled on his back on top of the bedspread, not underneath it as she'd anticipated. He still wore his jeans, but his flannel shirt was unbuttoned and askew, revealing the powerful chest that had unsettled her the night before. The steady rise and fall of that chest told her that he was still sound asleep.

His right arm trailed to the floor, where she could see one corner of a yellow legal tablet just beyond his outstretched fingers. So he'd found a way to write the night away, after all. A wave of tenderness engulfed her as she pictured him bent over his legal pad, totally engrossed in that magical world of creativity that inspired such wonder in her. She was so glad to have agreed to help him launch his career.

The legal tablet tantalized her with what it might contain, and despite her promise to herself, she was dying to find out what he'd composed while she slept. Perhaps he'd been working on *Primary Needs*. The story had captured her imagination, and it would be a thrilling treat to read the work as it came straight from Jack's mind.

He looked dead to the world. No doubt he'd kept his same schedule and had stayed up until early morning writing. She didn't want to disturb his much-needed rest, but a bomb would hardly wake him, from the looks of him.

Moving with great stealth, she crept out of the bedroom and around the coffee table to where the legal tablet lay. Sure enough, the top sheet was covered with Jack's bold script. He'd tossed his pen onto the carpet next to the tablet.

Sinking quietly to a cross-legged position, Krysta picked up the tablet and began to read. It quickly became obvious to her that Jack had been writing a love scene between the hero and heroine of *Primary Needs*. Krysta knew if she had any sense at all she'd replace the tablet and go take a shower—a very cold shower. She kept reading.

The politician had arrived unexpectedly at the home of the heroine, who was already dressed for bed and had pulled on a robe over her nightgown to answer the door. Inevitably, the politician took off the robe, and Krysta gasped. The heroine was wearing a soft nightie covered in daisies.

Just then a viselike grip surrounded her wrist, and her gaze lifted to meet Jack's.

His eyes were the color of a mountain lake, and just as cold-looking. "What are you doing?" His question rasped harshly in the stillness of the hotel room.

"I—I woke up, and looked out here, and—"

"That's mine." He took the tablet from her grasp and tossed it on the coffee table. "No one sees it until I say so."

At first his tone chastened her, but she quickly recovered with a complaint of her own. "But I'm in there! Or at least, my nightgown is!"

He continued to hold her wrist in a manaclelike grip as he skewered her with his gaze. "Of course that seductive little nightgown is in there. People are always asking writers where they get their ideas. Well, now you know! Did you think I'd see it lying on your pillow and not use my imagination? Imagination is my stock in trade, Krysta."

"I just never thought—"

"Well, think." His grip tightened. "I never intended to spend the night counting sheep. After seeing that nightie I lay here in the wee small hours fantasizing about it, and you in it. And out of it. But what I wrote still belongs to me until I say different."

Her heart thundered and her vocal cords constricted, but she was determined to stand up for her rights. "You invaded my privacy with your words, but I'm not allowed to read what you've written until you say so? That's not fair, Jack."

"Maybe not." The night's growth of beard made him look dark and dangerous. "But writers have been revealing people's secrets for centuries and insisting on the autonomy to do it without censorship. It comes with the territory."

His unexpected aggressive behavior intimidated her, but it stirred something passionate in her, as well. She'd never considered that Jack possessed the dark and compelling sexuality he was displaying now.

She fought to keep her breathing steady. "Well, you'll have to excuse me. I've never known a writer before." She glanced at his fingers still firmly clasping her wrist. "You'd better let me go if you want me to be on time for the limo."

Instantly he released her and lay back on the couch. As she got to her feet and started to leave, he closed his eyes and muttered a soft oath. "Krysta, I'm sorry. It's just that I'm not used to—"

"I have to go." In her present state she was far better off with his anger than his kindness. If he started being sweet, no telling what sort of foolish behavior she'd indulge in. She practically ran toward the safety of the bedroom.

JACK TRIED TO APOLOGISE several times during the next hour before Krysta left the suite, but he'd spooked her and she wouldn't stay still long enough for him to make amends. Finally, she whisked out the door, telling him she'd see him that night.

Once she was gone, he picked up the legal tablet and threw it against the window. He'd definitely overreacted when he'd opened his eyes to see her reading his rough—very rough, draft. Now that he'd adapted to a computer, he was even more critical of anything he composed on paper because a legal pad had no delete key. Compared with his polished work, the scribblings on the tablet seemed crude and embarrassing. Besides, he wasn't used to having anyone around who might chance upon his work before he was ready to have it read.

But that didn't excuse his barking at her. Part of his reaction had stemmed from his own guilt. He *had* invaded her privacy, and despite his defense of the practice, he was uneasy about it. The more he got to know Krysta, the less he wanted to reveal of her to the world. His nighttime writing effort had been more to relieve his frustration than to advance the action of his story. Yet he couldn't tell her that.

It was water under the bridge at this point, though. He couldn't stand there stewing about it forever when he needed to shave and vacate the room soon or risk having some maid discover him. While he was roaming the city today he might come up with a way to apologize that Krysta would be able to accept. He'd bragged about his tremendous imagination. Time to prove how good it was.

CARRYING HER TOTE BAG containing the tape recorder and Jack's proposal over one arm, Krysta entered the reception area of Manchester Publishing. It was smaller than she'd imagined, although a large brass version of the Manchester logo on one wall and numerous framed book covers left no doubt she was in the right place.

A young brunette with long permed hair and wire-rimmed glasses sat at the receptionist's desk. She smiled at Krysta. "May I help you?"

"Yes, I'm...Candy Valentine." Krysta had been practicing under her breath all the way over in the limo, but she still wasn't satisfied with her delivery.

The receptionist didn't seem to notice her hesitation. "Oh, Ms. Valentine! We've been expecting you. Have a seat and I'll tell Ms. Briggs that you're here." She picked up the telephone on her desk and punched a button.

Krysta sat in a sleek leather chair, reached into her tote bag and turned on the tape recorder.

The receptionist replaced the receiver. "She'll be right out. You know, you look exactly the way I pictured you would when I read your manuscript."

"You read Ja—my manuscript?" God, she'd have to be more careful. *She* was the writer now. It was *her* work, not Jack's, that she carried in the tote bag.

"My goal is to be promoted to editorial, so I offered to help read the Valentine's Day contest entries. I loved your story and sent it right to Ms. Briggs, along with a recommendation to publish." She looked very proud of herself. "My judgment was on the money, too."

"Then I have a lot to thank you for," Krysta said. She really didn't know much about this business, she thought. She'd imagined all manuscripts were read by editors, yet here was evidence that the first reader might just as easily be the receptionist in the outer office.

"Oh, no, I'm the grateful one. You should see some of the junk I've had to wade through. Your manuscript was a breath of fresh air. And *hot*, too." She winked at Krysta. "Just what I like."

Krysta managed a weak smile. She hadn't been allowed to finish the scene Jack had written the night before, but she had no doubt it had been steamy. And now she knew where he got his ideas.

"Besides that, my discovering you in the contest entries should be very good for my career."

"I'm glad."

"In fact, I'm keeping my fingers crossed that—" She stopped speaking as a tall woman in a gray wool suit walked into the reception area.

Krysta stood and was glad she'd worn three-inch heels. Otherwise Stephanie Briggs would have towered over her. From the cut of her slim suit to the casual perfection of her short brown hair and understated makeup, Stephanie was every inch the urban sophisticate. Krysta recognized a kindred spirit immediately.

"So you're Candy." Stephanie extended her hand. "I'm Stephanie."

"It's good to meet you at last." Krysta returned the firm handshake.

Stephanie's glance swept over Krysta and she smiled her approval. "It's even better to meet you and discover you didn't send us a twenty-year-old photograph. The marketing department will be very glad that you're as attractive as your picture."

Krysta thought about the inevitable day when the marketing department would learn that Candy Valentine was a man named Jack. "Are my looks really so important?"

"Ordinarily they're not. Most of our authors wouldn't make *People* magazine's list of the fifty most beautiful people in the world, and we really don't care. If you'd been homely, we still would have bought your manuscript."

"That's good to know."

"But we wouldn't have marketed the book, and you, the way we plan to under the circumstances. The fact that you're young and pretty is a publicity bonus, and we're going to make use of it. Now, come along, and I'll give you the fifty-cent tour of the place. The staff is dying to get a look at our next bestselling author."

As Krysta walked with Stephanie down the carpeted hallway she wondered how Jack would react to Stephanie's comments when he heard the tape. Viewing it from his perspective, he couldn't be very happy to learn that without Krysta, he might have been just another title on the rack instead of a highly promoted lead book. But she'd put the recorder in so that he'd know as much as possible about the plans for *Uptown Girl*, and he still needed that information even if some of it proved to be painful.

"I brought the proposal for my next book," Krysta said, lengthening her stride to keep up with Stephanie.

"Excellent. We need to start thinking about the book that will follow *Uptown Girl*. What's your premise?"

Feeling as if she were taking an oral exam, Krysta outlined Jack's story in a few sentences. Thank heavens she'd taken the community college public speaking course and knew how to present an idea.

Stephanie paused outside a doorway and faced her. "Good. Excellent. Do you have the outline with you?"

Krysta pulled the manila envelope containing the proposal out of her bag and handed it to Stephanie.

"I'll read it as soon as I can."

"Do you think you'll get to it before we—before I leave?"

Krysta thought it would be best if she negotiated this next contract for Jack, too, and right now, she had the perfect opportunity to strike while the iron was hot.

Stephanie's eyes widened. "I can see you're not going to need an agent with business initiative like that. Yes, I'll try very hard to read it before you leave." She winked. "I can always go over a few pages between acts of the musical tonight."

"That would be great."

Stephanie laughed and took her arm. "You and I are going to make quite a team, Candy. Now come and meet the rest of the editorial staff."

As Jack cut across to Fifth Avenue he realized he'd better have a terrific imagination if he intended to buy Krysta an apology present on his limited budget. Zipping his ski jacket against a sharp winter wind, he shoved his hands in his pockets and started window shopping to get inspired.

Something to do with Valentine's Day, he thought as he passed displays dominated by red, white and pink. Not candy, especially with the obvious play on his new pseudonym. He liked to think he was more subtle than that. Flowers were a cliché, and besides, anything he could buy would look pretty sorry next to the bouquet provided by Manchester.

A trinket from Cartier, perhaps, or a tasteful leather item from Gucci. Sure. First he'd have to buy a few things for himself, like a ski mask and a water pistol. He'd never cared much about being rich, but walking down Fifth Avenue looking for a gift for Krysta, he would have loved to have unlimited funds.

Figuring there wasn't much point in going into Tiffany's, he bypassed it and headed for FAO Schwartz. Maybe whimsical could take the place of expensive. He hoped so.

Some time later he came out of the store with his purchase. The bag was small enough to stuff in his jacket pocket as he headed back down Fifth Avenue toward Brentano's. In Jack's opinion a walk through the streets of New York wasn't complete without a visit to at least one bookstore.

He planned to wander the aisles and dream of the day his book would be on sale. True, it wouldn't have his name on the cover, but it would be his story people were buying, his words they were devouring on the subways, during lunch breaks, at home in the evenings after the kids went to bed. Just thinking about that put an extra spring in his step.

Then, above the traffic noise, he heard a shout from somewhere ahead of him. A man dressed in dark clothes with a navy stocking cap pulled over his ears ran toward Jack, knocking pedestrians out of the way in his flight. A couple of people screamed and dodged out of the man's way.

Jack had no time to think, but his football training still ruled his instincts. Crouching down, he used his shoulders to throw the runner off balance. As the man spun around, Jack launched himself at his knees. They both went down with a thud on the cold cement, and Jack's glasses, not particularly secure in the best of circumstances, skidded across the sidewalk.

The man struggled, but working on the shipping dock had kept Jack in decent shape. He held the guy pinned to the sidewalk and called out for someone to get the police.

A squad car arrived at the same time as a well-dressed, portly man in a suit and topcoat trotted up, puffing.

As New York's finest took over and returned the wallet to the man in the topcoat, Jack got up and looked around for his glasses. It wasn't easy considering the view had become very fuzzy.

The man in the topcoat finished giving his statement to the police and walked over to Jack. "That was heroic, son," he said. "I'd just taken out my wallet to pay the cab driver when this fellow swooped in. I owe you a great deal for stopping him."

"Then maybe you could help me find my glasses," Jack said. "They fell off when I tackled him."

"Here they are," volunteered a woman, coming toward

him with a mangled bit of plastic in her hand. "The lenses are smashed, I'm afraid."

The businessman stepped forward. "We'll take care of that in no time." He laid a hand on Jack's shoulder. "Come with me, my boy. My optometrist is excellent."

"Listen, I couldn't accept—"

"Nonsense. I had fifteen hundred dollars plus change in that wallet and the unlisted phone numbers of some very prominent people, not to mention credit cards and pictures of my grandchildren. I can't begin to imagine the mess I would have been in if you hadn't stopped that mugger."

"I'm glad I could help."

"You look like the type who would help out and then just disappear, like the Lone Ranger or something. I can't have that. I insist on replacing your glasses, at the very least." Without waiting for an answer, the businessman turned to hail a cab. "We'll pop on over to my optometrist's office right now."

"No, really. I'll just—"

As the cab pulled to the curb, the man glanced at Jack. "Listen, my wife will boil me in oil if she hears about this and discovers I didn't reward you in some fashion. Allow me to buy you new glasses and you'll save a forty-year marriage."

Jack decided further protest would make him seem ungrateful, so he followed the businessman into the cab.

Once they were moving through traffic, the man turned to him. "Now, don't take this amiss. I'm extremely grateful and I don't want to insult you in the least, but have you considered getting yourself a haircut?"

Jack leaned against the seat and grinned. "You sound like someone I know."

"Your mother, perhaps?"

"No, another...woman."

The man nodded. "It's up to you, of course, but my stylist is excellent, and it would be the least I could do. And as long as we're replacing those glasses, have you ever worn contacts?"

"Years ago."

"They've improved, believe me. I have the disposable kind, and they're a damn sight better than fooling with glasses. My optometrist could have them ready for you in twenty-four hours."

KRYSTA HAD WRANGLED two keys to the hotel room by convincing the front desk clerk that she was hopelessly absent-minded and needed a second key to avoid locking herself out. If the front desk clerk on duty was suspicious, he hadn't indicated it.

By the time she returned to the room that night, she was exhausted. A Broadway baby she wasn't, if that meant arriving for work at nine and continuing to be bright and perky until after midnight. She didn't understand how Stephanie and the two men from marketing who had accompanied them to the theater and dinner managed to keep such a schedule. If today was a typical example, New Yorkers definitely lived a faster-paced life than people on the West Coast.

The living room was dimly lit with only one lamp burning, and Jack was already asleep on the couch. Krysta was just as glad. After the grueling day she'd had, she wasn't up to matching wits with Jack. Her defenses were down, and that wasn't a good position to be in with somebody who appealed to her the way Jack did. She deliberately avoided looking at him as she came in, so that she wouldn't be tempted to snuggle down beside him and let nature take its course.

Moving quietly around the suite, she opened the courtesy bar and took out several of the nonperishable items so that she could store part of what she'd been able to smuggle out of Sardi's. Jack should appreciate the chunk of prime rib she'd managed to wrap in a napkin. Red meat was his kind of treat, and she'd ordered the prime rib with him in mind.

She left the napkin-wrapped dinner rolls on the banquet table, along with a couple of pats of butter. She probably shouldn't have indulged his high cholesterol habit with the beef and butter, but this trip didn't seem like the time to take a dietary stand. She had more critical issues to hold the line on. Like staying out of Jack's bed.

The extra food put away, she took some melatonin from the bottle on the wet bar, snapped off the living room light and walked into her bedroom. Someone, probably Jack, had turned on the bedside lamp so she wouldn't have to stumble around in the dark. Very thoughtful. She yawned and went into the bathroom to take off her makeup.

There was a fair amount to take off. Before she started, she gazed at herself in the mirror. A high-priced hairdresser named Emilio had taken a good three inches off her hair and styled it differently. He'd told her he wanted to transform her from wholesome to seductive. According to Stephanie and the two guys from marketing, Emilio had succeeded.

The makeup session with Rudolfo had left her with thinner eyebrows, more hollow-looking cheeks and a pouting red mouth. In one of the photos she'd been asked to bite into a ripe strawberry, not necessarily to use for the jacket picture, but to get her in the mood, the photographer had said.

Krysta had spent the morning trying to imagine herself as an author. By the end of the afternoon, she felt like a *Playboy* centerfold. Jack's book seemed to be nearly forgotten in the frenzy to make the supposed author glamorous and sexy. One day down and two to go, she thought wearily. But it was all for a good cause, and she still felt good about the contribution she was making to Jack's career. With luck she wouldn't make any major mistakes as she played out this role.

With her face finally washed clean and her soft daisy nightgown on, Krysta returned to the bedroom, and for the first time saw that something was propped against her pillow. She slowly picked up a rounded plastic heart that fit easily in the palm of her hand.

The casing was decorated with a laser design that sparkled when she held it to the light, and the white-tipped shaft of an arrow protruded from one side. A folded sheet of yellow lined paper lay on the bed where the heart had been resting.

Putting down the heart, she unfolded the note. Jack's bold script greeted her.

Dear Krysta,

I behaved in a heartless manner this morning. My heartfelt apologies.

Jack

She picked up the heart again and examined it. An opening indicated that the arrow was designed to go all the way through. She pushed on the shaft, and the tip of the arrow slid through the other side at the same time that a message emerged from the top of the heart.

Be My Valentine.

Her breath caught in her throat. *Oh, Jack.*

She pressed the little heart to her chest as the age-old message ran round and round in her head. She'd seen it hundreds of times today in her travels around the city, but the meaning had been obscured by the commercialism of the season. Now the phrase brimmed with meaning. And it demanded an answer that she didn't feel prepared to give.

8

JACK HAD BEEN AWAKE when Krysta had come home, but he'd deliberately played possum. He'd watched her through half-closed eyes as she'd puttered around the suite depositing the food she must have brought him from Sardi's.

The damned salon had cut her hair, which he would have vetoed if he'd had a vote. But there was something intriguing about the shorter style, too. It swung when she moved, drawing attention to the luster of her dark gold curls and giving her a sassy look he might even begin to like. Hell, who was he kidding? He'd probably find something to like if she'd shaved her head and put a ring through her nose.

The draw for him wasn't really her looks, although he enjoyed responding to that saucy smile and treasured gazing into her emerald eyes. It was her damned perseverance, her indomitable spirit, her optimism in the face of a challenge that squeezed his heart. He wanted to help shoulder her burdens, which was laughable considering he could barely shoulder his own at the moment. In point of fact, he'd had to ask her for help instead of giving it.

When she went into the bedroom, he listened intently for some reaction to his gift. Maybe she'd laugh. Maybe she'd wonder why he'd bother buying her such a cheap toy. Maybe he should have gone for a single rose, but that was Hamilton's sort of gesture, not his. Jack remembered seeing the rose on Krysta's desk the day she'd made the first call to Manchester. Nope, he didn't intend to follow in Hamilton's footsteps. Win or lose, and this was fast turning into a contest, he'd do it his way.

If he could write the end of this scene, Jack would have

Krysta become so overwhelmed by the little plastic heart and its message that she'd walk back into the living room and softly call his name, just in case he wasn't sound asleep. Then he could pretend to wake up, and then...

He lay waiting, hearing nothing but Krysta's preparations for bed. Then the light went out. Bitter disappointment seared through him as he realized that his attempt to connect with her had failed miserably. He sat up in frustration and shoved his fingers through his hair. There was a hell of a lot less of it to shove his fingers through than there had been that morning. Krysta wasn't the only one who'd gotten shorn today.

He might as well admit he'd accepted the businessman's offer of a haircut because of Krysta. Not that she'd really care all that much, other than to be pleased that he'd decided to take more pride in his appearance. He ranked somewhere in the area of a project, a fixer-upper and nothing more. Her real focus was on somebody who didn't need any fixing, except for the minor imperfection of his kissing technique.

Which gave Jack an idea. It was an idea he had no right having, but his ego had become involved and was demanding he accept this challenge.

Krysta would be gone all the next day, too, but she had to come home sometime so they could go over the tapes she was making for him. And it was, after all, February 14, a day devoted to lovers. He'd noticed that the subject of kissing flustered her more than a little because it threw Hamilton into a bad light and made her wonder if Jack might not be a better bet in that department. Tomorrow night he'd reintroduce that volatile subject and see where it took them.

For a campaign like that, one he hadn't engaged in for some time, he wanted to be well rested. He should probably try to alter his body clock to be more of a match with Krysta's. He stood, walked over to the wet bar and picked up her bottle of melatonin pills. Tonight he would sleep.

AS SHE SHOWERED and dressed the next morning Krysta decided she'd overreacted to the plastic heart. It was probably

Jack's idea of a cute little joke, asking her to be his valentine. She had come on this trip to be his "Candy Valentine," so it probably was a play on that theme rather than a straightforward request for her affections. Sure, he'd wanted to make amends for snapping at her the way he had, but that was only because he still needed her to be his "Candy Valentine."

Still, Krysta wasn't positive about her conclusions, and she would have liked to have a few words with Jack before she left the suite. Consequently she'd made no effort to be quiet while she got ready for an eight-thirty appointment. She even made coffee in the pot located on the wet bar, thinking the gurgling and the scent would awaken Jack.

He didn't stir.

Finally, as she stood sipping her coffee, she walked over and stared down at him to make certain he was still breathing. That was when she noticed his hair. Her gasp of surprise had been enough to startle him awake the morning before, but today it had no effect. He slept on.

She evaluated the haircut as best she could, considering he lay on his side with his back to her. Whoever had done the job had a practiced enough hand to contour his hair to make the most of its natural wave, and the back feathered nicely to his nape. Although she'd counseled him to cut his hair, she was glad he hadn't asked the stylist to make it supershort. It wouldn't have suited his maverick personality to have the clipped, almost military cut of someone like...Derek.

Derek's haircut reflected his kissing style, now that she thought about it. Well mannered, brief and efficient.

Thinking of Derek's efficiency reminded Krysta that she had a limo to catch in ten minutes, and it didn't look as if she'd be having a conversation with Jack this morning. She returned to the bathroom to finish applying her makeup.

She was curious as to why he'd suddenly had his hair cut, and a little annoyed that he'd chosen New York as the place to do it when he could have found a much cheaper salon in Evergreen. That was pretty typical of Jack's impetuous behavior, though, and she probably shouldn't complain, because af least he'd done it. Funny, but now that he had, she almost wished she had his long hair back. Fresh from the shower and clad in a towel, he'd looked quite impressive with hair reaching to his broad shoulders.

There was also the question of why he'd had his hair cut yesterday. Maybe he'd done it out of boredom, from knocking around by himself all day, but that didn't sound like Jack. She doubted that Jack, with his fertile brain, was ever bored, which meant that he might have cut his hair for her. He might have bought the valentine heart as a sincere gesture instead of a cute joke. He might, just might, be making a play for her. The thought made her heart beat faster, but it didn't look as if she'd find out the truth about Jack's feelings this morning.

Three minutes before she had to walk out the door she checked her appearance in the full-length mirror at the far end of the bathroom. Before the photo shoot, Stephanie had taken her to a clothing rental shop to pick out the little red leather suit and white silk blouse she wore. Stephanie had said there would be some photo opportunities the next day along with the local talk show that afternoon, and Candy Valentine should definitely appear in red and white on February 14, of all days.

The skirt was shorter than Krysta would have chosen, but Stephanie had insisted on the outfit and proclaimed that Krysta looked as chic and sexy as a runway model. Krysta had pointed out that she wasn't as tall as a runway model and that discussion had led to Stephanie's confession that she'd once been a model. Krysta was enjoying the growing relationship with Jack's editor and regretted that it was built on a lie. She would have liked to keep Stephanie as a colleague.

Picking up the tote bag containing the tape recorder, a fresh supply of tapes and her coat, Krysta walked back into the living room and over to the couch. Leaning down, she shook Jack's shoulder. "Wake up, Jack. I'm leaving now, and you'll have to vacate pretty soon, yourself."

He groaned and snuggled deeper into the pillow.

"Jack!" She shook him harder.

"Wanna sleep," he mumbled. "Having a good dream."

"Well, you need to get up. I'm leaving now, and the maid will be along any time."

Abruptly he turned over, his eyes wide open. "Krysta?"

"I'm sorry, Jack, but you have to get up. This is probably the first good night's sleep you've had in months, but we don't want the maid to find you here."

He gazed at her as a slow smile crept across his face. "Your stuff really works."

The shorter hair made a startling difference in his appearance. He looked far more cosmopolitan and worldly. She could imagine this version of Jack dining at Sardi's on paté. "What stuff?"

"That melatonin."

"So you finally took some. That was a good idea, Jack. Take some more tonight."

"I just might." His eyes glowed with a new intensity. "The dreams I had were incredible."

Belatedly, Krysta remembered one of the potential side effects of the herbal sleep aid—explicit sexual dreams. It hadn't happened to her, but apparently Jack was susceptible. Big surprise. Her cheeks warmed with embarrassment. "That sometimes happens with melatonin," she admitted. "I forgot to tell you about it."

"Too bad. I would have taken it sooner."

"Well..." She backed away from the sofa. "I really have to go."

"That's a shame." His gaze swept over her leather miniskirt and jacket. "Nice outfit."

"It's rented." Liquid fire ran through her at the look in his eyes.

"When will you be home?" he asked softly.

"I...I don't know." Her heart was beating furiously. He'd asked when she'd be *home*, not when she'd be back. The difference between the two closed them in an intimate circle.

"Any general idea?"

"Stephanie mentioned something about dinner, but I thought I might beg off."

The light in his eyes intensified.

"She and I will be going over the revisions for *Uptown Girl* this morning," Krysta hurried on, "and I'm sure you'd like to hear the tape of that."

"Yes, I would."

She backed away a few more steps. "I'll bet the limo's already down there waiting."

"Then, I'll see you tonight."

"Right. Oh, and I like your haircut."

"Same here."

"See you later." She turned and headed for the door.

"Krysta?"

"Yes?" She paused with one hand on the knob.

"Happy Valentine's Day."

She glanced around. It was a good thing people were counting on her to show up in a few minutes, she thought. Otherwise she would have turned around and run straight into Jack's arms, and that might be a very unwise move for both of them. "Same to you," she said, "and thank you for the sweet little heart." Then she walked out of the door.

THE BUSINESSMAN'S optometrist had loaned Jack some glasses to use until he picked up the contacts that afternoon. They were a major improvement over the taped ones he had been using. Once he was shaved and dressed he took note of the weather and discovered the sun was trying to break through. For the first morning in a long time, Jack was wide awake. After clearing away any evidence of his presence in the suite, he grabbed his jacket and legal tablet before setting out toward Central Park.

He found a vacant bench and sat down to people-watch and write descriptions of interesting passersby. Unfortunately, the only description he seemed able to write concerned a woman who was nowhere near Central Park, a woman who was currently sitting in Stephanie Briggs's office, a woman wearing a very sexy red leather suit.

His preoccupation pointed to a malady he wasn't ready to admit, so after a while he flipped the legal pad closed and walked over to the Metropolitan Museum of Art. Half an hour later he walked out again, disgusted with himself. The last time he'd visited New York he'd spent hours wandering through the exhibits and marveling at the sheer volume of creativity displayed there. This morning he'd spent the entire time musing in front of Rodin's bronze titled *The Kiss* and thinking about Krysta. He'd pretty much wasted the admission fee.

He couldn't see much point in going to the Museum of Natural History and wasting more money. Even the Statue of Liberty would probably remind him of Krysta in some obscure way. He wondered if he'd been obsessed with her for months but had been too exhausted to realize it. Now, after a good night's sleep, he was crazy with longing.

Finally he settled on walking the streets, although even that didn't help much. It was Valentine's Day, and everywhere he looked, he saw lovers—a couple hunched over an intimate table in a restaurant, another strolling with their arms around each other, still another kissing on a street corner while they waited for the light to change. It was the most romantic of days, and he was in the most romantic of moods, but Krysta wasn't here.

Eventually he picked up his contacts late in the afternoon and headed back to the hotel to wait for Krysta. Once inside the room he slapped his forehead as he remembered that she was supposed to be on a local talk show and he'd planned to watch. It was already five minutes past the time the segment was scheduled to air.

He grabbed the remote and turned on the set. Fortunately, he remembered the channel without having to search out the note he'd written to himself, and he pushed the buttons to tune it in. Sure enough, there was Krysta in her short little skirt and saucy little smile. Krysta and a female talk-show host were seated in front of a large red cardboard heart fringed in white lace.

"And although you admit your pseudonym is part of a marketing plan, it's obvious you don't intend to reveal your *real* name on this show."

"I don't consider it important at this point," Krysta said.

Good girl, Jack thought.

"So we'll drop that line of inquiry and move on to something we can talk about, your prize-winning book," the interviewer said. "Manchester supplied me with a few excerpts from *Uptown Girl* so I'd be acquainted with your style. You're a very sensual writer, Candy."

"Effective writing concentrates on the senses," Krysta said.

Nice line, Jack thought. He didn't remember telling her that one.

"I'm particularly impressed with your love scenes," the interviewer continued. "Where do you get your ideas?" she added, looking as if she'd come up with the most stunningly original question in the universe.

"I observe, and I've developed my powers of imagination," Krysta replied earnestly, as if the question had been a brilliant one.

"Beautiful," Jack muttered, admiring the hell out the way she gazed with calm confidence at her interviewer, as if she'd been on television for years.

"Women writers seem to have a particular gift for the nuances between a couple making love," the interviewer said. "Would you agree?"

"Absolutely not. Men are perfectly capable of writing sensitively about lovemaking."

Jack silently thanked her.

"They may be capable of it, but more often than not a male writer will give you a wham, bam, thank-you-ma'am type of scene."

"That may be true for some writers," Krysta said, "but it's still unfair to make generalizations that a man can't write about love."

The interviewer laughed. "Name someone."

"Jack Killigan."

Jack nearly fell off the couch.

"I've never heard of him," the interviewer said.

"Don't worry, you will."

"What has he published?"

Jack clenched his teeth together. She was going to spill the beans right on television. He couldn't believe it.

"He hasn't published anything yet," Krysta said, "but I'm certain he will someday. And he writes beautiful love scenes."

The breath whooshed out of Jack's lungs. That was close. Too close. She was improvising again, and he didn't like it.

"Sounds like the perfect Valentine guy to me," the interviewer said.

Jack leaned forward. Was it makeup, or was Krysta blushing?

"He is," she said.

Jack's heart beat faster.

"Well, we're out of time, folks," the interviewer said. "We've spent the past ten minutes with Candy Valentine, who made the most of this romantic season by winning Manchester Publishing's Valentine's Day contest for unpublished writers. Her sexy romance, titled *Uptown Girl* will be out in time for Valentine's Day next year, right, Candy?"

"That's right."

"And I can hardly wait. Folks, this is one hot read."

The station shifted to a commercial, and that was the end of Krysta's appearance on the show. Jack flicked off the set and thought about what he'd just heard.

Krysta had said he wrote good love scenes, but that was old news. The interviewer, not Krysta, had been the one who'd called him "the perfect Valentine guy," and Krysta had merely agreed with him. She could hardly have done anything else under the circumstances. It probably meant nothing, nothing at all. Unless she really *had* been blushing when she said it. Then it could mean that he'd just gained the whole world.

CONVINCING STEPHANIE that she needed to spend the night alone and order up room service had been difficult, but Krysta had finally managed it. The truth had worked—she was dead on her feet after two days of being a celebrity. Her tote bag over one arm and the huge heart-shaped box of candy she'd received from Manchester under the other, she fumbled as she tried to put her card key in the lock. The door opened, anyway.

She looked into the warm welcome of Jack's eyes and her heart turned over. "Hi."

"Hi. You look exhausted." He drew her inside.

He looked so damn good to her. For some reason he wasn't wearing his glasses, and with his newly styled hair, a recent shave and a decent night's sleep, he was quite a revelation. "To be honest, I am exhausted."

"You can be perfectly honest with me." He took her bag and box of candy and set them on the coffee table before helping her off with her coat.

"That's good to hear." As he took her coat she caught a whiff of his after-shave, and some of her exhaustion faded. "I've been tossing lies around all day. Maybe that's why I'm so tired." She stepped out of her heels and wiggled her toes in the carpet.

"How about a warm bath and some dinner?"

It sounded like a wonderful start. She nodded.

"I'll get the bath water running if you'll put in the dinner order."

She gazed at him and wondered how she'd missed noticing when they were growing up together that he was so handsome, so sexy. "Better put on your glasses so you can tell the hot tap from the cold."

He grinned. "Don't worry. I'll manage."

After he left the room she shrugged and picked up the menu. If he wanted to stumble around without his glasses, it wasn't really her concern. One thing was for sure, his magnetic gaze was even more powerful without that barrier of glass. The more she stared into those blue eyes, the more she longed to forget about Derek, forget about Jack's uncertain future, forget about her own financial burdens, and live out a fantasy in this hotel room with Jack.

She ordered the largest steak on the menu with the usual trimmings of baked potato, sour cream, butter and a dinner salad. She added a bottle of cabernet, a pot of coffee and a piece of chocolate cake. It wasn't her usual fare, but she wasn't in one of her usual moods. The room service operator warned her that the meal would take longer than usual to arrive because it was, after all, Valentine's night.

More time to soak, Krysta thought. Replacing the receiver, she started taking off her suit jacket as she headed for the bedroom.

The rumble of water pounding into the tub and soft music from the bedside radio greeted her as she came through the door. She sighed and went to the closet to hang up her jacket. Glancing at the bedside table, she noticed the plastic heart was still where she'd left it the night before. *Be My Valentine.* Perhaps tonight she'd find out exactly what Jack had meant. A shiver of anticipation ran through her.

The sound of running water stopped and Jack emerged from the bathroom. "I added some of your lavender bath oil to the water," he said.

"Thanks. That sounds—" She paused. "How could you tell what kind it was without your glasses?"

He leaned in the doorway and crossed his arms. "Opened the bottle and sniffed."

"Oh."

He pushed away from the doorjamb. "Better get in there while it's still hot."

"Thanks, Jack. By the way, dinner is going to take a while."

"I'm in no hurry."

"Good." The words fell about her like rose petals. *In no hurry.* Perhaps that was the most seductive quality this man possessed. All her life she'd felt the pressure of time. Here in New York had been even worse. But Jack was the sort of guy who took a relaxed approach to life. And right now, that appealed to Krysta very, very much.

"I'll call you if dinner arrives," he said.

"You're welcome to start listening to the tapes if you want."

"Maybe I will." He started out the door. "By the way, you were great on TV this afternoon." Then he closed the door after him.

So he had seen the show. Had he noticed how flushed she'd become when the interviewer had mentioned that Jack sounded like the perfect Valentine guy? If he had any clue as to how she was beginning to fantasize about making love to him, he hadn't let on. And although she'd seen some flashes of physical desire in his eyes when he looked at her, he might not want to start a relationship right now when he was on the threshold of a brand-new venture. If Krysta were in his shoes, that's how she'd think.

She took off her makeup, undressed and sank gratefully into the steamy water. Jack had known the perfect temperature to make it, which wasn't surprising considering his sensuous nature. And he'd added just the right bath oil to relax her. As she leaned her head against the rolled-up towel Jack had placed at the end of the tub, Krysta couldn't keep her thoughts away from the man in the other room.

He had a smart mouth, but she was starting to realize that was a coverup for his sensitivity. His ability to write so accurately about human emotions revealed his true makeup, which was warm, caring and very sexy. That glimpse into his psyche was certainly playing havoc with *her* emotions. She'd never been so turned on by a man in her life. Everything about him indicated he'd be a wonderful lover. And her curiosity was killing her.

9

LISTENING TO THE TAPES served both to distract Jack from the beauty bathing in the next room and to humble him about the greatness of his writing. Apparently Krysta's looks had contributed as much to the Candy Valentine project as his book had.

If *Uptown Girl* really took off, he'd need to do something special for Krysta. That might be difficult because nobody was supposed to know of her involvement, and by the time royalties came in her situation might have changed drastically. She could even be married to Derek Hamilton, purveyor of crummy kisses. Now, there was a depressing thought.

Fortunately Krysta had been selective about what she'd recorded, so by the time she emerged from the bedroom wearing a white terry robe, he'd made it through most of the first day.

He shut off the recorder and glanced up. "Feeling better?"

"Much."

She looked like a present ready to be unwrapped, and he wondered if he'd be able to keep his hands to himself. A knock on the door signaled the arrival of room service. Good. Another distraction. Maybe over dinner he'd be able to assess her mood and decide what to do. It had been a long time since he'd attempted a seduction, and he didn't want to miscalculate.

"Better go hide," Krysta said.

"Yeah." He retreated to the moist, fragrant atmosphere of the bedroom and saw that she'd tossed her discarded underwear on the bed, including lacy panties, bra and stockings.

Not panty hose, but stockings. He looked around for a garter belt and found none. Both the writer in him and the man wondered how she kept the stockings from falling down, so he picked one up and discovered the lace-decorated top was elasticized.

Rubbing the silky material between his fingers, he imagined her putting the stocking on. He saw her easing it over those pink toenails and guiding the material past her instep. He envisioned the nylon caressing her graceful calf and slender knee before smoothly encasing her thigh in a gentle hug. He laid the stocking back on the bed, closed his eyes and took a deep breath. Sometimes imagination was a curse instead of a blessing. He was thoroughly aroused, but the next step in the evening plan was dinner, not bed.

Behind him, Krysta opened the bedroom door. "Dinner's served."

He was in no shape to walk out that door. "Be right there. I'm going to wash up," he said, and headed for the bathroom. Turning on the faucet, he leaned both hands on the counter and stared at himself in the mirror. "Killigan, you are in danger of making a colossal fool of yourself tonight," he told the frustrated guy reflected back at him. "Take it easy, okay?"

Moments later he had himself under control enough to return to the living room—a room, it turned out, lit only by candles on the banquet table. He blinked.

"The, um, room service guy did this." Krysta stepped from the shadows. "I guess he'd been given the word from Manchester that Candy Valentine should have a romantic dinner tonight even if she chose to spend it alone."

Jack stood transfixed by his first view of Krysta by candlelight. Exquisite.

"You may not be able to see very well, especially if you'd rather not wear your glasses," she said uncertainly. "We can blow them out and turn the lights back on if this is too much atmosphere for you."

He snapped out of his trance. "No, this is great." He walked over to the table. "I just hope they're not planning to send up somebody from an escort service to make your evening complete."

Her eyes widened. "You don't think they would, do you?"

"I was kidding. I can't imagine anyone taking that kind of liberty if you made it clear that you wanted to be alone."

"Well, I did." She looked at him, but when he returned her gaze she seemed to lose her nerve and glanced away. "I knew we needed to listen to those tapes together, especially the one from the revision session this morning. Maybe we should hear that now."

"Since we don't have a strolling violinist, we might as well." For a moment there, in the candlelight, he'd imagined she might be thinking along the same lines that he had been, but then she'd steered them right back to business.

"I'll find the place on the tape."

He glanced at the table and noticed an open bottle of red wine. While she fooled with the recorder he walked over and lifted the lid covering the plate of food to find out what she'd ordered to go with it. "Steak and baked potato?" he exclaimed in surprise. "Has life in the Big Apple corrupted Krysta Lueckenhoff?"

She laughed. "No, you have."

How he wished that were true. "With one steak knife to our name I guess somebody better start cutting up this roast beast."

"Be my guest." She came over with the tape recorder and snapped it on as she sat across from him. "I think this is the part I wanted you to hear."

As he listened to Stephanie Briggs begin discussing changes she'd like to see in *Uptown Girl*, he cut meat and put it on a saucer for himself before giving Krysta the plate. She took the potato off and plopped it on his saucer, along with some bits of salad. He was listening too intently to question her divvying up of the food.

He ate without giving it much thought while he concentrated on the tape. Thank God Stephanie's suggestions for the book were reasonable and wouldn't require a lot of work, he thought. More than that, they didn't veer much from his original image of the characters.

Then the recorder picked up Krysta's response. *I disagree with your first suggestion,* she said with sickening clarity.

Jack dropped his fork and stared at his dinner companion. *Christine needs to be very angry in that scene with her father,* Krysta's taped voice continued. *And I don't think she should cry. That's a wimpy thing for her to do at that point, and she's too strong to break down in front of him.*

Jack hit the stop button on the recorder. "You *argued* with her?"

"Why not?" She seemed totally unrepentant. "Stephanie was wrong."

"But she's the *editor*."

"And I'm a *reader*. I've been buying romances for years, and I know what readers want."

"That may be true, but a first-time author doesn't argue with the editor. Especially not on her very first *point*."

Krysta shoved his hand aside and pressed the play button. "Listen to the rest, Jack."

"You mean the part where she cancels the contract because she realizes I'm going to be too difficult to work with? Krysta, you—"

"Just listen! She went along with it!"

And so she had. Jack gazed across the table at Krysta's smug little smile as Stephanie retracted her original criticism and agreed with Krysta's evaluation of the scene. He stopped the tape again. "Okay, so you got away with it. I sure as hell hope that was the only time you tried that."

"As a matter of fact, she changed three of her five points."

"My God."

"Jack, what's the matter with you? Don't you believe in the integrity of your work?"

"Not as much as you, apparently."

"Then it's a very good thing I handled the revision discussion. Ready to hear the rest of the tape?"

"I don't know if my heart can take it. You're a dangerous woman."

"And one you need, obviously." She punched the play button again.

"If you only knew," Jack murmured.

"What did you say?"

"Nothing."

"Stop your muttering and relax. Someday you'll thank me for being so assertive on your behalf."

He found relaxing almost impossible as Krysta and Stephanie chose to discuss a love scene next.

I'll bow to your judgment on this, Candy, Stephanie said. *But I wonder if Jake shouldn't be a little more frenzied as he makes love to Christine that first time. After all, he wants her very much.*

That's the beauty of his restrained approach, Krysta replied. *I can guarantee that women will go crazy imagining themselves being seduced so slowly and expertly. His controlled passion makes him even more exciting.*

Jack risked a glance at Krysta and caught her looking at him. Was that a gleam of desire in her eyes, or the candlelight playing tricks on him? He'd give anything to know if this conversation was doing the same thing to her that it was doing to him. She glanced away, and he could swear she was blushing. He barely heard the rest of the tape and hardly tasted the food on his plate.

When the discussion moved to the TV interview that afternoon, Krysta turned off the tape. "What do you think?"

I think I'll go crazy if I don't make love to you very soon. "I think you're amazing," he said. It was all he had courage for. "You did a great job with Stephanie."

"Thank you."

He sipped his wine and watched the candlelight caress her soft skin and lustrous hair. "That haircut really does suit you. I would have voted against cutting it, but now I see I would have been wrong."

Her eyes grew luminous. "I'm glad you like it."

Perhaps it was only the candlelight that put that welcoming light in her eyes. Maybe it was only the force of his own desire that made her look like a woman who wanted to be loved. He decided to bring up the television show. After all, she'd said publicly that he wrote great love scenes. "You mentioned something in your interview today that I—"

"Oh, I almost forgot! I have the proofs from the photo session, if you'd like to see them."

"Okay." Well, he probably had his answer. She wanted to stick with business matters. Taking the wine bottle and his water glass, he left the table. "Bring your glass, and we'll sit on the couch and go through them." He was glad he hadn't asked about the television show. He might not have liked what he heard.

"You'd better get your glasses for this," she said. "I'm supposed to give Stephanie my favorites tomorrow, and I want your input considering that one of these will end up on the dust jacket."

"I don't need my glasses." He snapped on a lamp next to the couch.

She blew out the candles and walked toward the couch, her wine goblet in her hand. "Look, I know they must bother you, with that tape on them, but I want you to be able to see these pictures, Jack. You can take the glasses off again when we're finished."

He sat on the couch and crossed his ankle over his knee before taking a sip of his wine. "I'm wearing contact lenses."

Her mouth dropped open. "I don't believe you." Still holding her goblet she sat beside him and peered into his eyes. "You *are*. When did this happen?"

"I picked them up today." Only a few inches and his lips would be on hers. His heart beat faster. But she wasn't offering to kiss him. She was only examining his new lenses. Yet her breathing seemed a little quicker, a little more shallow.

She moved back a bit and studied him. "You arranged for contact lenses in that short a time? You must have paid a fortune. The haircut was one thing, but buying contacts in a strange city on short notice is really beyond understanding."

The words sounded like Krysta, but her soft tone caught his attention.

"I didn't pay for them. I—"

"Oh, Jack. Don't tell me you put them on credit. That's even more ridiculous than—"

He pressed a finger against her lips. It was a subtle move, one that could go nowhere, or start them on a long, sweet journey. He'd know by her reaction to his touch which it would be. "Hey," he said gently. "Stop talking for five seconds and let me tell you how I got the haircut and the contact lenses."

Her eyes darkened a fraction.

A less observant man might have missed the change, but Jack had written about such moments, and he didn't miss it. Slowly he removed his finger, but he kept eye contact. He wanted to build on what he'd started. Briefly he told her about tackling the mugger, trashing his glasses and accepting the offer of the grateful businessman to pay for contact lenses and a haircut.

"You could have been killed," she murmured, her gaze never leaving his, her fingers tight around the stem of her glass. "You should never have tried to stop him."

"I acted on instinct. There was no conscious decision on my part."

"Now, that really scares me, thinking you might do something foolish like that again."

"Why?" he asked quietly.

She swallowed. "Because I care what happens to you."

"You mean whether I take my vitamins or get enough sleep? That sort of thing?" He heard the edge of frustration in his voice but couldn't control it.

"Well, that, and whether you're happy...and...and if you'll find someone special some day."

"You're worried about my love life?"

"Not worried so much as..." She closed her eyes and took a long, shaky breath. "I can't stand it another minute."

He noticed the tremor that passed through her, and hoped

he could guess what she was about to say. "Can't stand what?" His heart thudded wildly.

"Wondering." Slowly she opened her eyes, and they flashed green fire. "Can you kiss the way you wrote about it in the book?"

The blood roared in his ears. "Yes."

"Would you...show me?"

He turned away to set his glass on the coffee table. Then he took her goblet from her unresisting fingers and put it beside his before turning back to her. His hands shook slightly as he cupped her face with both hands, but the sensation of her warm skin beneath his fingers steadied him. He wanted nothing more than to kiss her the way she was meant to be kissed. If this was all he was ever allowed, it would have to be enough. And he would make sure that she never forgot the next few minutes for as long as she lived.

"Close your eyes," he murmured, gazing down at her. "Close your eyes, and empty your mind of everything else but this."

She looked more hesitant and vulnerable than he'd ever seen her. "I don't know if I can, Jack."

"You can."

"Should I...hold you?"

"No. I'll hold you." *For as along as you'll allow it.*

With a little sigh she allowed her eyes to drift closed.

"Happy Valentine's Day," he whispered. He started with her temples, brushing them with his lips before pressing his mouth against the gently beating pulse there. He breathed in the fragrance of her hair as he slid his fingers into the thick mass of curls.

Holding her with firm pressure, he tilted her head back and kissed her closed eyes, willing her to see only pleasure, feel only delight. He stroked his fingers through her hair to cup the back of her head, then guided her backward until her head rested in his hands and her throat lay exposed.

Beginning at the tender hollow that throbbed with excitement, he settled his mouth there, heating her already warm skin as he moved up the column of her throat with languid kisses. Her breathing quickened with each feathery touch. And each time his lips brushed her petal-soft skin, his soul became more enmeshed in the pure joy of loving her at last.

He drew out the moment, drew out the risk for both of them. Searching out the sensitive spot behind the lobe of her ear, he rejoiced in her tiny gasp of surprise as he caressed her there. He traced the line of her jaw in reverent detail, and as his path took him closer to the corner of her mouth, she began to quiver beneath him.

He teased her with a soft touch at one corner, a gentle kiss at the other. Her lips parted on a slight moan. He angled his mouth above hers, allowing her to sense him there, to feel his breath and to know he drew nearer. He touched down with the lightness of a breeze, the warmth of a sunbeam, and the gentle insistence of a man in love.

It was his secret weapon, the force that made a mockery of mere technique. He loved her, had loved her for months, perhaps for years. Slowly he took command of her mouth and tried to tell her. The message was gentle at first, as he molded his lips to hers and savored the velvet softness and the delicate taste of her. He paid homage as a supplicant might.

Until the fever took her.

With a groan of surrender she pulled him in deeper, and as supplication transformed to demand, and sweetness to desperate hunger, he lifted his mouth from hers and drew back, although his whole being rebelled at being denied the satisfaction of loving her completely and thoroughly. But that next step would not be taken mindlessly. Too much depended on what happened next to let themselves fall into bed without thinking. He'd asked her to empty her mind. Now he would ask her to think.

She didn't open her eyes at first, and it was all he could do not to return to those provocatively parted lips.

Then gradually her eyelids lifted to reveal a gaze that would melt steel. Her voice was blurred with passion. "Why did you stop?"

His breathing was none too steady. "Because it was the end of the kiss."

"I don't think so."

"You asked for a kiss. That's what you got."

Awareness dawned in her expression. "I'm supposed to ask if I want...more?"

"Yes."

Her voice was husky with passion. "And why is that?"

"Because I'm not the vice president of a company and probably won't ever be one. Because I understand perfectly why you want financial stability in a man, and I may never have that. Because I'm in no position to make promises. If I were a stronger man, I'd tell you to stay the hell away from me. I don't fit into your game plan."

A sultry smile tipped the corners of her well-kissed mouth. "Are you finished?"

"Yes."

"I liked the kiss, Jack." Her slow, easy speech was the exact opposite of the brisk way she usually talked. "I liked it a lot."

Apparently he'd transformed her into a seductress, he thought in wonder as he gazed at her and waited for the rest.

"And I was wondering..."

He lifted his eyebrows as she paused dramatically.

"I was wondering if you can make love the way you wrote in your book."

He thought his lungs would explode. "Yes," he said, and scooped her up off the couch.

As he carried her into the bedroom, the tie on her robe slipped and the garment fell open. He glanced down at the daisy nightie she wore underneath, then back into her face. "Did you plan for this to happen all along?"

"No." She smiled up at him. "But I thought if it did, you might want to do a little research on exactly how the nightie comes off."

"What you read that day's been destroyed."

"Jack! It was good!"

Pushing her discarded underwear aside, he eased her down to the bed and smoothed the hair away from her face. "This will be, too. And some things aren't meant to be in print."

10

KRYSTA TREMBLED in anticipation as she gazed up into Jack's face and realized that soon she would know what it was like to be loved by him. She thought of the scene in *Uptown Girl* when Jake had first made love to Christine. Jake and Christine. Jack and Krysta. She hadn't noticed before.

She touched his cheek. "The characters in your book—"

"Are not us."

"But the names. They're almost like ours."

"Almost." He trailed a finger across her lips. "I made those characters just enough like us to inspire me. But Christine's not you, because I hadn't ever... I didn't know you well enough."

Her mouth tingled where he'd touched her. "We hadn't ever made love."

"Only in my mind."

The idea that he'd imagined making love to her while he wrote took her breath away. "So Jake isn't you, either?"

"No."

"He's...a pretty sexy guy."

The corners of his mouth twitched as if he was holding back a smile. "Are you saying I'm in competition with somebody I made up?"

"Well..."

"Forget Jake. He's not real." He leaned down, his lips close to hers. "But I am," he murmured just before he carried her away with another mind-shattering kiss.

She tangled her fingers in his hair and invited him to deepen the embrace. When at last she felt the thrust of his tongue, desire shook her with a force that made her gasp.

He'd done nothing more than kiss her and she was already molten and ready for him, already fumbling with the buttons of his shirt. He caught her hands and finished the job far more efficiently than she ever could have. She ran her hands over the firm muscles of his chest and felt the answering shudder beneath her palms.

Lifting his mouth from hers, he gazed down at her with an intensity that tightened the coil of excitement deep inside another delicious notch. Moving from the bed, he finished undressing, his attention remaining focused on her the entire time. She remembered this part of his fictional love scene, remembered how Christine had responded to the first sight of her lover's body. In the soft light from the bedside lamp, Krysta feasted on the unveiling of Jack, thoroughly aroused, and very real. In that moment she abandoned all thought of fictional heroes.

He stooped to the floor and pulled some small cellophane packages out of his pocket before laying them on the bedside table.

So there was some premeditation involved, she thought. The idea excited her even more. "Do optometrists give out those little packages with new sets of contact lenses?" she murmured. "I suppose it makes sense. If you're sexier, you'll probably have reason to use—"

"You know what?" He levered his body to the bed.

The stimulation of having an unclothed Jack right there beside her made speaking almost impossible. She longed to touch him but was finding herself more than a little shy about where to begin. "No, what?"

"I'm amazed you didn't ask me about condoms before we ever came in here. I thought we'd have to discuss which brand to use."

It was a legitimate concern, but for some reason her brain didn't seem to be functioning very well right now. She cleared her throat. "Now that you mention it, wh—"

"Too late," he said, sliding off the sleeves of her bathrobe. "We're not going to discuss it now. It's a good brand."

"But—"

"Be quiet, Krysta." His smile was gentle. "For once in your life, relax and let somebody else take charge."

It was the sort of command she'd waited a lifetime to hear. And take charge he did. So this was what it was like to tremble in anticipation of a man's touch. She'd never known. But she'd never known a lover with instincts like Jack's, a lover who spurned the obvious and embraced the subtle, a lover who specialized in the art of surprise.

He stretched her arm out and stroked her fingers as if they were the most erogenous part of her. And for the moment, they were. Then he moved to her palm, and the inside of her wrist, igniting bonfires along his path.

As he brushed his fingers along the underside of her arm, she imagined that same touch on her inner thigh and moaned in anticipation. "Kiss me, Jack," she begged.

"I thought you were going to let me be in charge," he murmured.

Her breathing grew shallow as he continued his ministrations to her other arm. "Not even any...requests?" she asked.

"I'll consider them."

She let out her breath on a long sigh. "Then kiss me, Jack."

He did, sliding down the bed to place his lips against the arch of her foot. As he ran his tongue into the crevices between her toes, she began to throb with the intensity of wanting him. She trembled as he kissed his way with careful intent up her calf and behind her knee. When his lips caressed her inner thigh, she thought she might go out of her mind.

And still he hadn't removed her nightie. She was ready to tear the material off herself, but he'd clasped both her hands in his, intertwining their fingers as he approached the moist center so ready for him. And then he moved past that pulsing spot without touching her there and came back to her side again. She was wild to have him.

Releasing her hands, he drew the nightie over her head. Except for the slight trembling of his hand as he cupped her breast, he seemed to be in perfect control. She arched into his caress, desperate for his mouth to relieve the aching need swelling in her breasts.

She'd expected him to go slowly here, too, but it was as if he knew the moment for light caresses had ended. He took her breast into his mouth fully and deliberately, giving her such pleasure that tears filled her eyes.

The pace accelerated. His touch was more demanding than gentle as he slid his hand down to her waist. When he moved astride her, she thought he might sheathe himself and take her then and there. And, oh, she wanted that. The pressure had become so intense that all she could think of was having him fill her and end the sweet torture he'd begun.

But he didn't reach for the package on the bedside table. Instead, he trailed kisses down the valley between her ribs as he slid both hands beneath her bottom. Before she realized his intent, he'd lifted her to his waiting mouth for a caress that splintered all semblance of self-control. She could no more stop the cataclysmic response he brought forth than stop breathing. She cried out as wave upon wave took her with a force that left her gasping and limp in the cradle of his strong hands.

At last he lowered her gently to the bed and returned to her side. He smoothed the tangled hair from her cheeks as he covered her face with kisses. She had no breath, no words to tell him how he'd made her feel, but he seemed to know.

She felt dazed and disoriented as she looked into his eyes. "But I still want—"

"Good." He lingered a moment and brushed his mouth against hers. "So do I."

The taste of passion on his lips began the spiral of need all over again. "Now, Jack," she urged. "I want you."

He outlined her mouth with the tip of his tongue. "That sounds like an order."

She groaned in frustration.

With a soft chuckle he reached over to the bedside table for the condom. The soft snap of the latex as it covered his erection sent a hot new surge of longing through her.

"Come here," he whispered, slipping his arm beneath her and lifting her gently. She hadn't expected this would be what he'd want now, but she followed his guidance and positioned herself above him.

"Why this way?" she murmured.

His voice was ragged with need. "Because you need to be in control again."

She hesitated. Was there censure in his tone or was it merely roughened with desire? "Jack, I—"

"It's okay, Krysta. I'm man enough to let you lead."

"I believe you are." She gazed into his eyes as she slowly lowered herself, taking him deeper and deeper inside her. She'd never seen a blue so intense as the color of his eyes as she accepted him completely inside her.

He understood so much, including her need to give to him as he'd given to her. Bracing her hands on either side of his shoulders, she initiated a slow rhythm and watched his eyes darken. Knowing that she was bestowing pleasure built the tension in her once again, and although she concentrated on him, her own needs began to clamor for satisfaction.

But she wanted him to know that he'd already taught her something about making love. She pushed aside her own desires and tuned in to the sound of his breathing, allowing that to guide her into an ever-accelerating motion. She watched his eyes and listened to the soft groans of pleasure as his hips moved in concert with hers. And for a brief time she felt what he felt and knew just when to increase the pressure, when to ease away, and when, at last, to take him on a glorious ride over the brink. To her complete surprise, she careened over the edge with him, as if they'd truly become one mind, one heart, one soul.

As the pieces of her world slowly realigned themselves again, she sank to his chest and laid her cheek over his beating heart. She'd had no idea. Nothing, not even Jack's own words on paper, had prepared her for such cataclysmic lovemaking. She thought of trying to tell him all that was in her heart, but decided she could never do justice to what she felt.

Jack was the wordsmith, not her, and besides, he was so sensitive to her feelings he must know what he'd accomplished.

She closed her eyes and snuggled against him. He reached a hand to stroke her hair. For the first time in her life she felt completely, utterly at peace.

SHE WAS OBVIOUSLY planning to keep her reaction to herself, Jack thought with some impatience. They lay propped against the headboard, pillows behind them, and they'd turned on the other bedside lamp so they'd have plenty of light to study the photos for the dust jacket.

Jack wasn't quite sure how to interpret Krysta's silence about their lovemaking. She'd never been slow to offer her opinion of his behavior before. After they'd made love she'd lain quietly with him for several long minutes. He'd needed some recovery time, himself, so he hadn't been ready for an immediate critique. But he'd expected her to eventually make some comment about what they'd just shared.

He'd be damned if he'd ask her for one, though. That old "Was it good for you?" routine wasn't his style. He knew it had been good for her, and it had been spectacular for him. But he'd had the decided impression that he was on trial, and he'd sure like to hear the results.

That didn't seem likely. Whatever Krysta thought about his lovemaking, she wasn't talking. So he relaxed here in bed with her, hip to naked hip like newlyweds, the box of valentine candy open with brown candy wrappers scattered over the covers, and Candy Valentine's publicity photos spread before them. Krysta had suggested getting them out, which was when he'd begun to suspect she wasn't going to discuss her reaction to the obvious pleasure he'd given her.

So maybe they wouldn't talk about it. Maybe they'd just do it some more. He didn't think she'd have a problem with that. Perhaps he expected too much in the way of verbal reassurance. Not everyone was into words the way he was. Hell, almost nobody was.

If he'd been writing this scene he would give Krysta dialogue telling him that he was the best lover she'd ever had. Unfortunately he wasn't writing this scene. All along he'd been teasing her about wanting to be in control. Maybe it was time to admit his own need for control, which he exercised every time he wrote a book, and which he longed to exercise in real life, truth be told.

"I think this is my favorite." Krysta held up a five-by-seven proof of her sitting sideways on a stool in the leather suit, her legs crossed, her upper body turned toward the camera, and a decidedly come-hither look on her face.

Jack felt a twinge of jealousy. "How did he get you to look at him like that?"

"Did I say it was a male photographer?"

"No, but I'll bet it was."

"And you'd be right." She shifted slightly, which rubbed her silky thigh against him. "He told me to think of the sexiest guy I knew."

"Is that so?" He glanced at her.

Reaching down to pick a chocolate out of the box, she kept looking through the photos without seeming to notice that he was staring at her. "This one's not bad, either." She held up one in which she was leaning against a post while wearing a full-length white coat with a white fur collar that brushed her cheeks. She was holding the heart-shaped box of candy she'd brought home tonight. Narrowing her eyes at the picture, she took a bite of the chocolate, exposing a creamy center. "Classier, I think. Which one do you—"

"And who might that be?" Jack asked, not giving a damn about the pictures when they had more important matters to discuss.

"Who might who be?" She took another dainty bite of the candy.

"You know good and well. The sexiest guy you know." He took the proofs away from her.

"Hey!" She reached for the proofs. "We need to go over those."

"Later." He held them out of reach.

"Jack." She made another grab.

He dumped them on the floor, then took her by the shoulders and toppled her backward across the mattress. "Who's the sexiest guy you know?"

She laughed and squirmed beneath him. "Mel Gibson."

"Oh, yeah? On what grounds?"

"You obviously didn't see *Braveheart* or you wouldn't ask." She grinned up at him and popped the last of the candy in her mouth.

"I can see we still have a little trouble sorting out the difference between fantasy and reality around here." He shifted his weight so he had better access to her inviting body. "The sexiest guy you know isn't Mel Gibson."

"Yes, it is."

Putting a firm hand between her thighs, he kissed her smiling lips and tasted chocolate. Then he lifted his head as he stroked upward and probed deep. "You don't know Mel Gibson," he murmured. "All you know is the fantasy he creates."

She drew in her breath. "I suppose you're some sort of authority."

"I suppose I am. I'm in the fantasy business, myself." He'd aroused her in seconds. He could send her spiraling into orgasm in seconds more. That gave him some satisfaction, at least. "Who were you thinking of when the photographer took that picture?"

"I..." She shifted the candy in her mouth. "I can't think of anything when you...do that."

He leaned down. "You'd better give me that piece of chocolate before you choke on it," he whispered.

"No."

"Yes." He delved into her mouth with his tongue and captured the bit of candy.

"I want that," she murmured.

"But you want this more." The chocolate was sweet on his tongue as he massaged the tight little bud that gave her such pleasure.

Her fingernails dug into his shoulders as she drew closer to the abyss. "Jack..."

"So you thought of me when he took the picture?" Ah, she was nearly there.

"I...yes!" She arched upward.

"Thank you, Krysta." He settled his mouth over hers and drank in her gasps as he pushed his fingers in deep to absorb her contractions.

Afterward, she lay so quietly beneath him that he thought she might have drifted off to sleep. And he vowed not to wake her, even though he was hard and wanting her again.

Then her hand curled around his erection, and all his senses went on alert.

"You've wrung that confession out of me by devious means," she said, her voice silky as the stockings she'd worn that day. "And now I intend to get a confession out of you with the same method."

He'd tell her anything she wanted to know, but that wouldn't be much fun. "Good luck. I'm a past master at keeping my own counsel."

Her hand glided upward, then back down. "I want to know when you bought those condoms."

He sucked in a breath as she repeated her motion and lingered over the sensitive tip. "What difference does it make?" he asked.

"I want to know how long you've been planning this evening's entertainment." She wriggled from beneath him and continued her caress. She seemed to understand more about male anatomy than he'd given her credit for. "I want to know if this was part of the plan all along."

"I don't see that it..." He couldn't finish the sentence. In one graceful movement she arranged things so that she could take him in her mouth. "Matters," he finished, groaning.

After driving him very nearly crazy, she lifted her head to give him an angelic smile. "Oh, it matters." Her thumb had found his trigger point and she was using her knowledge to great advantage.

He clenched his jaw and closed his eyes as he fought to stay in control. It was a mistake. He opened his eyes when he heard the rip of cellophane. She'd used her teeth and one free hand to open the package, and now she was rolling a condom over his throbbing penis and torturing him every step of the way.

"Want to tell me yet?" she asked.

Not yet, answered his highly stimulated body. But when she was finished, he grabbed her shoulders and rolled her to her back.

Her eyes sparkled with fun as she gazed up at him. Her thighs remained clamped together. "Not until you tell me."

He'd never forced a woman in his life and he wasn't about to start now. He let her win. "I bought them when you agreed to come on this trip," he said.

"That long ago?"

"It was a wild dream, not a calculated plot. I was prepared to take every one of them home unused."

She opened her thighs and drew him toward her. "Doesn't look like that will happen."

"No, it doesn't." He claimed her with one quick thrust.

She gasped and her eyes widened in surprise.

"Did you think I'd always go slow and easy?" he murmured.

She cupped his face in her hands. "With you, I never know what to think."

He drew back and pushed in tight again. "That makes two of us." It was the closest he could come to asking her to talk to him.

She gazed at him in wonder. "You don't know how you've affected me?"

"I can only guess."

"I was sure you knew. You've taken me where no one else ever has. I—" She drew a breath. "Compared to you, I feel...inadequate."

"Inadequate?" He looked at her in disbelief. "But you're the most beautiful, most responsive woman I've ever—" He shook his head. "*Inadequate.* That word has no business being in the same room with you, Krysta."

She moved provocatively beneath him. "Love me, Jack. Love me until morning comes."

11

As Krysta yawned and stretched the next morning, her toe hit something that clattered to the floor. She leaned over the edge of the bed to discover the heart-shaped box of candy up-ended and chocolates everywhere. Then she glanced at her travel alarm on the bedside table. The travel alarm she hadn't set the night before.

"Oh, my God!" She leaped out of bed and stepped on a caramel cream and a chocolate nougat. "Dammit! Oh, yuck!"

"I gather you're not a morning person," Jack said, lifting his head off the pillow.

She hardly spared him a glance as she tottered on one foot and lifted the other while trying to scrape the chocolate from her sole. She lost her balance and staggered, only to step on a dark chocolate with a cherry center. "I hate candy!" she moaned.

"The food or the author?"

"Both, at the moment." She walked stiff-legged on her heels into the bathroom. "I have to be ready in fifteen minutes, Jack," she called over her shoulder.

"If memory serves, I can manage it in less time than that."

"Will you stop with the one-liners?" She held on to the door frame for balance and poked her head around it to glare at him. Her irritation evaporated at the sight of Jack lying there propped on one elbow, the sheet pulled up only as far as his waist, his hair deliciously tousled, and a seductive grin on his beard-stubbled face. She was falling in love with him. That might not be the prudent thing to do under her current financial circumstances, but the truth was inescapable. Jack was the man she'd dreamed of all her life.

"I'll be glad to take care of that chocolate for you," he said softly.

She was quite sure he would, and she'd love to let him. He might even smear more chocolate around just to give him an excuse to do something sinfully sensuous.

Not that Jack needed an excuse. He was a sexy rogue, no doubt about it, but somebody had to think of the business side of things this morning. That somebody would obviously have to be her. She'd taken on the responsibility, and she was determined to do the best job she possibly could of being his alter-ego.

"The limo will arrive in fourteen minutes to take me to have breakfast with Stephanie," she said. "Candy Valentine has established herself as a punctual person. I need your help."

"That's the trouble with reputations." He shifted his weight, causing his shoulder muscles to bunch appealingly. "You have to uphold them. I think maybe we should—"

"Jack, this is important. I'm pretty sure Stephanie will make an offer on your next book this morning."

He grew still. "You are?"

"I am."

His gaze narrowed. "And if she does, you're planning to negotiate the contract?"

"Of course."

"I don't like the sound of this."

"I'll be reasonable."

"Like last time when you demanded double the money?"

"You got it, didn't you? Listen, Jack, if I don't get down there in ten minutes, Stephanie will be sipping coffee by herself in the Rose Room of the Algonquin, and no matter how you look at it, that would be a mistake."

He threw back the covers. "Okay. Go take your shower. I'll talk to you while you're in there."

It took all the discipline she possessed to turn her back on his magnificent body and head for the shower. She consoled herself with the fact that she was doing it all for him. "Better pick up the candy first," she cautioned before she twisted the handles of the shower.

"Do you know that the Algonquin is where Dorothy Parker and a lot of other writers from the Roaring Twenties used to hang out?" Jack called over the sound of the spray.

"No," she called back.

"I'd guess that's why Stephanie's taking you there, so you'd better act impressed."

"Got it. Thanks for the tip." She took the shortest shower in history, and Jack was still kneeling on the floor searching for chocolate when she returned to the bedroom with a towel wrapped around her.

He glanced up. "This candy reproduced during the night. There's twice as much here as there was yesterday."

"It was a double-layered box." She stepped carefully as she walked past him toward the closet.

His hand circled her ankle.

She spared him a quick glance. "Jack, I—"

"Good morning."

Once again, she melted before the intensity of his gaze. What she wouldn't give to have set that alarm. "Good morning." The mere touch of his hand on her ankle reawakened her desire, demonstrating how close to the surface her passion for him remained, even after hours of making love. "So I've brought you to your knees," she said, her tone deliberately light.

"Yes."

She swallowed. The banter was gone from his expression, and the resistance nearly gone from her heart.

"Thank you for an incredible night," he said.

"It was incredible, Jack."

His thumb caressed her instep. "When will your breakfast with Stephanie be over?"

"I'm not sure." Heat surged through her. "How about this? No matter what the contract offer is, I'll tell her I want to come back to the hotel and have some time alone to mull it over. That way, you can have input."

A slow grin appeared on his handsome face. "Oh, Krysta, I like the way you phrased that."

She couldn't help laughing, even though it was shameful that he couldn't keep his mind on business at such a critical time. "You are incorrigible."

"It's one of my finer qualities."

"Let me go, Jack. I have to get dressed."

"More's the pity." But he released her ankle and went back to hunting for the chocolates. "Do you think we should eat these?"

"Absolutely not." She whipped through her dressing routine, throwing on underwear and a green linen pantsuit. "You don't know what's been on that floor. Rug-cleaning chemicals for one thing. Throw them away. Make yourself some coffee and I'll smuggle croissants or something back from the Rose Room."

"What about the maid finding me here? I don't want to leave and take a chance on being gone when you come back. Not when I've been promised input."

She tried to send him a reproving glance and failed miserably. "I'll put the Do Not Disturb sign out. She can make up the room later in the day, for once."

"Or not at all."

"Jack, you're a hedonist." She grabbed her coat from the closet.

"An incorrigible hedonist. That makes me pretty close to perfect."

"I'm outta here," she said, hurrying past him.

"Y'all come back," he said softly.

She gave him one last, yearning glance. "I will." He probably thought she was so regimented that it was easy for her to walk out of the room. Little did he know that her own hedonistic tendencies grew stronger every time he looked into her eyes the way he was doing now. "I'll see you soon," she said, and left.

STEPHANIE WAS, IN FACT, sipping coffee when Krysta arrived at the Rose Room a bare four minutes late.

Holding the tote bag containing the tape recorder she'd already turned on, Krysta glanced around. The breakfast crowd at the Algonquin was definitely upscale. She suspected Armani and Gucci were well-represented by the customers who sat on cranberry-upholstered chairs drawn up to white linen-covered tables. Ornate white molding, cranberry-colored walls, crystal chandeliers and gold-plated wall sconces completed the turn-of-the-century elegance.

"So this is where Dorothy and the gang hung out," Krysta said to Stephanie as the waiter pulled out her chair.

"I thought you'd appreciate eating here." Stephanie motioned for the waiter to bring Krysta some coffee. "Did you have a nice Valentine's night, all alone in your suite?"

Krysta grabbed her napkin and ducked her head while she made a big production of putting the napkin in her lap. "Very restful, thanks." She cleared her throat and looked up, hoping that she was revealing nothing in her expression.

"From the pink in your cheeks I'm beginning to wonder if you were up there watching adult movies. Is that how you get inspired?"

Krysta managed to laugh. Adult movies were as good an excuse as any for her reaction, she decided. "You've found me out. I really don't watch them ordinarily, but there I was with titles like *Cheeky Cheerleaders* staring me in the face, and I've always been curious about movies like that."

Stephanie regarded her over the rim of her coffee cup. "And?"

"Pretty repetitious, actually."

Stephanie nodded. "Most of them are produced by men for men, I suspect. If they've tried to appeal to women, they obviously don't know how, which isn't surprising. It's a rare man who understands what arouses a woman."

"Very rare," Krysta agreed. *And I've found one.*

"That's why books like yours sell so well, of course. We love to read about a man like Jake and imagine him making

love to us, just as you pointed out in our discussion yesterday."

Imagination pales next to the real thing, Krysta thought.

"I'd be very surprised if a man could ever capture the
erotic tone you've created in *Uptown Girl.*"

"Oh, I'm not so sure about that."

"Well, it doesn't much matter if they could or not. You've
done a wonderful job, Candy." Stephanie picked up the
menu and signaled their waiter. "Let's order, and then we
can talk."

Krysta noticed a selection that included croissants and ordered that, thinking that she'd find some way to put the croissants in her tote bag when Stephanie wasn't watching. It
wasn't great nutrition, but better than the chocolate chip
cookies Jack might filch from the honor bar in the suite.

She let Stephanie direct the conversation, and the editor
seemed to be in no hurry to discuss business beyond her ini-
tial praise of Candy's work. They covered politics, the climate
in the Seattle area, and Stephanie's love of houseplants.
Krysta enjoyed the conversation because she found she had
much in common with Stephanie, but she was itching to get
down to brass tacks. Then she could return to the suite, where
she could get down to...a few other things.

In addition to her eagerness to talk about Jack's new book,
she hadn't found a good time to slip the croissants into her
tote bag. Smuggling food was a lot tougher in this one-on-one
situation than it had been during the raucous group dinner at
Sardi's.

"I think we need more coffee," Stephanie said and turned
to locate their waiter.

Seizing the moment, Krysta grabbed the croissants from
the basket beside her plate and dropped them into the tote
bag.

Stephanie turned back more quickly than Krysta had expected. She glanced at the bread basket and then at Krysta.

Krysta knew she was blushing, knew she'd been caught.
"I—uh—was pretty full, but these looked wonderful. I didn't

think this was the sort of restaurant where one asked for a doggie bag."

"Of course you can ask for a doggie bag. In fact, I'll order more croissants and have them wrapped for you. Take those out and we'll add them to the batch."

Krysta wished the tote was big enough for her to crawl into after the croissants and disappear. "That's not necessary, really. Just these two will be fine."

"Heavens, don't worry about it. I think under the circumstances Manchester can afford a package of croissants." She gave instructions to the waiter, who nodded and went back to the kitchen. Then she pushed away her plate and rested her arms on the table as she leaned toward Krysta. "Your new book is wonderful."

Krysta didn't think she could be happier if she'd written the outline for *Primary Needs* herself. She beamed at Stephanie. "I hoped you'd like it."

"I love it, which I think you'll figure out when you hear the deal I'm going to offer you. Now, you still don't have representation at this point, right?"

Krysta went on alert. "Should I have?"

"That's entirely up to you, of course. With most authors I'd say yes, but you seem to have a real grasp of the contract process. I guess it's because of your work at Rainier Paper. But I can recommend a few people if you want to consider getting an agent."

"Not at the moment, but maybe eventually." Krysta realized that when Jack revealed himself as Candy Valentine sometime in the future, he might want to hire an agent to negotiate for him. He was far too subjective to do it for himself.

"In that case—" Stephanie paused as the waiter arrived with the wrapped package of croissants and more coffee. She waited for him to leave and Krysta to tuck the package into her tote bag.

In the process Krysta rearranged the tape recorder to make sure it would get all of this very important conversation.

"Here's what Manchester is prepared to offer for *Primary*

Needs," Stephanie said. She named a price that was higher than the amount paid for *Uptown Girl*, but not twice the amount, which was the figure Krysta had in mind.

Krysta picked up her coffee cup and took a slow sip. "This book has the potential to outsell *Uptown Girl*," she said.

"Once again, we're speculating. But I think so, too, which is why I went up on the advance."

"Up a little," Krysta added. "But not a lot."

"I think that's safer. For you and for us."

Krysta set her cup down with great care. "I'll take that into consideration. But if I agree to that amount, I want a raise in the royalty percentage."

Stephanie blinked. Then she leaned back and grinned at Krysta. "Maybe you *should* get an agent. I think I'd come out ahead."

Krysta smiled back. "And I also want a guaranteed advertising budget equal to the advance."

"You do realize that with this first book we're exceeding that."

"Yes, but that doesn't address what you'll do with the second book, does it?"

"Okay." Stephanie leaned forward. "One percentage point higher on the royalty rates, the advance I stated, and an advertising budget of at least that amount, although I suspect it will be higher. We'll want to ride this Valentine's Day promotion for at least another year. Do we have a deal?"

Krysta had her mouth open to agree to the terms when she remembered that hadn't been the plan. "It sounds very good," she said. "But if you don't mind, I'd like a few hours alone in my suite to think it over."

Stephanie looked surprised, but she quickly composed her features. "Of course. We can have dinner tonight and finalize everything then."

"That would be perfect."

"There is another matter I wanted to ask you about, but it can wait until tonight, if you'd like to get back to your hotel."

Krysta wanted to take as much information to Jack as possible. "Now is fine. What is it?"

"Did you pick out your favorite photos for the dust jacket?"

"Uh—" The last thing Krysta remembered about the stack of proofs was that Jack had taken them away from her, dropped them to the floor and pushed her back onto the mattress so that he could... She tried to wipe the vivid image from her mind. "No, not yet," she said hastily, and hoped the strained quality of her voice wasn't obvious to Stephanie.

Stephanie grinned. "Forgot about them while you were watching those movies, didn't you?"

"Yes. I'm sorry. I'll be sure to—"

"Doesn't matter." Stephanie waved a hand in dismissal. "Tonight's fine, since nothing would happen with them until Monday, anyway. But marketing got a set of those proofs, too. That, combined with meeting you, has convinced them we need to put you on tour for *Uptown Girl*."

As JACK DRANK COFFEE and munched on chocolate chip cookies from the honor bar, he wished he could figure out the next step with Krysta. These few days in New York had thrown them together in a crucible of fiery emotions, but it was something like a shipboard romance, minus the ship. Forty-five stories above Times Square in a suite neither of them could afford on their own was far removed from life in Evergreen, Washington. Krysta didn't give him credit for practicality, but he could be far more practical than she guessed.

Dressed only in his jeans, he paced the area in front of the windows and studied the traffic below every few minutes to watch for limos. It was a stupid exercise because limos were everywhere on the streets of New York. Seeing one near the hotel meant nothing, but watching for them gave him something to do.

He'd love to tell Krysta exactly how he felt and ask her to marry him, but that would be pretty selfish at this point. If Hamilton never suspected she'd found somebody else, she might be able to let him down gradually and still get that promotion she needed to finance her dad's care. But Hamilton might become vindictive if he discovered she'd turned right around and chosen a guy from shipping over him. He might even arrange to get her fired.

That wouldn't matter if Jack could be assured he was about to earn a ton of money. Yet no matter what grandiose predictions Manchester made, nobody knew how the book would sell until it hit the stores next year. He'd read enough industry magazines to get that message loud and clear. Candy Valentine was still a huge gamble and would be for many months to come.

He wandered into the bedroom yet again to check the time on Krysta's travel alarm. She'd been gone a very long two hours and he was going crazy waiting for her. Of course he was eager to hear about Manchester's reaction to his new book, but he'd been thinking about making love to Krysta far more than he'd been thinking about another book deal. He'd even put a condom in his jeans pocket so he didn't have to waste time looking for one. And still he had no answers about their future.

Finally he heard her card key in the lock. Heart pounding in anticipation, he set his coffee cup on the banquet table and walked over to meet her. Soul-searching would just have to wait.

She came in the door, a glorious smile on her face. "Jack, I have some wonderful—"

"Everything about you is wonderful." He captured her with one arm around her waist, took the tote bag with his other hand and kicked the door shut with his foot. "And I need all of it right this minute." He dropped the tote bag to the floor.

"Wait. I—"

"Can't." His hungry mouth came down on hers as he maneuvered her out of her green jacket and toward the middle of the room. She tasted better than any woman he'd ever kissed. He could live off of her kisses.

When the jacket was free he tossed it over his shoulder and started on the buttons of her blouse.

She framed his face in both hands and pushed his mouth slightly away from hers. "Jack, I think you'll want to hear—"

"I want to hear you whimper," he said, pulling the blouse from the waistband of her slacks. "And then I want to hear you cry out when I come inside you." He unfastened the catch on her bra and filled his hands with her breasts.

She moaned and closed her eyes. "Don't say I didn't try to tell you."

"I won't. Unsnap my jeans, Krysta. I need your hands on me."

She hadn't pulled his jeans all the way off by the time he'd slid her slacks and panties to the floor, but she'd accomplished enough to make everything possible. He guided her down to the carpet. Kneeling between her thighs he feasted on the silky warmth of her breasts. Sure enough, there was the whimper he'd been waiting all morning to hear. Rocking back on his heels he gazed at her as he retrieved the condom and put it on.

Lying there, pink and panting and disheveled, she was everything he'd ever dreamed of in a woman, in a lover, in a lifelong mate. Bracing his hands on either side of her, he lowered his hips and plunged deep, rejoicing that she was as hot and wet as if he'd spent hours touching her. With only a few swift strokes he was ready to explode. He gauged the level of passion in her green eyes and decided to go for it. One more thrust and she arched beneath him with the cry of completion he'd longed to hear. He emptied himself inside her with a groan wrenched from the depths of his soul.

Some time later, as sanity slowly returned, they abandoned their place on the carpet, gathered up their clothes and settled themselves in the king-size bed.

He stretched out beside her feeling sated, although he assumed the feeling wouldn't last long. He sighed. "That's better."

She smiled. "Better than what?"

"Anything. Making love to you is better than anything in the world."

"You may not think so when you hear my news."

"I'll still think so. But you might as well tell me this all-fired important info that you thought was more critical than a rendezvous on the rug. I don't want it to interrupt the proceedings again."

She lifted her eyebrows. "There will be more proceedings?"

"I believe there will be. So tell me. What did Stephanie have to say?"

"She loved the new book."

"That's great." Funny how anticlimactic it was after what he'd just shared with Krysta.

"You don't seem very excited, Jack." There was censure in her tone.

He positioned himself so he could nibble at her lower lip. "My priorities have changed."

"She offered more money, but not as much as I thought you deserved."

Jack leaned his forehead against hers and sighed. "Here we go."

"But I think we should take it, because I negotiated a one percent raise in royalty rates and a guaranteed advertising budget in the amount of the advance."

He wondered if she realized how she'd phrased that. *I think we should take it.* Part of him was overjoyed at the sense of commitment that implied, but the other part was terrified she was expecting too much from this fledgling career of his. It wasn't strong enough to keep them both afloat. Not yet, in any case.

"You're not saying anything, Jack. I think it's a good deal."

He raised his head and looked into her eyes. "It's a very good deal. Thank you. Getting a higher royalty percentage is a real coup. You do know your contracts, lady."

"There is one other thing. It has to do with *Uptown Girl*."

"I'll bet she asked you about that dust jacket picture. I remembered we hadn't picked one out while I was mucking out the bedroom and found the proofs on the floor."

"Stephanie did mention that, but I can tell her what pictures we've chosen when she and I have dinner tonight."

He frowned. "Do you really have to go to dinner with her? I was hoping—"

"I have to give her an answer about the contract, don't forget."

He'd thought they might take a walk through Manhattan tonight. It would be their last chance to do anything like that considering that the plane left first thing in the morning. Maybe by then he'd have worked out a strategy for them to spend time together during the next year without getting either of them fired. "Phone her."

She shook her head. "No, Jack. Now is not the time to appear unfriendly."

He approached her delicious mouth again. "I can testify that you're definitely not unfriendly."

"She wants Candy to go on tour for *Uptown Girl* next February."

He paused a fraction away from her delectable lips. "I hope you told her it was impossible."

"Actually, I told her I probably would."

His head came up again. "You did what?"

"I'm sure there's a way we can manage it. And I think without the tour the whole deal might go sour. I—"

"No." Dammit. Dammit to hell. He'd hoped to avoid a moment like this for a long time. If nothing else was required of her he could have somehow tried to keep the connection between them for the next year until he could be more certain of his publishing career. But this proposal of Stephanie's changed everything. He couldn't ask Krysta to jeopardize her career by making a commitment to go traipsing over the country masquerading as him. The outcome was too uncertain.

"What do you mean, *no?*"

"I mean you're not touring for me."

"Why not?"

"Because I won't ask it of you, and that's that."

12

KRYSTA WAS STUNNED at Jack's reaction. "Of course you can ask it of me! I would be happy to do that for you. Or have I embarrassed you so much during this trip that you can't trust me to represent you on tour?"

Pain flashed in his blue eyes as he reached for her. "No, no. Never that."

"Because I realize I haven't been perfect at this Candy Valentine business." She stumbled over the words, her heart aching because he wouldn't accept her help. "Just this morning Stephanie caught me smuggling croissants, which probably didn't improve Candy's image, and I know you think I'm too tough with the negotiations, but I'm only trying to protect your—"

He pulled her close and gazed earnestly into her eyes. "Krysta, you've been wonderful. We haven't discussed it, but I know you've put your job at risk by coming here. If Hamilton finds out you lied about the spa trip to spend the weekend with me, he might figure out a way to fire you. I'm sure he could dig up some ancient company policy about sexual relations among employees, even if he'd planned to violate the rule himself."

"He's not going to find out."

"I don't plan that he will, either. I'm prepared to go to great lengths to prevent his finding out. But if you went on tour, I'd have to go with you, and that will be nearly impossible to keep secret."

That was the part she'd looked forward to with the most relish. In fact, floating through the hours in a haze of love, she'd even dreamed that they might be married by then. It could all work out so perfectly that way. She'd keep her job at Rainier as insurance for a while, but she didn't expect to need it very long after Jack's first royalty check arrived.

Then gradually Manchester could discover that Candy had a writing assistant named Jack Killigan, and eventually they could learn the true author of the books so Jack could get his rightful measure of praise. Money wouldn't be a problem, because she was a good negotiator, a function she'd continue to fulfill, and Jack was a tremendous writer. They'd be a great team, and knowing Jack's generous nature, she knew her father would be provided for, as well.

"Maybe we wouldn't have to keep the trip secret," she ventured. "I could pretend I'd written the books for as long as you wanted to keep up the pretense, and then we could announce the truth when you were ready."

"And commit career suicide yourself? How long do you think Hamilton or his buddies would want to keep you on if they believed your heart belonged to the publishing world? He'd still be smarting from your rejection, and he'd just love to be able to question your dedication to the company in light of your new interest in becoming a bestselling author. He'd start documenting every slip you made."

She moved away from him. "You're letting that famous imagination of yours run away with you. You don't know that anything of the kind would happen."

"Don't I?"

Privately she had to admit he'd made some valid points. What hurt the most was his apparent refusal to consider the obvious—getting married and sharing in the success of Candy Valentine. But in order to propose marriage to someone you needed to love them, and he'd never spoken those words to her. Words were his strength, his magic wand, his sorcerer's power. He'd used words to tempt her into loving him, but he'd withheld the words she most wanted to hear.

Apparently she was only the means to fulfilling a fantasy for Jack. Once he'd discovered what was under the daisy-patterned nightie, he was compelled to move on to more imaginative conquests. She'd never known much about artistic personalities, but she seemed to be learning in the school of hard knocks this weekend.

She turned onto her back and closed her eyes to stem the flow of tears. She would not give him the satisfaction of seeing her cry. She didn't want this scene to end up in a Candy Valentine novel. She swallowed. "What—what would you suggest I say to Stephanie about the tour?"

He put a hand on her bare shoulder. "Krysta."

She opened her eyes and stared at the ceiling. "Everything you said is absolutely on target, Jack. I don't know what I was thinking of. I guess I got carried away with pretending to be you. I wanted it to go on...forever. But of course that's—"

"I wish it could, too."

For the first time since she'd known Jack, she didn't believe him. She figured he was jollying her along, getting her used to the notion that the party was over. Well, she was a grown up and she didn't need that sort of coddling. She, of all people, understood how the world worked. Jack was about to become famous, and he was hesitant about making commitments at a time like this. One never knew where the road to fame would lead. One needed to keep one's options open.

But she had to convince Stephanie to abandon the idea of a book tour for Candy's first novel. She had no clue how to do that. She took a deep breath. "I just need some ideas, Jack. Some reasons why a book tour would be a bad idea."

"All right," he said quietly. "Remind Stephanie that some very successful authors don't tour, like Danielle Steel, for example. Tell her that you think an air of mystery would be as beneficial as having you out there. And if none of that works, tell her you have motion sickness and nothing cures it. Tell her you barfed all the way to New York and you'll probably barf all the way home."

She just might, at that, Krysta thought. She continued to gaze up at the ceiling. "I'll try those things. I can't guarantee that it won't affect the deal, though. She seemed really keen on this idea of a book tour. But I'll do the best I can."

"With you, that's a given." He shifted his weight and moved the upper part of his body over hers, bracing his hand beside her head so that she was forced to look at him. "I want you to know something. I wish circumstances could be different. But you need to hang on to your job at Rainier if you hope to be able to help your father. My future is very...uncertain. I can't have you hitching your wagon to a star that might very quickly fall to earth."

"You won't fall to earth, Jack."

He smiled. "And you're prejudiced."

"Maybe, but I've been hearing what Stephanie says, and you're..." She blinked. The tears were very persistent. "You're really going to make it," she finished, and turned her face toward the pillow.

"Hey," he murmured, touching her cheek. "Please don't— my God, you're crying."

"No, I'm not!"

"Krysta—" He turned her face back toward him. "Krysta, don't." His lips covered hers.

A woman with a stitch of pride would push him away, she thought. So what if his kiss moved like velvet over her bruised lips? So what if he knew just how to comb his fingers through her hair so that she felt treasured for all time? He didn't mean a bit of it. He was a fantasy lover, just like the heroes in his books. He'd needed her to play a part for him, just like he needed the heroines of his novels to play a part each time he started a new book. And now the role was complete. But he wasn't a mean-spirited person, so he didn't want her to feel sad about it. She just wished she could stop crying.

"Hush, Krysta," he crooned, taking her more fully into his arms. "It's been a rough few days. Everything will be okay. I've expected too much. I'm sorry. There, now. I'm right here."

Which only made her cry harder. Of course he was right here. But after tomorrow, when the plane took them back to Washington, where would he be? Oh, she might see him in the company cafeteria now and then, but soon he'd leave Rainier to write full time and become a bestselling author. And she would be a memory. A sweet memory, perhaps, but part of his past, part of his beginnings, before he became rich and famous.

"Krysta," he murmured, kissing her damp cheeks. "Please, sweetheart. Please don't cry."

She could only think of one way to make herself stop. Taking his head in both hands, she brought his mouth down on hers. She might not have Jack Killigan for long, but she had him now.

He needed very little urging to make love to her again. At least she still had the power to ignite his lust, she thought with some gratitude. Maybe there was even a little bit of love mixed in there, too. She imagined there was as she gazed into his blue, blue eyes while he moved gently within her. Funny how she'd once thought Jack was beneath her notice. Now he seemed beyond her reach.

JACK FELT LIKE a first-class heel. Damn Stephanie Briggs for making it seem as if Candy Valentine was only a step away from the *New York Times* bestseller list. Damn Stephanie for suggesting a book tour for Candy, which forced him to take a protective stance with Krysta, who naively thought he was a shoo-in for fame and fortune. He could try to tell her his future as a novelist was far from secure. But he was quite sure he could tell her until the cows came home, and she'd never believe him after the way she'd been dazzled by Manchester. She thought he was putting her off, delaying a commitment, because he didn't care enough. The truth was he cared too much.

So because he didn't feel free to say it all—that he loved her and wanted to spend the rest of his life with her—he said nothing. Instead, he spent the rest of that day giving her pleasure and praying that she'd absorb the depth of his caring through his touch. His heart wrenched with the knowledge that she loved him, but felt she couldn't say the words any more than he could. Each of them existed in a self-imposed prison, and the only communication they allowed themselves was a physical expression of desire.

When at last Krysta left for her dinner with Stephanie, Jack had never felt so sexually satisfied in his life. Or so unbearably heartsick.

KRYSTA SAT ACROSS the table from Stephanie within the jeweled interior of Tavern on the Green in the midst of Central Park. From the kaleidoscope of multicolored crystal and stained glass inside to the fairy lights and Chinese lanterns outside, the restaurant sparkled with an intensity befitting Stephanie's vision of Candy Valentine's future.

"Believe me, you're going to be big. Very big," Stephanie said as dessert was served. "But the tour is all part of the plan. We're not just selling the book, we're selling you, and the idea of an author as delicious as a box of chocolates. You're perfect to promote that image. I can't believe you're turning your back on it."

Krysta had tried all of Jack's arguments and none of them had worked with Stephanie. She'd dismissed the Danielle Steel comment as irrelevant in today's market. Steel already had her audience, she'd said. Candy Valentine had to build one, and not by appearing mysterious, but by appearing accessible. When Krysta had finally played her last card, Stephanie had promised to find her a specialist on motion sickness who would certainly cure her of nausea.

Krysta was out of ideas and out of energy. Abandoning the argument for the time being, she pulled the photo proofs from her tote bag and she and Stephanie spent the rest of the time in the restaurant deciding which one to use. They ended up with the shot of Krysta in the full-length coat.

Finally the meal was over and Krysta hoped to be allowed to go back to the hotel with the matter of the tour on hold, at the very least.

"I think I'll just share a taxi with you as far as the Marriott," Stephanie said.

Krysta groaned inwardly, knowing the campaign would continue in the cab. Sure enough, it did.

When the cab driver opened Krysta's door at the hotel entrance, Stephanie got out and paid the fare.

Krysta glanced at her uneasily. "Aren't you taking this cab home?"

"I just had a better idea. How about a nightcap?"

Under the bright lights of the Marriott's portico, Krysta felt as if she were standing on stage and she didn't know any of her lines. "I'm a little tired, Stephanie. Sorry."

"Just one. A brandy would go perfectly right now, don't you think? A farewell toast, so to speak."

No, Krysta didn't think so at all. But Jack's career depended on the goodwill of this woman. She wouldn't get Candy to go on tour, so Krysta decided maybe a farewell toast was required. "Why not?" she said.

"Excellent." Stephanie smiled and took her arm as they walked into the hotel and headed for the elevator.

As they waited for an elevator to be free Krysta turned toward Stephanie. "Would you rather go to the lobby bar or the revolving one on top of the hotel?"

"I think it would be much cozier if we just went up to your suite and ordered room service. I'm interested in what sort of room Manchester reserved for you."

Krysta felt as if Stephanie had just doused her with ice water. "Oh, let's not," she said quickly. "The place is a mess. Truly. I'd hate for you to see what a slob I am."

Stephanie laughed. "What nonsense. I'm not going to be the least bothered with a few articles of clothing lying around."

You might if they belonged to Jack, Krysta thought. She mustn't panic. There was a way out of this. "I haven't been to the rooftop bar yet," she said. "I'd really like to see it."

"Next trip." The elevator arrived and Stephanie walked inside. "Coming?"

Krysta hurried into the elevator after her. "Look, Stephanie, this is a very bad idea. I don't feel well. I think I'm coming down with something. Something contagious."

"I know what your problem is. You're afraid I'll convince you to go on that tour. That I'll wear you down. What floor?"

Krysta panicked. "Stephanie, please—"

Stephanie stood with her hand on the Door Open button, which held the elevator in place. *"What floor, Candy?"*

Krysta hadn't seen this side of Stephanie, the side that wouldn't take no for an answer, but it explained her attaining such a position of power with Manchester Publishing at a relatively young age. Krysta had the feeling that if she didn't go along with Stephanie and take her up to the room, she might cancel Jack's contract, unreasonable though that might be. "Forty-fifth," she said. "But I insist you give me thirty seconds to pick up the place before I invite you in."

Stephanie punched the button and the glass elevator started up the terraced atrium of the hotel. "Goodness, anyone would think you had a man hiding in your room."

Krysta tried to laugh and started to choke.

Stephanie pounded her on the back. "You *are* a bundle of nerves. A shot of brandy is exactly what you need. I'm glad I thought of it. I know it can be disconcerting, attaining this level of success after years of struggling in obscurity, but I'm going to get you past this paranoia, Candy. I've been dealing with authors for years. You're not the first one to run screaming from the thought of doing a little publicity."

Krysta sank against the elevator wall and tried to imagine how she'd get out of this mess.

Stephanie crossed her arms and gazed at her. "I used to be just like you, afraid of success, but I conquered that fear and I've never looked back. You're going to thank me someday for giving you a little push, Ms. Candy Valentine."

Krysta resisted the urge to laugh, afraid that she'd lose control and lapse into hysteria. For the first time she understood how Jack must have felt during all those lectures she'd given him in the Rainier cafeteria, and how she must have sounded to her brothers over the years she'd helped raise them. Stephanie was using exactly the same tone, and it made Krysta feel like a wayward child. She didn't much like the experience.

The elevator doors slid open at the forty-fifth floor and Krysta hurried out. "Don't forget. I get thirty seconds to tidy the place up."

"To tell the truth, I'm not surprised you're worried about that. You have definite perfectionistic tendencies. I can see it in your work."

"You can?" Now that was something to think about. Surely Jack didn't have perfectionistic tendencies. Or did he? Perhaps she'd been too blinded by her own assessment of him to notice.

She dug in her tote bag for the key as she tried to outdistance Stephanie. It didn't work. Stephanie's long stride kept right up with her even though she was practically running down the corridor. She pushed the card key into the slot and prayed that Jack wouldn't meet her at the door.

"Be right with you, Stephanie," she said, a little louder than necessary as she opened the door about a foot. She slipped through and slammed the door in the editor's face.

Jack leaped up from the couch and threw down the book he'd been reading. "Who?"

She rushed over to him. "Keep your voice down," she muttered. "She insisted on coming up to the room for a nightcap."

He stared at her.

"I tried to avoid it, Jack, believe me. Finally, I was afraid she'd cancel the whole deal if I didn't let her come up here. And I've used all your arguments against the tour. She's not buying a single one of them."

"Do you think she's on to us?" he murmured.

"I don't think so. I hope not. Just take your book and go hide in the bedroom. I'll get rid of her as soon as I can."

"Right. And don't agree to that damn tour, no matter how many nightcaps you have."

She put her hands on her hips. "I am not in the habit of getting drunk and giving in."

"Yeah, I know. I tried that." With one last glance, he went
into the bedroom and closed the door.

Krysta took a quick inventory of the suite and was about to
let Stephanie in when she saw Jack's running shoes lying beside a chair. No way could she explain size twelve Reeboks.
She grabbed them and ran to the bedroom door. She flung it
open and heaved them in the general direction of the bed
where Jack lay reading. As she closed the door she realized
that Jack had been forced to duck. And maybe she'd meant
for him to.

Taking a deep breath, she walked to the hall door and
opened it.

ONCE HE HEARD VOICES out in the living room, Jack left the
bed and went over to sit on the floor beside the door and listen as best he could to the conversation. Krysta was ticked.
She'd heaved those shoes right at him, and he didn't think it
was an accident.

Hell, he didn't blame her for being furious. He'd started
something he wasn't in a position to finish. Yet during the
evening as he'd waited for her to come back, he'd been unable to dredge up any regret for what had happened in the
past three days. All his fantasies about Krysta had come true
except the part about living happily ever after, and he wasn't
giving up on that one yet, although he couldn't tell her.

As for Krysta, he didn't think she'd settle for somebody like
Derek Hamilton after this weekend, and that was a plus. Jack
might still lose her to somebody with a better portfolio, because she had to consider her responsibilities to her father.
But at least now she'd demand a guy who knew something
about how to treat a woman. He hadn't allowed himself to
contemplate the idea of her with someone else, though, which
had served the useful purpose of keeping him from punching
holes in the hotel walls.

He leaned against the door and heard Krysta order a bottle
of very good brandy from room service. He shouldn't have
made that crack about having too many nightcaps and agree-

ing to the book tour. She would never allow herself to get tipsy under these circumstances and he knew it.

The stupid remark indicated how frustrated he was becoming with the whole situation, but that didn't excuse it. He'd apologize after Stephanie left. Then maybe he'd ask if he could keep seeing Krysta once they returned to Evergreen, although they'd have to be careful not to run afoul of Hamilton for a while. Maybe if Jack kept coming around, she'd begin to understand that he wasn't avoiding a commitment, just postponing it until the right time.

He concentrated on the conversation between Stephanie and Krysta, and from what he could tell it centered around an illuminated billboard visible from the hotel window. He vaguely remembered the billboard, a shirtless guy who was modeling designer jeans.

"Looks like a candidate for a Candy Valentine hero to me," Stephanie said clearly.

"He is pretty cute, at that," Krysta said, almost as if she'd raised her voice for his benefit. "Nice pecs."

Jack gritted his teeth. She sure knew how to get under his skin.

"You should see some of the cover models," Stephanie said. "Really yummy. I already have somebody in mind for Jake in *Uptown Girl*. I think we'll show him shirtless, like that guy on the billboard."

"I can see that for the cover," Krysta said.

"You know, it would be fun if you could be around for the cover shoot. Hey, maybe you'd like to meet the model I have in mind. You two would probably hit it off great."

"Sounds nice, but we'll have to see," Krysta said.

Jack's breath hissed out through his teeth. He could have done without the sounds *nice* part.

"Do you have a guy waiting for you back home, Candy?" Jack tensed.

"No, nobody," Krysta said.

Jack leaned his head back and closed his eyes. *Nobody*. But there was, dammit. She just didn't understand.

The brandy arrived, and there was some clinking of glasses and laughter as they apparently got comfortable with their nightcaps.

"I'm just not going to take no for an answer on that book tour," Stephanie said. "You're doing it, and that's that."

"I really can't," Krysta replied.

"All right. I didn't want to play hardball, but you're forcing me to. Unless you agree to the book tour, we'll have to reconsider our publishing program for you. We need that tour to help assure Candy Valentine's success. You scratch our back, we'll scratch yours. That's the way it has to be."

Jack surged to his feet, ready to go out and tell Stephanie what she could do with her program. His hand was on the knob as Krysta gave her answer.

"Then, of course I'll do the tour."

13

JACK FROZE IN PLACE. She was willing to make that kind of sacrifice for him, even if she thought he didn't care enough to offer her a wedding ring? He'd get her out of the tour somehow, of course, but if he stormed out there now he'd diminish the value of her gesture and make her look like a fool in front of Stephanie.

"I'm glad you came to your senses," Stephanie said. "Now, before I leave, I'd like to use your bathroom, if I may."

Grabbing his shoes, Jack headed for the closet with no time to scan the place for any other signs of his presence, but he had a bad feeling that a pair of Jockey shorts were lying somewhere on the floor. He had to crouch down to fit under the top shelf, but he managed to close the closet door after him before Stephanie walked into the bedroom. From what he could tell, Krysta was right on her heels.

"Now you'll really embarrass me," Krysta said. "I'm sure the bathroom is a disaster."

Jack could picture Krysta, her heart pounding as she visually swept the area.

"I'm not on an inspection tour," Stephanie said. Then the bathroom door closed.

Jack stood with Krysta's white silk blouse caressing his cheek on one side and the powder-blue suit she'd worn on the plane rubbing his shoulder on the other side. The whole closet was filled with her fragrance, and he wanted to hold her so much his arms ached.

"Jack," Krysta whispered from just outside the closet. "You in there?"

"Yeah," he whispered back. "Did you find anything of mine on the floor?"

"I kicked your Jockey shorts under the bed. Jack, I had to agree to the tour."

"I know."

There was the sound of the bathroom door opening again. "Krysta?" Stephanie said. "Are you okay?"

Krysta's footsteps headed away from him. "I'm fine," she said. "Why?"

"When I came out, I could have sworn you were talking to the closet."

"Just verbally going over my wardrobe," Krysta said. "Making sure I had something to wear back on the plane."

"With the closet door closed?"

"That's right. You caught me standing there muttering to myself. Authors are strange ducks, as I'm sure you've discovered over the years."

"You're right, I have. By the way, I noticed you use a man's razor and shaving cream on your legs. I've found that works better, too."

"Yes, it certainly does." Krysta closed the bedroom door after them.

Still holding his shoes, Jack emerged cautiously from the closet and crept over to listen at the door again. Stephanie seemed to be in the process of taking her leave, thank God.

"It's been a fascinating few days," Stephanie said. "I feel as if we're very much alike, you and I."

"I think so, too," Krysta agreed.

There was a pause. "You're sure you don't have a special someone back in Evergreen?"

"Yes, I'm very sure."

"Then maybe that special someone is right here in New York with you?"

"I—I don't know what you mean," Krysta stammered.

Jack held his breath.

"Don't be embarrassed about it," Stephanie said. "I probably would have brought my boyfriend along for support on my first trip to New York. But next time, come alone. You're a big girl now, and you can make your own business decisions."

"Stephanie, I—"

"With the kind of drive you've shown thus far, it didn't make sense to me that you'd fight the idea of a tour so vigorously, especially after you indicated originally that you'd do it. Besides that, the arguments you came up with sounded a little rehearsed. Finally, I put all the evidence together and came up with the answer. I've edited a fair amount of mysteries in my day, too."

Her comment was met with dead silence. Jack could imagine Krysta standing there completely dumbstruck.

"Some men can't handle it when their women threaten to become independent and successful," Stephanie continued. "If this guy of yours is telling you it's okay to make a lot of money, but not okay to get out there and promote your book, please don't listen to him. Soon you'll have your pick of gorgeous men. You don't have to settle for a chauvinist."

"I—I'll keep that in mind."

"And I'll be in touch. It's been a pleasure, Candy. Good night, now."

Jack slumped against the doorjamb and waited until Krysta came and opened the bedroom door.

She stood there, looking exhausted. "Did you hear her? She thinks Candy Valentine was bush-league enough to drag her hometown sweetheart to New York with her. And that he's the reason she won't go on tour."

"He is."

Tired though she obviously was, Krysta lifted her chin in defiance. "Well, too bad. I'm going on that tour. This whole house of cards will collapse if I don't. Furthermore, I see no reason why you have to come along. I've got the routine down well enough. It's not as if I have to speak in literary phrases or anything. Maybe I'll even take a community college course in literature, just to beef up my conversation on the subject of writing and writers."

He rolled his eyes. "You're crazy. You don't have the time to—"

"I believe in finishing what I start, as I've said to you before. When the tour is over and your first book is a success, you can decide what to do about the entire charade. But if I don't do this for *Uptown Girl* next February, your career won't be launched."

"Sure it will. Maybe not with as much fanfare, but the book will still be published. Stephanie won't change her mind about that."

"Maybe not, but she'll think Candy is a wimp who listens to her boyfriend instead of standing on her own two feet."

"Who cares what Stephanie thinks?"

"Well, you should, but that's only part of the problem with not doing the tour. I realize after this very informative weekend that it takes more than a good book to make somebody a bestseller. You may never have such a golden opportunity to get your work in front of an audience as you do right now. I don't want your failure as a writer on my conscience."

Her tone was reminiscent of the lectures she used to give him in the Rainier cafeteria, but tonight he wasn't amused. He was frustrated as hell at her bullheadedness. "Krysta, think of the consequences to you. You'll have to lie to Hamilton again, and this time it will be an even bigger lie. You'll have to pretend you're going on a book tour for your first book, because the word might easily get back to him if you're going to be that visible. And you'll have to tell the same lie to your friends and your family. Everybody you know will be led to believe that you're Candy Valentine. That's nuts."

"In your view. Not in mine. Now, if you'll excuse me, I'd like to go to bed. We have a plane to catch in the morning."

The ice dripping from her every syllable told him that she intended to go to bed alone.

He lost control. "You're being a damned martyr, Krysta! Hamilton will crucify you and you'll be left with nothing! What about your career? What about your father?"

A dangerous-looking light came into her green eyes. "I can handle Derek, Jack."

His blood ran cold. There was only one way he could imagine her handling Derek Hamilton. He'd been so sure she wouldn't settle for a guy like that, but maybe he'd been wrong. "Don't do it, Krysta."

The crack of her hand against his cheek resounded in the stillness that followed. "How dare you?" she whispered at last, her whole body trembling.

As he stared into the fury and hurt of her gaze, he had no answer. And where Krysta was concerned, he had no rights, either, considering he wasn't ready to step forward to claim her himself. "Okay, maybe that was out of line."

"*Maybe?*" She stormed past him into the bedroom.

"Okay, it was definitely out of line." He couldn't demand that she not go back to Hamilton. He could only hope she wouldn't.

She paused by the bedside table with her back to him. When she turned around she had something in her hand, and tears were streaming down her cheeks. "Here, Jack. Catch!" She hurled the plastic heart across the room.

He caught it with one hand and the plastic arrow shaft bit into his palm.

"Now get out of my sight."

He left the room, and walked out of the suite. Outside in the hall he paused to put on his shoes. His jacket was still inside, but he didn't care. He trotted toward the emergency exit door and pounded down the stairs, the downward spiral perfectly matching his mood. Once outside he hit the pavement running, welcoming the cold. As he ran he tried to crush the fear that he'd just hurled Krysta right back into Derek Hamilton's arms.

BY THE TIME KRYSTA opened her bedroom door the next morning, Jack was already packed and gone. Somehow he also avoided her in the airline terminal. Although the flight home was a blur of pain as she worked to blot out thoughts of the man sitting back in the coach section, she forced herself to think through her options.

If she planned very carefully, she would get her promotion, provide for her father's care and do Jack's book tour. It was a lot to handle, but if she'd learned one thing in life, it was how to shoulder responsibility. Because she had no intention of becoming a martyr or Derek's mistress, she had to find a way to make herself more valuable to Rainier Paper.

Her first move after returning to work on Monday morning was to pay a visit to marketing department head Denise Terkel to present some of the ideas she'd picked up while schmoozing with the marketing department at Manchester. Advertising was advertising, in her opinion, and it was time she concentrated on a transfer to a department where promotion was more likely.

"EXCELLENT IDEAS, KRYSTA." Denise, a redheaded dynamo who stood barely five feet tall, smiled at Krysta across the cluttered expanse of her desk. "Did you dream those up while you were soaking in a mud bath at that spa you went to?"

"You might say that."

"I didn't realize we had such a creative mind sitting down in the contracts department."

Krysta absorbed that statement and its possible implications. "I guess you've forgotten I was the one who suggested doing infomercials promoting Rainier's research into alternative sources of paper material," she said carefully.

Denise frowned. "I thought that was Derek Hamilton's idea."

So Derek hadn't given her credit. No wonder there had been no action on her request for a transfer to advertising. "Well, we sort of brainstormed it together," she said. "He must have forgotten to mention that."

Denise steepled her fingers and gazed at Krysta over the tips of her manicured nails. "I guess he must have."

"I'd really love to work in this department, Denise."

"Considering that you're a bundle of innovation, I don't see why that can't be arranged. Juliet won't be happy to lose you in contracts, but Rainier likes to make the most of an employee's potential."

"That's good news. Now I'd better get back to my post." With a firm handshake, she left Denise's office and went straight to Derek's. He was in a meeting, so she left word for him to call her.

By lunchtime she still hadn't heard from Derek. She went out to a small café with Rosie rather than chance going down to the cafeteria and running into Jack. He had transformed her entire view of the world, but the less she saw of him now, the better. Her wounds were still too fresh.

When she and Rosie returned there was a message on her desk from Derek, who said he'd pick her up at six for dinner. She tried to reach him for the rest of the afternoon to beg off, but he was never available. Finally, she decided to have dinner with him, after all. At least she'd be able to confront him about taking credit for her idea. She'd handle it diplomatically, of course, but she couldn't just let it go.

At her apartment after work she dressed carefully in a modest black knit and pearls. She'd told Jack she would handle Derek, and Derek himself had given her the means. He probably never imagined she would talk to Denise about the infomercial. Assuming he'd taken credit for her idea, which Krysta was pretty sure he had, she could express disappointment but let him know she hadn't spilled the beans to Denise. But she'd use his behavior to put him on the defensive so he couldn't object when she ended their relationship.

Derek arrived promptly at six, every hair in place, his top-coat over his arm and his navy blazer free of even the slightest speck of lint.

Krysta marveled that she'd once found his brand of fault-less grooming attractive. She picked up her coat and purse from a hall table near the door. "I'm ready."

"Before we go, I have something to discuss with you." Derek moved past her into her small apartment's tiny living room, which held only two chairs, one lamp and a television set.

"All right." Krysta put down her coat and purse and closed the front door. "I have something to discuss with you, as well." Maybe she wouldn't have to sit through a dinner with him, after all.

He laid his topcoat carefully over the back of a chair. "If you don't mind, I'd like to go first. I did a little checking and discovered you went to New York City this past weekend."

She was instantly on guard. She wasn't sure how he'd found that out, but she'd might as well not deny it. "The spa was outside the city, but I flew in there, yes."

He gazed at her. "Jack Killigan was on that same plane. Did you know that?"

She tried her best to stay calm. "Really? What a coincidence."

"Don't dig yourself in deeper, Krysta." He approached her slowly, like a cat stalking its prey. "You've had lunch with the guy on a regular basis and you told me he comes from your hometown. I'm not going to buy the story that you didn't know he was on that plane with you. I have only one question. Are you and Killigan having an affair?"

"No." It was the absolute truth.

He stepped closer. "That was uttered with conviction, which gladdens my heart." He put his hands on her shoulders and gazed into her eyes. "What happened? Did you discover a common laborer wasn't the kind of man you wanted in your bed?"

She brushed his hands aside and stepped back. "I demand an apology for that remark, Derek."

He shrugged. "All right. I apologize. But you'll have to forgive me for being upset. For weeks you've been putting me off every time I tried to get close to you, and then I discover you've apparently run away for a weekend rendezvous with one of the dock workers. So if you're not having an affair with him, what's the story? How did you two end up on the same plane?"

Fear for Jack roiled in her stomach. Derek wouldn't hesitate to fire Jack, who could be replaced easily. He might not be so quick to get rid of her, because she was an important part of the daily operation and he knew it. His superiors would demand reasons for her dismissal, but they wouldn't give a second thought about Jack. Her brain felt like a pan of scrambled eggs.

"Jack had no part in it," she said, desperate to come up with a plausible story that would take the pressure off the man she loved. "I found out he was going to New York to see a friend from college, and I booked myself on the same plane." She laughed. "All my life I've gone out with brainy guys like you, Derek. But lots of women, me included, have a fantasy about the brawny type. I thought I might talk Jack into satisfying that fantasy. But he turned me down flat."

Derek came close again and placed his hands at her waist. "You know what? Crazy as that story sounds, I believe you. I've always sensed something wild and rebellious in you trying to get out." His thumbs kneaded her waist.

She tried not to shudder, or worse yet, become sick to her stomach.

"I can satisfy that wildness, Krysta, if you'll only let me."

In your dreams, Charlie. She tried to ease away, but he gripped her harder.

"It's time, Krysta," he murmured, trying to bring her closer. "I can't have you prowling around after dock workers when I can take care of all your needs."

"Let go of me!" Unable to stand his touch another second, she wrenched away.

He started after her. "Now, let's not be shy. We both know what you want."

She clenched her jaw. This wasn't going well. "I'm sorry, Derek. I'm not interested in having a physical relationship with you."

He paused, looking genuinely puzzled. "But I thought we were getting along, you and I."

"We were—are. Were. But not in that respect. I admired

you as a colleague but found that romantically we...just didn't click. Then today I discovered that you apparently presented the infomercial idea to marketing as yours alone."

His face turned pink. "So that's it. You're mad at me because of that. Okay, I'll go back and tell them you had some part in it, if that's all you want. Denise called me today and asked me to approve your transfer to marketing. I'll recommend you for it. Happy now?"

She took a deep breath. "Thank you."

He took a step toward her. "You can do a hell of a lot better than a mere thank you, Krysta."

Jack's warning rang in her ears. She hadn't wanted to believe him. "Surely you don't expect that I'll go to bed with you because you're treating me with the consideration every employee deserves?"

"Now, that would be crass of me, wouldn't it?"

Relief swept through her and she smiled. "I knew you wouldn't—"

"I expect you to go to bed with me because we belong together. We're two of a kind, and it's about time you recognized the fact."

"I disagree. We don't belong together. I'm sorry, Derek, but we really don't."

He grabbed her before she realized what he intended to do. Holding her with a strength that surprised her, he shoved his face close to hers. "You stubborn little bitch. You obviously don't know what's good for you, but I'm going to try and teach you the error of your ways. Either we go into that bedroom now, or your story about chasing to New York after Killigan goes in your file, along with every single mistake you make from here on out. You'll be gone in three months."

She curled her hands into fists to keep from scraping her nails across his face. She'd save that for later if she needed it. "I won't be gone in three months, Derek," she said, her voice quivering.

His expression cleared. "Now you're making sense."

"I'm gone now." She pushed with all her might, and the element of surprise freed her from his grip. "I resign."

He stood and stared at her. "You're crazy."

"You're not the first person to tell me that recently." She felt a wonderful sense of freedom. Later remorse would probably hit full force, but at the moment she felt glorious.

"I know how much you need this job."

"Not that much. Don't let the door hit you on the way out, Derek."

He snatched his topcoat from the chair and stomped past her. "You'll regret this."

"Probably, but right now it feels fabulous."

His response was to slam the door so hard her living room window rattled.

Krysta gazed at the door and wondered why she didn't feel grief-stricken at having just sawed off the limb she was sitting on. Jobs weren't that easy to come by in this neck of the woods. Instead of a bigger paycheck to help pay for her father's care, she had no paycheck.

Yet something deep inside told her she'd done the right thing, both for her and for her family. Self-annihilation didn't set a very good example for her brothers. She'd try to get a job that paid better than the one at Rainier, but if she couldn't, she and her brothers would work things out. Having Stephanie take charge of her life in the same way she'd so often taken charge of her brothers' lives had been an illuminating experience. Perhaps she needed to allow her brothers the freedom to make their own decisions about their education and helping out with their father.

And if she didn't get a job, there was another consideration. She'd have plenty of time to go on tour for Candy Valentine.

14

"I STILL SAY IT'S LAWSUIT time." Rosie stood, feet braced and hands on her hips as she watched Krysta clean out her desk. "In case you haven't noticed, it's not quite so easy for men to get away with sexual harassment in the workplace these days."

"I'll think about it." Krysta put her family beach picture into a cardboard box before glancing up at Rosie. "But it was only one incident, and there were no witnesses, so it could turn into a 'he said, she said' kind of thing. I went out with him for several months, so building a case might be tough."

"I still think you should try. I know it's easy for me to say, but if we don't stop the Derek Hamiltons of the world, who will?"

"You're right. I really will think about it." Krysta regretted telling Rosie that she was quitting because Derek had demanded sexual favors in exchange for a promotion. It was the nearest to the truth she could come with Rosie, who had been a good friend and didn't deserve to be stonewalled. But Krysta hadn't made any reference to Jack. A lawsuit against Derek would undoubtedly result in unmasking Jack as the real Candy Valentine. A court case was out of the question under the circumstances, but she couldn't tell Rosie why.

"I wish Juliet hadn't picked this week to go over to China and finalize the adoption of her little girl. She'd back you on this, and she's got clout with the rest of the brass."

Krysta interwove the flaps on the box. Then she addressed her friend with great care. "Don't forget that what I told you is confidential. I don't want anyone else to know about Derek's behavior."

"I promised, and I won't break that promise, but the whole thing stinks, if you ask me."

Krysta rolled back her chair and stood. "Try looking at it from a different angle. Maybe, now that I'm free of Rainier, there's a better job waiting for me out there, one with greater chances for—"

"I don't even want to hear it. I believe if some cloud showed up without a silver lining, you'd have it recalled. Don't you ever get mad and just want to punch the hell out of someone?"

Krysta remembered vividly the last time that had happened. She'd hit the man she loved. "That doesn't solve anything, Rosie."

"Maybe not, but it sure can make you feel better."

"Not necessarily." She walked over to the coatrack.

"Then that's where you and I are different, Mother Teresa. Don't forget we're going out tonight for a cholesterol binge. I'll pick you up right after I blow this miserable joint at five."

Krysta walked over and gave Rosie a hug. "Don't let my experience sour you on Rainier. It's a good company, and except for Derek, the management's the best."

Rosie hugged her back. "And we're gonna get that SOB sooner or later."

"Yeah." Krysta decided to leave it at that. "See you tonight." She was almost out the door with her box when Rosie called after her.

"Are you gonna go say goodbye to Jack Killigan?"

Just the mention of his name almost made her drop the box. She sure hoped Derek hadn't started rumors about her already. "Why?"

Rosie's expression was innocent. "Just wondering. He's a nice guy, and he seems to think a lot of you."

"Then maybe I will stop by the shipping dock before I leave." On the way out to her car in the drizzle of a February afternoon, she contemplated the wisdom of going to see Jack. She didn't intend to tell him she'd quit, just that she'd arranged the time off for his book tour. Because they were avoiding each other these days, he wouldn't discover her absence at Rainier for quite a while.

By the time he did, she'd be set up in a new job, a better job. The last thing in the world she wanted from Jack was pity.

After depositing the box in the passenger seat of her car, she locked the door and trudged back through the rain to the entrance nearest the shipping dock. On her way in she met the foreman, Bud.

"You're here to see Jack, I'll bet," he said.

"That's right."

"I'll get him for you."

Wish you could, Krysta thought wistfully as the foreman walked through the door onto the noisy dock. But Jack Killigan was a shooting star traveling at light speed away from her.

Jack came through the door wearing his blue coveralls and yellow hardhat. Of course, she'd known his hair was short now and his glasses had been replaced with contact lenses, but she still blinked at the transformation it made. Even his movements seemed more purposeful, his gaze more direct. And he was so gorgeous she caught her breath.

He walked toward her. "You've been out in the rain."

All I have to offer is a kiss in the rain. She swallowed the lump in her throat and tried to keep her voice steady. "I had to put some things in my car, and then I decided to stop by and tell you that I'm cleared for the book tour."

"Dammit, Krysta, I didn't want you to—"

"Nobody knows anything about Candy Valentine, Jack. Not yet, at any rate."

His eyes narrowed. "Then how did you get Hamilton to give you that much time off?"

"That's my business."

A muscle worked in his jaw and he swore softly under his breath as he stared up at the ceiling.

She could almost read his mind. He thought she'd slept with Derek to get this favor. But she wouldn't stoop to defending herself against the unspoken accusation.

When his gaze returned to hers, it was bleak. "And now you're all prepared to go on tour for me."

"This is for the best, Jack."

His laugh was bitter. "What a typical rose-colored glasses remark." A pulse throbbed in his temple as he glanced away and his chest heaved. "I had no idea you'd work so fast, but I should have known." He rubbed a hand over his face. "I just wish to hell you'd waited another twenty-four hours. Maybe you can trade that time off for a promotion, or maybe some company stock."

"What are you talking about?"

He glanced back at her. "I called Stephanie Briggs this morning. I tried to get her yesterday, but she wasn't available."

She felt as if she'd just swallowed a large chunk of ice. "Why did you call her?" But she knew. He'd abandoned the charade, abandoned her.

"Turns out it's no big deal, after all, Candy Valentine being a guy," Jack said. "Stephanie and I had a good laugh over it, and everything's cool."

"I see." She'd known her usefulness to him would end someday, but she hadn't expected to be discarded quite so soon. She waited for the heartrending pain to hit, but apparently the news had left her numb. She felt nothing.

"Dammit, Krysta, couldn't you have been a little less efficient?"

At last her anger kicked in. "And couldn't you at least have notified me of your intentions?"

"Couldn't you have notified me of yours?"

Fury bubbled in her veins. "You mean my intentions regarding Derek?"

"Yes." His jaw clenched. "I deserved to know. You can't convince me he blithely gave you three weeks off, months in advance, for no good reason."

"Of course he wouldn't do that." Suddenly she wanted him to believe the worst because it would hurt him, and she wanted him to hurt. "But don't think it was all self-sacrifice on my part. I enjoyed every minute of it."

"Liar! Three days ago we were—"

"I'm not lying." She didn't want to be reminded of what had been happening three days ago. And besides, she was telling Jack the truth. Resigning in the face of Derek's demands had been one of the best experiences of her life. By giving herself more autonomy, she was able to grant more to the members of her family.

Jack looked as if a paper bale had just fallen on him. "I can't believe it," he said tonelessly.

"I'm not one of the heroines of your novels, Jack."

His gaze intensified. "My mistake. Apparently you're not. And it seems that Hamilton is getting exactly what he deserves."

"I think he will. Goodbye, Jack. Best of luck with your writing career." She hurried down the hall and out into the rain.

"DON'T GIVE ME THAT innocent little smile, babe." Jack took a swig of his fourth long-necked beer and scowled at the poster above his computer. "Enjoyed yourself with Hamilton, did you? I suppose you were planning to tell me you put a bag over his head and thought of Candy Valentine."

He took another long swallow and frowned. "But of course when you found out today that Candy's dead, there was no reason to pretend you did it for the good of the cause. You could tell the truth and shame the devil." Jack stared at Krysta's smiling face. "So ol' Derek's a real studmuffin. Who would have thought a guy with a fake Rolex could get it on?" He raised the bottle in the poster's direction. "Thanks for sharing, Krysta."

His cat jumped into his lap.

"Well, here's a nonpartial observer ready with an opinion. Tell me, cat, can you believe Krysta Lueckenhoff would jump into bed with the likes of Derek Hamilton two days after making mind-blowing love to yours truly?"

The cat meowed and began kneading her claws into the denim of his jeans.

"Well, I can't, either, no matter how mad she was at me. She even told me it was so, told me straight out, and I still can't buy it. Maybe in about fifty years I'll understand what happened."

The cat circled his lap and settled down.

"Oh, and by the way, I've changed your name back to 'cat,'" he muttered, stroking the tabby's golden fur. "Then you and me, we're goin' on a trip, living off the land, like I did before. That's after I tell Mr. Fake Rolex where he can put a very large paper bale, which will likely get my ass fired."

The cat began to purr.

"You like that idea, do you? You'll purr out of the other side of your mouth when we run out of Tender Vittles."

The cat gazed up at him with eyes that were a familiar green.

"And to answer your question, no, you are not going to be a famous author's cat. Not unless I decide to opt for a sex change." He scratched behind the tabby's ears. "Krysta was right. They'd bought the whole package, and now I'm relegated to the bottom of the list. No display dump, no book tour. They were royally ticked at me, cat. Indignant city."

Jack sighed and tipped the bottle back to drain it. Then he lined it up next to the three empties on top of his computer terminal and reached for another. Four down and two to go. The computer screen, gray and lifeless, reflected his grim expression as he unscrewed the cap.

PUTTING ON RAIN GEAR the next morning seemed stupid to Jack when he was on his way to get fired, so he threw on his ski jacket, jumped on his Harley and took off through the downpour for his showdown with Derek Hamilton. Even if Krysta had enjoyed it, Hamilton couldn't get away with asking a woman for sexual favors in exchange for privileges at work. Not if Jack had anything to say about it, and as a matter of fact, he had plenty to say. He arrived in Hamilton's outer office completely soaked.

The secretary eyed him with distaste as he dripped on the carpet. "Do you have an appointment?" she asked.

"Mr. Hamilton and I have had this appointment for months," Jack said. "We just hadn't settled on the exact time."

"Let me check with him." She picked up the receiver on her desk phone. "Your name?"

"I'll announce myself." Jack headed for the closed door of Hamilton's office.

"Just a minute, Mr.—"

Jack ignored her and walked in, locking the door behind him.

Hamilton half rose from behind his desk, his expression startled.

"Hello, there, Derek." Jack approached the desk. "I'm here to talk about Krysta Lueckenhoff."

"Oh." Hamilton seemed to recover himself somewhat. "Don't worry. She's been dismissed."

"She's been *what?*" Jack roared.

Hamilton drew himself up to his full height, which still lacked a few inches to allow him to go eyeball-to-eyeball with Jack. "We can't have that kind of behavior from employees here at Rainier. It was quite embarrassing, really."

"You slimeball. You dangle special company privileges in front of her so she'll sleep with you, and when she does, you *dismiss* her?" Jack reached across the desk and grabbed Hamilton by the tie. "I was going to tell you exactly what I thought of you, and I'm damn good with words, but sometimes words aren't enough." He clenched his fist.

"Sleep with me? Hell, she turned me down!"

"What did you say?"

"She was after you, you numbskull!"

Jack let go of Hamilton's tie. "What do you mean, after me?"

The vice president sank back into his swivel chair and loosened his tie, but kept his gaze riveted on Jack. "You're fired, Killigan."

"Yeah, yeah, I know. Just tell me what you were talking about a minute ago." A warm glow suffused the region of his heart. Maybe she hadn't gone to bed with this bozo, after all.

"I'm sure you know the details far better than I do. She followed you to New York and tried to seduce you. Surely, despite your limited intelligence, you would notice a woman of Krysta's caliber throwing herself at you."

"Who told you she did that?"

"She did, after I confronted her with the fact that you'd both been on the same plane to New York. She confessed that she'd followed you on purpose when she learned of your travel plans. She had a taste for brawn over brains, was the impression I got. We can't have people in the organization who are ruled by their hormones, so I let her go."

Jack folded his arms to keep from reaching for this sorry excuse for a man one more time. "And just when did this little interchange take place, where she confessed and you fired her?"

"This discussion is over, Killigan. You're lucky I haven't called security."

Jack lost the battle to control himself. In one swift movement, he grabbed Hamilton by the front of his white silk shirt and lifted him from the chair. *"When did you fire her?"*

Hamilton turned pale. "Monday night."

"Let's review our conversation." Jack narrowed his gaze as he peered into Hamilton's pale eyes. "Contrary to your opinion of my intelligence, I have an excellent memory for dialogue. Right before I was ready to punch you in the nose, you blurted out that Krysta *turned you down.* Do you happen to remember that statement?"

"You misunderstood."

Jack tightened his grip and lowered his voice. "Wrong. I understood perfectly. You've just admitted to sexually harassing a female employee, then firing her when she wouldn't cooperate." He shoved Hamilton back into his chair. "If Krysta will testify, we have grounds for a lawsuit."

"*We* have grounds? How come you're so chummy all of a sudden? I thought you didn't even like her!"

"What I feel for that woman goes way beyond liking, and it's time I quit wasting my breath on you and told her so." He turned to go.

"You're still fired!" Hamilton shouted.

"Fine with me. I wouldn't want to work for you, anyway." Jack kept walking.

"And I didn't fire her!"

Jack paused and glanced back. "You didn't?"

"No." Hamilton straightened his shirtfront and adjusted his vest. "She quit."

"I don't think that's going to help you much," Jack said. "But you have no idea what it does for me." He left Hamilton's office and took the fire stairs two at a time down to the floor where the contracts office was located. On the way down he let out a yell of jubilation that echoed in tune with his rapid footsteps on the metal stairs.

Rosie glanced up and raised her eyebrows when he burst in. "It's about time."

"Where is she?"

"Home typing up her résumé and nursing a slight hangover. If you hadn't shown up I was going to use my coffee break to come and get you, Mr. Candy Valentine. I was planning to tell your foreman all about this little sideline of yours, and watch you squirm."

"I gather Krysta told you what's been going on."

"She told me enough, after I plied her with some wine, to make me wonder if my first favorable assessment of you was mistaken. You may be the best lover God ever created, but—"

"Did she say that?"

"I'm not telling. I just have one question for you, loverboy. Are you going to do right by that woman, or will I have to ask some friends of mine to work you over?"

Jack's smile was grim. "Save your efforts for putting Hamilton away."

"Now, *there's* a cause I could get into. I asked around a little yesterday, and I don't think Krysta's the only one with a complaint."

"That's music to my ears. But Hamilton can wait. I need directions to Krysta's apartment, assuming you're pretty sure she's there right now."

Rosie leaned her chin on her hand and looked up at him. "I'm not giving directions to some guy who's going to use and abuse my good friend and then abandon her when he finds out he's about to become rich and famous."

Jack groaned. "I would never abandon Krysta. I'm crazy about her."

"How crazy?"

Jack leaned both hands on Rosie's desk and gazed into her brown eyes. "Give me directions to her apartment and I'm sure you'll find out the next time you ply her with a bottle of wine."

"Uh-huh." Rosie gazed back at him. "I'm beginning to see what that girl was raving about. You do have a way about you."

"I'm going to marry her, Rosie."

"Oo-wee!" Rosie wiggled her shoulders in delight. "I love stuff like this. Come around the desk and pay attention while Rosie draws you a map, Mr. Valentine."

15

IT WAS A TOSS-UP which ached worse, her head or her heart, Krysta thought as she sat in front of her word processor and updated her résumé. The rain pattering against her apartment windows fit her mood perfectly.

Already bored with the morning's assigned job, she decided to amuse herself by typing "Stand-in for Male Romance Author" as her most recent position. Under "Duties" she listed contract negotiation, revision consultant, dinner companion, roommate...lover. With a sigh she hit the delete button. She'd been a good Candy Valentine, dammit. Not everyone could have performed the role as well as she had. Even Rosie had said so.

She probably shouldn't have gone out with Rosie, although it had temporarily eased her distress to talk about her troubles and drink more red wine than was good for her. But this morning there was no Rosie, no wine, no job and definitely no Jack Killigan.

She'd forced herself to shower and dress, despite having no office to go to and no boss to satisfy. For the time being, her dining room table would be her office, and she would be the boss in charge of the great Krysta Lueckenhoff job search. She had a meager savings account that could take her through a few weeks if she scrimped.

She stared at the small screen on her word processor and longed for the computer she'd used at Rainier. Rosie had offered to put together her résumé for her and run it off on the laser printer in the office, but Krysta hadn't been that sort of employee and she didn't want to become that sort of ex-employee. Despite Rosie's insistence that the company owed her that much, she'd turned down the offer in favor of using her own word processor, limited though it might be.

She heard a motorcycle outside her living room window, and for one wild moment thought maybe...but, no. She'd have to stop imagining the sort of ending to this story that Jack would write in one of his novels. He'd even been the one who'd told her to separate fantasy from reality.

When her doorbell buzzed, she jumped and knocked her chair over. Telling herself it was either the Avon lady or a magazine salesman, she walked toward the door, her heart pounding. Then she squinted through the peephole and her heart threatened to stop altogether.

With a trembling hand she unlocked the door and opened it to the wettest, most magnificent man in the world. "You're soaked, Jack."

He grinned at her and stepped inside. "And you're hung over, Krysta."

She backed up. "And how would you know?"

"Do you deny it?"

"You've been talking to Rosie, haven't you." She backed up some more. He looked too appealing, and she didn't want to fall victim to that magnetism when there was no future in it.

"Among other people." He shortened the distance between them again.

"I'll bet you come down with a bad cold, riding around in the rain like that."

He advanced, his blue gaze intense. "If I do, will you be my nurse?"

"Absolutely not." She retreated farther. "Why aren't you at work?"

"I was fired." He stepped closer.

"Fired? But Jack, your book won't be out until next year! What will you do until then?"

He shrugged. "Something will turn up."

"That is so typical of you." She tried to break eye contact, but the old fascination with Jack remained and she couldn't do it. "I suppose you have no plan whatsoever."

"Oh, I have a plan."

Her blood thrummed through her veins. "You...do?"

"I do. But first I have a few questions. Did you tell Rosie I was the best lover God ever created?"

Heat climbed into her face. Doggone that Rosie. She was supposed to be her friend. "That was the wine talking. In point of fact, I think you're—"

"I'll take it, wine-induced though it might have been. Did you go to bed with Hamilton?"

She opened her mouth to say yes, but the lie wouldn't come out. "No."

A gleam of triumph shone in his eyes. "Then why did you tell me you had?"

"I didn't."

"Oh, yes, you did. I distinctly remember you shoving my nose in the fact and adding that you'd enjoyed it."

"I never told you specifically what I enjoyed." Her chin lifted. "You jumped to conclusions, and I let you jump. Served you right."

"You're right, it did." His expression gentled. "It would also serve me right if you refused to forgive me for having so little faith in you. But I'll ask, anyway, because I'm a desperate man." He paused. "Please forgive me, Krysta."

When he looked at her like that, all the anger seeped right out of her. "I guess you had your reasons for thinking that way."

"More instincts than reasons. When I thought Hamilton might get the woman I wanted, I turned into a complete jerk."

A quiver ran through her. "The woman you wanted? I don't recall you ever mentioning that you wanted me for more than a weekend in New York."

"Right again. Because I felt I had nothing to offer you."

"Nothing to offer?" All her anger and frustration came rushing back. "You must take me for a fool. You're going to be a bestselling author!"

"I know Manchester's enthusiasm convinced you of that, but I've read hundreds of magazine articles about this business. You *never* know if a book will be a success. You can't count on the income it will bring. It could be fantastic, or it could be a total mirage, and like a mirage, you won't know until you get there."

Under the glamorous spell of that weekend in New York, Krysta hadn't been able to consider such a truth. But today, back home in Evergreen, it seemed more logical to her. Yet she hated to give up the certainty of Jack's stardom so easily. "I still say you're going to be famous."

"Your faith in me is wonderful, but there was no guarantee of that then, and there's even less now."

"What do you mean? They're putting book dumps in the front of stores, and they—" She paused when the meaning behind his statement hit her. Oh, no. "Jack, what's happened?" She was afraid to hear his answer.

He ran a hand through his damp hair and glanced away. "Manchester isn't very happy to discover that a guy wrote those books. Some of the publishing plans are changing."

"But you said—"

"I know what I said. I wasn't completely truthful yesterday because I didn't want you to worry. What's done is done, anyway."

"Oh, Jack! Why on earth did you tell them?"

"Because I thought if I didn't, you were going to risk your career to go on that damned tour. But I was too late."

Her stomach clutched. "You mean that everything we went through has been for nothing?"

His startled gaze met hers. "Nothing?" He gripped her by the arms. "You're calling the most fantastic weekend of our lives *nothing?*"

"I was talking about your publishing career, Jack! That's the important thing right now."

"No, it isn't." He pulled her against his soggy jacket, dampening her blouse. "To hell with my publishing career."

"Don't say that. Don't ever say that."

"It's a free country, Krysta. I'll say whatever I want. I'll even say I love you."

She looked into his eyes and felt as if someone had just knocked the breath from her lungs. "Jack..."

He stepped away from her and caught her by the hand. "Come here," he said, starting toward the door.

She pulled back. "Jack, are you crazy? It's cold. And it's raining out there."

"Precisely." He tugged her through the door and closed it. The storm door slammed after them. Then he pulled her, sputtering and protesting all the way, out into the drizzle.

"Now." He stopped and drew her into his arms.

She shivered in the cold. "I wish you'd tell me what this is all about."

"The first lesson a writer learns is 'show, don't tell.'" He tilted her face up.

"Jack, I'm getting rain in my eyes."

"Then, close them, Krysta," he murmured.

And then she understood. His mouth touched her rain-cooled cheeks, warming them. His tongue followed the path of a droplet to a corner of her mouth. She drank in the rain, drank in the moist caress of his lips, drank in his love.

As happy tears joined the cascade that had become a benediction, she forgot the chill in the air, forgot the cars whizzing by on the street next to the apartment building, forgot the neighbors who might be staring out the window. But she remembered what he'd once said to her. *All I have to offer is a kiss in the rain.* It was more than enough.

He lifted his head and gazed down at her. "I love you, Krysta. I'll do whatever it takes to keep us together. I'll work extra jobs to help pay for your father's care."

"No." She swallowed and blinked back tears. "I won't have you sacrifice your writing for that."

"If I can't be with you, my writing holds no joy for me."

She cradled his face in both hands. "I won't be the burden that keeps you from writing, Jack."

"No, you'll be my inspiration, just as you have been for

months." His mouth hovered over hers. "And I really need some inspiration, Krysta." This time his mouth descended with less delicacy and more hunger. His embrace became more urgent, his tongue more demanding.

She managed to wrench her mouth from his. Their hot breath clouded the air as they gazed at each other. "We'd better go inside to continue this discussion," she said, sliding her fingers through his.

"Good idea."

Krysta ran with him up the steps and pulled at the storm door. It was locked. She glanced at him and started to laugh. "We're locked out."

"Let me try." He grasped the handle and pulled hard.

"It's no use. Sometimes the lock just clicks into place by itself. I've told the landlord, but so far he hasn't fixed it."

"I don't suppose you've left any windows open."

"Nope."

"Then there's only one thing left to do." He took off his ski jacket. "Put this on," he commanded, guiding her arms into the sleeves.

"Jack, what about you?"

"You're going to keep me warm. Come on."

Moments later they were on his motorcycle headed along the streets of Evergreen. Krysta wrapped herself tightly around him in an attempt to keep him from freezing to death. She wasn't sure how he was doing, but the friction of their bodies as Jack navigated the turns was keeping her toasty, not to mention extremely aroused. And she'd thought motorcycles were stupid.

At his apartment, he parked the bike and whipped her up the stairs almost at a run. A tabby cat greeted them at the door. "Krysta, my love, meet Krysta, my cat," Jack said.

"You named your cat after me?"

He shrugged. "She has your eyes."

"Oh, really?" Krysta tried to look into the cat's face, but Jack pulled her toward the bedroom.

"Take off your clothes," he said.

"What happened to all that romance you're supposed to be famous for?"

"There's nothing romantic about catching cold together. We're taking a warm shower." He winked. "Now *that* might get very romantic."

It did. Jack's ministrations under the warm spray soon left Krysta too weak to stand. Afterward, he toweled her off, swept her into his arms and carried her to his bed, where he finished what he'd so adequately started.

As they lay sated in each other's arms, he reached over to the bedside table and picked up a small object. "I think you left your heart in New York," he said, handing her the plastic toy he'd bought.

She sighed and took the heart. "I sure did. You don't know how I puzzled over this when you gave it to me. I couldn't decide if it was a clever joke or a real request."

"It was a real request." He pushed the arrow shaft in, and the *Be My Valentine* message popped up. "Will you?"

She smiled at him. "You're eleven months early."

"I believe in getting a head start. Which reminds me." He took the heart from her and put it back on the bedside table. "I have a new proposal ready."

"You do?" She ran her fingers through his damp hair. "Goodness, Jack. You must have been working night and day to come up with one that fast."

"Actually, this one took longer than it should have, but then, it's the most important proposal of my life, so I guess that's okay."

"Is it a romance?"

His gaze was tender. "You bet it is."

Her breath caught in her throat at the look in his eyes. "We're not talking about a book, are we?"

He shook his head.

Her pulse quickened in anticipation.

"Krysta, I—" He stopped and cleared his throat. "Damn, I want to get this right."

"I don't think you could possibly get it wrong."

"Wanna bet? I may have written these scenes but I've never tried it out in real life." He gave her a sheepish grin. "Okay, here goes." He took a deep breath. "Krysta, will you—"

The phone beside the bed rang and Jack frowned. "Ignore it. The answering machine in the other room will pick it up." He turned back to her as the phone stopped ringing and his voice on the answering machine message filtered in from the living room. He spoke over it. "Krysta, will—"

"Jack, that's Stephanie Briggs on the phone! I recognize her voice!"

"Who cares? I'm in the middle of something very important. I'll call her back later."

"Later?" She extricated herself from his arms and started to climb out of bed. "That's not very wise if you're about to take on the responsibilities of a wife, Jack."

"I didn't even ask you yet!"

She grabbed a towel and wrapped herself in it as she hurried out to the living room. "I'm going to answer that phone. Then you can ask me. And I'll tell you in advance my answer is yes."

"Krysta!" Jack roared.

She ignored him, punched the stop button on the answering machine and picked it up, interrupting Stephanie in midsentence. "Hello? This is Mr. Killigan's personal assistant and I just walked in the door. May I help you?"

"Candy, is that you?"

"Uh, my name is Krysta Lueckenhoff."

"Your name is Candy Valentine," Stephanie said. "Or at least it was a few days ago. I never forget a voice. Listen, you and your friend Jack threw us all for a loop around here, and now I'm in charge of damage control. Obviously I can't send a guy on tour as Candy Valentine."

"Obviously," Krysta agreed. She glanced over her shoulder as Jack came in with a towel draped around his hips.

"Unfortunately, I didn't get a look at your Jack. I should have just opened the closet door, but I, of course, thought he was some hayseed you'd dragged along with you to New York."

"He's no hayseed," Krysta said.

Jack lifted his eyebrows.

"What does he look like? Is he presentable?"

Not at the moment. Krysta stifled a laugh. "If you dressed him right, he'd look pretty good."

Jack scowled at her.

"Is he sexy?"

Krysta gave Jack the once-over. "Definitely."

"How about compared to Fabio?"

"He'd give Fabio a run for his money. He's even been known to wear his hair long."

Jack started forward. "Now, wait just a damn minute. I'm not shaving my chest or—"

Krysta twisted away from him and walked the length of the cord.

"We may be able to salvage this situation yet," Stephanie said. "If he photographs well, we can do a promotion billing him as Jack Killigan—Mr. Valentine."

"I think that sounds like a terrific idea," Krysta said.

"We'll have to fly you both back to New York, I guess. The accountants won't like that, but I'll handle them."

"Both of us?"

"Both of you, Candy. Or Krysta, or whatever your name is. It's obvious you've got a head for the business, and I've enjoyed dealing with you. No telling what I'd run into with Mr. Valentine, there."

Krysta danced out of Jack's reach. "You have a point."

"Okay." Stephanie heaved a big sigh. "I'm rescheduling the twenty-city tour and crossing my fingers."

"I think we can do twenty-five cities."

Jack gaped at her and began waving his hands in the air.

"Is that right?" Stephanie asked. "You're a regular little hustler, aren't you."

"I believe in Jack's talent. He's going to be big."

"Well, fortunately for you, I believe in his talent, too. I'll see about extending the tour. And when I have dates for the return trip to New York, I'll let you know. Are you both at this number?"

Krysta winked at Jack. "We're both at this number."

"Good. He needs you. I'll be in touch."

Krysta hung up the phone and turned to Jack.

He folded his arms across his chest. "Looks like I've been preempted."

"On what?"

"My proposal."

"Oh, Jack, do you really mind?" She crossed to him. "My answer is yes anyway."

"What, no negotiating?"

"What on earth would I negotiate? I love you so much, that I—"

He placed his hands on her shoulders. "Hold it right there."

She paused and glanced up at him.

"Back up that train. What did you just say?"

She ran her palms over his chest and gazed into his eyes. "I love you so much."

He closed his eyes. "Say it again. Slower."

She stood on tiptoe and wound her arms around his neck. "The first rule of writing, according to someone who should know, is 'show, don't tell.'"

With a groan of impatience he pulled her close. "You can show me in a minute. Tell me now. I need to hear it."

"I love you, Jack. I want to be your wife, your friend, your lover, your business consultant, your personal assistant, your contract negotiator, your—"

"My everything." He gazed down at her and shook his head. "Twenty-five cities?"

"You never know what you can get unless you ask."

"Is that so?" He leaned down and whispered an extremely provocative request.

"Perhaps that can be arranged." She began to unwind the towel from his hips.

"Just promise me one thing."

"Anything, my love."

"That I won't have to shave my chest."

"You won't have to shave your chest," she murmured as her own towel dropped to the floor.

"You're sure?"

"I'm sure." She caressed him intimately. "You're in my hands now, Mr. Valentine."

Dear Reader,

I've often wondered what my life would be like if I'd pursued my second reading passion and tried writing something other than romance. How different might my professional life be...and how might my work affect my personal life if I'd tried writing another type of book altogether?

I'm referring to horror novels.

I love to be scared. I love Halloween (as you probably know if you read my last Temptation novel, *Trick Me, Treat Me.*) And there are days when I come up with a particularly gruesome plot idea and wish I could somehow work it into a romance novel.

Thrill Me allowed me to do just that. I got to throw in some fiendish scenarios, as envisioned by Sophie Winchester, my horror-writing heroine. The way her writing affects her personal life is at the core of this slightly twisted tale. Throwing in a straitlaced small-town police chief really stirred things up and the end result will, I hope, thrill *you*, too.

The icing on the cake was knowing this story was going to be paired with one of my all-time favorite Temptation books, *Mr. Valentine,* by my all-time favorite Temptation author, Vicki Lewis Thompson. Talk about the perfect happy ending for me.

I guess that reinforces the decision I made in my writing. I am a sucker for those happy endings. So, long live romance!

Happy reading,

Leslie Kelly

THRILL ME
Leslie Kelly

To Vicki Lewis Thompson.
Thank you for giving me so much reading
pleasure, as well as your deeply valued
friendship. You are the ultimate Temptress.

And, as always, to my editor Brenda Chin.
You keep me sane. You keep me sharp.
And yet somehow you still manage to
make this fun. I thank you for more reasons
than I can ever express.

1

SOPHIE WINCHESTER was skilled at only two things. She could type 120 words per minute without a single error.

And she was damn good at committing murder.

It was lucky she had the latter skill, because with the advent of voice recognition software, the typing game didn't look to be a great long-term career plan. That was okay. She'd take murder over note-taking and typing any old day.

It was just too bad secretarial work was so darn respectable. While murder...wasn't.

The shrill whine of her alarm clock returned right on schedule, as it had tauntingly promised nine minutes ago when she'd smacked the snooze button. "Too bad I can't figure out a way to murder inanimate objects," she muttered. Unplugging the stupid alarm just wouldn't give her as much satisfaction as pulverizing it to a bloody pulp, particularly after a night like the previous one, when she'd had only four hours sleep.

Unfortunately, she couldn't murder an alarm clock. Oh, sure, she could murder someone *with* an alarm clock, particularly if there was a glass of water and a frayed wire nearby. But that still wouldn't allow her to stay in bed past six-thirty on a Thursday morning.

Punching at the off switch to cease the whine, she started making deals with whomever was listening. "I'll confess, I'll come clean, I'll stop this double life. For an extra hour's sleep I'll cop to everything."

Mugs, her fat orange tabby, wasn't impressed by her typical early morning gripe session. She shot him a glare as he delicately licked his paw. He nudged her head out of the way

so he could commandeer himself a spot on her pillow, which
he knew she was about to vacate.

"Lazy thing," she mumbled, giving him a scratch behind
the ears and getting a throaty purr in response. Mugs scooted
closer, silently ordering her off so he could get more comfy.

She stumbled out of bed and padded to the bathroom,
practically sleepwalking through her typical routine. After
her shower, she French-braided her long, light brown hair
and clipped it with a pretty, understated gold barrette. Then
she faced her standard dilemma over whether she should
wear panty hose under her plain navy slacks or risk panty
lines.

Her boss, Pastor Bob, was too nearsighted to notice a panty
line or two. But his sister, Miss Hester—who served as his
hostess at the First Methodist Church of Derryville—would.
And she'd sure have something to say about it. Miss Hester
always had something to say, which was becoming a problem.
Because Sophie was finding it more and more difficult to
keep her tongue glued to the back of her teeth these days.

Being diabolical sometimes made it tough to be discreet.

"Panty hose," she mumbled, too tired to come up with reasons why she shouldn't just quit her day job and be done with
it. Let the world in on who she was, on the things she'd done,
and tell them all what they could do if they didn't like it.

Shrugging off the pleasant thought of how Miss Hester
would react if she ever came back at her with what she *really*
thought, Sophie finished dressing and left her bedroom. She
walked into her bright yellow kitchen, made herself a cup of
strong coffee, and glanced out the window over the sink.

"Still January," she said with a sigh. Spring hadn't made a
miraculous appearance three months early. Slushy gray snow
still covered much of her pretty little lawn, keeping her mood
as gray as the landscape.

And suddenly, as always, Sophie began to play the game.

"I wonder how hard the ground is."

She sipped again.

"How much would the temperature have to go up for

someone to be able to dig a hole?" She smiled. "A really big one." *Miss Hester size.*

Mugs, who had grown bored on his pillow perch and followed her into the kitchen, hopped up onto the counter. He pressed his warm kitty nose against her arm, demanding attention.

"What do you think, Mugs? How would you get rid of a body in the dead of winter with the ground frozen hard?"

A shovel? Backbreaking. Front-end loader? Too loud, too obvious. Wood chipper? Messy...and overdone, she thought, particularly after the movie *Fargo*. Pickax? She discarded the idea, knowing it would break through the hard earth too slowly to allow for quick burial.

Then she lifted a brow. A pickax wouldn't work on the frozen ground, but it would create a nice opening in the surface of a frozen lake. An opening big enough to slide a body through. By the time the spring thaw came, who knew what condition the remains would be in.

How perfectly, deliciously morbid. She chuckled, imagining someone ice fishing in the middle of winter. How might that someone react if he looked down while chugging his sixth can of beer and saw the grinning face of a corpse staring sightlessly at him from the other side of the ice?

By the time she got in her car to drive the short distance to the church, Sophie had already envisioned the whole thing. From gunshot, to pickax in the ice, to shocked fisherman, the scenario appeared fully fleshed out in her brain.

She just had to put it on paper.

Or, rather, her alter ego, R. F. Colt—the fastest-rising star of the horror fiction world—had to put it on paper.

Wishing she could get right to work, she sat in her still-running car in the church parking lot. She wanted to capture her thoughts about the scenario she'd come up with, so she wrote some notes in a small spiral notebook she always carried in her purse. She started a new notebook with every project, so this one wasn't too cluttered yet. By the time she finished the novel, the notebook would be jam packed with snippets of dialogue, potential suspects, plot points, not to mention crime scene descriptions, complete with blood spatter...and weapons.

Speaking of which... "Gotta go to Draper's Hardware and measure the circumference of the sharp end of a pickax," she muttered, adding that notation.

Or maybe not. Draper's was located right here in town. Sometimes her research earned her a few second looks from people whose radar she'd rather fly beneath. In Derryville, everybody knew everybody else's business, so she should probably avoid Draper's and drive over to Margate, the next town over.

But not yet. First, Sophie Winchester, the sweet-smiled, quiet, small-town church secretary had a full day's work to accomplish. She'd schedule meetings, type sermons and co-ordinate the community garage sale. She'd phone in a lunch order for Pastor Bob's favorite deli sandwich, and write an article for the monthly newsletter. She'd lend a sympathetic ear to the parishioners who stopped by to chat about the horrible state of affairs today, when teenagers could terrorize people on the street by driving so *fast* and playing their awful music so *loud*.

She'd be the Derryville sweetheart she'd always been, the one everyone loved. She'd play her role of the girl next door who'd left home for only a few years to attend college and had come back where she belonged, scared away from the big bad city.

If only they knew.

But no one did. No one in Derryville knew the real Sophie Winchester. They never suspected that each night she left the church and spent hours in front of her computer, constructing her next fiendish plot.

They were familiar with the pretty, nice twenty-six-year-old who never wore her clothes too tight, her makeup too heavy, or her emotions on her face. Not the woman dubbed by *People* magazine as the author most likely to give Hannibal

Lechter nightmares. They didn't listen, didn't pay attention, didn't *see*. Which was exactly the way she liked it.

She had both her worlds. She was Sophie, from the most respected family in Derryville, Illinois, who loved the security and low-key small-town happiness that had always been the foundation of her life.

But she was also R. F. Colt, the gruesome author who was poised to break into the number-one slot on the *New York Times* bestseller list with her first hardcover novel. The one who'd just sold the movie rights to her second book to a Hollywood production company. The one whose agent swore would be a millionaire before age thirty.

Two worlds suited her fine for now, at least until she could decide how to let her family and the town know who she really was. She certainly had the best of both worlds—a happy, respected place in her community, *and* an outlet for the creative juices that had churned inside her since she was a middle schooler addicted to Stephen King books.

Sophie simply wasn't ready to move from the role of local girl to big-name horror author. She liked her privacy. Liked her old traditions. Liked Sunday dinner with her parents, and a chat with the mail carrier every day. She was able to write what she did *because* of the simpleness in her life, not in spite of it. She needed that calm, normal safety net to keep her grounded by day because, by night, she let loose the reins of her imagination and allowed it to run wild.

She also didn't want people to look at her differently, or, heaven forbid, treat her differently, just because she happened to know about a thousand ways to murder somebody. Even long-term friends might give her a second glance at that one.

So, two worlds it was. If both her worlds were just a little lonely, void of male companionship, well, that was the price she'd pay to retain her privacy. Besides, she'd never met a man yet who would want a sweet, small-town girl, and wouldn't care that behind her big blue eyes churned a mind always contemplating bloody murder.

And she probably never would.

DANIEL FLETCHER SAT IN A booth in the front window of Ed's Diner, sipping his coffee, watching the world come to life on another winter morning in small-town U.S.A.

Life doesn't get much better than this.

Two months ago, his day would have started at a cluttered desk, in a dingy, crowded precinct, with him typing yet another report about the drug bust he'd made in the predawn hours. He'd be bleary-eyed, pissed off, stressed, overworked, underpaid and lonely.

Not anymore. He much preferred this type of morning. If nothing else, the coffee was a damn sight better at Ed's, in Derryville, Illinois, than it had been at the eighth precinct in Detroit. And somehow, the stress that had hung around him like a rotten smell back in the city had disappeared in the clean, wholesome air of suburbia.

"More coffee, Chief?"

He didn't turn immediately, but continued staring out the window at the church parking lot across the street, wondering who'd driven up in the little white sedan. The driver had pulled into a spot a good ten minutes ago, but hadn't yet gotten out. He could see the exhaust fumes curling up from the tailpipe into the cold morning air.

His cop instincts pinged as he assessed the situation. He mentally catalogued the number of cars at the intersection, the people crossing the street, the Wilson kid walking his dog. He noted the proximity of the bank, the pharmacy, and the preschool on the corner.

Then he almost laughed at his overly suspicious reaction. Probably the person in the white car was someone who had clothes to drop off for the rummage sale, or meals-on-wheels to pick up for delivery to the elderly. There was no big mystery, no crime about to take place just because of an idling car.

His big city cop instincts were *all* out of whack. They had been ever since he'd moved here right after Thanksgiving.

"Chief?"

That was pretty whacked, too. He still couldn't get used to the loss of his name. He'd been known as Daniel all his life. Officer or Detective Fletcher for the last decade. But since he'd moved here to Derryville, he was called Chief by everyone from his landlady to the guy who pumped his gas at the one and only gas station in town.

"I'm okay, Deedee, thanks."

"You're sure I can't get you...*anything* else?"

He finally turned to look up at the waitress, who'd served him coffee just about every morning since he'd moved here. He noted the pursed lips, the deliberately provocative stance. Yeah. She wanted to give him something else. Shit, so did half the other women in Derryville. "No, I'm fine, thanks."

Deedee leaned down, her breast brushing against his shoulder as she deposited his check on the table. "Come back for lunch, Chief. I'll be sure to save you a piece...of cherry pie."

Daniel again ignored the innuendo in her voice and gave her a noncommittal smile. "Sorry. I bagged my lunch today."

She pouted, then turned away.

Fresh meat. That had to be what it was. Daniel knew he was a decent-looking guy, but cripes, the women around here acted like he was movie star material. It had to be because of a shortage of bachelors in the area. *Any* man under sixty with a pulse and decent-smelling breath would probably get as much attention from the females of Derryville as he did.

Too bad he wasn't in the market. Getting involved with anyone at this point wasn't on his agenda. The last thing he needed to do in this small town was get mixed up in a fling with someone he'd run into all the time afterward. This wasn't like Detroit where he could avoid a bar or Laundromat because he knew which of the women he'd dated were regulars.

Besides, no one here had piqued his interest.

Except her.

He tried to thrust off the thought as the memory of blue eyes and long light brown hair swept through his mind. But her image wouldn't fade away. He'd only seen her once, just a flash of her face as she'd walked past the drugstore window while he'd been talking to the owner about some teenage shoplifters. She'd been alone, her head down to shield her cheeks from the December wind. It had been a day or two before Christmas, so it had probably been the twinkling white minilights in the store window that had caught her attention. She'd looked up. Their stares had met for a moment, just long enough for the little lights to illuminate her beautiful blue eyes, her delicately featured face. Then she'd walked on.

He couldn't leave the store fast enough to follow her, and he hadn't been able to get the owner to turn around quickly enough to identify the woman. He hadn't seen her since, though he'd kept an eye out for her every single day.

Just as well. Romance wasn't in the cards right now. He'd never been able to make it work with a woman in Detroit because they couldn't get past the cop to see the man, so he doubted he'd find someone here in Derryville. Not yet, anyway.

No, he was no longer a vice detective. And yeah, he was walking the line a little closer to the Andy Griffith in Mayberry type of policeman, rather than the Dennis Franz in *NYPD Blue* variety. Still, he'd been a big city cop for nearly a dozen years. It was in his blood. It would probably take a while before he could ease into his new role as small-town chief, to let his always-on-alert attitude ease up enough to get involved with a woman. Especially considering the women here most likely wanted nothing more than holiday picnics, walks in the park, kids and church socials.

Someday, he told himself, he'd want all that too. *I hope.*

He turned to stare again toward the parking lot across the street, and finally saw someone emerge from the driver's side door of the white car. Bundled up from head to toe because of the cold weather, the person could have been male or female. The height told him it was probably a woman.

She walked carefully up the icy sidewalk, carrying a large box in her arms. The box obscured her view, and she alternated between peeking around the side to watch where she was going, and down at her feet to avoid slipping on the ice. She was being very precise, very cautious.

So precise, she had no way of seeing what Daniel was seeing. The Wilson kid lost his grip on the leash of his St. Bernard. The dog tore across the snowy church lawn, and, as if fate had planned it, ran directly into the path of the woman.

One step. That was all it would have taken to get out of the animal's way. But she didn't see him.

Then dog and woman got all tangled up in a mass of legs and fur, leash and parka. The big dog won the wrestling match and then bound away as the woman dropped like a rock on the icy sidewalk.

2

Sophie didn't know what had hit her. She just had the impression of shaggy fur before she struck the ground. Hard.

For a moment or two...or twenty...she lay there on the sidewalk, staring up at the cold blue sky. Her breath had escaped her lungs when she fell and by the time she could suck it in again, the freezing air stung her chest. She hacked out a cough and slowly sat up, only to have the monster who'd plowed into her trot back over and begin to lick her face.

"Ugh," she muttered, noticing the icy cold drool coating the big dog's snout. "Get away from me, Cujo. You've done enough damage and I don't forgive you."

The dog gave her a hurt look with its big brown eyes. God, Sophie was a sucker for big brown eyes. "All right, you big drool machine, I do forgive you, but you have to promise not to kiss me again. I already had breakfast and don't need a dog slobber chaser."

"Let me help you up."

She'd been expecting no more than a woof in response. For a second, she was startled, wondering if she'd been struck hard enough on the head to hallucinate about talking dogs. Then she realized she and the Cujo lookalike weren't alone.

"Miss? Are you all right?"

She turned away from the dog and found herself staring at a pair of men's khaki pants. Slowly lifting her eyes, she prayed those long legs, lean hips, and that broad, leather-jacket clad chest didn't belong to the person she suspected they belonged to.

But, of course, they did.

"I'm okay," she told Chief Daniel Fletcher, the new cop in

town. The one she'd seen several times, usually from a distance, but had avoided for a variety of reasons. Cops had a way of figuring out secrets. This one in particular had a dangerously confident smile that said he always got his man. Or woman.

She'd been intrigued by Chief Fletcher since she'd first heard his soft, husky laugh from behind a book stack in the library. No doubt, with his looks, his build, and that warm, throaty laugh, he could probably talk a woman into admitting anything from her real dress size...to her secret identity.

Not someone she should be getting to know better, as much as she wished she could.

Besides, with a newcomer, it would be a lot harder to maintain her sweet Sophie persona. People who'd known her all her life never looked any further than her kind smile and accommodating demeanor. So they never heard the sometimes biting sarcasm and keen wit she might slip up and fail to hide. This man, she suspected, would notice a lot.

It hurt to crane her neck back, but she had to because the man was so darn tall, especially with her sitting on her butt on the sidewalk. His incredibly handsome face, framed with a head of thick dark hair, looked down at her with real concern. When she didn't try to stand up, or reach for the hand he extended, he crouched beside her. As their eyes met fully, his big brown ones widened in surprise. He flinched, his own feet slipping out from under him until he landed in the snow beside her.

"My hero," she muttered.

The dog, who'd finally figured out Sophie didn't want any of his apologetic kisses, immediately turned his big head toward the chief and laid one on him but good.

"Eww," Fletcher said, wiping the back of his arm across his face. Then he shot a glare at the dog's owner, who'd finally worked up the courage to trot over to assess the damage. "Todd, get your dog outta here."

"Yes, sir, Chief," the boy said, wide-eyed as he stared back and forth between the two adults sitting on the frozen ground. Quickly grabbing the dog's leash, he hurried away, probably thrilled he was getting off so lightly.

Then the chief really surprised her. "I've seen you before. Outside the drugstore, two days before Christmas."

"It was Christmas Eve," she replied. She cursed her tongue for the admission.

He looked pleased by it. "You remember."

"Um...sure," she said. Then she hurried into a reasonable explanation, which was nowhere near the truth. "I remember because of the Torrence twins. They got arrested for shoplifting. But the store owner dropped the charges when he found out they'd been trying to get a present for their baby sister since their mother couldn't afford one."

He nodded, looking slightly disappointed that she'd remembered for no other reason. She didn't correct his assumption. Truthfully, she'd never forgotten her first glimpse at the man every woman in town had been talking about. He was one *fine* looking specimen.

"Is his name really Cujo?"

She tilted her head in confusion, not sure what he was talking about.

"The dog. You called him Cujo."

Uh-oh. He'd heard her less than sweet-natured mutterings to the big mutt. "No. I was kidding."

"Oh. Because, I mean, probably a lot of St. Bernards were named Cujo after the book came out."

She raised a brow, trying to look artless and innocent. "Book? I wouldn't know about that, but I saw part of the movie once, on cable." She shivered delicately. "Scary."

He nodded. "Yeah. Probably not your thing."

If only you knew.

The chief finally rose to his feet, almost slipping again on the ice before planting his feet in the snow instead. "They ought to salt this sidewalk."

She frowned. "Miss Hester slashed the budget for salt. It's only spread on the front sidewalk used by the parishioners." She shook her head in disgust. "And, of course, the one be-

'ween the residence and the church. Heaven forbid *she* slip
and fall. The Fire Department would have to bring in a crane
to get her up."

He let out a bark of laughter. Sophie cursed her own tongue
and gritted her back teeth. "Oh, that wasn't nice, I'm sorry.
Miss Hester's a dear old thing. She just worries so much
about keeping the church money to help the poor."

He gave her a quizzical look, as if confused by her sudden
change in tone, but didn't press her. He extended his hand.
"Let me help you."

She stared at it for a minute, that big, masculine hand. He
wore no gloves for protection against the cold. Nibbling her
lip, she slipped her gloved fingers into his and let him pull
her to her feet. Once standing, she was about to extend her
thanks when her shoes skidded again. She reached out for the
closest thing to grab. And because fate had a cruel sense of
humor, immediately found something.

His shoulders.

Crashing into him, until they were chest to chest, separated
only by the padding of her thick parka and his leather jacket,
she found herself staring up into those chocolate-brown eyes
of his. She caught a whiff of spicy aftershave from his
smoothly shaven cheek. She was also close enough to notice
the most incredibly kissable lips she'd ever seen on a man.

"Thank you," she whispered, "I'm awfully clumsy today."

He gave her a slight smile. "My pleasure."

She didn't pull away. Not because she couldn't easily stand
on her own, but rather, because it felt so very nice to lean
against his long, hard body. They stood there, right outside
the church, in broad daylight. Two strangers, practically
wrapped in each other's arms, just staring at each other.

It had been a long time since she'd been in a man's arms. A
long time since a *lot* of things. And she'd missed those things.
Particularly missed being kissed with deep, wet intimacy.
Right now, she suspected she wanted that from this stranger
more than she wanted to hit number one on the *Times* list.

She licked her lips. "I'm not usually this clumsy."

"It's slippery," he replied in a low voice.

"Slippery," she repeated, wondering why her body felt so weak all of a sudden. Now she leaned against him out of necessity because her legs felt too weak to support her.

"The ice," he clarified. "It's slippery."

She swallowed. "Yes, slippery. Dangerously slick."

He tightened his grip on her hips. His fingers curved around her with gentle possession that confirmed they were both playing a sensual word game having nothing to do with the ice.

Some devil made her add, "And hard."

Sophie heard a soft sound that might have been a groan from deep in his throat. His jaw tightened and he closed his eyes briefly, as if needing to regain control of himself. He finally said, "Do you need me to carry you inside?"

She felt hot blood rise in her cheeks as she ordered her feet to move. Stepping back, she said, "No. I, uh…needed to take a second." Struggling to find a reason for clinging to the man like a helpless, twitty female, she mumbled, "I just hurt my, I mean, I fell on my butt." *Oh, God, shut up, Sophie!* "I mean, I'm fine now." Fine, hell. She was a babbling idiot.

Though it didn't spill from his lips, she saw the laughter in his eyes. He kept a hand on her elbow. "Think you can walk?"

She nodded, clenching her teeth to keep any more stupid words from coming out of her stupid mouth.

"My name's Daniel Fletcher."

"I know who you are." Then, grudgingly, she added, "I'm Sophie Winchester."

"Winchester…"

"Yes. *That* family." Her family was very well known in Derryville, having lived here for more than a century. Her grandfather had been the chief of police for years.

"There are pictures all over the walls of the station of your grandfather doing good deeds."

She nodded. "And my uncle, too, I'd imagine." Her uncle had followed her grandfather in the role of chief. They'd fully expected one of the members of the current generation to follow in their footsteps. Her cousin, Jared, *had* gone into law enforcement for a while—working with the FBI—but had left to become a writer. Not fiction, like Sophie, but true crime novels. Happily, he'd recently returned to town and gotten engaged to one of Sophie's friends.

Carefully bending down, she began to gather up the pieces of clothing that had fallen out of the box she'd been carrying from the car. "For the rummage sale," she explained when he bent to help her. "I cleaned out my closets."

She spied a glittery pile of red fabric and reached out to grab it, but he beat her to it. Sophie scrunched her eyes shut, hoping he wasn't paying attention to the clothing he picked up.

No such luck. "Hmm. This doesn't look quite like the typical Derryville church social dress."

Shoot. She couldn't believe she'd been foolish enough to leave the sequined red halter dress in the box. She'd meant to pull it out, knowing Miss Hester would have a fit if she saw it. It wasn't something "sweet Sophie" could easily explain.

Sophie had gotten the dress from a working girl in Chicago, who'd helped her research a book about a serial killer prostitute. The woman had mailed it to her as a gift, telling Sophie she'd inspired her to go back to school. Sophie had been touched, though she would never have worn the dress unless she had some reason to dress up as a hooker. Or a drag queen.

"Halloween costume," Sophie muttered, reaching to grab it out of his hands.

He wasn't letting it go so easily. "It's definitely not your size." He straightened. "Too big for you."

She shot him a glare, wondering if he meant the ample bodice of the dress. Because busty she wasn't. "I know."

He eyed her from head to toe. "It would be way too long."

Okay, maybe she could forgive him for the size crack. Besides, wrapped up in this thick parka from shoulder to thigh, he couldn't have any idea what kind of figure she had, even though she had been in his arms a few moments before. With this much padding, she looked and felt about as curvy as the abominable snow monster.

"Thanks for your help," she said, determined to get away from this man now, before he could fluster her even more. Somehow, she could barely keep a thought in her head under that warm, brown-eyed stare of his. He'd already seen or heard a lot more of the true Sophie than she ever usually revealed.

"Let me carry the box for you."

Hearing the firm tone in his voice, she lead the way to the office. After unlocking the door, she preceded him inside and flipped on the light switch. Luckily, no one else was in yet. She took the box from his arms and deposited it on her desk.

He looked surprised as she flipped on more lights and unlocked the door to the inner office. "You work here?"

She nodded.

Then he took a nearly imperceptible step back, suddenly looking a little pale. "Are you a...minister or something?"

She hesitated, easily able to read his dismay at having played sexy word games with a female minister. Then she relented and set his mind at ease. "No. Just a secretary to one. Thanks again for your help."

"You're welcome." Then he tsked. "It's so *cold* in here. I can see my breath better now than I could when we were outside."

"Miss Hester," Sophie muttered, knowing the older woman had once again turned the thermostat completely off last night, instead of lowering it. No matter how many times Sophie explained it, the woman didn't seem to realize it probably cost every bit as much to bring the office back up to a reasonable temperature as it would to keep the heat running on low all night. "She's very frugal."

"Maybe I should start calling you Bob Cratchit," he said.

She grinned. "That'd make Miss Hester Scrooge, right? If any ghosts visited her in the night, she'd scold them for being wasteful by using too much chain."

"So why do you keep working here?"

She thought about it, particularly since she'd been wondering the same thing, just an hour ago. Not that she could tell *him* her real reasons for staying. "Pastor Bob's a dear. And Miss Hester's not really bad...just a bit eccentric." She thought of the characters she'd based on Miss Hester in recent books, who had provided some comic relief, which her readers seemed to enjoy. She gave him a secretive smile. "Let's say she inspires me." Unable to resist, she added, "To do murder."

He laughed, low and long. That laugh. Oh, Lordy, she couldn't resist his low, masculine laugh. For a moment she'd almost forgotten how much she liked the way this man sounded. As much as she liked the way he looked.

This will never do.

"I have a lot of work to do. And it wouldn't be great for Miss Hester to find us in here alone." God, wouldn't that give the old woman something to gripe about? "So, thanks again."

He stiffened, obviously taking the hint. She cursed her own lack of tact, knowing he probably thought her an uptight, prissy church secretary. But wasn't that what he was *supposed* to think?

She should have felt relieved when he gave her a curt nod, then turned and walked out into the cold morning. Somehow, instead of relief, she felt a vague sense of disappointment.

DANIEL DIDN'T KNOW Sophie Winchester well, but he didn't mind. *Because nobody else does, either.*

For the rest of the day, he opened up his ears, listening to conversations on the street, in the bank, in the break room back at the station. Her name came up a few times. And every time, within sixty seconds, somebody would comment on how sweet the youngest of the Winchesters was. Sweet, biddable, small-town-loving, and wasn't it an almighty shame that she hadn't found the right local boy to settle down with?

That thought made him sweat even more than his two dozen reps with the free weights that night. She was single.

He didn't usually drive over to the gym in Margate on

Thursday nights because it was an hour away. But tonight, he'd needed to pound some metal. Derryville boasted a YMCA with one-hundred-year-old weights and a treadmill used by every resident. His feet had sunk into the two tracks on the thing the one time he'd tried using it. He'd joined the gym in the next town the same day.

During the drive, and his workout, he'd thought about nothing except the woman who'd practically thrown him out of her office. "There's gratitude," he muttered as he bench-pressed his last set. "After I saved her butt when she fell on it."

She puzzled him. And like any true cop, he was fascinated by puzzles. Her expression could be so tender, but her wit so biting. She'd been friendly, then aloof. Saucy, then proper. She was a walking contradiction—getting flustered and embarrassed as hell when she'd fallen against him. But then she'd played sexy little word games while wrapped in his arms. He only regretted that they'd come to their senses. He had the feeling he could have kept holding her all day and not had his fill.

Though she'd been wearing a thick winter coat, he'd been able to feel the slightness of her body. The delicacy of her hands, jaw and neck gave evidence of a petite figure, and she'd fit just about perfectly tucked underneath his chin.

Damn, he was losing it. Sitting here getting hot and bothered while he worked out in a sweaty gym.

Finally, having pushed himself enough to pound the woman out of his thoughts, at least for now, he toweled off and headed toward the showers. The place wasn't crowded this late on a weeknight, which meant he should find the locker room nearly empty. He pulled his tight tank off his body as he walked down the corridor from the weight room, anticipating the way the cool shower would feel against his heated skin.

Then something caught his eye. A group of women were working out in one of the closed-in exercise rooms, doing some kind of aerobics with karate moves. He recognized one of them.

"Holy...." He froze, staring through the window. "So I'm not the only one who cheats on the Derryville YMCA," he whispered, his lips widening into a grin.

Because Sophie Winchester, clad in skintight spandex and looking like pure neon sin, was working her cute fanny off.

3

SOPHIE WAS AWARE of the titters and whispers long before she realized why the other women around her were tittering and whispering. She'd been completely focused, following the instructor's moves as she demonstrated this week's steps in her Tae Bo class. But she could no longer ignore the fact that something had distracted her classmates.

"Oh, Lordy," someone whispered.

"I wouldn't mind trying a full body roll with him."

Casting a quick look around, she wondered just what would make the other participants completely forget they were supposed to be working out. The faces of most of the women in the room wore the same titillated expression. And they were all looking in the same way. Toward the window.

She couldn't restrain her curiosity, and glanced over. "Oh, shoot," she muttered when she saw who had prompted the women's whispers. Chief Fletcher. "What are the odds?"

She quickly looked away, refusing to let her eyes shift toward the window again. She knew he still stood there. Watching.

Of all times to bump into him, it had to be once again when she was at less than her best. This morning she'd been on her rear on the ice, wiping off dog snot. Now she was a hideous mess. Sweaty, working out in her loudest, most obnoxiously bright yellow neon workout clothes—tight shorts and a thong type bodysuit worn over them. Since she dressed so sedately at home, she enjoyed going all out with her clothes when she knew she wouldn't be running into anyone from Derryville. So far, in the ten months she'd belonged to this gym in Margate, she never had. It appeared that tonight her luck had run out.

"I think we're about done, ladies," the instructor said. "Don't forget to stretch out to cool down."

"If I take this class twice a day, every day for three months, you think I can look good enough to get a man like him?" This from a fiftyish woman who, Sophie knew, was a divorced mother of four.

"Hands off, girls. I saw him first," said a perky redhead. Her words were teasing, but her tone held an edge. She meant it.

Shocking. The women were acting like they'd never seen a man before. Then Sophie gave into temptation and peeked again. This time, she understood why the women were so...um...distracted.

"Whoa, mama," she muttered, forgetting she was in the middle of a stretch. Her jaw dropped open at the sight of Daniel Fletcher, bare-chested, dripping sweat, pumped up, looking like he'd stepped out of the pages of a sexy woman's magazine.

Pure, undiluted hunger made her dizzy. Which wasn't a good thing since she was standing on one foot. Her other was tucked up under her bottom, her knee bent for a stretch. She wobbled. Groaned. Then, gravity kicked in full force.

It was almost karmic that the second time she interacted with Daniel it would be because she fell. Right there, on the mat, on her butt, in a roomful of gawking woman.

"Ow," she muttered, not knowing whether it hurt more that she'd fallen. Or that he'd seen her fall.

"You okay, Sophie?" the instructor asked.

"Yeah, you okay, Sophie?" said a deep, slightly teasing voice.

Seeing his sneaker-clad feet and thickly muscled calves with swirls of dark hair, she groaned again. Had he really strode into this group of sweaty, panting females, dressed... or undressed...like that? The women in this place were probably lining up to collapse at his feet.

He'd probably like it. What man wouldn't?

None of my business if he did. I wouldn't care a bit. Maybe if she kept telling herself that, she might start to believe it. Because, though she'd only known the man for hours, it nearly pained her to think of him scooping some other woman up off the icy ground or the padded gym floor.

"I'm okay," she muttered. Finally, she raised her stare up his body, gulping as she took in the loose nylon gym shorts. They clung to his lean hips. From this perspective—at his feet—she had a really good view of all the impressive bumps and bulges in the black nylon. Big bumps. Inspiring bulges.

Her breath escaped her lungs in one long, shuddery whoosh.

"We really have to stop meeting like this," he said. She heard the laughter in his voice.

She continued her visual inspection, tilting her head back to see that, yes, he was still bare-chested. His stomach was washboard flat, rippled, and glistening. He'd obviously just finished lifting weights because she could see the quiver of his muscles under all that hot male skin.

She'd never, in her life, wanted to nibble on a man's belly as much as she did right now.

He had a white cotton shirt slung over his incredibly broad shoulders. Even the muscles of his neck shone with energy, as did his dark, slightly bristled face.

"Don't tell me you need help getting up again. This mat's not as slippery as the ice." He bent down next to her, lowering his voice. "Not as slick. Definitely not as hard."

No, no, no. No sexy word games with the chief. Once a day was quite enough. Once a lifetime was enough with a guy who could make her this tongue-tied and brainless.

"I'll be fine."

He raised a brow. "Just sitting out a set?"

She nodded.

He tilted his head and quirked a brow. In a low voice, he said, "But everyone else is gone."

Jerking her head up, she saw he was right. The other eight

or ten women from the class had scooted out of here, probably the minute this hunk of man had come in. Heaven forbid any other woman be caught looking sweaty and un-made-up after a grueling workout. No, that was Sophie's job.

One woman—the giggly redhead—was standing right outside the door, so obviously eavesdropping Sophie had the urge to say something salacious, just go give her something to stew over. *Aww, hell, admit it, Sophie.* She had the urge to say something salacious because, dammit, that's how this man made her feel!

"You certainly know how to empty a room," she muttered, taking her own mortification out on him.

"Must be because I haven't showered yet." A grin played about his lips, telling her he knew full well the reaction he'd gotten from the other women.

"Yeah, you're pretty ripe. Hit the showers, big guy."

He drew an offended hand to his chest...*oh, that chest.* "The human banana is telling me I stink?"

She looked down at her bright yellow workout clothes and chuckled. "Help me up since you're the reason I fell."

"At least I'm not as slobbery as Cujo."

Charmed against her will by his teasing, she put out a hand and let him pull her to her feet.

Then it was his turn to stare. He cast a long, assessing look over her, from head to toe. And suddenly, Sophie realized it wasn't necessarily such a bad thing to have a man see you in workout clothes. Particularly when the spandex was scooped deep to make the most of meager bustlines. And when the bodysuit did remarkably saucy things to her hips and tush.

He noticed. Whew, judging by the way his jaw clenched and a pulse started ticking in his temple, he definitely noticed.

"So, why do you come all the way here to work out instead of staying in Derryville?" His casual tone did nothing to ease the thick tension between them in the empty room. Sophie glanced over and saw that even the redhead had given up and left, apparently realizing Daniel and Sophie knew one another.

But not as well as she'd like to know him.

"For the same reason you do?" she finally replied.

"Because the equipment at the Y was purchased when Roosevelt was in office?"

"No, I meant because I don't want to work out with someone who will report to the woman under the dryer next to them at the beauty parlor how many reps I did or how I look in spandex."

He glanced down. "Not a problem."

She liked the way he said that. With quiet certainty and a boatload of masculine appreciation.

"So you don't really like the Derryville grapevine? I find it kinda charming that the waitress at Ed's Diner knows how I take my coffee and that I like my eggs over easy," he said.

Mental note: eggs over easy for breakfast. Just in case she ever, um, needed to know. Then she thought about what he'd said and smirked. "Deedee? Oh, yeah, she knows how you take your coffee." Crossing her arms in front of her, she tilted her head and gave him a pitying smile. "She also knows you wear a 34 pants, under which are some nice tight-fitting boxer briefs."

His jaw dropped.

She ticked off the rest on her fingers. "You don't wear pajamas, you don't go out much at night, you don't eat enough vegetables, and you sleep in a queen-size bed, which she'd very much like to see up close and personal."

He gawked. "Wha..."

"Don't you get it?" She almost felt sorry for him because he looked so stunned. "You're living in a small town, Chief. Everybody knows, everybody tells."

"But...."

She knew what he was asking. "Mrs. Pearce, your landlady?"

"Yeah?"

"Her sister is Tina Laudermilk, the bank teller."

He blew out a puff of air in visible impatience. "So?"

"Mrs. Laudermilk was maid of honor for Joanie Simmons."

"Sophie..." he growled.

"Joanie Simmons is Deedee's aunt. Well, not her real aunt, but her step-aunt, because Joanie was once married to Deedee's Uncle Rufus, who used to get drunk as a skunk and pee in the streets before he crashed up his motorcycle and died."

"Sophie!"

She chuckled. "You don't follow me?"

He blinked. Then it began to sink in. "Excuse me, did you just establish a chain of evidence on the rumors about my freakin' underwear?"

Ahh...he got it.

"Yep."

He ran a hand over his eyes, then swept it through his sweat-dampened hair. The movement highlighted every powerful flexing muscle in his arm.

Sophie gulped, then drew in a shuddery breath. "Gym's closing soon. We'd better get out of here."

He didn't move, still appearing shocked to learn just what the sweet little old Derryville grapevine could do. For someone who hadn't grown up in this kind of community, it probably was a shock. She suddenly felt badly for being amused by his reaction to learning just where his new job had landed him: Derryville, or, as Sophie liked to call it, Peyton Place does Mayberry.

"Chief..."

"Daniel," he murmured.

She cleared her throat. "Daniel, are you okay?"

He shook his head. "I don't know."

Unsure where she got the courage to actually do it, she reached out to give him a comforting pat on the shoulder.

Only, oh, goodness, that shoulder was warm. And hard. And slick. And for some reason her hand didn't comfortingly pat so much as it seductively caressed. She couldn't seem to pull her fingertips away from his skin.

Sophie couldn't say she was mindless, lost in a haze of lust.

Oh, she lusted all right. That was definitely lust, not post-workout stress, making her legs all wobbly and her tummy roll over. But she wasn't mindless. She knew what she was doing, could see the whiteness of her own fingers and the pink polish on her nails so startling against his golden brown arm.

He finally seemed to realize. The look of consternation on his face was quickly replaced by one of awareness. Heat.

Remove your hands and step away from the hunka-hunka burning man, Sophie. But she didn't.

"Checking my pulse?" he asked, his voice a thick growl.

Her fingers were close to his throat. He'd practically issued an invitation. Or was it a dare?

Without giving it too much thought, Sophie followed his implied order and moved her fingers to his neck. She easily found his pulse; it was raging against her touch, as if his heart had suddenly begun to race. Like hers had.

His breath grew choppy and he nearly growled. "Sophie..."

"You must have worked out pretty hard," she whispered.

He stepped closer, sliding one foot between hers, until their legs were nearly touching. "It wasn't the workout."

They were both sweaty, hot and panting. And Sophie suddenly knew exactly how he felt. She would be feeling the same way with this man even if she hadn't just worked out. "I know."

He moved again, until this time she felt the heat and crisp hair of his legs brush against her bare skin. Their calves touched, their knees too. And it was the simplest thing in the world to slide her arms around his neck and pull him close.

Just one kiss. Just one simple, tiny brush of the lips to get it out of her system so she'd stop all this wondering.

But her good intentions fled when she finally felt the man's lips against hers. Pure desire, insistent and demanding, erupted between them. Their mouths opened, tongues tangling in a quick, hot exploration that raised more questions than it answered.

His flimsy shorts did nothing to conceal his reaction, and Sophie moaned as she felt him grow hard and insistent against her belly. He pressed harder, answering her moan with a low growl. When he dropped his hands to her hips, making a delicious detour against the side of her breast, she nearly fell to the floor.

No, kissing him hadn't answered a damn thing. Particularly because she now had a new question. *God, if that feels this glorious through clothes, how would it feel skin to skin?*

He finally pulled away and they both sucked in a few deep breaths. "You're killing me here. I'm not going to be able to walk out of this place for a good ten minutes."

She raised a saucy brow. "You're telling me it would only take ten minutes?"

He tsked and shook his head, looking amused by her naughty wit. "I meant, it'll take me that long to calm down." Lowering his eyes, he stared at her mouth, then further down her body. Her chest heaved with ragged breaths, and her spandex clothes did nothing to hide the taut tips of her breasts. "Believe me, sweetheart, if we were in a more private place, it'd take me *hours* to finish what I want to do with you."

Good Lord.

Then she realized she really had engaged in a passionate embrace with this man, who was practically a stranger, in a public place. "This was crazy."

"No, just inevitable."

"That too," she admitted.

"So why'd you freeze me out of your office this morning?"

She didn't pretend ignorance—that's exactly what she'd done. "It's...complicated."

He shook his head in visible disapproval of her reply. "Nothing this instinctive can be too complicated, Sophie."

He didn't have to elaborate, she knew what he meant. There was something between them. There had been since the minute their eyes had met through the drugstore window on Christmas Eve.

It just remained to be seen what they did with that something. And when. And where.

Not here. Not yet.

And though she hated to think it, since reality had set back in, she had to concede the truth. *Maybe not ever.*

Somewhere a door slammed and women's voices echoed from down the corridor. She pulled away, wondering where she'd found the strength. "I think it's time to leave."

"Let me take you home." It wasn't a request.

She shook her head. "I have my car."

"Let me *follow* you home."

That almost wasn't a request, either. He'd handed her an opportunity to finish exploring what was happening between them. A woman would have to be stupid, committed or frigid to turn it down. She was none of the above. She was just plain chickenshit.

A kiss was one thing. Inviting into her home, into her bed, would mean inviting him into her private life, which required more thought. "No. I'm sorry, I can't. Not...not yet, Daniel."

He studied her face searchingly. Finally, apparently realizing she meant it, he gave her one brief nod. "All right, Sophie. Not *yet*."

She focused on the "yet," knowing he meant to collect on the implied promise.

Hopefully, by the time he did, she'd be ready to make good.

4

DANIEL KEPT HIS eyes out for Sophie on Friday, but didn't see her all day. He even cruised past the parking lot of the church once or twice, just in case she needed rescuing from a slippery sidewalk.

If he'd been stupid with attraction for the woman the day before, things had gotten downright ridiculous after their encounter at the gym. Just remembering the softness of her lips against his and the sweet but spicy way her skin had smelled had left him smiling. And the thought of how her curvy little legs, hips and rear had looked in that tight, unforgiving spandex had him shifting in his pants more than once today.

He wanted her. He'd known her thirty-six hours and he wanted her like he'd never wanted anyone in his life.

"Ready to call it a day, Chief?" Carol, the dispatcher he'd inherited along with the scratched, solid oak desk and the cluttered office, had stuck her head in through the open door. "It's quitting time."

Quitting time. Five o'clock. Another surreal aspect of his new life here in Derryville. He really *did* go home at five o'clock, even on a Friday. Sure, he remained on call pretty much 24/7, but so far, in two months, he'd never been called in by the night dispatcher.

"Yeah. I guess." Then, before Carol could duck back out and go home to her truck-driving husband, Daniel figured he might as well take advantage of the Derryville grapevine that discussed such things as a man's underwear preferences. "Carol, what do you know about Sophie Winchester?"

Carol smiled. "Sweet little Sophie? She's just about the nicest girl in this town. Good family, too."

Sweet. Good family. *Yeah, tell me something I don't know.* There was more to her than sweetness. *Much more.* That's what he wanted to learn about. "What else do you know about her?"

Carol wagged her eyebrows. "She's a pretty little thing. You interested? I know she's single, doesn't date anybody, keeps to herself most of the time. One of the best students Kennedy High ever had—went to college on a scholarship. She's gentle, quiet, shy. Just the kind of girl you've been looking for."

Daniel raised a brow. "I haven't been looking for a girl."

Carol smirked. "Well, it's about time you did. And since she's the first one you've mentioned, I gotta guess she's exactly what you're looking for."

Daniel didn't try arguing with her reasoning, knowing he'd just give the maternal woman more excuses to try her hand at matchmaking. "Forget I said anything."

"Why don't you ask her brother about her, if you're really interested?"

"Her brother?"

"Sure. Aren't you working with Mick on your new house?"

Mick. Of course. Another Winchester. He had been working with Mick's real estate company on finding a small house to buy in Derryville. His first *real* house—not rented, not a big city dive with screaming neighbors upstairs and a drug dealer around the corner. Just a nice house he could make into a home. Hell, maybe he'd even learn how to fix leaky faucets and put up wallpaper and homey crap like that.

He'd had his eye on a little rancher west of town and was going to see it again with Mick tomorrow. Sounded like the perfect time to ask the man about his sister. Because if anyone else could see beyond the woman's "sweet" reputation, it would certainly be her own brother. At least, he supposed that was the way it worked. Having been raised an only child, by workaholic parents who seldom seemed to notice his existence, he wasn't exactly sure how the sibling thing went.

That was something else he suspected about Sophie. For

some reason, he got the feeling she was a loner. Like him. No, she hadn't grown up a big city latchkey kid. She was surrounded by people who liked and cared about her. But there was an aloof quality, maybe even just the way she always seemed to be playing a role, rather than being herself, that told him she kept people at a distance. She practically ordered no one to get close.

Daniel never had been very good at following orders. That was one of the reasons he'd left the force in Detroit—because all too often his superiors issued orders that covered their asses and got in the way of investigating crimes.

Bidding Carol good-night, he locked up his office. He spoke to the night dispatcher and greeted Skip and Chuck, the two officers who worked the night shift. Both were young and eager kids. They wouldn't last a week in the city. For here, though, they were fine. Respectful, efficient. They knew the folks in Derryville and were hard-working and dedicated.

The biggest problem was they were cousins. They looked and sounded so much alike, he sometimes had a hard time telling them apart. Like those Baldwin brothers, the actors.

"Night," Daniel said as he headed toward the door. "Stay alert for any criminal types. You never know when someone might decide to take Ed hostage at the diner and order him to make a steak that doesn't taste like boiled shoe leather."

His officers nodded, their eyes sparkling with eagerness.

Daniel sighed. "I was kidding, guys."

"Oh," Chuck said. "Good one, Chief." Then he frowned, visibly disappointed that he was not likely to face a hostage standoff tonight, after all.

"Yeah," Skip echoed, sounding equally disappointed. "Good one, Chief."

Shaking his head, Daniel headed home. He didn't even bother to take his squad car, which was parked out back. His temporary apartment was right above the travel agency, less than a block away. As he walked there he was greeted by at least a dozen residents. He didn't think he'd known the names of *three* of his neighbors in Detroit.

Maybe someday he'd get used to it and not wonder why people in small-town America were so darned friendly all the time. It didn't feel quite as unnatural as it had the first few weeks in town, but he wasn't sure he'd *ever* be completely comfortable with everybody knowing his business. Particularly not business like what he wore under his jeans or how often he changed the sheets on his bed: boxer briefs, and every weekend. Sophie's revelation the night before had stunned him into taking another long look at the town he now called home.

He still liked it. But he thought he'd like it better from a slight distance. Hopefully, the apartment wouldn't be home for much longer and he'd get some privacy in the new house on the *outskirts* of town.

Inside, he stripped off his uniform, pulled on a pair of jeans and a sweatshirt, then grabbed himself a beer out of the fridge. He'd just had time to twist off the top and bring it to his lips when his phone rang. "Fletcher."

"Chief, we got trouble."

Trouble? In Derryville? "What is it, Skip?"

"This is Chuck."

Like he was supposed to be able to tell the difference? "Sorry. What's going on?"

"You better get down here. I think someone in town is about to get murdered."

THE VERY LAST PERSON Sophie expected to see when she answered a knock on her door Friday evening was Chief Fletcher. She shouldn't have been surprised—after all, the man had inhabited her brain for the past two days. She'd been unable to think of much else...not her new book, not Pastor Bob's sermon, not Miss Hester's penny-pinching. Nothing but Daniel Fletcher with his long, lean body and bone-melting laugh.

Last night, after getting home from the gym, she hadn't even been able to rid her mind of him long enough to get any writing done. And when she'd finally given up and gone to bed, her night had been filled with the most erotic dreams imaginable, starring Daniel Fletcher.

Which made her that much more shocked to see him at her door just after she'd gotten comfortable for the night. She'd changed into a pair of faded jeans, torn at the knee, and a sweater. With her face scrubbed clean and her hair in a pony-tail, she knew she didn't resemble the pinch-faced church sec-retary. Not that she'd much resembled her at the gym, either. Since she'd been about to make herself some dinner, she'd even answered the knock while holding a big soup ladle.

"Chief?" she said, then cleared her throat because her voice sounded so weak. "What on earth are you doing here?"

"May I come in? I need to speak to you, Miss Winchester."

This wasn't a random knock to ask for money for the be-nevolent brothers of the force, or a meet-the-chief home visit. Could he be here to follow up on the unasked, unanswered questions from the gym? That set her heart into overtime.

Of course, there were other possibilities. If she were a sus-picious-minded person—and she *was*—she'd be concocting a dangerous plot right about now. Maybe he was a psycho killer posing as a cop. Maybe he'd left a string of dead bodies, rather than just broken hearts, when he'd moved here from Detroit.

Cool it. Maybe she ought to stop the mental grasping and see what the man wanted.

"Sure," she said, knowing she was being as stupid as any woman in one of her novels. The ones who opened the door to the sexy stranger, then disappeared off the face of the Earth. Well, disappeared for a while at least. R. F. Colt's au-dience expected blood and body parts, so no one disappeared forever.

"Thanks," he said, stepping inside the foyer. He filled it, his broad shoulders and tall form seeming to take up all the space in her quaint house. "I'm sorry to bother you at home."

"How did you find out where I live?"

He smiled. "This is Derryville."

"Enough said." Heck, in this town, he wouldn't have even had to know her last name to get her address. She was the only Sophie around now that old lady Semple had retired to Florida.

She led him into her living room. "So is this an official visit?" Part of her hoped he'd say no, that he had simply tracked her down because he was overwhelmed by her beauty and feminine charm. A bigger part of her already knew better.

"Yes. I don't want to alarm you, but a situation has come up tonight and I'm afraid it might involve you."

Sophie raised an inquisitive brow. "I'm intrigued." By a lot more than any risky situation. She was intrigued by the man, darn it all. She had no business being attracted to anyone here in Derryville, but there was no help for it. She'd been hooked on this guy since before she'd ever seen his face. And now that she'd been with him, spoken to him, been held in his strong arms—*seen the way he looked while sweaty and almost naked*—she knew she was in way over her head. Drowning. And the sexy cop was the only one she wanted to save her.

He hadn't continued, merely watched her watch him. She wondered if her face was so easy to read, because she noticed the pulse in his temple pick up its pace. His face flushed slightly and he parted his lips to draw in a deep breath.

She nearly had to grab the back of a chair for support, imagining sharing that breath with him. Falling into his arms, as she had yesterday morning, and giving in to her impulse to taste his sensuous mouth again, let their tongues meet and tangle. She wanted to wrap herself around him and remember what it was like to be a woman.

He was just as aware. Just as in tune with the strange currents in the air. The pulse of something deep and instinctual pounded between them; she could almost taste it. She saw in his eyes that he felt it, too.

"You're getting wet."

Oh, God, yes, she probably was. Every one of her senses was at full alert, though how he could have known that she had no idea. She couldn't believe he'd said such a thing, even though it was entirely true. The man had more confidence than anyone she'd ever known. "How...what..."

"The ladle." His voice was as throaty and thick as hers.

Glancing down, she noticed she *had* been getting wet. From dripping chicken broth. It had landed not only on her pants, but on the floor.

Soup. She was getting wet from *soup.* She closed her eyes, almost groaning, thankful she hadn't admitted the truth of her very naughty thoughts. Lucky for her she hadn't done what the normal woman in Derryville would have done had a man said what she had *thought* this one had been saying to her: slap his face.

Sophie's first impulse had been to throw her arms around his neck and her legs around his waist and prove him right.

"Let me get something to clean it up." Hurrying to the kitchen, she dropped the ladle on the counter and grabbed a handful of paper towels, trying to grab some self-control along with them. *Get a grip, woman.*

She hadn't realized he'd followed until she turned around to see him standing in the doorway. "Smells good. You can cook?"

"Not much beyond burnt toast," she muttered before pushing past him to clean up the floor.

He leaned against the jamb, with one hand carelessly thrust into his pocket. He was dressed casually in tight, faded jeans and a Detroit Pistons sweatshirt. Better than the glistening, bulked-up, hot and luscious half-naked look he'd had going on the night before. But still not as good as the uniform. It was easier to remember how off-limits he was when he wore the standard khaki brown.

Looking again at the sweatshirt, she realized he'd taken off his leather jacket. "Sorry, I didn't even offer to take your coat," she said.

He pointed, and she glanced up, seeing his jacket hanging beside her parka. "I made myself at home. Hope that's okay."

This was a man who didn't wait for invitations. Somehow,

she liked that about him. In Derryville, most men followed proprieties, played by the old-fashioned, small-town rules. It sometimes made her want to scream, to shake them, tell them to wake up. Was she the only woman around who didn't always want a man to do nothing more than kiss her cheek after a first date? The only woman who longed to meet a man who didn't wait to be asked for permission to go further? Not that she'd met anyone who interested her enough to go further. But it would be darn nice to think she someday might.

People who only saw her as nice little Sophie would probably be shocked. Those who knew her as tough, bloody, hard-edged R. F. Colt, probably more so. But sometimes she fantasized about being swept away by a powerful man who didn't ask because he wasn't about to risk hearing no.

She sensed Daniel Fletcher might be such a man.

No. Don't even go there.

These were dangerous thoughts. Not that he, himself, seemed dangerous. Just determined. Strong-willed. Passionate.

Enough, Sophie, you hardly know the man.

"There's more right here." He pointed to the floor near his booted foot. His lips were curled slightly in a half smile, as if daring her to come close enough to wipe it up. The spot would put her almost face-to-face with one lean, masculine hip.

Sophie hadn't been dared to do anything in a long, long time. She stood, stepped closer, not letting him see the way her hand was shaking, not to mention her legs. Meeting his steady stare, she pointed to the floor. "Right there?"

He nodded. Then, before she could crouch down to get the spot, he grabbed the wad of paper towels from her hand and bent down himself. Sophie nearly groaned, looking at the top of his dark head, inches from her thigh. When he'd finished wiping up the drops, he looked up and gave her a cocky smile, as if he knew—just *knew*—how he was affecting her.

"Thanks," she managed to squeak out.

"Think nothing of it. I obviously interfered with your dinner plans." He rose slowly, with deliberation and masculine grace. "So who made the soup? Smells too good to be from a can."

Still staring at the fine way he filled out his jeans, she shook her head, trying to snap out of her daze. "My mother. She brings me food a lot. They're on vacation right now, so my freezer's completely full. I think she's afraid I'll starve to death on my own cooking."

She was probably right. Even Sophie couldn't stand her own poor attempts in the kitchen.

"Your whole family lives around here?"

She nodded, not particularly interested in talking about the Winchester clan. "I should throw those away," she said, reaching for the wet paper towels. He let her have them, brushing his fingers against hers in a move too deliberately sensual to be an innocent, accidental touch.

She had to scoot past him to get through the doorway into the kitchen, but he made no move to get out of the way. There was enough room, their bodies didn't touch, didn't come closer than a few inches to one another. But Sophie felt as though they had. The electric awareness snapped between them as she moved past him to drop the towels into the trash can.

He seemed to notice, too. He continued to stare at her, a look of intensity pulling his brow down, as if he couldn't figure out what was happening here any more than she could.

Chemical reaction. Instant attraction. Maybe even just static electricity on a cold winter night. Or it could be raw lust from a woman who hadn't been touched intimately by a man since her last visit to the gynecologist.

She cleared her throat. "Um...you said something about a problem that might involve me?"

He nodded slowly, remaining silent.

"What is it?"

"Maybe we could talk over a cup of...coffee?"

She felt sure he hadn't been about to say coffee. She had a

feeling the hunky chief was angling for an invitation to share her soup. *What the hell.* "Have you eaten?"

He shook his head.

"Sit down," she said, knowing she was crazy for inviting him to stay. Having him in her house for a moment longer than required was risky. At any time he might ask to use her bathroom, might walk down the hall and peer into the spare bedroom, which she used as her office. Might see the police procedurals, the collection of horror novels, the shelves loaded with R. F. Colt books. Might wonder why a church secretary had *Gray's Anatomy* open on her desk, with red-inked notes in the margins, calculating blood loss or angle of entrance wounds.

Had she even shut the door?

Maybe. Maybe not. Somehow she couldn't muster up the energy to care. Something was happening here, between her and Chief Daniel Fletcher. It had started when she'd practically fallen into his arms on the church sidewalk. It had grown stronger when they'd kissed at the gym. It had intensified even more when he'd shown up at her door. And brushing past him on her way into the kitchen had ratcheted the awareness level up ten times.

It was risky for him to stay. But God help her if he left.

5

DANIEL HADN'T BEEN hinting around for an invitation to dinner. Well, okay, maybe he had. The hot homemade chicken soup smelled pretty darn good to a bachelor who usually ate out of a can or a microwave. But his real motivation in sharing Sophie Winchester's meal was not driven by hunger. Instead, he just wanted to spend time with her, get to know her, before he dropped the bombshell about the real reason for his visit.

The thought of someone hurting her made his gut clench. *No way.* Nobody was going to do anything to hurt this woman as long as he lived and breathed.

"Is everything all right?" she asked. "You ready to talk about this big issue?"

He shook his head. "Let's wait until after dinner, okay?"

As soon as he told her the truth, that someone had found a small notebook detailing what looked like a murder plot against her, Sophie would likely freeze up. He wanted to get to know her now, while she wasn't on guard, afraid and worried. Maybe by becoming her friend, he'd be in a better position to protect her as this case went on.

He wasn't being selfless. Something intense was happening between them, and he wasn't ready for it to end. He wanted to be with her, to watch her continue to pretend she wasn't staring at him, wasn't as physically aware of him as he was of her.

And he was. Whew, big time. Holding her so briefly yesterday, when she'd been blanketed in her thick parka, hadn't prepared him for the sight of sweet little Sophie in her wickedly curve-hugging workout outfit from last night. Nor for tonight's jeans and loose sweater that skidded over the gentle curves of her body.

No makeup, hair in a ponytail, yet she didn't look like the fresh-scrubbed, all American girl next door. This woman made the look somehow seductive. Sinful. Probably because of the way she used those big blue eyes of hers to study everything around her. When she looked at him, Daniel felt positively devoured. He only wondered what she could do with her hands and her mouth if she could make a man feel that way with just a stare.

"I picked up some fresh bread, too," she said. "I'll heat it up, then we can eat." She put the loaf in the oven, then took some veggies from the fridge and began to prepare a salad.

"Let me do something to help."

She eyed him, then nodded toward the cabinet. "You can grab some silverware and dishes."

He did so, setting the kitchen table. "I like your house."

She looked surprised. "Thanks. It's small, and old, but I love it. The yard's really pretty in the spring when the perennials come into bloom."

"Perennials?"

"Flowers that come back every spring."

"Oh. I guess I need to learn that kind of stuff if I'm going to buy a place of my own."

"Are you looking to buy a house?"

He nodded. "Actually, your brother's helping me."

"Is that the reason you came out to talk to me?" She leaned against the counter, looking at him, a half smile on her lips. "The *situation?* What has Mick done this time?"

Interesting. She thought her brother might be in trouble. He made a mental note to check out Mick Winchester. "Nothing to my knowledge. Why?"

"Mick's left some angry women behind over the years. One of these days, somebody's going to pay him back but good."

He heard the good humor in her voice. "Sounds like you don't think that's such a bad thing."

She snickered. "Nope. As his sister, I love the louse to

pieces. But as a woman, I hope somebody blows him right out of the water one of these days."

Again, Daniel realized, she didn't sound like a small-town, quiet, good girl. That was making him like her more and more.

She turned away to finish the salad. Realizing dinner was almost ready, he asked, "Can I wash up?"

She nodded, pointing absently toward the hallway. But before he could even leave the kitchen, Sophie let out a scream.

His blood froze.

"Stop right there," she ordered. "Don't take another step."

Daniel swung around, immediately on alert. "What's wrong?" he asked, turning his head to eye all the corners of the room.

Had she heard a noise? Seen a face in the window? He muttered a quiet curse for leaving his weapon locked up at home. Hell, he'd never had a need for it since he'd moved here...until now.

She didn't answer. Instead, she rushed past him. She darted down the hallway, then yanked a door shut. Giving him a weak smile, she explained, "The spare room. It's a mess." Then she pointed to a door directly opposite. "There you go."

"Thanks for scaring me half to death."

She nibbled her lip, looking sheepish. "Sorry. I'm just horrified of anyone finding out my dark secret."

"Secret?" he asked with a raised brow. He was very interested in any secrets Sophie might be keeping. Particularly any naughty ones. *Stow that, this is business.*

"Yeah. I'm not a great housekeeper. I just throw all my stuff in there. It's a nightmare."

Made sense, he supposed.

Not.

She might sound completely innocent, sweet-smiling Sophie, but he suspected there was more to the story than some dust bunnies or unfolded laundry. If he didn't know better, he'd think Sophie Winchester had something she wanted to hide in the guest room. Not a man, he was quite sure. No way would she have invited him to stay for dinner if she was entertaining someone else. But something didn't ring true about her explanation about the spare room. Heck, the whole house had a cluttered, lived-in look that he already liked, if only because it was so unexpected from the put-together church secretary.

The bathroom was no exception. It wasn't done up in prissy spring colors, with flowers or dried stuff that smelled like peaches. No, Sophie's powder room was a screaming bright yellow, with black fixtures and funky framed comic book art on the walls. He liked it. It suited her—the Sophie he was coming to know—the girl who wore the same shade of yellow when she snuck away to work out in the next town.

And this Sophie, he sensed, was not necessarily the girl the whole town seemed to think she was.

Returning to the kitchen, he found her dishing out two large bowls of soup. "I don't think I've ever eaten homemade soup in my life," he admitted as he sat down.

"My father brought the canned stuff home once and I thought my mother was going to brain him with it." She laughed softly. "She's old-school Italian."

As they ate, they were joined by a fat orange cat who sauntered into the room like he owned the place. He gave Daniel a look that clearly asked just what he thought he was doing in the cat's domain. Daniel smiled as he finished off his bread. "Your cat seems surprised to see me."

Sophie shrugged. "Mugs is the only male who's eaten in this kitchen since I bought the place." Seeming to realize how her admission sounded, she hurried on. "I mean, like I said, I can't cook. I don't typically have men over for dinner." She nibbled her lip, backpedaling again. "I mean, we would usually, um, go out or something."

A charming flush pinkened her cheeks and Daniel brought his napkin to his mouth to hide a smile. "To Ed's, I'm sure. I hear their steak special is something else."

She frowned. "Something special if you like beef jerky."

Yeah. She'd had Ed's steak special. "So where do you go on your...*dates?*"

She waved an airy hand. "Lots of places. Tons."

Tons of places on her scads of dates. Riiiiight.

So, she didn't want him to think she didn't have an active social life, which meant she was thinking of *him* in terms of her social life. That, in his opinion, was a good thing.

"Mugs, go take a nap or something," she said when the cat attempted to charm his way up onto Daniel's lap. The cat ignored her, giving Daniel a plaintive mew. After pushing his bowl away, Daniel scooted his chair back and invited the cat to jump up.

Sophie scowled. "Mugshot, you're being very rude."

"Mugshot?"

She raised a brow. "What's the matter? Not the name you'd expect for a spinster church secretary's cat?"

He nearly fell out of his chair at that one. "*Spinster?* You're all of what, twenty-three? And, uh, I don't think there is such a thing as a spinster in the twenty-first century." No way was this woman destined to be alone. Not with her sweetly curved mouth and those blue-enough-to-swim-in eyes. "Besides, you go on *lots* of dates, from what I hear."

She shot him a withering glare. "I'm twenty-six."

"Positively ancient," he murmured.

"And I know you know I was lying about my social life. The pope goes out more than I do."

"I'd imagine he goes out quite a lot, actually. Saving souls, doing good works and all."

She harrumphed. "I meant on dates."

"I somehow suspect you could go out with as many men as you want, as often as you like, if you chose to."

"You might not know as much about me as you think." Her voice held both secrets and challenge, as if she was practically daring him to figure out the puzzle that was Sophie Winchester.

He wanted to. Wanted to figure her out, know her, get inside her head. Raw heat made him admit that wasn't the only part of Sophie he wanted to get inside.

He wanted to make love to her. He'd wanted her physically since the minute he'd seen her passing by the store window on Christmas Eve. He'd never been hit as hard by instant attraction in his life as he had been by this woman sitting across from him, daring him to understand what made her tick.

Their eyes met, and he knew damn well she'd read his thoughts. The electric awareness which had faded somewhat during their amiable dinner returned in full force. They just looked at one another across the small kitchen table. He continued to stroke the cat, liking the softness of the animal's fur against his fingers. Sophie finally lowered her gaze, watching him, her face growing pinker as she studied the movement of his hand.

She was thinking of being touched by him. He knew it.

"I know a lot about you," he said softly.

She visibly swallowed, then shook her head.

He ticked off his impressions, everything he'd learned since meeting this unpredictable woman. "You live here alone with your cat. And you don't invite men over," he said, challenging her to correct the picture he was painting of her life. "You donate boxes of clothes to the needy. Your mother keeps you fed. You're pushed around by your boss's sister, and everyone thinks you're the sweetest thing in town."

Bull. All of it was bull. He knew it down to his bones.

"Sorry, babe. I don't see the spinster church secretary with a cat that everyone else in Derryville sees." Letting Mugs hop off his lap, he leaned back in his chair, extending his legs in front of him. He crossed his arms and gave her his most disarming smile. "Honey, that might be what you're selling to the rest of this town. But I, for one, am not buying it."

SOPHIE WAS IN REAL trouble. Good Lord, one meal with the man and he'd already seen through the careful facade she'd used to fool everyone in Derryville throughout her adult life. Her jaw dropped open, then snapped closed again. She took a deep, steadying breath, trying to keep her cool and not give him more proof that she was not a sweet woman, but one with a temper and a sharp tongue.

It took a lot of effort.

"Maybe you're right about a few things."

"Just a few?"

She didn't relent. "Maybe I'm a spinst...*single* woman...by choice. Women in the twenty-first century choose to be single all the time. We don't have to gauge our success by the number of men we date."

"Uh-huh. Why don't you just admit you don't *want* to go out with anybody in this town because not one of them sees you for who you really are?"

She froze at that one, because he'd struck at the heart of the matter. He was exactly right. God, how could he see so much, know her so well, after such a brief acquaintance? She'd love to find out, love to see if this big city cop had been using his analytical skills on her, or if he was just one perceptive guy.

"Who I really am?"

He nodded, then pushed the dishes out of the way to lean across the table, making sure he had her complete attention.

Uh, yeah, he definitely did.

"I see the real you. I want to see a lot *more* of the real you."

Her breath caught as he leaned even closer, close enough that they were sharing breaths. Then closer...closer...until his lips brushed hers in the lightest, faintest kiss that left her trembling, shaking, and dying for more.

He pulled back the tiniest bit and she struggled to remember her name. "What was that for?" she finally whispered, her lips still tingling where they'd brushed so delicately across his.

"That was a thank-you for the soup."

She emitted a shaky sigh. "Gee, I'd love to see how you'd say thank you if I'd actually cooked anything."

"Since you told me how you cook, I can't say for sure."

She hid her disappointed frown. Barely.

"But if you did even a tiny bit better than burned toast, i
would probably inspire something like this."

She didn't have time to hide her reaction this time. Because
before she knew what was happening, Daniel had slipped his
hands into her hair and gently cupped her head. He pulled
her forward and took her mouth in a sweet, wet, hot kiss that
did more to fill her up than any other meal she'd had at this
kitchen table.

She'd been kissed before, even by him. But last night at the
gym had been about raw, sweaty desire and attraction.

Tonight was about seduction. A sensual caress of lips and
tongue. He teased her, tasted her, slipped his tongue against
hers in a delicate, intoxicating dance that left her shaking in
her seat. Somehow, this slow buildup of tension and delicious
intimacy aroused her every bit as much as last night's carnal
embrace. He had touched her with nothing but his mouth but
her whole body was alert and dying for more.

Finally, he pulled away and sat back in his chair. They
looked at one another across the table. Sophie had a quick
mental flash of sweeping the dishes to the floor and diving
across the table to leap on him.

They weren't her *good* dishes, after all.

"Well?" she asked, knowing he understood the question.

He licked his lips. "Oh, yeah."

Yes! Her libido answered. Her mind had shut off com
pletely.

Then he ran a hand over his eyes and shook his head. "But
first we need to talk. I think it's even *more* important now that
I'm coming to know the real Sophie Winchester."

Her mind kicked back into gear, to her great regret. "Back
to that again?" She crossed her arms, more to keep herself
from reaching across the table and grabbing him than any
thing else. "Okay, Chief, who am I, really?"

"You're also a woman who has the softest lips I've ever felt
and kisses like sweet, sugarcoated sin."

She gulped. *Whoa.*

He rubbed his hand on his jaw, staring at her intently. Then his eyes narrowed. "Who you really are is a smart-mouthed, naughty, imaginative woman with a slightly twisted sense of humor who can't cook, probably can't sew, knit, iron or do any other housewifey crap most men in this town would expect."

She couldn't restrain a laugh. He'd pretty much pegged her, all right.

"Luckily," he added with a sexy, playful grin that stole her breath right out of her mouth, "I'm not from this town."

No, he wasn't. And the kiss they'd just shared should have had her jumping up singing hallelujah for that fact.

But what he'd said had cut through the hazy desire clouding her mind and brought her back to reality. He did know her. Dammit, he really did. So how much of a stretch would it be for him to find out the rest? All of it?

She couldn't afford that.

Sometimes life was so unfair. Because here was a man she'd love to get to know better. A *lot* better. And she couldn't. Couldn't be around him, couldn't get to know him, couldn't jump his bones and make love to him from here to next week.

It was too risky. She'd known it before; tonight merely confirmed it. "Okay, maybe you're right about some things. But truthfully, why I stay to myself is my own business." Swallowing hard, she told the biggest whopper of her day. "That's the way I like it, and that's the way it's going to stay. So whether you're from town or not really makes no difference to me. Anything else..." *wild kinky sex on the kitchen table* "...would be short-term. Temporary. So it probably isn't the best idea."

He watched her for a moment, gauging the truth of her words. She tried hard to meet his stare, knowing how quickly a cop would peg her a liar if her eyes shifted away. Finally, though he didn't look convinced, he apparently decided to let her get away with throwing up barriers. He sat back in his chair. "Okay, Ms. Winchester. I guess I get the point."

She told herself to be glad she'd handled this so responsibly after their kiss, rather than throwing herself across the table and begging him to take her. She'd done exactly what people would have told her to do.

Unfortunately, in spite of what most people in this town would think, Sophie never had liked being told what to do. Her brother Mick was probably the only one who'd understood that about her when they were growing up.

After all, she was the one who usually came up with ways to break the rules. He was just the one who got caught.

"So," she said, "maybe you'd better tell me what it is you came here to tell me. It's getting late."

"All right," he finally said, rising from the chair to stand over her. "Let me go get something."

Sophie immediately stood too, clearing the dishes off the table while he left the kitchen. By the time she'd put the bowls in the sink, he was back, watching her from a few feet away.

"I have something I want you to look at."

That was a loaded comment, considering what she'd really wanted to look at all evening was him. Naked. Sweaty. Howling with pleasure.

Enough.

His next move stunned her out of her lustful dementia. He held up a small plastic baggie. Inside was a 3 x 5 spiral notebook. *Her* notebook. The rat had gone into her office!

"What is going on?" she asked, wanting to know who he thought he was to invade her privacy like that. Damn, what else had he nosed through while he was supposed to be in the bathroom?

She was about to threaten lawsuits over illegal search and invasion of privacy, when he shut her up with six words.

"I think you're in danger, Sophie."

"Danger?" she repeated, not understanding what he meant.

"Yes. I think someone's planning to kill you."

6

"YOU'RE CRAZY."

That was her response after he explained the whole situation to her. Daniel didn't take offense. Most potential crime victims didn't believe they were targets at first, especially in a place like Derryville. It seemed even less likely when it involved the town sweetheart. "I'm very serious about this, Sophie."

She didn't take her eyes off the notebook. Daniel had wrapped it in a plastic baggie after examining it at the station this evening.

Sophie looked confused, bewildered and more than a little anxious. "Where did you say you got the notebook?"

"Mrs. Madigan, one of the tellers from the bank, found it in the road not far from the church on her way home from work yesterday evening. She turned it in this afternoon."

Though she reached for the notebook, he didn't let her have it. "Evidence."

She frowned. Pointing to the small marks on the dinged-up red cover, she asked, "What are those little holes? Looks like teeth marks."

He tried to ease any concerns she might have that she could be dealing with a biting sicko. "Don't worry, they're obviously not human."

She gave him a look of exasperation. "I'm not an idiot—I know what human teeth marks would look like. But what kind of animal made these?"

He briefly wondered why she'd know what human teeth marks would look like. "Something was at it. Maybe a squirrel, chipmunk."

"A big stupid dog," she muttered.

Daniel nodded. "Could be."

She rolled her eyes. "Cujo."

"Again, it's possible. But just because that dog was near the church yesterday doesn't mean he's the one who was at this notebook. We have no idea whether it was dropped near the church, or carried there by whatever animal had it." He hated to mention it, but had to make sure the woman had all the facts and would remain on guard. "It's possible the person had been near the church, watching you." He hurried to ease her fears. "But not definite. And I don't think this could have been out in the elements too long. The pages are nearly dry and the snow didn't do much damage."

"No, just the drooly dog. What about fingerprints?" she asked.

"Nothing traceable yet. Couple of partials. We haven't hit anything on the crime database."

She nodded slowly. Sophie seemed to be taking this whole thing very well, not getting panicked, not asking a million un-answerable questions or getting even the slightest bit hyster-ical. She remained thoughtful, analytical. Pretty much what he'd come to expect from her.

"So, do you know of anyone who might want to harm you?"

"Nobody wants to harm me."

"The notes in here say otherwise."

She ran a hand through her hair, then pulled her ponytail off. "Look, whatever's in that notebook, what on earth makes you think it's about me?"

He frowned. "There are specific mentions in here about the church, the office, the time 'she' would leave."

She muttered something under her breath.

"What?"

Crossing her arms, she raised a brow. "I'm not the only woman who works in the church office. How do you know it's not referring to Miss Hester?"

"Not likely." He didn't tell her *why* he didn't think it

likely—that being because the whack-job would have to be stupid to think of disposing of a woman the size of Miss Hester through a hole in the icy lake. Christ, to make a hole that big with a pickax would take days.

She pressed him. "But how can you be sure?"

"Trust me, Sophie. I know my job."

She blew out an impatient breath, rolled her eyes and plopped onto the couch. She didn't exactly look like the patient, sweet and smiling secretary the town knew. She looked more like someone who seriously wanted to punch something.

Probably him.

But he wasn't going to tell her any more than he had to. He didn't want to talk to Sophie about the kind of stuff this sicko had written in the notebook. Right down to how he'd dispose of the body. She didn't need to hear about things like pickaxes and wood chippers.

"Fine. You won't tell me anything. But, how can you possibly know it's not just some big...misunderstanding? Or a joke?"

"I tend to take things like entrance wounds, weapons and body removal very seriously."

She let out a nearly inaudible groan, looking down at her own hands. "I can't believe this."

She was finally getting the point. She looked weary, so damn vulnerable it almost hurt to watch her. When he'd started this job, he'd resolved that nothing was going to happen to an innocent victim here, like it so often had in the crime-ridden big city he'd recently left. Not on his watch. Not in his town.

And definitely not to this woman.

THE ONLY WAY SOPHIE COULD get Daniel to leave that night was to promise to lock all her doors and windows, and keep her cell phone by her side at all times. When he finally accepted that she was *not* going to go visit friends for a day or two, he went over a long list of don'ts and do's. Even after that, the stubborn man insisted on doing a final search of her house. She managed to keep him away from her office without threatening bodily injury, but it was a close call for a minte.

"This is unbelievable," she muttered when she looked out her front window the next morning, seeing the police car slowly cruise down her street. He'd said he'd have a patrol going by throughout the night. She'd seen it at least four times before she'd finally been able to fall asleep.

This protective stuff was going to get old really fast.

"And to think you wanted to meet a take-charge kind of guy. Next time be careful what you wish for," she muttered.

She had no idea how to handle this latest situation. She wasn't in any danger, for heaven's sake. Well, not for the reasons Chief Fletcher might think. Her physical well-being wasn't threatened. But if the truth came out, her nice, anonymous, orderly world might well be.

So much for keeping a low profile, maintaining both her worlds for as long as she could.

"What a mess," she muttered.

In more ways than one. Yes, the current situation was bad. The police chief thought someone was going to murder her, and soon enough the whole town would know it.

But somehow, the other issue—the personal issue—was what had really kept her up last night. She was *way* too interested in Daniel Fletcher for her own good. Cripes, she hadn't even realized her notebook was missing from her pocket, probably because she'd been thinking of nothing else but the chief since the minute they'd met.

She figured she must have lost the book when she fell on the ice outside the church. The big slobber-mobile masquerading as a dog had probably snatched it up before romping away with his owner.

The fact that she hadn't even *noticed* told her more than she wanted to know about where her mind had been since Thursday morning. Not on work. Not on her deadline, her P.R. campaign, her print run, her movie deal.

No. She'd been thinking of one thing. Him. Mister hunky-nosy-over-protective-drool-worthy-helluva-kisser police chief.

She had to figure out a way out of this mess, hopefully without having to interact too much with Daniel. Not that she'd necessarily *mind* interacting with him, in certain ways at least. But that was impossible.

If she kept quiet about the notebook, he'd be darn well furious when he eventually found out. And he *would* find out.

If she told him the truth about who she was, well, his reaction would probably be even worse.

Sophie had had a few experiences with the big, strong, over-protective type of man. They all had one thing in common. They couldn't wrap their arms—not to mention their minds or hearts—around the kind of woman who plotted and fantasized about gruesome murders all day long.

Either way she lost. If she came clean and told Daniel who had really written the notebook, he'd back off, all right, in every way possible. Since she'd already decided she couldn't possibly get involved with him, that should have been a relief.

It wasn't.

Deep in her heart, during the dark, lonely hours in her bed, she had admitted the truth. She didn't really want him to back off, except on this murder investigation nonsense. She hated the thought of him exiting her world completely, becoming just another townsperson she nodded to while in line at the grocery store checkout. She wanted him in her life.

"Be honest," she muttered. "You want him in your bed."

Well, that was true too. But it was more than that. She liked him, liked his wit and his smile. His intelligence and his courtesy. And good God she liked the way he kissed.

"Maybe..."

Then she shook her head. No, not maybe. Even if she told him, came clean, and he somehow, amazingly, didn't mind, it would still ruin things eventually. Sure, she could ask him to keep what she told him in confidence, but just canceling the investigation would raise some eyebrows. His officers would want to know why. The rumors would start. Sooner or later, the truth would come out. And the way gossip spread in this town, she'd have a line of readers at her front door wanting autographs, and a group of picketers across her driveway protesting the violence in her books.

Sophie almost preferred the physical threat of a real stalker. She knew how to take care of herself. Several years of self-defense courses, as well as visits with the FBI, DEA and State Police had exposed her to the world of personal protection.

But she was clueless about dealing with fame. Or infamy.

"Well, Mugs," she said as she absently gave her cat a good-morning scratch. "It looks like we're about to get a crash course."

She just hoped that somehow, while she figured out how to deal with her professional life, she'd find some answers for her personal one.

"CHIEF?"

Daniel reached for the radio on the dash of his squad car Saturday morning. Usually he didn't bother going on patrol on weekends, unless there was a particularly popular local band playing at the honky-tonk out by the interstate. Then he and every man on his squad worked overtime to make sure no one tried to drive home after a little too much celebrating.

Today, however, with a genuine case to investigate, he'd been up and at work shortly after sunrise, learning everything he could about Miss Sophie Winchester. So far, he hadn't found much he didn't already know. She'd been born and raised here, moved away for a few years to go to college. Bought her house six months ago, had good credit, had never been arrested or even charged with as much as a speeding violation. No violent ex-boyfriends. No explanation about where she learned to kiss like an angel.

Why the woman would have an enemy out for her blood, he had no idea.

He told himself he'd be just as vigilant with any other potential victim in Derryville. But, deep down, he knew it was his concern for this particular one that had left him restless and unable to sleep the night before.

If he were a better cop, or a stronger man, perhaps it would have only been his concern about her that had filled his mind overnight. But that wasn't the case. He'd also tossed and turned due to more erotic thoughts. Those thoughts had been present since the first time he'd seen her, back before Christmas. Their too-brief kisses had made things a lot worse.

God, a woman had never affected him so instantly, so powerfully. He hadn't so much as dated a woman in months, and throughout the night he'd thought of doing a lot more than *dating* the town sweetheart. He'd wanted to climb on top of her right there on her kitchen table and make love to her amid the bowls of chicken soup, with her cat watching from below.

"Chief, are you there?"

"Sorry. Go ahead."

"Goldilocks has left the cottage. Repeat. Goldilocks has left the cottage."

What the.... "Excuse me?"

"Goldilocks..."

"I heard you, I mean what the hell are you talking about, Chuck?"

"It's Skip, Chief. But I think in sensitive cases, we should maintain radio anonymity. So call me Papa Bear."

Okay, either some teenagers from the high school had hitched a joy ride in one of the squad cars and were goofing around with the radio, or else one of his officers had gone completely mental.

"Skip, just tell me in plain English what's going on. Who is Goldilocks?"

"Our intended victim."

"Sophie Winchester?"

"Affirmative."

Daniel responded with the first thing that crossed his mind. "Her hair's not gold, it's brown."

"Told you," he heard from in the background. "She should

have been Belle from *Beauty and the Beast*. She had brown hair," Chuck, Skip's partner in overactive imagination said.

"But there wasn't any big bad wolf in *Beauty and the Beast*," Skip replied, obviously forgetting he was on the radio with his boss. "And no bears, either, so our nicknames would have been stupid like the French candle guy or the clock."

Daniel muttered a four letter word that he technically wasn't supposed to say across an open radio channel. "For God's sake, would you two shut up? There wasn't any damn wolf in *Goldilocks and the Three Bears*, either, so just cut the fairy-tale crap and tell me what I need to know."

After a brief silence—during which Daniel figured Skip and Chuck were glaring at each other like two kids caught trading notes in the classroom—Skip finally replied. "Uh, Gold...I mean, Sophie, left her house a short time ago."

He was instantly interested. "Alone?"

"Affirmative."

"No one followed her?"

"That's a negative, Chief. All secure on her street. No perps in sight. Perimeter is all clear."

God almighty, these two had been watching too many cop shows. "Where'd she go?"

"Downtown. We're parked outside Ed's right now. Our source tells us she ordered a coffee, two cream, two sugar. And the Saturday Sunrise special, eggs scrambled, toast wheat, hold the scrapple."

Beyond having a quick thought that the two of them had one more thing in common—a dislike of an unidentifiable mystery meat called scrapple—he ignored the inane food details and focused on what else Skip had said. Lowering his voice, he wondered if his two officers could hear the anger in his controlled tone. "Your *source* inside?"

Whether they heard it or not, they instantly went on the defensive. "Carol, boss. She knows the case and was going into Ed's with her husband, so we have her keeping in contact on her cell phone."

Oh, that had to be inconspicuous. Carol spent her days

fighting to be heard over her brood of children, or the noisy cops at the station. Even her normal speaking voice was a few decibels shy of being a hearing hazard. Ed would probably hear the woman's phone conversation over the sound of the deep fryer in the kitchen.

"Don't do a thing," he finally said as he turned his car toward downtown. "I'm almost at the diner. I'll go in myself and see just how bad things have already gotten."

7

DANIEL KNEW the minute he walked into the diner that his officers' "source" had not kept quiet about their big case. He'd no sooner set foot in the crowded place before a number of heads went together and the whispers started. He heard the word "killer" and knew this little drop of a town had been stirred up into a great big boiling pot of gossip.

He knew he couldn't blame Carol. Considering the Derryville grapevine, the story of the notebook had probably circulated two minutes after Mrs. Madigan, the woman who'd found it, had turned the thing in at the police station. He imagined the Friday night bridge games, movie dates and bingo parlor had been abuzz with nothing else but the news that a killer was on the loose in town.

So much for keeping a lid on things and doing some quiet investigation. Damn, he hadn't even had twenty-four hours to get ahead of this thing before it became public knowledge.

But if *he* had it bad, well, the person sitting at the booth closest to the black velvet Elvis portrait had it a lot worse. Sophie looked ready to *commit* a murder, not become the victim of one.

"Morning, Chief. You here to protect Sophie? Don't you worry, we've been keeping a close eye on her. Any time you need to start up a posse, or a SWAT team, or something like that, you just let me know. I already got a half-dozen volunteers."

He merely sighed and shook his head as he walked past old man Shin, former town barber and current head of the citizens' patrol group.

He reached Sophie's table just in time to hear Deedee, the

waitress, say, "Hey Sophie, honey, you sure you don't want anything else? Stay a while, pumpkin, no need to go out on the street. You stay right here where you're nice and safe."

"No, thanks, Deedee."

The waitress shrugged and walked away, probably not hearing Sophie mumble, "Who's going to keep you all safe from me when all this concern sends me postal?"

Daniel plopped down in the empty seat across from her. "Would I do?"

She flushed, obviously realizing she'd been overheard. "Can you get me out of here?"

He nodded once. Then he reached across the table, took her hand and pulled her to her feet. Conversation in the diner ceased and every set of eyes turned in their direction.

"Good plan, Chief. You be her bodyguard," Mr. Shin said with an approving nod.

Knowing it was probably a vain effort, he responded, in a louder than normal voice. "Miss Winchester isn't in need of a bodyguard. I don't know why there's so much talk circulating, but she's not in any danger here in Derryville."

He took Sophie's arm and began leading her toward the door.

"Then why's she holding on to you like she's Linus and you're her blankie?" the waitress, Deedee, asked, her expression speculative.

Daniel paused, looking down at Sophie who was, indeed, holding tightly to his arm, focused only on the door. Then he smiled, figuring he'd give the gossipers something else to carry out to the town. Giving Deedee a confident look, he replied, "Well, why do you think?"

Then, in spite of the crowd, the whispers, the voice in his head that told him he was reacting on a personal level, rather than a professional one, he turned to face Sophie. Tracing the tip of his finger against the fine, smooth skin of her jaw, then her mouth, he forced her to look up at him.

And right in front of everyone, he dropped a possessive kiss on her surprised lips.

SOPHIE HAD TO HAND IT to Daniel. If there was one way to get the patrons of Ed's Diner to stop gossiping about a potential murder on a busy Saturday morning, it was to get them talking about a potential romance. Her romance.

Good grief.

"You do realize what you've done, don't you?" she asked him as they walked toward his patrol car. And she wasn't just talking about the way he'd almost stopped her heart and made her jeans feel uncomfortably tight.

"Yep."

"They'll be planning for a Valentine's wedding before we have our seat belts buckled."

He didn't seem too concerned. "Valentine's Day is overdone. I always thought if you were going to have a holiday wedding, you should go for something more unique."

She chuckled. "Like Halloween, with all the guests in costume."

"Yeah," he said as he unlocked the passenger door of his car. "Or April Fool's Day with everyone playing practical jokes during the reception."

She couldn't believe she was sharing this easy, casual conversation with the man who'd just publicly branded her as *his* back in the diner.

Somehow, when she thought of it that way, she wasn't quite as dismayed. There was something rather delicious about the thought of being his. In the most elemental way possible.

Once they were inside the car, Sophie turned in her seat. "However you did it, thank you for getting me out of there. I didn't think I was going to get past Mr. Shin unless I agreed to come to his house to let him teach me some karate moves."

"Scary."

"Or going with Deedee to borrow her brass knuckles."

"Scarier."

"They mean well," she admitted with a heavy sigh. "They think they're protecting me."

That comment cut through the playful mood. "Which brings us back to our little problem."

"The notebook."

"Right."

The damn notebook. She didn't know whether to be angrier with herself for carrying the thing in a loose coat pocket, or with Miss Hester for not letting the sidewalk be salted, or with the big dog who had nailed her Thursday morning.

Then again, if it weren't for her untimely fall, she wouldn't have had this amazing man swoop in to help her up.

"Have you given it any thought since last night?"

She almost laughed at that. She'd thought of nothing else but how to handle this predicament. She nodded. "Yes, I have. But can we put this off for a while? Just not talk about it right this minute? It's not like I'm in any danger sitting here in your car."

He started to shake his head.

"Please, Daniel." She put her hand on his arm. His muscles instantly flexed in reaction. He was apparently very aware of the touch, even through his coat. Pulling her fingers away, she gulped and added, "I can't deal with this right now. We'll talk later, okay? Can we just...just drive?"

He turned in his seat and looked into her eyes. She stared back, not even trying to hide her weary dismay over the whole issue. No, she wasn't concerned for the reasons he might think—certainly not out of any fears for her physical well-being. But this nightmare was making her pretty miserable.

"Okay," he finally said. "Let's do something to take your mind off it."

She sat back in the car, enjoying being in the confined space with him, breathing the same cold morning air, catching a hint of aftershave from his morning-smooth cheeks. How was it possible that in spite of everything that had happened in the past few days, she was so glad to have met him? Glad to have spent time with him, gotten to know him?

Kissed him.

Definitely that.

She hadn't figured on being back in Daniel's company so soon after last night, when he'd left her so confused. But one thing was certain...she'd already admitted to herself during the late-night hours that she didn't want him out of her life. However this turned out, she wasn't going to regret whatever happened between her and Chief Daniel Fletcher.

"So, where to?"

She should go home. She had a ton of pages to produce to make up for getting no work done Thursday and Friday night. But it was a beautiful, sunny morning. Cold and crisp, with the sky a brilliant blue and white puffy clouds holding no hint of snow or rain. Much too lovely a day to stare at a computer screen or the poster-covered walls of her office.

Before she could answer, they both heard the trill of a phone. Daniel checked the caller ID. "Whoops, it's your brother. He's supposed to be showing me a house this morning."

Her brother Mick. She began to smile. Because, though he was known throughout three states for being a cad and a player when it came to women, her brother had a quick mind, a killer sense of humor and a protective heart.

She'd come close, so many times, to telling him the truth about who she was and what she was doing. The only thing that had kept her quiet was that she knew he'd hate having to lie to their parents to keep her secret—Mick truly loathed liars. But now, maybe it was time to come clean. And she couldn't think of anyone better to ask for advice than her own big brother.

DANIEL DIDN'T KNOW exactly why Sophie had agreed to leave with him, instead of just asking him to walk her to her own car so she could go home. He took it as a good sign. Maybe she'd changed her mind and was trying to take down some of the barriers she'd thrown up so hastily between them last night.

Whatever the reason, he was thankful. Last night, sharing

an intimate dinner, then a kiss, had definitely whetted his appetite for more of Sophie Winchester.

"Well, something came up with your brother and he can't meet me until tomorrow morning," he told her after a brief conversation with Mick. "Do you want to go somewhere for a while?"

"Anywhere," she said. "We can just drive as far as I'm concerned."

"And talk."

"Uh-oh."

"Hey, you blew me off last night. But now I have you at my mercy."

She responded with a tiny grin, obviously reading the double meaning of his words.

After they'd buckled up and he'd started the car, she said, "I didn't exactly blow you off."

"You threw me out, Sophie."

Her reply was so low he could barely hear it. "I regretted it all night."

He swallowed hard and shifted in his seat. Not many women would come right out and admit something like that. Then again, Sophie wasn't like most women. That's what he liked so much about her. "Let me make sure I follow you. I get the feeling you're not saying you regret making me leave because of your safety."

She chuckled. "No. Your physical protection wasn't what I was thinking about most of the night."

He took a deep breath, trying to slow his suddenly racing heart as heat dropped straight into his lap.

"So, do you care to tell me what you were thinking all night?" he asked in a low voice, though he knew he was playing with fire. He was behind the wheel of a damn patrol car. Playing sexy word games with her could leave him too distracted to drive.

She shot him a glance that said she, too, knew they were treading in dangerous territory. "That's probably not a great idea." Then she added, "At least not while you're driving."

He hit the brakes, stopping in an intersection, eliciting a hearty laugh from her and a honk from the driver behind him. After giving the impatient man an apologetic wave, he stepped on the gas. "Okay, so, if we're looking for a topic of conversation, there's always the notebook."

She turned in her seat, looking at him as he pulled his cruiser onto the highway. The road was clear of snow, with big piles of the stuff on either side. The crisp morning air and brilliant blue sky made it a perfect day for a drive.

"I don't suppose you'd just, uh, take my word for it that I'm not in any danger."

"Nope."

She blew out an impatient puff of air. "Look, I'm serious about this. No one is out to get me."

"You can't be sure."

"I am." She reached out and put her hand on his arm until he glanced over. "I am certain. Can you just trust me on that?"

She sounded certain. But there was no way she could be, not any way he could think of, at least.

"What do you say? Would you consider letting this drop?"

He shook his head. "Not until you tell me how you're sure."

"I can't. It's not something you'd understand."

He shot her a look out of the corner of his eye while he sped up to pass a slow-moving tractor trailer. The driver had hit his brakes when he saw the light on top of Daniel's cruiser. Typical.

"Is this your big secret? The thing you keep hidden from everyone?" He sensed he was onto something when she looked away, staring out the window as if she'd never beheld a highway sign before. "The thing you think nobody will understand?"

"I'm sure of it."

Thinking back to everything he'd learned about Sophie, to his own impressions, and right up to her insistence that she knew she was in no danger, he reached only one conclusion.

He didn't necessarily buy it, but he knew there were cops out there who did.

Sophie thought she was clairvoyant.

"It's okay, I think I *do* understand."

"You do?"

"Yeah. I have an idea what it is you're hiding, and why you think other people wouldn't be able to handle about you."

"Really?" she looked both curious and surprised.

He had to be honest with her. "I mean, I don't particularly care for that stuff myself, but know there are people who do."

"That stuff?"

He shrugged, trying not to sound like he thought she was nutty. Though, he did wonder for a brief moment.... "You know, um, that ESP stuff."

Her jaw dropped open. "You think *I* think I'm clairvoyant?"

"Isn't that what you were talking about?"

She began to chuckle. "Oh, sure, I'm a mind reader. Didn't you know? Gee, I've helped the police with hundreds of cases."

She was joking but didn't sound overly offended. "Okay, so can you read my mind right now?"

She closed her eyes. With one hand, she made a circular motion over her head, and the other patted her stomach.

"That's a kid trick."

"Yes, but it helps me concentrate. You see, I first learned about my abilities when I read the lunch lady's mind in fifth grade and realized what exactly was in meat loaf surprise."

"Yum. Sounds as good as Ed's steak."

"Stop talking, you're distracting me."

"Okay," he replied, thoroughly enjoying her mischievous mood. Daniel was unable to resist her bright smile and laughter. Sophie had left her more reserved, quiet persona behind as the miles widened between the car and Derryville. Like that night at the gym, or when she was safe at home in her own house, she was being the real woman who'd so attracted him from the start.

He wanted to hold on to her as long as he possibly could.

"Now, concentrate. Think hard about something...whatever's been most occupying your mind lately."

He did, unable to hide the thoughts that had been most on his mind. They were full of heat, passion, and raw, hot and heavy sex. And they starred her.

"Naughty boy, Chief."

Shit, maybe she *was* a mind reader!

"You're thinking of how hot Deedee looks in her waitress uniform, especially with the purple eye shadow she wears."

He made a buzzing sound. "Way off."

She scrunched up her brow and tried again. Then she gave a theatrical gasp. "Oh, my goodness, how wicked!"

Wicked. That sounded interesting. He wondered if she really was turning into him, because pure uninterrupted wickedness sounded pretty damn appealing to him right now.

"It's *Ed* you're picturing in the uniform and purple eye shadow."

He snorted. "Smart-ass. How the hell did you ever get a reputation for being a sweet, good girl?"

"You mean I'm not?"

"If you are, then Ed in drag really is my dream date."

Her expression said she was pleased someone recognized the true Sophie.

He continued to drive, and they continued to talk, to laugh, to open up and get to know each other better. The miles slipped by unnoticed, and he honestly couldn't have said, after a few hours, what state they were in.

Neither one of them cared. Inside the quiet, cocooned police car, they seemed to exist in a void, where it was just the two of them. No family, no town, no creepy stalkers or gossiping landladies. Just Sophie—the *real* Sophie—and Daniel.

Finally, they stopped for lunch at a roadside tavern, sharing greasy burgers and fries. Sophie challenged him to a game of darts, and he proceeded to beat the pants off her.

He already sensed she wasn't the kind of woman who wanted any man to let her win.

When they got back in the car, she confirmed it. "You're good at darts. I would've taken you down if I could."

Taken him down. Hmm...he couldn't resist sharing the quick, wicked image that had flashed through his mind. "I wouldn't have minded being taken down. Maybe on the pool table?"

She looked as if she didn't understand for a second. Then she shook her head and laughed. "I walked right into that one."

"Yeah, you did."

Their eyes met and held, both of them recognizing that something had changed this morning. They certainly weren't long-term pals, or lovers, but they'd left the place where they were strangers, or mere acquaintances. Sometime during their drive, they'd become friends.

That was a strange realization for Daniel. Because he'd never found himself staring at the cute, jean-covered ass of a *friend* while playing darts. He'd never looked across to the passenger side of his car and been tempted to haul *a friend* across the gearshift onto his lap so he could kiss her. Taste her. Explore her. Touch every inch of her.

His gaze shifted lower to take in the creamy color of her sweater against her neck. She hadn't zipped her jacket and the soft fabric of her top hugged the even softer curves of her body. The car suddenly felt too close, too small, too...hot.

Her chest moved as she drew in deeper and deeper breaths. Raising his eyes to meet hers, he realized she, too, had noticed the air growing charged, heated.

"I don't think you ever thanked me properly for getting you out of the diner this morning."

She half lowered her lashes and gave him a coy look. "I remember how you like to say thank you."

Recalling the way he'd kissed her to thank her for the soup, he nodded. "That's how I like to *hear* thank you, too."

Her lips parted.

"So, what do you say, Sophie? Are you going to say thank

you, or are you just going to sit there staring at me and licking
those perfect lips of yours?"

Before he could even think of how she might respond, Sophie gave Daniel her answer.

She climbed right over onto his lap.

8

SOPHIE HAD BEEN going out of her mind being so close to Daniel throughout their morning drive. Occasionally, during their conversations, she'd gotten past the crazy, hungry feeling she had for the man. But it had always been there, right below the surface, making her edgy, aware, anxious. And hot. Oh, Lordy, so hot, in spite of the crisp, cold day.

When he made his flirtatious comment about her getting him on top of a pool table, she'd been unable to resist any longer. She'd thought about his kisses long into the previous night. Now she wanted to experience them again.

"Well, you must really not have liked Ed's Saturday Sunrise Special if you're *this* grateful," he said, laughter on his lips when she'd climbed onto his lap.

Then nothing was on his lips except *hers*. She caught his mouth in a hot, wet kiss which answered all the questions that had taunted her through the night. Yes, his mouth did taste both sweet and intoxicating, like a mint julep she'd once sipped. Yes, his breath, mingled with hers, sent a path of pure warmth down into her lungs with every inhalation. Yes, his tongue could do crazy, incredible, intensely erotic things with hers. Mimicking what else he wanted to do.

What she *wanted* him to do.

When he moved his hand to the waistband of her sweater, she whimpered. At his pause, she realized he'd thought she was protesting. "Don't stop," she whispered against his lips, pulling his hand close again, almost sighing in relief when she felt his fingers move beneath her sweater to touch her skin.

Like everything else about Daniel Fletcher, his fingers were hot. Incredibly erotic. He caressed her waist in tantalizing touches from tummy to back. He'd pause to reach below the waistband of her jeans, teasing her hip or the curve of her rear.

She shivered then, shivered and pressed closer, shifting until she faced him in the seat. Then she moaned, low in her throat, feeling his erection pressing hard into the apex of her thighs. Her jeans felt tight and achy, and she wanted them gone. Wanted nothing separating them but whatever cold air could manage to squeeze between their naked skin.

"This is crazy," he murmured as he plunged his hands deeper into her hair, cradling her head for another deep, erotic kiss.

"I know. But I want more," she whispered when he drew away.

He, apparently did, too. Before she even realized what was happening, she felt cool air on her belly, that had before been warmed by his touch. He lifted her sweater slowly, caressing her midriff, then finally reaching the under curves of her breasts.

Sophie was suddenly very thankful she wasn't wearing a bra. He growled when he realized it.

"Oh, God, yes," she whispered, dropping her head back as he cupped one breast in his hand and slid his fingers over its tip.

He didn't respond, merely bending his head to replace his fingertips with his mouth. He sucked her nipple between his lips, and Sophie jerked against him in instant response.

She didn't know how far they might have gone, how crazy things might have gotten. But they were suddenly interrupted by a beeping horn. Jerking apart, they looked out the window and saw a car full of teenagers, laughing and giving them a thumbs-up sign.

Fortunately, Sophie had been sitting with her back toward the window, so they hadn't gotten too good a look at her.

But they'd definitely interrupted the moment.

Rather than being mortified or frustrated at having been

caught making out in his squad car, Daniel began to laugh. "I don't think I've done anything like that since high school."

"No car make-out sessions in your recent past?" she asked as she tugged her sweater down. Speaking without revealing the tremble in her voice proved a real effort.

He gave her one last kiss, then helped her scoot back over into her own seat. "Nope, but, believe me, I'm remembering the appeal." Then he sighed. "And the drawbacks."

"Definitely," she said, sitting back in her seat and thinking about how close she'd come to making love with Daniel.

Close, but so damn far, she ached.

DANIEL WASN'T SURE whether Sophie would retreat into an embarrassed silence after their heated encounter in the car. He half expected her to, knowing she didn't totally trust him yet, nor trust what was happening between them. Fortunately, she didn't. No, she didn't exactly curl across the seat and keep her hand on his thigh, giving him some kind of hint about what could happen between them when he took her home. But she didn't clam up and pull the silent treatment either.

They talked about a little of everything. They had more in common than he'd suspected, beyond their mutual dislike of mystery meat—scrapple or meat loaf, it didn't much matter. Like him, Sophie was a hockey fan. Though he teased her about being disloyal to her geography, he let her get away with saying she preferred the Flyers to the Redwings.

She talked about her family, filling him in on the Winchesters. Her grandfather sounded like a real character. According to Sophie, he was conducting a scandalous affair with Hildy Compton, the 85-year-old co-owner of a local B&B.

Finally, when she prodded him, he admitted a little about himself. When he told her he hadn't spoken to his parents in a few years, not by design, but due to their disinterest, she looked almost teary eyed. "Have you tried keeping in touch?"

He shrugged. "We do the Christmas card bit."

"Do they even know you've moved?"

Come to think of it, he hadn't sent them a change of address card. "I'll let them know."

"Sad. I can't imagine not having a family support network. Being alone, disconnected."

"You can't, huh? None of that appeals to you? To the Sophie who nobody really knows, really sees?"

She thought about it, then nodded. "I hadn't thought of it that way. It would be easier being myself if I was completely on my own. No more of this sweet Sophie nonsense."

She didn't have to tell him why. Living a double life had to have been damned hard for her. Never having been close to his parents and having no other close relatives, Daniel had never felt tied down to the expectations of family. But he could see what Sophie had gone through. Her brother, Mick, was the town bad boy. The rumor mill said he'd gotten into lots of trouble, usually involving a female, from the time he was a kid.

So Sophie had stepped into the role of the good girl, the golden child. It had probably been expected of her from the time she was a baby. What choice did she have but to conform? The only way out would have been to leave Derryville. And in spite of her sometimes sarcastic wit about her hometown, he sensed she truly loved it and didn't want to leave.

"You really like living in Derryville, don't you?"

She nodded. "Believe it or not, I do. It's home."

Home. He'd never felt that way about a place. Not a building, not a house, not any address. Certainly not a town.

"How about you? Getting used to the small-town life?"

Because he seemed to have broken through Sophie's shell, the one that protected her true self, he wasn't ready to admit the truth. The last thing she needed to hear from someone she'd finally opened up to was that he didn't know if he'd ever find what she'd so easily taken for granted. That feeling of hearth, home, security and warmth, all associated with a place.

The move to Derryville was supposed to be the start of that. So far it hadn't happened. But he still held out hope.

"Oh, yes," he replied. "It's amazing. Big change from the city. No red-light district. No drug dealers outside the school yard." He shook his head. "No sickos thinking up twisted, unusual ways to hurt other people."

That, of course, reminded them both of one thing. The notebook. The issue she wasn't ready to talk about. And the one issue he wasn't ready to let go of.

He assumed that was why Sophie suddenly fell quiet. Because she pulled away, almost imperceptibly, until her right side hugged the door of the car. Whatever intimate connection had lasted throughout most of the day was gone now.

He told himself he should be glad, that it was for the best since she was a potential victim and he responsible for her safety. It didn't work. Convincing himself of that was tougher than when he'd tried to make himself believe, at age seven, that there was no Santa Claus, as his dad had informed him.

When they got back to Derryville, he took her downtown, to her parked car. There had been one more moment of awkwardness, which probably wouldn't have occurred if he'd driven her straight to her house. If he had driven her home he suspected she just might have let go of the self-protective aura and invited him in. And who knows how their day might have ended.

As it was, they stood outside on a downtown street, with prying eyes probably peering between the dusty blinds covering the windows of every storefront. They'd said goodbye, exchanging only one long look that hinted at the heat-and-emotion-filled day they'd shared. Not as heated as he'd have liked it. But, he had to admit it, emotionally something was happening between him and Sophie Winchester.

Something he'd never figured would happen to him.

As hard as it seemed to believe, Daniel was falling in love.

SOPHIE REPLAYED DANIEL'S words about big city crime versus small-town values throughout the night. He disliked imaginative sickos who thought up new ways to hurt people.

Uh...that pretty much described her, didn't it? No, she didn't actually go out and act on those sick scenarios, but she sure did profit from them.

"More proof he should be off-limits," she told herself Sunday morning as she headed for church. She'd have rather slept in, considering her string of sleepless nights lately. But she knew Miss Hester. The woman would be merciless Monday morning if Sophie hadn't spent a penitent Sunday.

Besides, Sophie usually spent the church service doing some serious people watching. It was amazing how much was revealed by body language and whispered conversations during a church service.

The Millers were having marital troubles. He owned the bakery. Judging by the way Mrs. Miller pulled her hand away every time he tried to hold it, he'd been letting his bread rise in the wrong oven.

The Flanagan kids were menaces who shot spitballs out of their rolled-up church bulletins. Mr. Henry, who used to sell Sophie's father his cars before the used car lot closed up, had a disgusting habit of picking his nose. Sophie made sure never to sit in a pew he'd occupied the previous week.

The most interesting people watching this particular Sunday morning was seeing the interested looks on the faces of the single woman all around her. She didn't even have to turn around to know why. The whispers, the smiles, the women who sat up, sucked in, and stuck out told her everything she needed to know.

The new chief had mended his heathen ways and come to Sunday service.

"Room for me?"

The pew was half-empty. Pastor Bob's 8:00 a.m. services were too fire-and-brimstone for most people. Most parishioners preferred to wait until 11:00 when he was tired and hungry and ready to rush through the sermon to get to the coffee and donuts outside.

"Sure."

She scooted over, certain every pair of eyes in the place was glued to the back of her head. She couldn't help wondering whether their brown hair—his dark, hers lighter—combined to make a nice picture. Then she pinched herself for caring.

"You're up early," he whispered.

She nodded, barely glancing over as the music started.

"I never slept," he admitted, not looking at her, but facing directly forward as if focused on the service. "I was thinking about you. What happened. All of it. All night long."

His husky voice, so full of want and sweet seduction, made her almost melt into a puddle of molten Sophie right there on the floor of the church. Two problems with that. First, she didn't want Mr. Henry flicking any of his nose-gold on her. And second, the janitor was a sweet old guy and had enough to do without cleaning up melted Sophie guts.

"Well?"

"Shh," she whispered.

"Come somewhere with me after church."

She shook her head, noticing a few people looking at them.

He raised his voice. "Please."

Seeing more people including her own grandfather and some of her other relatives looking over, she shot him a glare.

"I'll say it louder," he threatened.

"Oh, all right," she snapped, just wanting to shut him up.

She couldn't say she was entirely displeased, particularly when she learned where he wanted her to go. He wanted her opinion on the house he was considering buying. No, it wasn't exactly a quick dash to the nearest hotel for a Sunday afternoon sexual smorgasbord. Somehow, though, this seemed more intimate.

Helping a man pick out his house. That was something Sophie had never been asked to do.

"SO YOU'RE SURE YOU like it?" he asked after they walked out onto the back porch again.

"I do. It's not only bigger than mine, but it has a better yard and one thing my in-town place lacks."

He nodded. "Privacy."

"So, you want to make an offer?" Mick asked. "I think we could really do some dealing on this property since it's been available a while."

Daniel nodded, but also said he wanted to check out a few more things first. That left Sophie alone with her brother for the first time since they'd arrived.

Mick hadn't seemed surprised to see her with the chief. He'd given her one quick grin, then accepted her presence without a word. Typical Mick. Because he had a revolving door love life, he figured other people did, too. Somehow he'd apparently never noticed that Sophie's door had gotten stuck in the closed position somewhere back in the nineties.

Maybe that could change....

No, she reminded herself. She and Daniel were friendly and cordial. She was helping a newcomer just as she might help anybody else who'd recently moved to Derryville. Just because they'd shared some hot kisses and he'd sucked on her nipples until she'd forgotten what planet she lived on didn't mean they were involved.

Yeah. Right.

But, she had to admit, the hardest part about seeing the house with Daniel was the way she kept picturing things she'd change, as if she someday might be living in it. *Ridiculous.* She had her own little house, and she and Mugs would probably live happily there for a very long time. Long after Daniel Fletcher met and married some sweet young Derryville girl who truly was the friendly, uncomplicated, home-and-hearth little darling she appeared to be. Not the bloodthirsty murder-mongerer. Not the kind of twisted person he so seemed to loathe.

"You're quiet today," Mick said as the two of them waited on the porch while Daniel checked the condition of the AC unit.

"Haven't you heard? I'm always quiet."

Her brother obviously heard the note of resignation she couldn't keep out of her voice. "Says who?"

"Everyone who knows me."

"Nobody knows you," he said. "You shoulda been an actress."

"Boring."

"A secret agent. You're awfully good at blending into your environment and can keep a secret better than anyone I know."

They shared a look and both burst into laughter. "I think we'll leave that job to Jared."

"He sucked at it."

They chuckled again, remembering the way their cousin, Jared, had spent his Halloween weekend—with amnesia, thinking he was a secret agent on a dangerous mission.

Jared. He'd understand. Sophie realized there *was* someone else she could talk to. Her brilliant cousin. She'd grown used to him being gone, traveling the world, researching his next true crime novel. So she sometimes almost forgot he'd recently moved right back here, to Derryville. He was planning to marry Gwen Compton, Sophie's friend, who ran a local bed-and-breakfast.

Gwen and Jared had met during his Halloween adventure and had apparently fallen in love at first sight. The fact that Jared was a writer, not the next James Bond, hadn't changed Gwen's feelings for him. In fact, they both shared such fond memories of the way they'd met, they were busy getting their inn, the Little Bohemie, ready for in-character weekend adventures.

Jared was one person who would understand and have some advice on how to balance the line between an unusual career and a normal life. Not that life in the Little Bohemie Inn was truly normal, considering it was haunted. But close enough!

"Can you drop me off at Gwen's?" she asked her brother, knowing she needed to talk to someone now, before the urge to confess everything to Daniel became too strong to resist.

"You're not leaving with Daniel?"

The deceptively uninterested way he asked put her on guard.

"There's nothing going on with us."

"Sure there's not."

She shot him a glare, then realized something. If Mick thought she and Daniel were a romantic item, that meant he probably hadn't heard the rumors circulating about the big murder plot. "Have you...heard anything about us?"

"You know I don't listen to rumors."

She arched a brow and gave him a sympathetic look. "And I know why, too."

"Why?"

"Because ninety-five percent of the time the gossip includes you."

His boyish laugh said he wasn't too surprised by her claim. "Not exactly ninety-five percent. And most of it's bullshit."

She quickly calculated. "So, if it's only seventy-five percent about you, and most of that's bull, that still leaves, oh, about twenty percent of the true gossip, in a town of five thousand people, focused on one man."

"Sometimes, I wish you'd never stopped playing with Barbie dolls and decided to admit you had brains."

She rolled her eyes. "I never played with Barbies."

"Sure you did. You just usually had them tied to the tracks of my train set. Or else you'd shaved their hair, then put their little plastic heads on sticks so you could use them as shrunken head bookmarks."

"One man...out of five thousand," she taunted, knowing he was trying to distract her.

He continued to shake his head. "Shoulda never let you do my algebra homework for me when I was in high school. You're too good at math."

"That's pretty pathetic, considering I was ten."

"Exactly. So when is the rest of the world going to find out how damn smart you are inside that pretty head of yours?" He looked serious now. They'd had this conversation a few times over the years. But since Mick did his own fair share of hiding the real man behind the public persona, he'd never pushed her to be more true to herself.

She shrugged. "Stop trying to change the subject. You just don't want to admit I was better than you at math by the time I was in preschool and figured out *two* nickels was *not* more than one quarter."

"Sucker."

"Louse."

"Ahh, the sounds of siblings bickering on a Sunday morning. What could be more homey than that?"

Daniel hadn't heard what Sophie and her brother were sniping about, but he did notice the sparkle in her eyes and the grin on her lips. Sophie liked arguing. She probably didn't get the chance to do it very much.

Damn, he loved a woman who could hold her own in a blowup, then who'd want to make up in the most passionate way possible afterward.

She didn't look pleased at having been caught behaving in a manner not suited to sweet Sophie. "My brother is a know-it-all."

"And my sister is a fraud."

"Bossy man."

"Controlling woman."

"Cad."

"Smart-ass."

Daniel held up his hands, breaking up their lighthearted argument. God, he liked the way they talked. It made him wonder, not for the first time, what it might have been like to have siblings. To have a brother or sister who knew him so well they always understood his moods, his thoughts. His wishes.

He envied them. As strange as it seemed, considering he'd always considered himself happy with his life, he found himself envying them for their sibling relationship, something he'd never had, but which they took for granted.

"Okay, I think I'm ready to make an offer on this place," he admitted to Mick, suddenly uncomfortable with the direction his own thoughts had taken. Now wasn't the time to reevaluate his life, his relationship with his family—particularly with the parents he'd long assumed hadn't been around because they hadn't cared to. "You want to go back to your office and talk about it?"

"Yep," Mick said. "But can you give me an hour or two?" He raised a brow and quirked a grin that Daniel supposed women would find irresistibly charming. Hell, Mick had the kind of open personality that said he could be a good guy friend, too.

"Sure," Daniel agreed, glad to have more time with Sophie. They had never talked about the notebook the day before during their ride back to town. And as much as he'd liked putting it aside for a while, he could not longer afford to.

"Good. Meet me at my office at noon."

"Done."

"In the meantime," Mick continued, with a mischievous look at his sister, "I think Sophie wanted to take you out to our cousin's place, to show you the town's famous haunted inn."

Surprised, he looked at Sophie and saw a flush on her cheeks. She obviously hadn't wanted Daniel to take her; she'd likely asked her brother. Too bad. Because Daniel was more than ready to step in as the man in Sophie Winchester's life.

He just had to make her want him there, too.

9

"OH, MY GOD, Sophie, you're telling me you are R. F. Colt? You're the one who came up with Detective Mike Michaels? Your brain came up with the story about the psycho who killed brides and grooms at their own wedding receptions?"

Sophie nodded, wishing Gwen, her friend and her cousin Jared's fiancée, hadn't spoken so loudly. Almost as if she hadn't been able to control her own tongue, Sophie had spilled her story to Gwen once she'd learned Jared was out of town for the weekend.

Daniel was somewhere in the house, being given a grand tour by Gwen's grandmother, Hildy Compton. Sophie and Gwen were sitting in the quiet kitchen of the inn, sharing a pot of tea...and sharing secrets.

"I loved that book! I told you months ago it was my favorite Colt book and you made some comment about it being weak."

"It is," Sophie replied, ever critical of her own work. "My worst. The climax was flat and the villain's goals and motivation weren't laid out well enough."

"I don't know what you're talking about. All I know is I had nightmares every time I started planning my wedding."

"Sorry," she replied. "But remember, you can't tell anyone."

Gwen nodded. "Of course I won't. Wow, I should have figured it out...the pseudonym is a dead giveaway. Colt, Winchester, makes perfect sense. What does the R. F. stand for?"

"Really Female."

Gwen snickered. "Wow. Can I have your autograph?"

Sophie had to pause at that. "I've never had someone ask me that before."

"Is that a yes?"

She nodded. "Okay, as long as you promise you won't tell anybody. I still can't believe I told you. I came here intending to talk to Jared, because I figured he'd understand."

"And since he's out of town you spilled your secret to me instead. You must be dying to talk about it if you risked telling me when the police chief is in the house." Gwen nibbled her lip. "Not to mention Hildy and her *friends*."

Sophie knew what Gwen meant. Her grandmother, Hildy, was an eccentric who knew everything, thanks in part to her Casper-type friends who haunted the Little Bohemie. Sophie had often hoped to meet one of the gangster ghosts, believing Gwen and Jared when they said the stories were true. So far, no such luck.

She wondered if Daniel believed in spooks. Given his lack of faith in ESP, she figured not.

"So what are you going to do about this notebook/murder plot thing? I heard people talking about it at the store yesterday."

"Oh, great. Were they all picking out which flowers they'd send to my funeral?"

Gwen wrinkled her nose. "Old man Shin claimed lily rights."

Sophie made a face. "Ugh. I hate lilies."

"I know," Gwen replied with a grin.

Before Sophie could comment on the flowers she'd prefer on her casket after she was murdered, Hildy Compton entered. The "little old lady" lived up to the label physically, but definitely not when it came to her personality. Hildy was a feisty, tart, outrageous old woman who'd apparently lived quite a life in her younger years. Sophie didn't know the details, but she knew Jared was including Hildy in a book about organized crime of the twenties.

"I got an idea," the old woman said as she came in and helped herself to a cup of tea. She carried it over to the table, carefully balancing it with her wrinkled, slender hand, then sat in a chair next to Sophie.

"You have an idea about what?" Sophie asked, almost afraid to hear the answer. "And where's Dan...Chief Fletcher?"

"Locked in the attic. Wanted to get rid of him for a bit."

Sophie leapt to her feet. "What?"

Hildy waved her back down into her seat. "He'll be fine. Lots of interesting stuff to get up to in our attic. Eh, Gwen?" Gwen's face turned an interesting shade of pink, telling Sophie she'd had firsthand experience with attic adventures. Sophie had the feeling she didn't want to know any more, since they probably involved Jared. That'd be almost as bad as hearing about her own brother's romantic escapades.

"Why did you lock Daniel in the attic?" Sophie asked.

"Oh, I didn't," the old woman replied with a cackle. She slapped a bony knee with her bonier hand, probably not doing much damage through the black leather pants stretched over her skinny old lady limbs. "Moe locked him in. Then he told me what you two have been talking about."

"Moe?"

Gwen nibbled her lip. "A ghost."

Ohhhh...right....

"Here's what you do, sugarlips," Hildy continued. "Write an anonymous note to the police, apologizing about the notebook. Tell the truth—that it was just ideas for a book, never meant to scare anyone, blah, blah, blah. And that you didn't want to come forward because you feel foolish about everyone knowing you're trying to write a novel."

Sophie thought about it, realizing the old lady was onto something. The explanation was plausible. The note could have been from anyone in town, but would be linked to the notebook because of her handwriting. "You're brilliant."

"Well, you don't think it's just my stellar good looks and talent in the sack that hooked your grandpa, do ya?"

Okay, mental note: There was definitely something worse

than hearing about the romantic escapades of her cousin or big brother. Hearing them about her grandfather.

Judging by the look on Gwen's face, she didn't want to think about that, either.

Then Sophie thought about Hildy. The old woman had come into the kitchen knowing what they were discussing. Meaning..."Did a ghost really tell you what we were talking about?"

Hildy nodded. "Oh, ayuh. Moe likes your books. Thinks they'd make good movies. He says he wishes Clara Bow wasn't dead because she'd be great in the one you wrote about the beautiful teenager murdering all the teachers at her prep school."

Sophie could only shake her head, not quite sure what to believe anymore. One thing was sure, though. Somebody had locked Daniel in the attic. And somebody was going to have to go up and let him out.

DANIEL DIDN'T GET A chance to see Sophie during the day on Monday. After his attic adventure at the local inn—he still couldn't figure out how he'd gotten locked in there, or why the owner hadn't even noticed he'd disappeared from her tour—he'd driven her back home so he could go to Mick's office.

After he'd made the offer on the house, he'd spent the rest of the day thinking about the sudden twists and turns his life had taken in the past few days. He was buying a house. He was finally aware of what living in a small town really meant. He was questioning his family life, his childhood, his relationship with his parents. His past. His future. Everything.

And all because of her.

He was falling in love with Sophie Winchester. He had never held out much hope that it would happen, since he'd never come close to anything beyond affection, liking, or the hots for any woman he'd ever dated.

He'd moved to Derryville hoping he'd eventually like small town life. Hoping at the very least to find someone who interested him, someone he felt comfortable enough to settle down with. He'd certainly never expected to find real love, the kind that made his palms sweat and his heart trip over itself when she smiled. The kind that filled him with abject terror, which no man ever wanted to admit having, when he thought of something happening to her.

Something happening...well, that worry seemed to be over now.

Daniel still wasn't *totally* convinced, but the note that had been slipped under the door of the police station overnight certainly looked reasonable. It matched the handwriting in the notebook, of that he was fairly certain. Whoever wrote it swore he or she had never meant any real harm to Sophie, claiming the whole thing had been some kind of crazy research for a book.

He just wished the writer had come forward in person. He didn't completely buy the idea that the guy was just embarrassed to have anyone know he was trying to be a writer. In Daniel's opinion, starting a murder panic in a town the size of Derryville should have at least deserved an in-person visit to the police station. Not to mention an apology for the long hours he and his crew had logged since last week.

Besides, something about the note—one particular sentence—had been niggling in his brain all morning. Just the way the writer had asked that they "let this case die its own natural death" had been driving him nuts because it had seemed both unusual and familiar. But he couldn't figure out why.

In any case, he had to let Sophie know about this latest development. He hadn't wanted to talk to her at the church, where people came in and out all day, so he'd called her instead, asking if he could meet her at the house that night.

He'd heard a tiny hesitation in her voice. "Is this a personal visit? If you're hoping for more soup, I'm afraid it's all gone. And my mother is still out of town, so my cupboard is pretty bare."

He chuckled. "Burned toast is okay with me."

She fell silent again, obviously thinking. He wasn't even aware at first that he was holding his breath, waiting to see if she wanted the visit to be personal.

But he finally admitted, "Look, something has happened with this notebook thing, and I'd like to talk to you about it."

"Okay," she said softly. "Come by at seven."

So a few hours later, at a few minutes before seven, he stood at Sophie's door, holding a bag filled with cartons of Chinese food, and a bottle of wine.

Her eyes widened when she saw them. "Fried rice, egg rolls and wine? You're sure this isn't a social visit? That ranks right up there with chocolate and roses for me."

"I'm saving you from a night of burnt toast or cat food."

Mugs suddenly stuck his head around the corner and me-owed, sounding insulted. Loudly. Damn, it was the cat, not his owner, who had ESP.

Following her into the house, he thought of how quickly he'd become comfortable here, and with her. Quite a change from just the other night, the day after he'd met her.

While she got out some silverware, he opened the wine and poured two glasses. As they ate, he told her about the note.

"You're sure it's the same handwriting?"

"I'm not an expert, but I'm sending it to one at the Illinois Crime Lab to make sure of it. But I've studied the notebook and the note for hours, and I'd say, yeah, I'm almost certain one person wrote both of them."

She breathed a visible sigh of relief and sat back in her chair. "Then I'm in the clear."

He shrugged, still not totally convinced, but not wanting her to think he was an overprotective caveman.

He had a feeling, when it came to Sophie, he could be one.

A variety of emotions crossed Sophie's face. There was cer-tainly relief, but also something that looked like a flash of re-gret, or sadness, as if she wasn't entirely pleased with the good news he'd delivered to her. He had a feeling he under-stood why. In spite of how concerned he'd been about her, a part of Daniel hadn't minded the need to keep Sophie close by.

He wasn't nearly ready to let her go.

"So," she said as she later cleared away the mostly empty cartons of food. "I guess that's it."

"I guess so."

She wouldn't meet his eye as she tidied up the kitchen. "You'll be back to your regular routine, I suppose."

"Uh-huh." He murmured, unable to take his eyes off the simple but graceful way she tucked a long strand of her dark hair behind her ear. Sophie had a way of moving that made him just want to stop and watch. "And you will, too."

"Right," she said. "Back to my normal life." Then she added, in a voice so soft he almost couldn't make out her words. "Whatever that is."

He understood what she meant. Her words further confirmed what he'd suspected. He wasn't the only one who'd fallen fast and hard here. He couldn't explain it, or try to make anyone else understand, because he'd never have believed it possible, himself. But it was true, nonetheless. He'd fallen in love with Sophie Winchester, the sweetheart with the acid tongue, the sexy-as-sin church secretary. The woman who'd made his world pause for a minute the first time he'd set eyes on her.

And she, apparently, didn't want to lose him, which meant she had feelings for him, too. That explained her hesitation tonight. It explained everything.

He stood.

"I guess you're leaving now." Her voice sounded so vulnerable, so regretful, that he almost relented and told her he wasn't going anywhere.

But not quite yet.

"I can't go without doing one more thing."

Dropping the dish towel on the counter, she turned to face him and raised an inquisitive brow. "I thought the case was solved, that everything was over."

"The case is apparently solved. But things are definitely not over."

Stepping closer, he finally let her see the intensity in his eyes, the hunger that had been clawing at him since she'd practically fallen into his arms Thursday morning. His pure, undiluted desire for her.

"I'm afraid I'm not going anywhere until we get one thing settled."

"What's that?" she asked, her voice a breathy whisper.

"Well," he said, coming even closer until one of his legs slid between hers and their breaths mingled, "I'm afraid I can't do anything until I decide whether I'm going to make love to you right here on the kitchen counter, or just pick you up and take you straight to your bed."

SOPHIE FROZE, HER LIMBS immobile as her breath caught in her lungs. Daniel had changed the subject so quickly, not even giving her time to realize old Hildy Compton's idea about a note had worked. Sophie had added the touch of leaving it at the police station, hoping to get this thing resolved as quickly as possible. Apparently, she had.

She'd barely had time to acknowledge that fact, or to regret the continuation of her deception with Daniel, whom she was beginning to care deeply about, when he'd totally changed gears on her.

"Um...did you say what I think you said?"

He nodded and stepped closer, like a big, lithe cat, stalking its prey. "I did."

She sucked in a breath, deeply, inhaling the pure, sensuous promise washing off Daniel as easily as she took in oxygen.

"Oh, Lord, finally," were the only words she could manage. Then she slipped her arms around his neck and tugged him down.

"Kitchen it is, then," he whispered as their lips met in a mating of hunger and sweet emotion.

Then there weren't any more words, just long, deep, wet kisses that tore the veils of doubt from her mind and the emptiness from her body. He filled her from toe to tip with just his kiss. She couldn't even imagine how full of delight she'd be once he actually made love to her completely.

His hands fell to her hips and she ground against him, almost cooing as she felt the rock-hard reaction of his body.

"You nearly fried my brains in the car Saturday morning. If those teenagers hadn't beeped, this would have happened then. In broad daylight. Right there in the car."

"I know," she mumbled, frantically reaching to tug his shirt from the waistband of his pants.

He was doing the same, pulling her sweater up and off, tossing it away. Mugs would probably be lying on it in twenty-two seconds, unable to resist the soft angora any more than Sophie had been able to. But right now, she didn't give a damn.

Daniel seemed to touch and caress her everywhere at once. Softly at her waist, teasingly over her belly and midriff, then running the tips of his fingers against the soft underside of her breasts until she quivered with sensation. Finally, unable to stand it, she grabbed his hands and pulled them up, demanding that he ease the ache in her nipples with his touch.

"Impatient?"

"Dying."

He chuckled as he finally caught her nipples between his fingers, squeezing delicately until her legs went weak and she sagged against him. He lifted her onto the counter so he could taste her; his mouth left a trail of heat from her earlobe, down her neck, across her collarbone, until finally he drew one taut tip between his lips and suckled deeply.

She jerked and moaned, feeling restless. "I'd love to finish right here, but we need to go into the bedroom," she whispered, remembering the lone box of condoms burning a hole in the bottom drawer of her nightstand.

"Covered," he muttered, moving his mouth away only to suck on her other breast. "You don't really think I came over here without shoving a fistful of condoms in my pocket, do you?"

"You were that sure of me?"

He pulled away to meet her eyes, saying more with his expression than he did with his voice. "I was that sure of us."

His words made her hesitate for a second. Sophie hadn't been thinking much beyond this, this incredible pleasure, this delight, this release of the pressure that had been building between them for days. She hadn't thought of tomorrow. Of any kind of tomorrow for them. Because their tomorrow would come after a today when she'd continued to lie to him.

"Don't think about it, Sophie," he urged her, obviously seeing the indecision on her face. "Whatever happens afterward is for then. Now, there's just this."

He nibbled on her neck, running his tongue along her jaw before catching her mouth in another one of those crazy-wild kisses that made her body limp and loose. And wet. Very wet.

She might not have tomorrow. But she was damn sure going to take today while she had a shot at it.

Instead of telling him, she showed him. She reached for his shirt again, which she'd never gotten around to removing, and tugged it up, sucking in a breath when she caught site of the solid ripple of muscles across his middle. Then she pulled higher, admiring the swirl of dark, spiky hair on his massive chest. He lifted his arms so she could push off the shirt, and she couldn't resist running her hands over those hard shoulders, and those massive arms. "Good God, you're amazing," she whispered, unable to decide which part of his body to look at next.

Then she knew. A wicked smile crossed her face as she reached for his belt buckle.

"You're going too fast," he admonished. But he didn't try to stop her, giving in with a throaty growl when she unzipped his pants and caressed him through his tight briefs.

He seemed to realize she meant to have him right here, right now, and didn't want to wait. Because Daniel pushed up her jean skirt, and when she lifted her bottom off the counter, pushed it up around her waist. He hissed when he saw the thigh-high stockings she wore beneath. "Wicked."

She smiled. He made the word a compliment. Then her smile faded and her mouth fell open as he reached up to tug her tiny white panties off her hips. His fingers scraped across the curls between her legs, taunting, teasing, raising the tension and her desire. "Oh, yes." She was incapable of anything more coherent.

He grabbed a condom out of his pocket, then pushed his khakis and briefs down. When she saw his thick erection, and realized he'd be inside her in mere seconds, she moaned. Loudly.

He caught her moan with a hot kiss. Then reached between her thighs. "You hide these soft sexy legs, just like you hide the real you, don't you, sweet Sophie?"

Sweet Sophie. For the first time in her life, she actually liked hearing that expression on someone's lips. She wasn't entirely sure why. But perhaps it was because he didn't make it sound like an expectation. Or a half-condescending nickname.

"I like the way you call me that," she admitted. "Because I know you don't mean superficial sweetness..."

"I mean how sweet your little whimpers sound to my ears," he said as he nibbled her throat. "How sweet your skin tastes. Right...here." He lowered his lips to her breast and suckled her nipple, sending hot sensation charging through her body.

Then he pulled away to look into her eyes. His were dark, intense, full of passion. "How sweet and wet and hot you feel against me." This time, he moved his fingers between her legs and plucked at the flesh there, making her whimper and jerk. "This is incredibly sweet, Sophie." He groaned as he slid one finger deep inside her, his thumb remaining on the explosive little bud of sensation that swelled at his touch. He kissed her neck, his rough cheek feeling so incredibly good against her soft skin, his whispered words driving her wild. "And I'm looking forward to tasting you there, to see just how sweet."

Waves of pleasure washed over her in a warm, electric

pulse, her orgasm brought on as much by his words as by his touch.

"Sweet Sophie," he whispered again, watching her climax.

That was it. That was why. From him, the term sounded like both a sensual demand and a carnal acknowledgement. He knew her intimately enough to call her sweet for all the right reasons.

"You can call me sweet Sophie any old time you want," she managed to say between breaths as she slowly returned to sanity.

He kissed her again, deep and long and wet. And when he pulled away, she knew she had to have him inside her, had to be joined with him as deeply as humanly possible.

"Now, Daniel, please," she whispered.

Not even removing his clothes, he sheathed himself, and pulled her down so her legs circled his hips. Then he slid into her with one long, deliberate stroke. She stayed still, savoring the fullness, the overwhelming connection. The completion.

As he began to move, holding her, cradling her, rocking against her, Sophie felt another climax wash over her in waves.

"I won't be far behind you this time," he said. "I've been wanting you for weeks, since the first time I saw you."

"We've got all night," she told him, holding onto his broad shoulders as he backed her against the refrigerator and drove into her again and again.

And finally, after he threw back his head and groaned at his own powerful orgasm, he said, "*That* was the sweetest thing ever."

10

DANIEL WOKE UP first the next morning, after a long, endless night of lovemaking in Sophie's bed. And he woke up sure, absolutely certain that, for the first time in his life, he'd found the woman he loved. He loved her sense of humor, her naughty wit, her innate goodness, her sassy comebacks. He loved looking into her eyes when he was buried deep inside her body.

Loved the way they'd connected. From the very beginning.

She barely moved as he sat up and checked his watch. "Sophie, we need to get moving."

"Mmm?" she mumbled.

Her cat jumped up onto the bed, sending a glare in Daniel's direction that said exactly what the cat thought about having his spot in the bed usurped the previous night. Then he ruined the effect by walking in circles and making himself a comfy bed...right in Daniel's lap.

"I think your cat likes me."

"He's not the only one," she whispered with a big, satisfied yawn.

"You really awake?" he asked, seeing her eyes drift closed again. "It's a workday. Miss Hester's gonna pull out the whips and chains if you're late."

"Miss Hester can..."

"Ahh-ahh...that's not very sweet of you."

"I'm never sweet in the morning until I get my coffee."

He bent over and pressed a light kiss on her nose, then her lips. "Coffee it is. How do you take it?"

"Loaded. Double cream, double sugar. And don't use the skim milk, that's just for tubby Mugs here."

The cat sniffed and looked up. Daniel wondered again if the creature understood what was being said.

He grabbed his pants off the floor and pulled them on, shivering in the cold January morning. Padding barefoot into the kitchen, he checked the thermostat on the way by. They hadn't noticed the lack of heat during the night. Now, however, it was at the very least uncomfortable.

He found her coffee and put a pot on, then opened the refrigerator to look for milk. Skim only. "Sophie, you're out of your milk. You want Mugs's?"

She didn't reply. "Don't go back to sleep!"

Again, no reply.

Chuckling, he grabbed the skim, figuring he'd add a little extra sugar to compensate. Closing the fridge, he noticed a note-sized piece of paper under a magnet—a grocery list. Seeing a pen on the counter, he grabbed it to add milk to Sophie's list.

Then he paused. Stepped closer. Took a really good look at the handwriting on the list. And recognized it.

He'd been studying it for four days. First in the notebook. Then in the note left at the police station overnight.

Sophie had written this list. "And the notebook. And the note."

He swallowed hard, accepting all the implications as they flooded his mind. She'd threatened herself? Then canceled the threat with her note?

She'd never been in any danger. There'd never been any stalker or imaginative novel writer. It had all been Sophie. Always Sophie.

"Why?" he whispered.

What possible reason would she have for doing it?

Though he'd been speaking to himself, she answered him from the doorway to the kitchen. "Why what?"

He turned, the list still in his hand, and looked at her. She was clad only in a long sleep shirt, with her hair wildly tangled around her face. Her lips were reddened and swollen from a night full of erotic kissing. Her cheek was pink where his had scraped against it. Her eyes were dreamy and satisfied. She looked like a well-loved woman.

Until a few minutes ago, when he'd seen the shopping list, he would have said she was. But could he really be in love with a woman who'd do something like this? Then lie to him about it?

"Why'd you do it?" he asked, holding up the note.

"Uhh...because I'm out of laundry detergent?"

"I wasn't asking why you started a shopping list. I'm talking about the notebook. The note." He waved the paper and it made a soft fluttering sound. "The handwriting's the same."

The color faded from her cheeks and she sucked her lip into her mouth. Her eyes grew wide. She reached out one hand in supplication. "Daniel, I'm sorry, it's not...I didn't mean to cause any of this trouble."

He leaned against the kitchen counter, stunned by her admission, even though he'd already figured out the truth. "So you really did it. You wrote the notebook and left it to be found."

"No," she insisted. "I didn't leave it intentionally. It must have..."

"But you wrote it," he pressed, not even letting her finish. "What I want to know is why."

She looked away. "I can't explain."

"You're going to have to. We opened an official police investigation into this matter, Sophie. This isn't just about you and me."

"You and me?" She sounded wary as she obviously began to grasp just how furious he was.

"Yeah. You, lying to me, and me trying to make sense of it."

She stepped closer, again reaching out her hand, but he just couldn't bring himself to take it. He turned away and he grabbed a mug, then poured himself a cup of coffee. Sipping at it, he inhaled the steam, hoping the hot liquid would clear his head.

He still couldn't wrap his brain around it. But he did venture one guess that had leapt into his mind. "Since I've moved to this town, I've been given pies. And I've had fake calls about Peeping Toms. I've saved kitties from trees for their scantily dressed owners." He shook his head, remembering some of the nutso schemes some of the single women of Derryville had invented to try to get his attention. "Were *you* trying to get my attention? Christ, Sophie, you had that from the minute I saw you."

She began to shake her head, denying it. "No, no, not that."

"Then what? You want to tell me this note thing was the truth? That you sit home at night and think of sick and twisted ways to kill people in your spare time because you wanna be famous? The next Stephen King?"

She stiffened, but kept her lips set in a tight line.

"Sophie, talk to me."

She shook her head. "I can't, Daniel. I can't tell you everything that drove me to write the notebook. All I can say is that it must have fallen from my pocket accidentally Thursday when the dog knocked me down. I never meant to cause trouble. The note under the door was just a desperate attempt to try to make the whole thing go away."

"And it never occurred to you to just come clean? To trust me enough to tell me the truth?" He closed his eyes, sucking in a shaky breath to try to regain his composure. Because when it came down to it, her lack of trust in him hit harder than any damn notebook or handwriting sample.

Even after last night, she still didn't trust him.

That hurt. Big time.

He walked past her toward the bedroom. She didn't try to stop him.

"You're leaving?" she asked softly, not even turning around.

"Yeah. I'm leaving."

SOPHIE WATCHED HIM DRESS, watched him go, and didn't say a word to stop him. How could she? What was she supposed to say? *Oh, no, Daniel, I'm not some stupid, manipulative female who wanted to try to trick you into needing to protect me because I was hot for your body.* No, she was much worse, in his book, wasn't she? She was the one with the twisted mind who thought up ways to kill people. Even if the bad guy always got caught, even if the police or P.I. always triumphed.

Her books held a lot of blood. A lot of violence. A lot of what she'd once prided herself on as incredibly unique ways to commit murder. Which he'd find revolting.

She almost wished she could say she'd been just a lovelorn, lonely woman seeking out the new cop in town. It would probably be a little more palatable to him. But there had been enough lies between them. Her lies.

It wasn't until after he left that she began to cry. Big, fat tears fell from her eyes as she lowered herself to the bed they'd been sharing less than a half hour before.

He hadn't said goodbye. Hadn't said he'd see her soon. Hadn't said they'd talk later. He'd just given her an even, assessing look, then walked out her front door.

"Damn, damn, damn," she muttered, punctuating each word by slamming her fist on the bed.

Good old Mugs, so intuitive, seemed to know she needed some comfort. Instead of his snooty cat response, he came over and crawled up her front to give Sophie little kitty kisses on her face. He purred as she rubbed her fingers in his fur, offering an instinctive animal kindness that she gratefully accepted.

"You're an angel, honey, but you can't help me with this one. I don't know if anybody can."

But eventually, as the morning wore on, she realized there might actually be someone who could help. So she picked up the phone and dialed a familiar number.

"Jared?" she asked, when he answered the private line in his office at the Little Bohemie Inn. She said a silent thanks that he'd returned from his weekend away.

"Hey, Soph. What's up?"

"I need you."

And within thirty seconds, she stopped crying. Because he'd told her he was on his way.

DANIEL RECOGNIZED THE handwriting on the envelope the minute Carol brought it into his office that afternoon.

"Kid delivered it to the desk."

He nodded his thanks. She didn't leave, waiting expectantly for him to open it. "Well?"

"Thanks, Carol, you can go back to whatever you were doing."

He didn't want anyone watching him open the note. Because the whole subject of notes and Sophie's handwriting brought him right back to the state of disappointment and anger that he'd finally shaken off after half a day.

The anger surged back. The disappointment had never left.

Finally, unable to resist, he opened the envelope and drew out the single sheet of paper. "Sophie Winchester is really in trouble this time. Please come back."

He shook his head, not surprised by her gutsy move. No fiddling around with weepy phone calls or sappy e-mails. She'd gone right back to the source of their problems.

Her notebook. The threat against her.

"No can do, babe," he muttered. He wasn't ready to go talk to her. Oh, he intended to, he'd planned to do that even before he got the note. No way was he letting this relationship go. He'd walked out this morning to give them both a chance to cool off and regroup. She hadn't been ready to talk. He hadn't been ready to be brushed off with weak explanations and apologies.

But that didn't mean he hadn't planned on going back tonight. For the first time in his life, he'd fallen in love with a woman. He damn sure wasn't going to let that go without a fight. Until he got her to admit the truth about what was going on, he wasn't giving up on them.

Another note came an hour later. Same routine. Carol's eyes were round as she watched in curiosity. He again ignored her until she finally left his office, closing the door with a huffy sigh.

"We're talking life-threatening danger here. Sophie Winchester is in real peril," the note read. He shook his head, this time almost laughing at her melodrama. After stuffing the note in his drawer, he went back to his paperwork on a petty theft case.

The third note, which arrived at three, was more blunt. "Get over here or I won't be responsible for what happens to Sophie."

Sweet Miss Sophie had an impatient streak, did she? This time he did laugh, wondering what the residents of this town would think of sweet little Sophie being so insistent. He sat back in his chair, remembering ways she'd been insistent the night before. No, she wasn't a selfish lover, far from it. His pulse sped up just thinking of some of the ways she'd wanted to give and receive pleasure.

She definitely hadn't been the innocent virgin type in bed. She'd been wild. Insatiable. A perfect match for him.

When Carol walked into his office an hour later with yet another familiar-looking envelope, he couldn't wait anymore. He wanted to know the truth, wanted to hear from Sophie's own lips what had happened.

He steeled himself for the worst as he drove over, but even as he did so, he knew it couldn't be too terrible. The woman he loved might think it was. But no matter what, it wasn't as bad as not having her in his life.

When he arrived, he found another note on the front door. "Let yourself in," he read aloud. Testing the handle, he found it unlocked. That old police instinct kicked into gear, making him cringe. He hadn't left his door unlocked since he'd had his own tree house when he was seven.

"Sophie?" he called out.

She didn't answer. But he saw a few more pieces of paper on the floor, making a trail. On the first one was the word "follow" written in large block letters.

He followed, until the single-word notes led him right to the closed door of her secret room. The second bedroom she'd been so anxious to keep him from entering the other night.

He sensed it was all connected.

Half wondering if she had an insane first husband locked in the room, he reached for the knob, twisted it, and entered.

"An office. It's just an office?"

He stepped inside. That was when he saw the posters. Blown-up book covers, as it turned out. All with books by the same author. One of his all-time favorites, in fact. R. F. Colt books had been popular stuff back at the station in Detroit. Mainly because the guy made the cops out to be intelligent and effective. Unlike some others who preferred to paint the police as bumbling modern-day versions of the Keystone Kops.

He froze, looking around again. Colt books filled a couple of shelves on a bookcase against the wall. Multiple copies of each one. Along with police procedurals, *Gray's Anatomy*, criminal exposés.

On top of the computer monitor was a little statue of Lucy from the old Charlie Brown comics. The sign above her head said, "The author is in. A nickel a story."

And he finally got it.

SOPHIE STOOD OUTSIDE in the hall, watching Daniel survey her office. She knew he'd figured things out when he dropped his head back and muttered a nearly inaudible, "Oh."

"Yeah," she whispered.

He whirled around. "It's you."

She nodded, nibbling her lip, praying he'd understand. Jared had sworn that he would. Her cousin had told her more about his relationship with Gwen, how unsure he'd been that any woman would really love a guy who was so fascinated by serial crimes, dead case files and the like. It had sounded so much like Sophie's situation that she'd finally listened to him.

Jared hadn't suggested the notes. He'd told her to march right into Daniel's office and get the whole story off her chest. But Sophie didn't have quite that much courage. So she'd gone back to the heart of the thing with her notes.

Daniel didn't look angry, or confused. Merely serious. "You're R. F. Colt."

"Yes, I am." She looked away, staring out the front window, like she did when she was writing and was stuck on a particularly tough scene. "I'm the one with the twisted mind who thinks up new and ingenious ways to murder people."

He shook his head. "Sophie, I didn't mean..."

She held up a hand to stop him. "You did. You said what you felt. I didn't take offense. But you see, don't you, why I couldn't, just *couldn't*, tell you right away?"

"You don't want the truth getting out here in town," he replied slowly. "I should have known. Something about the way the note said to let the case die a natural death seemed familiar."

"Detective Mike Michaels has said it in a couple of my books. I can't believe I wrote that in the note. Stupid."

"Maybe you subconsciously wanted to get caught." Then he shook his head. "It would have been easier just to tell me the truth then."

She stepped closer, meeting his steady stare, ordering him to listen. To believe. "I didn't want to lose you before we had a chance to see if something could work between us." She moved closer still, until their bodies nearly touched, separated only by an inch of air, and the mess that had come between them. "I wanted you to get to know the real me, the real Sophie that absolutely no one on this Earth knows. I wanted you to see me for who I am before you had to decide if you really wanted to be with this woman who *isn't* the woman who caught your eye when you came to Derryville."

"The one I who caught your eye?"

"Bad enough I'm not the sweet-faced, small-town girl who's going to have your roast beef and potatoes on the table when you get home at five-thirty."

"I don't like potatoes."

"Shut up. I'm not finished."

He didn't respond, but he did smile gently.

"Where was I?"

"Telling me to shut up," he offered helpfully.

She shook her head and rubbed her hand over her eyes, trying to get her thoughts back in order, trying to think of everything she'd planned to say to him before he'd arrived.

"Okay," she finally said, knowing it was useless to try to

stick to some kind of script. Instead, she spoke from the heart. "I'm not the housewife type and I never will be. But I love family, and I love this place, because of its small-town quirkiness, not in spite of it." She gulped for courage before taking this next step. "Daniel, I know it's very soon. But I have to tell you—I've already fallen in love with you."

He waited, not responding in any way to her admission.

"I want you to have the kind of life you never had growing up. Kids, a warm house full of laughter. Growing old together in a small town, living our own secret life behind closed doors."

His grin faded and his expression grew tender.

"You already know I'm not sweet Sophie. But can you live with the fact that I'm also R. F. Colt? That I do think up pretty sick stuff?" Unable to help it, she added, "And, come to think of it, I make a damn good living doing it!"

He stepped closer, erasing that bit of space between them. His voice was thick with emotion as he said, "I love you, too, Sophie. Or R. F. Or whoever you want to be."

She sagged against him, so relieved, so exhausted from the emotional roller coaster she'd been riding for days. Then he kissed her, sweetly, tenderly, telling her as much with that soft touch as he did with his words or his eyes just what he was feeling. When their mouths parted, she tilted her head forward to rest her forehead on his shoulder. "I'm sorry I wasn't honest with you from the beginning. I'm not a liar, I promise."

"I've been hiding the truth myself," he admitted. Lifting her chin with the tip of his finger, he added, "I tried to make myself fit in here. To like this life, to be the same as everybody else." He shook his head. "But I wasn't cutting it. Until I met you, I wondered if I was gonna make it. I needed you to spice up my life with your sharp tongue and your tight workout clothes and your fake sweet-Sophie smile that hides your outrageously naughty thoughts." He kissed her forehead, smoothing her hair from her brow.

Standing on tiptoe, she pressed her lips to his, kissing him again and again. "So you mean it?" she asked. "You can stand a woman with a pretty vivid imagination?"

He looked down at her. "I read fiction, Sophie. I even read thrillers and good cop books. When I was talking about people thinking up ways to hurt others, I was talking about the bad guys. Not authors."

She nodded, accepting his explanation. "And you want to stay here? Want to let me show you how to enjoy all the crazy quirkiness this place has to offer?"

"Oh, yeah. I'm not letting you go." He emphasized the promise by kissing her again. A long, deep, wet kiss that reminded her of all the things they'd done together the night before. And that promised more. Much, much more.

"There's only one problem, Sophie. I don't think I'll ever get used to people spreading rumors about my underwear."

Reaching for his belt buckle, she gave him a wicked smile and pulled him toward her bedroom. "Don't you worry, big guy. From now on, I'm the only woman who's going to know what you've got under your sexy cop uniform."

He gave her a throaty laugh. "Considering I was in a rush this morning, I'm afraid I have to admit the truth." He nibbled her ear and whispered, "Absolutely nothing."

All Sophie could think was, *How sweet.*

* * * * *

Don't miss Mick Winchester's story, in Leslie Kelly's
Harlequin single title debut,
KILLING TIME.
When reality TV comes to Derryville,
the town bad boy might never be the same.
Coming Summer, 2004.

*If you enjoyed these two stories,
you've got to check out...*

Don't miss:

961 CUT TO THE CHASE
by Julie Kistler
*Available next month wherever
Harlequin books are sold.
Here's a preview...*

1

ZOE KIDD BREATHED in the scent of sandalwood from her meditation candles. Lovely. Soothing. Cleansing.

Sitting there on her new purple yoga mat, she maneuvered her legs into the full lotus position, balancing her elbows on her knees and curling her index fingers and thumbs into the proper O's.

She closed her eyes and concentrated. *Breathe the sandalwood*, she ordered herself. *And don't think.*

Yeah, right. Don't think about the fact that today was supposed to have been her wedding day and tomorrow was supposed to have been the day that she and that snake Wylie left for their honeymoon on the Explorers Journey.

He was the one who'd wanted to get married, damn it. She was perfectly happy to live together. Or not even, just to co-exist peacefully in their separate apartments.

"Did you ever have any intention of doing the Explorers Journey with me?" she asked out loud. "And if not, why the hell couldn't you say so before I paid for the damn thing?"

Well, there she was, with her eyes wide open, not calm or relaxed or *cleansed* at all. And her right ankle was starting to kill her where it was mashed between her other leg and her lap, not to mention the fact that the backs of both thighs were plastered to her mat.

Well, she wasn't feeling particularly meditative, was she? Maybe a few rounds with her tarot cards would help her get in touch with her higher power and stop all the angsting.

Refastening one reddish-brown braid back over the top of her head, she started rooting around on her bookshelves for her pack of Enchanted Tarot cards. The deck was on the bottom shelf, and she was bent over, reaching for the last card, which had slipped to the very back of the shelf, when she heard the clomp of footsteps coming up the stairs to her apartment.

She raised her head, planning to call out to whoever it was to just come on in, but she lifted up too quickly, cracking her head squarely on the next shelf.

"Yeow!" she cried, stumbling back, scattering a waterfall of tarot cards like something out of *Alice in Wonderland*. There was only one card left in her hand.

"Come—" she began, but she only got the one syllable out

"Stop, police!" a very male voice announced. "Don't move!"

"What? Stay where I am?" Bent over with her backside in the air? Frozen to the spot, she stared at him through her legs. Good God, he had a gun! Kinda cute, but scary, with both his arms outstretched and that creepy gun pointed mostly at the floor. But he wasn't wearing a uniform. "Are you really a cop? Show me your badge!"

He immediately pulled out a shield and flashed it at her. Jake Calhoun. Okay, good. So he really was a cop.

"Were you shouting at someone?" he asked, in a calmer voice, relaxing his stance a little as he surveyed the empty room.

"No. Myself, maybe," she offered. "I hit my head and then I dropped my cards and... Do I have to stay like this? All the blood is running to my head. I feel like I'm going to faint."

He backed off, putting the gun away, thank goodness, shutting her front door quietly. "No, no, get up. Please. Whatever. Sorry."

"Whew." Slowly, carefully, Zoe straightened, lifting a hand to her head. Yes, she was still a little lightheaded, but not too bad. Meanwhile, his gaze was positively glued to her bottom. It was probably not his fault, she allowed, considering how brief her shorts were, especially when she'd been bent over like that.

But how humiliating. The only cute boy who'd been in her

apartment for weeks, and he barged in while she was woozy, sweaty, upside-down, and had half her butt exposed. She ventured a glance his way. He didn't look too upset by the short shorts problem. In fact, he looked positively...intrigued. Zoe swallowed. Yep, he was still looking at her.

Careful to avoid all the spilled cards, she edged around so that at least her front side was facing him. And then she gave him a real once-over. Okay, twice. Because the view was that good.

Light brown hair, cut short. Good, clean jawline. Blue eyes. There was a sort of speculative, suspicious look in those eyes she found oddly attractive. That and his mouth. He had these quirky lips, kind of narrow and clever, fuller on the bottom. She liked the look of those lips. A lot.

He was tall, maybe six-foot-one or -two, with broad shoulders, and a real *presence*. Nothing she could put her finger on but... Alive. Vital. Rooted. He looked like the kind of guy you would run to when a tornado just blew your house away and you didn't have a thing left in the world and you didn't care because you had *him*.

Zoe's eyes met his. Good Lord, he was cute. In a very traditional, button-down, authority-figure way, of course, which was not her type at all. *So* incredibly and completely not her type. He'd pulled a gun on her, for goodness' sake!

She lifted her chin. "Why in the world did you come barreling in like that? Pointing that thing at me!"

I heard thumps and a scream. The door was open, there was a definite haze in here, and it smelled like marijuana." He looked kind of grouchy as he scanned the room again. "How many candles are you burning? And why?"

"I don't think how many candles I'm burning is any of your business. And it's sandalwood, not marijuana."

"I thought there might be a burglary in progress, or maybe some kind of drug party gone bad," he explained curtly. "That does not smell like sandalwood. You're not burning the candles to cover the pot smell, are you? Is anyone else here? Is there a back door?"

"No, no, and no. I'm alone. The candles are supposed to b good for meditation. I don't have a back door." She took sniff. Good grief. He was right. It didn't smell like sandalwood. No wonder she wasn't getting any calmer. "I'n going to have to have a talk to the lady at the New Age stor downstairs. She swore these were sandalwood."

"Uh-huh."

"Well, it's true." She tried to plant her hands on her hip and look menacing, but her hand hit the smooth, hard edge o the tarot card poking out of her back pocket. Hmm... She pulled it out of her pocket and glanced down.

"That's odd," she murmured. It was a swirling pink card with two pretty swans outlined by a heart, with two tin kissing cupids at the top. The two of hearts.

The True Love card.

Her heart did a flip, but she ignored it. Instead she glared a the card in her hand. Talk about adding insult to injury. Ever her tarot cards were mocking her. So where was this Tru Love supposed to pop up? Between her and...

"Hello?" the cute cop interrupted. "If you're done playing cards, I need to talk to you."

Him? She gulped. Those beautiful blue eyes were staring a her, burning more steadily than all her candles. Her hear started to thump, beating to the most bizarre rhythm. *Tru love. True love. True love.* She felt all tingly and her face wa flush with heat.

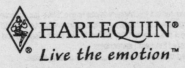

Don't miss the exciting February 2004 Harlequin Temptation lineup!

HARLEQUIN®

Temptation.®

CUT TO THE CHASE by Julie Kistler
BACK IN THE BEDROOM by Jill Shalvis
LEGALLY MINE by Kate Hoffmann
COVER ME by Stephanie Bond

Save $1.00

off any February 2004, Harlequin Temptation title

5 65373 00076 2 (8100)0 11118

© 2003 Harlequin Enterprises Limited
™ and ® are trademarks of Harlequin Enterprises Limited

HTCOUPNCPUS

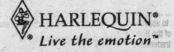

HARLEQUIN®
Live the emotion™

Visit us at www.eHarlequin.com

Don't miss the exciting February 2004 Harlequin Temptation lineup!

HARLEQUIN® Temptation.

CUT TO THE CHASE by Julie Kistler
BACK IN THE BEDROOM by Jill Shalvis
LEGALLY MINE by Kate Hoffmann
COVER ME by Stephanie Bond

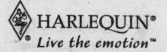

HARLEQUIN®
Live the emotion™

Visit us at www.eHarlequin.com

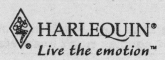

HARLEQUIN®
® *Live the emotion*™

Give in to the indulgence

...during The Decadent Escapes promotion.
Collect original proofs of purchase
from the back pages of:

LIP SERVICE 0-373-83630-9
BEYOND SUSPICION 0-373-83631-7
STRANGERS IN PARADISE 0-373-83632-5
READING BETWEEN THE LINES 0-373-83633-3

and receive free books from our most passionate authors!
Each author-led bonus collection is valued at over $9.00 U.S.!

Just complete the order form and send it, along with your proofs of
purchase from two (2) or four (4) of the featured books, to
The Decadent Escapes National Consumer Promotion, P.O. Box 9071,
Buffalo, NY 14269-9047, or P.O. Box 609, Fort Erie, Ontario L2A 5X3.

098 KJV DXHY

Name (PLEASE PRINT)

Address   Apt. #

City   State/Prov.   Zip/Postal Code

Please specify which bonus author collection(s) you would like to receive:

❏ I am enclosing two (2) proofs of purchase to receive 1 bonus collection
containing 2 FREE books by Lori Foster and Jill Shalvis
❏ I am enclosing four (4) proofs of purchase to receive 2 bonus collections
containing 4 FREE books by Lori Foster, Leslie Kelly, Julie Elizabeth Leto and Jill Shalvis

And don't miss out on exciting travel discounts that can be used all around the world!
Send us two proofs of purchase and check the box below to receive a Preferred
Member Hotel Accommodation Card for savings of up to 50% at hotels worldwide.

❏ I am enclosing two (2) proofs of purchase to receive 1 (one) Preferred Member
Hotel Accommodation card.

Visit us at www.eHarlequin.com